Operation
Quiet Thunder

Doug Hedman

Rolling Rock Publishing

Operation Quiet Thunder

This is a work of fiction. Names, characters, places, and incidents either are the product of the author's imagination or are used fictitiously, and any resemblance to actual persons, living or dead, businesses, establishments, governmental affairs, events, or locales is entirely coincidental.

Note that this writing includes themes and terms, including common and slang words and concepts, which were in use during the late twentieth century.

3241

Foreword

Thank you to those I have met along the way. You led me through life by lending your experience, your patience, your education, and your strength to my journey. You are not forgotten.

The story that you are about to read is a reflective view of a journey that touched our generation of Baby Boomers in so many different ways. The 1970s suffered the hangover of the 1960s. It was a time to move on from the past, and in trying so, we forgot many of the elements that tied our society together and enabled the events of the 1960s to be played.

In respect of our generation, and those who gave so much to it, including so many lives, I offer that we recognize our journey as an important one in history and one which critical values for our society have been brought ahead by the unselfishness of so many citizens.

This story takes us back four decades to an era that, we are told, was a simpler time; but in fact, nothing could be farther from the truth.

* * *

I met some friends along the way that I did not expect to meet.
Doug Hedman

Acknowledgements

Thank you to the patient people who gave me comments, critiques, and so many reviews along the way, including Kate, Gordon, Mary, Randy, Gerry, Barry, Irene, and Dave. Without your advice and encouragement, I would still be stuck in the editing circle. A very special recognition goes to Mary at Rolling Rock Publishing for her coaching and the heavy lifting on this project.

Finally, I thank my family for unselfishly affording me the time to spend typing words into a computer.

Contents

Operation Quiet Thunder

Chapter 1

25 miles west of Da Nang, Vietnam
February 1, 1971

"Hey Larry, I got a week of R&R and I'm heading to Bangkok on Friday. Gonna drink tequila on a beach and see my Lulu," announced the operations sergeant through his radio headset to his helicopter pilot.

"Well Tex, I guess that means another visit to the doc and a shot in the ass when you get back," replied the pilot. "Is he ready yet?"

"Hey Binh, ask him," Tex ordered the Vietnamese translator sitting a seat away.

Binh unbuckled himself from the fold down, took off his headset, and bent down to look eye to eye at the Viet Cong prisoner sitting on the bench seat with his hands cuffed behind him.

Speaking in Vietnamese, Binh yelled at the man and pushed his finger into the POW's chest to emphasis the question.

The translator received a wad of spit in his face as a reply, for which he retaliated by slapping the side of the handcuffed VC's head.

Tex witnessed the exchange. The short fused and broad sergeant unbuckled himself from his seat. Grabbing the prisoner by his black shirt forced the man's back to be pulled away from the bench. Since he was not harnessed, the man flew off the seat with the pull of Tex's thick right bicep. With his left hand, he grabbed the short chain between the handcuffs and spun the POW around so he was looking out the doorway. Tex buckled himself into his seat with the open door view.

1

"Larry, looks like this one needs some help remembering. A good view out the port door might help."

"You ready?" the pilot replied.

"Go for it."

The Huey UH-1, with the gun posts removed for today's flight, made a steep banked turn to the left, forcing the machine to tilt sideways on a 30-degree slope. Inside the cargo bay, Tex held the Viet Cong soldier by the chain between the handcuffs as the small man's body leaned toward the earth a mile below, giving him a sufficiently clear view of the napalmed forest. Urine flowed along the floor and outside to spray the side of the helicopter, drying immediately. Fifteen second later, the chopper was flying level.

"Binh, ask him again," Tex said as he turned the short man toward the translator.

Binh yelled at him, prompting a reply from the prisoner who had just witnessed his future accommodation if he did not answer.

"Says they're an hour walk west of the Ta Bat airstrip. There are two burnt out tanks before the camp," Binh replied.

"Do you believe him?"

"He pissed himself. He was scared enough to tell the truth."

"Yah, okay. Tell him if he is lying, I'll break his neck," Tex warned as he tossed the man toward the bench seat. "Larry you better order up some film of the area, I never trust anything a VC says. . . What the fuck! Unbelievable man. Charlie just jumped out the door."

"For Christ sakes. Tex you didn't push him did you?" Larry asked the man behind him in the cargo bay.

"No way man, he jumped by himself. I didn't touch him. Hey man, we need that film now. I don't have a good feeling about what he said," Tex warned the team as they flew toward their base at Da Nang.

* * *

The next morning in Da Nang, at C-Team Headquarters, Colonel Benson was in his office waiting for his field report on last night's mission. A double knuckle rap on the windowless door was followed by a man entering the room.

"Grab a chair, Field," offered the grey-haired colonel as he sat upright in his chair behind his desk.

Major Field, a tall man, still dressed in his soiled fatigues from the previous night's operation, moved three different piles of documents to the side of the desk so he could rest his arms on the wooden desk. His right forearm bandage showed silver dollar sized dried blood spots in the center. His piercing green eyes focused on the colonel, while impatiently waiting for the man to get on with the purpose of the meeting.

"Field, you did well last night. Your team recovered all five of our men taken prisoner last week. Two of those men are not ours, they are CIA, and they are valuable men to our operations over here. You run a hell of a team."

"Sir," Major Field started, "with due respect, all of our men are valuable. We recovered five valuable men, to use your words."

"Yes, yes, all of our men are valuable. Of course they are. It is always interesting to talk with you, Field; you're a unique man. You uphold the conviction of our Special Forces well."

The colonel rolled back in his leather chair so he could get up and walk to the bookshelf to the left of his desk. "Want a drink?" he asked as he poured himself three fingers of Jack Daniels. I ran out of shine, so Jack will have to do until I get another care package from my brother.

"No, thank you, sir," not the least bit surprised to see the colonel having his first of the day before 0800, "I still have to meet with the men and go over the reports."

"Ah, of course you do," pausing to finish the shot. Deciding another one was needed he poured it and turned to his man. "One thing you shouldn't include in your reports is the method your men used to get the location from Charlie. There are new orders coming down on how we need to change our ways to appease the people back home. It's bullshit, but Washington thinks we need a *kinder war*— whatever that means."

Anger swelled within Field resulting in new blood spots to show through his bandaged arm. "What the fuck do they expect us to do? This is war, man. The VC don't have any rules on how they kill us.

Maybe those chicken shit office boys should come over here and take a look at our men going home in bags."

"Yeah you're right; I don't know where all of these new ideas are taking us. It isn't the same Army I joined thirty years ago. No sir, it is not the same Army anymore. . ." The colonel paused as he drained his glass.

"On another matter, I find myself in a difficult situation. The CIA has requested two men from my operations. I don't know the details of the mission, but they asked for my best men. Some hotshot general even called me and told me that the CIA will get my best men, and well, I must at least try to accommodate them. Your name came up right away, Field. The CIA chief will be here soon, and I want to brief you before he gets to you."

"Do I have a choice?"

"Sure, I have final say on this matter. If you don't accept the reassignment to work on his mission, then I'll keep you here. I'll deal with the general; it won't be the first time that we have been at odds. While I don't want to lose you, I am damn sure that if this chief is onto anything useful to us, then I sure as hell want good men working on it."

"What do you know about him?" Field asked.

"Not a lot. CIA men are hard to follow. I made some calls. I don't understand why, but no one knows what Chief Baxter's actual title is, or exactly what he does. He seems to be on a long leash over here. Baxter is not what you expect from the CIA. He is a Korean War vet. He is smart, and he flies below the radar. Whatever he works on, he keeps it quiet. The man is thirty-eight, has been in CIA and military operations most of his life, which in itself is a testament to his survival skills. He gets his hands dirty, and you can't say that about a lot of them from Langley."

The colonel paused as he looked back at him, witnessing the stare Field had which made you feel as if he was looking right through you.

"The choice is yours, but you've done and seen enough of our work already—a change in operations will be good for you. I wouldn't want you to get bored over here and decide to leave. The replacements aren't made from the same stock as you and me."

"You said this chief asked for two men. Do I choose one, or do you volunteer one?"

"Sure, go ahead and tell me if you have someone in mind."

"You bet. I'll take Johnson with me."

"I kind of figured he'd be your choice. They mentioned his name after yours, but I thought you had better decide that one. I'll lose two of my best men, yet I'd make the same choice," the colonel replied, as there was a knock on his wooden door.

"That'll be Chief Baxter. We need your answer before he leaves. As I said, I'll deal with the general, if you choose not to go. But think about it. This war might just need you working a different angle to end it. I know you're the man who can lead such a challenge," the colonel said as he turned to the door and announced, "Come in, Chief Baxter."

"Good morning, Colonel."

"Good morning, Chief. This is Major Field."

"Your reputation precedes you, Major. You're doing a hell of a job over here. I don't know how you did it but you brought back five men last night. That is a hell of an accomplishment. Great job," Baxter said as he put out his hand toward Field.

"Thank you Chief Baxter. I'm fortunate to have a great team to work with. They're the ones who did it," Field replied as their handshake ended.

The short man in the basic green fatigues did not resemble any senior CIA agent whom Major Field had ever met. This man could step right into roll call and carry on into a patrol. His firm handshake suggested they might just be able to work together.

After a short meeting with the colonel and the chief, Major Field returned to his tent where he met his pilot, Captain Johnson.

"Hey Farmer, you were with the Old Man for a while. What's up, boss?" Johnson quizzed Field.

"Well, Larry, my man, they just made up a new rule—you can't take Charlie for a helicopter ride to help him remember where he's holding our men."

"What the hell! Why not?" replied Larry.

"Beats me, it seems like they are coming up with new rules around here everyday." Field lit up a smoke, and after inhaling a long drag, he continued, "The good news is that we got volunteered for a new assignment. Since we have the rest of today off, I have a bottle of Wild Turkey I'm going to crack. A couple shots will make the day go a whole lot smoother. One of those dollar cigars from your stash would make the bourbon taste even better."

Larry tossed Farmer one of his thick Cubans.

"Okay boss, that works for me. Top it up," he said, as he held out his black metal coffee cup for the liquor.

Chapter 2

Six years later

Southern British Columbia, Canada
Sunday, June 26, 1977

The portable sign warning of "Paving in Progress for next 5 miles" had been accurate. This was the third stop in the last mile. The lineup of vehicles ahead of him stretched 500 yards and around the curve in the road. He had been waiting for thirty minutes when a large, rotund, man in blue overalls walked down the road toward him.

"Hey, how much longer?" the man was asked by drivers as he passed them.

"Don't know, I just drive truck," he said in reply to the repetitive questions.

When the trucker approached the 1971 Yellow Mustang, bearing California license plates, a young, wiry man climbed out and asked him, "Hey mister, do you live around here?"

"Yep, have all my life," replied the truck driver as he adjusted his grease marked cap on his round head.

"Cool man. Do you know Gerry Field? He's supposed to have a farm somewhere around here."

The truck driver wiped his sweaty forehead with his bare arm, "Yeah, I know Gerry. He and his friends live about twenty miles from here. He goes by the handle 'Farmer' and his hippie friends call his commune 'The Farm'. Stay on this road for another five miles and take

7

the crossroad to the right. The road into his farm is about a mile past the sawmill."

"Great, I should be able to find him," the Californian said as he nodded before slipping back into his car.

The long row of cars started moving slowly ahead of him. The coverall-clad truck driver leaned down, placing his sweaty hands on the window frame, "California, watch out for the cops, they don't exactly understand Gerry's hippie friends—with good reason too, since some of his friends aren't packing a full load."

"Okay, thanks man," replied the driver of the Mach 1 Mustang. After starting the 429 cubic inch motor, the car vibrated as the engine rocked side-to-side while on a rough idle. Driving slowly ahead with the traffic, the potent fumes from the molten asphalt were inhaled by each motorist until they had passed the trucks and paving machines.

The convoy of vehicles increased in speed and dispersed along the highway once out of the flagman's control.

The young driver drove steady at 55 miles per hour, the legal speed limit. Inhaling the first drag from his Marlboro cigarette, he glanced at his reflection in the rearview mirror. His brown hair hung down around his thin face, and a sparse goatee covered his chin. The black circles under his eyes showed how little he had slept lately. At 26, he was 5'11", 165 pounds, looking much younger than his age. The nicotine relaxed him sufficiently to realize the peacefulness of the drive and the beauty of the British Columbian scenery.

The two-lane asphalt highway cut into the side of the mountains, following the natural shoreline of the lake below. The trucker's directions were correct. In five miles, he turned onto the secondary road. Fifteen minutes later he drove past the Blue River Lumber Company sawmill.

Dropping down into third, then second, he slowed down in order to find the road to Gerry's farm. The two-lane gravel road was where the truck driver said it would be. He turned onto the road and crawled across a cattle guard made of round metal pipes welded into position to straddle the fence line. On the right side of the road was a large plywood sign, painted in a rainbow of colors, with the words, *The Farm* in bright blue letters, outlined with bright yellow paint. Below the large sign was a smaller sign stating, *Private Property. No trespassing, man.*

Loose gravel on the road bounced off his low-slung chrome side pipes, making musical-like pinging sounds as he proceeded in first gear, diligently trying to protect his recently repainted car from the rock damage.

While lighting up another cigarette, his eyes witnessed a flash of movement in the bushes alongside the road. Onto the road, directly in front of him, emerged a brute of a man dressed in camouflage gear. He wore a cloth covered metal helmet with protruding branches, his face was coated with black paint marks above his beard, and his clothing included clumps of grass and other brush inserted into the military camouflage suit. His left hand held a Sako 308 sniper rifle wrapped in black and green cloth.

"Hey man, you lost? This ain't a good place to go sightseeing," the man's authoritative voice commanded

"No, sir, I am not lost," he replied respectfully to the man with the thick biceps, holding the long barreled rifle in his hands. "I'm looking for Gerry Field. I understand he has a farm nearby."

"What do you want with Gerry? He doesn't need any hassles. He's a busy man."

"I'm not here to hassle him. Dad sent me here to meet with him."

"Why would your dad send you here to meet Gerry?"

While looking at the camo paint on the man's face, he replied, "Don't really know the full answer. Dad told me to come up here and meet with Gerry. I'm Ken Schmidt and dad is James."

The camouflaged man looked closer at Ken and then formed a narrow smile crossed his face. The man was not easy to read and he did not know if the smile was a good thing or bad.

The buzz of two Honda 90 motorcycles approaching him changed his focus. They parked in front of his car, effectively blocking his forward approach.

The muscular man, with his rifle pointed toward the ground, spoke to the shirtless ponytailed man wearing jeans covered in faded colored patches who was driving the orange motorcycle. A thin young woman wearing cutoffs and a small flowered bikini top drove the second bike. Long blonde pigtails hung down her chest accentuating firm breasts beneath the too small top. Her tan contrasted beautifully with her blonde hair. It proved to be a test of restraint not to stare at the woman.

"Well, Ken Schmidt, your chaperones are here. They'll take you in to see Farmer. Nice Mach 1 you got there. Go slow so you don't chip the paint from the rocks." Then he walked away, vanishing from sight in the thick brush and trees.

For the next couple of minutes, he followed the two motorbikes down the gravel road. The road widened as they approached a row of buildings indicating the start of an old mining town. A mural was painted on its sidewall, facing the road, so it was the first thing you saw when you entered the town. The mural depicted a wide meadow, leading to a majestic green forest against snowy mountains and a clear blue sky. In the middle of the sky, white clouds spelled out the single word, 'Respect'.

Ken parked in front of the first building, right behind the motorcycles.

An imposing man spoke to the hippie with the ponytail, driving the Honda, while Ken collected three envelopes out of the glove compartment. When he climbed out of his car, he was met by this new man, who stood above him and was nearly a quarter wider in his shoulders.

"I'm Gerry Field. What do you need to see me about?"

"My father asked me to stop by and talk to you. I'm Ken Schmidt, Shelby's son," he said as he extended his hand and shook Farmer's hand.

Farmer returned a gripping handshake.

"I see," Farmer replied. "Good to meet you. Last word I had on you was you were in the army. What gives?"

"Finished my tour and now I've got to figure out what I want to do next."

Satisfied with the answer, Farmer, with a nod, dismissed the ponytailed man and his woman.

On the other side of Main Street was the official town hall, adorned with white painted letters above the door. Farmer led Ken into the recently painted pastel blue building, topped with a new peaked metal roof.

The century old building had retained its museum like eeriness, complemented by decades of stale air trapped inside the sawdust-insulated walls. The spacious open room had been segregated into two parts by the arrangement of the furniture. On the right side was a ten-foot long oval table with office chairs placed around it. At the other end was a large old wooden desk, flanked by two rows of oak file cabinets. Books and ledgers filled the shelves on the far wall from the floor to ceiling. In the center of these shelves, a glass cabinet held pictures and memorabilia of the old town and the extensive mining history.

"Give me a minute to finish up a couple things," Farmer said as he sat into the leather-padded chair behind the desk and flipped through the pages in the open file. He paused at the last page and began checking each line with his pencil.

In the meantime, Ken approached the glass cabinet in the center of the wall and picked out a wooden frame. The faded Polaroid showed three soldiers in green army fatigues, standing in front of a military helicopter. "Is this a picture of Dad with you?" he asked Farmer.

Farmer put down his pen after signing the last page and closed the file. Looking at the picture he commented, "Yes, that's Shelby, Larry and me, after we finished our Special Forces training in August of '69. Yeah, we called ourselves 'the Enlisted' because all three of us enlisted in 1968. We each had deferments because of our jobs in the States, so we wouldn't be drafted—besides we were getting to be too old by then anyway. As we learned later, each of us volunteered for the same reason—the daily newsreels from the '68 Tet Offensive. Old Walt could sure tell the nightly news.

"Yeah, the reporting hit each of us and made us become a bit more patriotic. Somehow, we had each convinced ourselves the Army needed us to help them win the war—the crazy, dumb fucks we were. Your dad was thirty-eight when he enlisted, ten years older than Larry or me. He didn't need to go, but he wanted to be there. He never let his age affect him, he always had to try and beat us at everything we did."

"Yeah, that's Dad for you, he always pushes to the limit. Everything is a competition to him."

"Back then, the army was dealing with draftees who didn't want to be in Vietnam and volunteers who shouldn't be there. They were backed up for Warrant Officers. They must have been damn happy to find two experienced helicopter pilots walk in and enlist. Someone with brains brought them in as Officers though. They did the same for me. God was watching out for our dumb brains when they pointed us over to Fort Bragg. Christ that seems like a lifetime ago now; man the years fly by. . ... How is Shelby doing anyway, he's been light on the letters lately?"

"Not good, Gerry—he was in remission and the cancer came back. The doctors at the clinic can't do anything for him, so he is in the VA hospital. All they can do now is ease his pain. He lives on bags of IV fluid, shots of who knows what, and a lot of morphine. There's no treatments left for him."

"Call me Farmer. Only my mother and my wife still call me Gerry." Farmer paused as his mind shot to the war. "Yeah man, we went through hell and back together; it's not fair he caught this damned disease. He doesn't deserve it—he earned much better than what he received," Farmer said, choking on the last few words.

"I've spent a lot of time with him lately. Only since Christmas, he started talking about Vietnam. Before then, he never said anything about his time in the army or in Nam. It was like he pushed it all out of his life."

Farmer looked again at the picture in Ken's hand. "That old picture brings back a lot of memories, not many of them are good ones I want to remember, except for the friends we were with. I try to bury the bad stuff away too. Yes, it was some kind of fate that brought us together."

"Dad told me you and he were both MIT graduates. You were a physicist who worked on research on designing nuclear power plants at MIT. Dad never understood why you would leave the cushy job of being a tenured professor to go to the snake infested jungles of Vietnam."

"Yeah, well he has a good point there—sometimes I still wonder why, too. Hell, it happened, and you know. . .it was the right thing to do at the time. Yes, it was the right thing to do at the time. Hey, for that matter, your dad wasn't that much different from me. Look at what he did! He was an engineer and a hell of a helicopter pilot, so he had a sweet deal with Boeing. I heard he was a legend as a helicopter designer and test pilot. I think that is the reason he enlisted. He figured he could make things better for all the pilots flying helicopters, if he flew in their machines and saw what worked, and what was broken, so he could come up with an improved product. It's the bullshit of the real war that tricks you, man. He never did get to do the *improving part* in the army though."

"He said something along the same lines to me. I think he really believed he could make a better machine for the men," Ken replied.

"I get why dad was called Shelby, after his prized Shelby Mustang. Did he call you Farmer because of this farm?" he asked.

"No, this place wasn't even in the plans back then. I grew up on a farm in Columbus Junction, Iowa. My dad was killed in Okinawa in '45, when I was five, so my mother and my uncle ran the old farm. I grew up working the farm and uncle taught me how to fix machinery and cars. He insisted I could be more than a mechanic so he pushed me to do well in school. I liked math, which got me into MIT. I picked the best of mechanics and mathematics and studied physics. I was just a hick kid from Iowa, with the name of Gerry Field, who wound up for basic training. Your dad made the nickname 'Farmer' for me. It stuck with me.

"Do you want a coffee? It's fresh."

"Sure, black works for me, replied Ken."

Farmer poured two cups of coffee from the Mr. Coffee machine, passing the blue metal cup to Ken. "Now you've got me wondering, what has your dad said about Larry?"

"Larry Junior Johnson! He says 'Larry's the most difficult man in the world to understand.' Is this him?" he asked as he pointed to the third soldier in the picture."

"Yes, that's Larry alright; the same guy that showed you his rifle when you met him on your way in here."

"No way! That was Larry. There is no way that fits, man. Dad said Larry was an engineer with Bell Helicopters, and was one of the best pilots ever to fly in Vietnam. He told me he once asked Larry why he left Bell and he said, 'it was the fucking meetings'. Dad said Larry was damn good in designing improvements into the helicopters, too good, because he found the better he did his design job, the less flying time he got and the more time he had to spend in meetings with accountants. He hated suit and tie meetings and all the politics inside the big company; he just wanted to fly helicopters. In '68, he walked away from the big job at Bell and enlisted so he could fly helicopters."

"Yeah, that's about it. He's a cool dude though; Larry has been my best friend since we met back in '68."

"How come he doesn't have a nickname? Dad always calls him Larry?"

"Well, you know, as tough as Shelby, or the army, was, nobody ever came up with a nickname for him. No one wanted to give him a label and risk pissing him off. You really do not want a pissed off Larry around you. I wasn't dumb enough to put a thorn in his side," replied Farmer.

"Dad said you two are the kind of men you want on your point. From what I saw of the man out in the field today, I can see why."

"At one time, we worked together well." Farmer paused and looked at the picture again, "Man, why did Shelby have to get sick? It just isn't right!"

"Dad sent me up here to bring you some letters he said you and Larry needed to read. I don't know what they are about, but he wouldn't send them in the mail; I had to deliver them to you in person.

"He received a letter in the mail a few weeks ago. Two weeks ago, he received a telegram. He also wrote you a letter," Ken explained as he pulled out three envelopes from his hip pocket and handed them to Farmer.

"Thanks man. Wow, that's quite a trip you made to deliver these to me."

"Well, dad told me this was really important, and you know what he's like, no sense arguing with him, he's getting worse as he gets older. Anyway, I took his order and headed up here."

"Good point. Shelby hasn't changed a bit."

Farmer wondered, *what the hell was Shelby up to,* as he removed his Buck knife from his hip holster to use the razor sharp blade to slice open the envelope from Shelby. Shelby had written the one page note with a shaky hand making the writing look more like calligraphy than regular penmanship. *How humbling and shattering for an engineer to degenerate to the state that he could barely write a note anymore,* he reasoned before squinting to make out the words on the white paper.

June 17, 1977

Hello my old friends:

You have finally met my boy. Ken he has a doctorate in Asian Economics and he finished his year of service. He is a free man again. Get this Farmer, he also has a brown belt in karate—an academic and a warrior. Larry will get along fine with him.

I'm on my last run. This cancer keeps eating away at me. Soon there will be nothing left to eat. How is this for luck? An enemy I can't even see, or fight, is taking me down.

Last week I received a letter from Birdman. It isn't good news. I will soon take our history with me, so our team is now down to you two. I believe Birdman's assessment. I'm certain he was careful enough to prevent any fallout.

What chews me up is learning they never sent in a cleaner. If Birdman couldn't make that happen, no one could. Washington wants to forget about Asia.

As I was laying here in this hospital bed trying to figure out what to do with Birdman's letter, I received a telegram from Billy Bob, with more bad news.

Farmer, no one should ever have to go and clean up that damn mess. I wish I was strong enough to be at your point. No one volunteered to do what remains.

To when we meet again, in a better place,
Shelby

Wiping his forehead with the back of his hand removed the sweat that had beaded. His palms were dried on his jeans as he walked away from Ken. He pictured his friend's face, topped with his old green hat with the red 49'ers logo patch, but the vision was immediately replaced by a wrinkled old face below the cap. He shook his head to clear the image.

The dry desk drawer squealed when opened. *Got to oil this drawer someday*, thought Farmer. A 26'er of Knob Creek rolled to off the side of the loose papers in the drawer. At the bottom of the pile was an old Polaroid that had been creased, but was now flat again. The photo had been taken at Christmas in Bangkok, in '71, just before their last operation together. All five men were dressed in Hawaiian shirts while sitting at a table with their beer bottles lifted in the air—playing the part of tourists very well. It was unimaginable before today that the Shelby in this picture would be on his deathbed. Surviving Vietnam, to die at home, just didn't make sense. *They couldn't ever be together again,* he realized as he stared at the days of their past; any one of them could be taken away at a whim. With a heavy heart, Farmer returned the Polaroid back into his desk drawer.

"I may be here for a while as I go through these letters," Farmer said as he opened the front door and called to Fred, the ponytailed man from the orange Honda. The shirtless man was sitting across the road having a sandwich with his woman on the bench in front of the bakery. After kissing her on the forehead, he crossed to find out what Farmer wanted.

"Fred, can you show my friend Ken around the place? He's going to set up at my house so I'll hook up with you later on. Give him a good tour, he's cool, man."

Farmer turned to Ken, "I'll catch up with you later. It's a fine Sunday afternoon around here, and Fred is a hell of a tour guide. Take your time and enjoy our little town. Are the keys in the Mustang?"

"On the floor."

"Okay, I'll drive her over to the house when I'm done here," replied Farmer.

* * *

Sitting at his dark brown mahogany desk, Farmer tried to clear his mind of his thoughts about Shelby dying. The second envelope included a neatly printed address to 'Mr. James Schmidt, 1759 Grapa Street, San Francisco, California'. There was no return address in the top left corner, but on the backside flap, a small picture of a bird had been drawn. The letter was from Robin Baxter, nicknamed *Birdman*.

June 6, 1977

My dear friend Shelby:
    The Lord knows that we should be able to move on in our lives; however, today is not a kind one.
    Harley is dead. On his way to his home in Portland, he drove off the rock bluffs and rolled down into the deep canyon. He did not suffer, I am told.
    I have left no loose ends. No written record of our team exists; they wanted it that way. With Harley gone, I am the only connection they have to our team. They didn't want to know who was on the team, and we never told them. The existence of our last operation, and the identity of our team members, is known by the four of us. I have chosen to take my history with me so they can never know about us. You will be able to travel safely from now on.
    Despite many attempts to organize a cleaner to pick up behind us, they would not send one in. They wouldn't risk any more assets on the lost land. Therefore, it is still there.
    I ask you to advise the others accordingly, on my behalf.

May no man ever carry the burden we have, for our country,
Birdman
Room 714, Watergate Hotel, Washington DC.

Farmer shook his head as he re-read the letter from Birdman. Harley was a hell of a rider; he lived for his collection of Harley Davidson bikes. Harley did not drive off the bluffs without help from someone.

Farmer read the letter for a second time. Harley and Birdman were the only two contacts between the Roadmen and the Central Intelligence Agency. No one in the military knew of the Roadmen since the CIA authorized the whole mission. No records were kept. It was a dark operation. Only Birdman and Harley knew the contacts with the

CIA and only Birdman and Harley knew the members of the Roadmen team. They were the top down and bottom up buffers.

Farmer unfolded page thirty-nine of the June 8, 1977, edition of the Washington Post, which had been inserted into a small envelope inside Birdman's letter. Shelby had circled the small printed notice with his red pen.

> A Mr. Robin Baxter, of Washington, DC, was found dead of
> natural causes at the Watergate Hotel, in the evening of
> Monday, June 6, 1977. Police interviewed at the scene stated
> foul play is not suspected.

'Birdman did himself in to protect us', was scribbled in his shaky handwriting below the newspaper notice.

It was as if an icicle had been stabbed into his spine sending a chill through his body after he realized what Baxter had done to protect him. Birdman had killed himself to forever sever the connection to the Roadmen and thereby cut off the potential that the CIA, Washington, the Pentagon, or anyone for that matter, could pursue the surviving Roadmen team: Larry, Shelby, and Farmer.

Birdman took his own life to save theirs.

The final document was a simple telegram typed on Pacific Union yellow telegraph paper:

> June 16, 1977
> Shelby. Elephant awakening. Machines close. Come now.
> Billy Bob

Birdman's comments echoed though his mind, *they never sent in a cleaner crew. Why?* His shaking hand popped off the cork stopper on the bottle of Knob Creek as he took his first swig and followed with a second shot. His body didn't acknowledge the warmth, which should have hit him from the aged liquor flowing down his insides. After the third swallow, he capped the bottle. His mind now felt numbed. He put his hands over his face in an attempt to block out the light of the room and conceal the realization of what he had to do.

* * *

As they walked down Main Street, Fred provided a vivid narrative on the history of the area.

"This used to be a mining town called New Pontiac. Hey man, imagine naming a town after a car," he said laughing at his own humor. "Yep, this town started in 1891. They mined gold and silver out of the mountains and brought the ore down to the river to send out on boats."

"Want a smoke, man?" Ken said as he lit up a Marlboro for himself and offered Fred one.

"A Marlboro, I ain't had one of them for a while," he replied as he took a drag off the cigarette. "Farmer's uncle wound up owning the place and almost all the land around here and up the valley. I understand he bought it from the mining company years ago, after they shut the mine down. He was a major shareholder and he got his choice of what to buy. He bought it all. He didn't pay much for it, but he must have known it had value for other reasons. Farmer owns all of it now."

Fred kept on talking as they walked down the street, past a variety of buildings. Ken listened and observed the people and surroundings as Fred spoke. They met up with a man with a long grey beard, in short pants, no shirt, and wearing sandals over his bare feet, walking with a young woman dressed in a bright orange tie-dyed wrap. The man pulled a Radio Flyer wagon with a small child sitting inside.

"Peace, Doc," Fred nodded to his friend.

Doc returned a wave, saying "Peace, Fred."

Fred continued, "This town is real neat. In the building, across from Farmer's town office, we have our own bakery that makes the best bread in the world. We grow our own wheat. Chelsea, my woman, works in the fields. And here, is Possum Street," he said as he pointed to the road on the left. Doc lives in the last house. Yeah, man, he's been here a long time. He is a great doctor."

"What's he doing here?"

"Doc didn't want to go over to Nam, so his dad told him to head to Canada. His dad was friends with Farmer's uncle, and he let Doc come up here. He started this town up again, probably a dozen years ago—not sure exactly—but it was a while ago. His woman is a nurse, too. She works with Doc delivering babies and helps him fix up people."

The buildings they walked past were painted in pastel colors of blue, green, red, orange, and yellow. They stopped in front of an odd shaped yellow building. A large Peace sign sat on top of a cylindrical addition at the side of the building. A polished silver bell hung inside the steeple.

Sitting down on a bench in the shade, Fred pointed to the building and announced, "This is our Church. Reverend Bob lives on the top floor of the Church, or else he lives at his woman's house, depending on how they are getting along. Reverend Bob is a cool dude. He teaches us to help each other and to be friends with all. A lot of us either went to Nam and wound up here, or just came here instead of going to Nam. We also have many Canadians who needed a better place to be. It's all good. Reverend Bob says we are all equal, we are all made of good and have suffered pain. He tells us to look ahead to make the world a peaceful place. Yeah, Reverend Bob is a smart dude—you know what made him so smart?"

"Okay, I'll bite, what?"

"Reverend Bob was on his third tour. He became a real sky pilot to all of us, helping us get through the rough stuff that gets stuck in your head. Yeah, he had worked in base camps and he saw the sick and wounded men coming in from the jungle. He said he watched too many people die and got so used to death, he forgot about life. One night he hooked up with our patrol as we were leaving camp. Sarge watched him enter the line and said, 'Evening Reverend, welcome to our walk in the woods tonight.'"

"You see, no one could go on patrol without a gun. Reverend Bob carried an old Colt .45 someone had given him. We used to joke with him how we always figured God would carry a Winchester lever action 30-30 rifle, like the Rifleman. He didn't like us talking about God and guns together."

Fred paused for a minute as he shivered and his hands began shaking. A minute later, he was okay again.

Fred continued, "About an hour later we were ambushed. The patrol got shot up real bad. Reverend Bob wound up in a ditch beside

Sarge. It was a cloudy night, but there was enough moonlight for him to see that Sarge had been hit bad and he was in real rough shape.

"No one could move until we knew what was around us. We stayed low, just lying in the dirt trying to locate their bunker. The brush ahead of us was thick and I figured the VC were hiding somewhere in there. I couldn't give up my position by taking a reckless shot their way, though."

Another Marlboro was accepted by shaking hands.

Exhaling his first drag, he continued, "I was the point gunner and had my M-60. Crawling on my belly, I set up behind a log ready to hit them whenever I figured out where they were. I loaded a clean roll of ammo before Reverend Bob stood straight up, only ten feet away from me. He had something swinging in his right hand, it was Sarge's grenade belt, and he put it around his neck. He walked toward where he thought the gunfire had come from. I guessed they were about fifty yards away, but Reverend Bob walked in my line of sight, and I couldn't fire without hitting him. I think Charlie couldn't believe anyone would be dumb enough to walk toward them without a rifle, so they just watched him walk at them."

Taking a long drag off his Marlboro, Fred wiped his eyes with the back of his hand. "When he got to their bunker, he must have pulled the pin on one of the grenades and threw the whole belt at them. Charlie's machine guns started flashing as they tried to shoot him, but those grenades blew the hell out of their bunker and leveled the jungle around it. The burning brush gave more light, but I still couldn't see much. Then Reverend Bob comes walking out of the smoke and fire, straight at me. He didn't stop; he kept on walking past us."

"Hey, some wild trip, man."

"Yeah, it was. After he got back to camp, he took off all his clothes and poured gasoline on them. He threw his Zippo onto his clothes pile and sat naked on the ground beside the fire. By morning, he was on his way back to the States."

"How about you, were you okay?"

"I didn't know I was so fucked up. They worked on me through the night; my arm only needed some stitches, my leg was in bad shape but the Doc sewed it up the best he could. I also had a bullet stuck in the right side of my skull. It must have been a ricochet or a poor load, cause I should have been dead if it was a direct shot through my helmet. They patched me up, but my head wasn't working right and my eyes were blurry. Morphine was good for the pain, but my eyes bugged me. After three weeks, they sent me to San Francisco. My head still wasn't working right, but the Docs found part of another bullet still stuck inside my brain. They took it out and I started getting better."

"That's some bad shit you went through. Are you okay now?"

"Yeah, I'm fine now. Back in the states, I met Reverend Bob in the hospital again, but he was different. He was strong—real strong—his sermons were even deeper than before. He had a new fire in his belly and he had to tell everyone about it. When I was leaving the hospital, he asked if he could come with me. We hitched up to Seattle to hang out with my dad. We stayed with him for about a year. It was a real weird time though, people were protesting the war, and we got tired of being hassled by jerks wanting to know why we went there to kill women and kids. That hurt a lot." Fred paused as he cleared his throat.

"So how did you wind up here?"

"We came here in the spring of '71. Everyone is equal here. Reverend Bob really helps us. He says, 'You don't have to believe in God, you just have to be able to believe in some greater direction.'"

"Man, you've had a rough trip," Ken said as he looked at Fred who had his eyes closed.

Fred nodded. "Were you ever in country?"

Ken had been asked this question a thousand times before. He still hung his head when he answered, "Nope, sorry man, I wasn't. I was in the reserves while I went to university, but the war ended before I graduated. I just finished a year in the Philippines, working for Military Intelligence out of Clark Air Force Base."

"So, you are one of the brains. Intelligence, yeah, that must have been a hoot. Well, you didn't miss much by not being there. I've never been the same, man. It was hell over there. There should never be another war." For the first time during the walk, Fred was silent.

They turned into Farmer's driveway where a rainbow of color variety flowers lined the gravel driveway. Encased by a border of tall fir and thick cedar forest, the two-story A-frame house was at one with local environment, utilizing cedar shakes for the roof and cedar shingles for the siding, which in their weathered condition now matched the color of the grey bark of the cedars in the surrounding forest. A woman's touch was clearly at work with the hanging flower baskets along the porch and the cedar garden boxes brimming with greenery under the windows. The long row of chopped and stacked firewood under the protection of an aluminum roof, lined the closest wall of the workshop behind the residence, confirming that Farmer prepared well in advance of the winter.

Farmer opened the front door before Fred could knock on it. A striking Vietnamese woman stood beside Farmer. "Ken, meet my wife, May."

In a mild British accent, May said, "I am pleased to meet you, Ken," as she extended her delicate hand to him.

"It is a pleasure to be here, thank you," he replied after shaking her silky smooth hand.

"Please come in Ken. You've travelled a great distance. Your room is ready. Gerry has taken your bags up for you."

The scent from the vase of freshly cut flowers enhanced the comfort of the warm pine paneled walls of the bedroom. After pulling off his leather boots, he slumped backwards and lay on the twin bed covered with a bright orange afghan. With a cooling breeze blowing into the room, the temperature was cozy. Birds chirping outside lulled him to close his eyes while he recounted Fred's story and Reverend Bob's journey. The two men's experiences led him to ponder the ramifications of a war that had been fought so far away, yet its spirit would remain a burden on his generation, and on all others that it had touched.

* * *

He dozed until Farmer knocked on the door. It took him a moment to realize where he was in the unfamiliar surroundings. "Yes, I am awake, come in."

Farmer opened the hand-carved cedar door informing Ken he should prepare to join them for dinner at the community hall tonight; they'd be leaving in an hour."

Sitting up on the edge of his bed, he ran a comb through his hair, and pocketed a new pack of Marlboros from his bag, threw on his boots and joined Farmer in the living room.

"Ken, Sunday nights around here start with a sermon from Reverend Bob at 5:00."

"Yeah, Fred told me about his friend, Reverend Bob. Why is the service so late in the day?"

"Well, Reverend Bob is a sharp dude. He used to hold church in the morning, but not many people showed up, so he moved the service to 2:00, however, even fewer people joined him since they had other things to do in the afternoon, too. The guy is persistent and came up with a new plan to combine the service and a potluck dinner. Now we have the service at 5:00, followed by a community potluck at the hall. He hit a home run; a lot of people go to hear him at church and afterwards they get a fine meal."

Lowering himself into a brown suede-covered chair, Farmer pointed to one for Ken to sit in. "How was your tour with Fred?"

"Great. He's an interesting guy."

"You bet. Fred has thrived here and fits right in. He works hard at the mill and for our community. He's my right hand man at the sawmill."

"He didn't mention a sawmill."

"That's strange. He must have run out of time. Anyway, we run the Blue River Lumber Company sawmill. The mill does pretty well for the area. She keeps people busy, we make our own lumber for our houses, and we even sell enough to pay for everything we need. I'll take you on a tour tomorrow and show you how it all works. I think you'll be interested to see how the operation gives purpose to many."

Dressed in a yellow cotton wrap-skirt, and a shimmering beige polyester blouse, carrying a casserole in a white bowl with a bamboo cover, May joined them in the living room. At 5'6", she was tall for a Vietnamese woman, but she had a natural bearing of elegance and grace that radiated energy. Farmer took the casserole dish from her in his left hand and held the door open for them with his right hand.

As they walked down the flower lined driveway and onward to the church, May took Farmer's available hand in her own. They made a unique couple.

When they arrived at the church, May carried on with the other women to deposit the food at the hall before the sermon began. She passed by a group of children playing at the side of the church, apparently led by a young woman.

Inside the church, lit candles sat in polished brass candleholders along the sidewalls. A large center chandelier hung from the ceiling with all its white candles beaming through dozens of shimmering glass beads. Below the chandelier was a smooth stone circle etched into the wooden floor. Inset blue opal stones made the shape of the peace symbol; the ten-foot diameter peace symbol set the tone for the church. Jasmine and patchouli incense burned in holders at the front adding soothing aromatherapy to the atmosphere.

Men and women continued to enter the church. The men shook hands, while the women hugged each other. Soon, over a hundred people had arrived and taken their seats in the pews.

A towering, burly, man, wearing a full black satin robe with a gold sash cord tied around his waist as his belt, in his bare feet within leather sandals, entered the stage from the side door. Reverend Bob had arrived. He raised his arms above his head and before spreading them wide apart.

"Welcome my friends. We are truly blessed. My brothers and sisters please join hands and start tonight with a moment of prayer to the guiding path in your life."

The congregation joined hands and bowed their heads. Each prayed to their own guide, be it Buddha, the Lord, a friend, or some other spirituality they pursued.

After a minute, Reverend Bob continued with his sermon. "My friends, we live in a time of change. The world is large and not all parts of the earth change at the same time. Blessed are we, with a community in which we each can participate in making our world a strong and better place. We've all seen other parts of our world that do not care about this. Each one of us can make our world a better place. We can use our goodness to help others."

He paused to let people reflect upon the words.

"I have good news for you. Last week the mill completed a special run. For two days of production, they cut fir beams for the new arena in the City of Cedar Falls. The order had a special meaning to us. With the $7,200 profit from the sale, they chose to donate the entire amount to our Open World Missionary project. We now have hit our goal of $10,000. We made it. Hallelujah! This money will now go to UNICEF, and they'll be able to take this money and purchase medicine, food, clothing and supplies for the hospital, school, and orphanage they operate in Laos. This is truly a thankful day. My friends, we can make a difference, and we have made that difference in the lives of others."

He raised both hands in the air in a salute to the Lord.

When he lowered his hands, he asked, "Please join hands as we pray for those we can help with this work. Doc, will lead us."

Doctor Ray took to the stage. The parishioners looked at the gentle man who had helped many of them. In a soft voice, he spoke, "I've thought about how to thank you for what you've done to help so many people, in a land that has so little. He continued in a soft, but direct voice, "I don't have the words to describe how this offering will touch these people. Instead, I offer you an image. Join me by closing your eyes. Imagine you see a young baby crying from devastating hunger. His malnourished teenage mother is so small and sick she has no milk to feed him. As the baby whimpers from hunger, a hand reaches toward the emaciated infant, clutched so tightly in his mother's weak arms. Now picture a nurse holding a bottle with milk, and while the baby is crying, the nipple of the bottle enters his mouth. He stops crying as he sucks in the warm milk. As one nurse takes the baby from the mother and sits with the child beside his mother, a second nurse gives the young woman a bowl of rice with meat and vegetables. These are the first meals the mother and baby have had in days."

Ray paused on purpose to let the image settle.

"And you, my friends, sent them these meals and they will be healthy. You've given them the food, the tools, and the seed, to grow their own food. They will not be hungry again. They will have medicines they need to remain healthy. You've made a difference."

Reverend Bob shook Doctor Ray's hand. "Blessed are those who can help others in need. Thank you, my friends," he offered as he turned to his congregation.

A tall man sat to the right of the podium with his guitar. He started playing an A and D chord sequence moving into Pete Seeger's song, 'Where Have All the Flowers Gone?'

"Thank you, brother Charlie, for the deep tune." Reverend Bob moved away from the podium and toward the front of the stage.

"I now must change our thoughts this evening. Today, I reflect upon the death of a friend. Robert died on this day two weeks ago, but only last Friday I received a note from his mom telling me of his passing. Although I knew Robert for so many years, as I reflected today on our experiences, I realized I barely knew my good friend.

"Now, you might ask me, 'how can you not know a good friend?' Well, friends—brothers and sisters—I remind you, we make ourselves complex as humans. We can love, and we can hate. We can respect and we can kill each other. We are a conflicting mass of feelings and emotions and actions. Each one of us is capable of good, yet each of us is also capable of evil. So instead, I ask you, how well, yes, how well, do you know yourself?"

A short pause gave effect of his words.

"But, I digress. Robert was like your friend Bill, or Mary, or Jim. We hold respect for our friends, and we help our friends as we would like to be helped."

Reverend Bob took a deep breath. "In a place a long way from here, my friend Robert Fleming, Captain Robert Fleming, helped me. He taught me to open the light in my mind. Yet for all the good he did in his life, his reward was he had his leg severed by a Claymore. I do not understand why these events happen. I've thought a lot about Robert over these past few years, I suppose he was always with me, he just wasn't here."

He looked to the ceiling and paused. "While I was lamenting the loss of my friend, I fell into a deep funk yesterday. I questioned the merit of perseverance; I questioned the reason to be. Then, as if she was sent on a mission, Mary came along and asked me about my confusion. I explained the challenge to her. She listened and reminded me that each one of us has a job to do to make this a better place. She told me she would write a poem for me. She's offered to share her thoughts with all of us tonight. Mary, please."

Mary walked up to the stage taking the microphone in her hand and stretching the cord over to the podium. From the yellow piece of paper, she read her poem.

> A Friend is the one,
> who listens until you are done.
> A Friend helps you hear,
> the sounds that are not clear.
> A Friend clears your sight,
> when you just can't see right.
> And so we all believe,
> that our Friend will never leave.
> But when he rides the last train free,
> he takes with him a part of me.

The congregation applauded Mary at the conclusion of her reading. After she handed the poem to Reverend Bob, he held her tight and kissed her forehead.

Reverend Bob rubbed his eyes. Looking at Mary he said, "Thank you, my dear Mary. You helped me through my time of challenge. May peace be with you, my friend."

Mary had a smile of complete contentment on her face as she set the microphone down on the side chair and walked off the stage to take her seat at the front row.

"Now I ask for your respect for my friend Captain Robert Fleming with a moment of silence. I ask you to think about a friend of yours during our silence and ask yourself, 'Am I friend of him or her?'"

After the silence, he continued, "Reflecting is a challenge. Reflecting is also a reward."

The side door opened whereby a short woman waved her hand at Reverend Bob.

"Our Sunday dinner is ready," concluded the Reverend. "Before we leave tonight, I ask you to turn to your neighbor and thank them for being your friend. Be safe and proceed with respect in your journey. Travel in the pursuit of a good life, my friends."

The departing parish members shook hands, hugged, or kissed each other. They were in no hurry to depart—dinner would wait for them until they got to the hall.

Outside the church, Fred caught up with Ken as he walked towards the hall. "What do you think about Reverend Bob?"

Ken looked straight at Fred and replied, "He is not the man I expected, but he is the man he should be."

"Cool, man. Deep. . .real deep!"

* * *

The former concentrate dry storage building had been cleared years ago and finished inside. The high open ceiling was the result of the addition of a steep steel A-frame roof. The mural depicting people dancing in a field of wild, colorful, flowers filled the south wall. Pastel blue and orange colors adorned the other walls. The hall served as a multi-purpose place for dinners, dances, and meetings. The residents had given the building the respectful title of *The Pontiac,* after the name of the original town and mine. Some also viewed the facility as their own version of *The Apollo* theatre.

Tonight The Pontiac was stocked with tables of potluck dishes brought in earlier by the families. People were working the lines and putting the food onto their plates. The hall could seat nearly two hundred, but with the warm evening air, most chose to sit outside in the garden area behind the hall and eat their dinner.

Ken, Farmer, and May sat outside on a carved cedar bench in the garden. Benches were scattered around the central pond and along the stream connecting the lower pool. The garden was blooming with fragrant flowers and colorful small bushes. One could not help but feel the tranquility of the area and its communion with nature.

Ahead of the first bench, the guitar player from the church played, accompanied by a young woman with a grand shiny wooden harp.

After dinner, Ken was separated from his hosts as he watched a group of teenagers lighting the bonfire in the main fire pit in the center of the park. A grey-bearded man handed him a large mug of his home-brewed beer. Most of the men were drinking the cold beer, poured from large plastic pop bottles. Ken sat on his bench and looked into the flames of the fire in the fire pit. The homebrewed beer was going down just fine as he watched the hypnotic dancing flames and took note of the residents of the farm coming and going.

To the left of Ken, a young man and his girl were toking up as they cuddled each other. To his right, men were immersed in a discussion about politics. They invited Ken to join them, and after brief introductions, they continued their discourse. The group's conversation focused on how the new president of the United States, a Democrat, would be able to get rid of the corrupt establishment that the right-wing conservatives had made of the government. The discussion became a heated debate, amongst normally calm men; men who believed nuclear plants would shut down, wars would end, and all would live in harmony with nature.

Ken listened, nodded, but avoided putting his opinion into the mix. Republican views wouldn't mix well into the conversation. He didn't have the desire to debate these points at this time, or in this place.

Rescued by a tap on his shoulder, he turned to meet the radiant face of a woman dressed in a loose white blouse and a blue cotton wraparound skirt. He backed up a step in reaction.

"Hey, Ken. What brings you to this part of the world?"

Momentary paralysis replaced surprise as he took in the willowy woman. In a voice, void of emotion, he responded, "Hello Leanne, it's been awhile."

"Wow, I can't believe you found me here. God I'm glad to see you again. It's been too long," she said as she stepped forward to wrap her arms around him, adding a kiss to his lips as she rubbed her hands along each shoulder blade.

Mechanically, he reciprocated the hug, but didn't respond to the kiss. She always was a touching person, a quality he used to enjoy.

Undaunted, she continued her conversation, "Ken, I know it's been a while. I've thought a lot about you over the years, but I never got myself together enough to get a hold of you. Man, I can't believe you're here."

"Uh, yes, hey, you look great. . .as always."

"Now, Ken, no I don't. I'm five years older, but some days I feel like its fifteen. I think I even found a wrinkle on my forehead. Getting old sucks. Hey, how did you find me anyway?"

After looking down to watch his boot kick the gravel, he leveled his head to gaze into her sparkling green eyes, "Leanne, I never could lie to you. I'm visiting a friend of Dad's. Meeting you here tonight is an unexpected bonus for me."

"Come walk with me," she said as she took his hand and began leading him along a pathway beside the stream.

Curiosity and intrigue won over the bitterness he had harbored deep inside for too long, as he kept beside her on the trail.

"You know, Ken, I really did mean to get a hold of you. I wish we would have connected after school, but, well, it was a rough time for me. I hurt you and didn't give you any reason to care about me again. I'm so sorry for what I did to you—for what I did to us."

He tried, but he couldn't think of anything appropriate to add to the conversation. The awkward pause caused them to stop walking.

"I really messed up. I wanted to tell you that I was so sorry, and so wrong. I wrecked the best thing in my life, but I was so screwed up and couldn't." She clenched his hand tighter.

"Leanne, that was a long time ago. We were both. . .younger. We never had the answers back then."

"I always meant to tell you that what I did was wrong, and it only happened once. I was so pissed at you for signing up and sought revenge on you in the meanest way I could, by doing Patrick in our bed, right when I knew you would be coming home. I was mad at the fucking war and the fucking government for being in the war. Then you went and signed up. When you walked in on us, I realized I had done the worst thing I could ever do to you. I wanted to hurt you, but I wrecked us."

She paused as glistening tears rolled down her face. She lifted her head to look directly into Ken's eyes.

"I was not right. I've lived every day wishing I hadn't been so stupid; I lost the only man who ever mattered to me."

Compassion replaced bitterness as he held both of her hands and pulled her closer. "Hey, that was a long time ago. I was selfish, and I registered for me. Signing up paid for university. I really screwed up by not talking to you about what we were going to do.

"Did you finish?"

"Yeah, I finished my doctorate. I paid them back by working my ass off in training and during my tour of duty this last year. My service was the right thing to do, for me. I love our country; I just don't understand where we are going with it."

As if a switch had been turned off, she stopped her tears. "Oh Ken, why did we go off the track? Do you know that after school in '72, I got a job for 'The Man'? Can you dig the irony in that—me working for the IRS? Well, like the story of my life, I managed to screw that up too. I liked my job, and my boss liked me. I was there for six months until his wife caught us in his office. Then I moved on. I worked a few bars. Hey, money was good. Undo a button, wear a tight top, or show some leg, and the tips got even better."

They stopped walking when some frogs hopped across the path in front of them. The stop caused Ken to visualize Leanne working the bars. Her tip jar would have overflowed.

"I met a guy playing in the band at the bar. Yeah, Max was the real dude. Wild, fun, and didn't care a damn about the system and the government, never mind politics. He gave my brain a rest.

"Max was spoiled and young. The free life of travelling and staying with friends kept us going at the start. After only three months together, Max fucked up. Hell, it had to happen eventually; he was with me, so you knew he was going to fuck up."

After taking a deep breathe, she calmed down.

"Yeah, he got caught carrying coke in his guitar. Then I learned that he hadn't turn up for his draft medical two years before and he was probably going to jail.

"Max's dad paid the $25,000 bail. The next day we were on the Greydog to Canada. His dad sent us money to live, and we just hung around Vancouver. It was a wild time. We had cash, drugs, and good times. That didn't last too long, though. After three months of partying on Max's allowance, his dad messed up on some operation, or something at the hospital, and he was sued. He stopped sending us money. We were broke in no time. A chick told us about this place, so we hitched a ride here. Max's dad never did send any more money."

Compassion came easier now. "Hey, Leanne, life was different then. You've had a rough trip getting here, but I'm glad I found out where you wound up. This is a good place. It's a safe home for you."

At the wooden bridge, they stopped to watch the red fish swim upstream against the rippling current.

She became warm and cheerful again, "Hey, Ken, I have a daughter. Christina is walking. She's my everything."

Without giving him a chance to comment on this news, her voice lost its enthusiasm and she continued, "Yeah, life was falling into place for us here. I got a great accounting job at the mill. Max couldn't hold down a job. Instead, he kept on working on his music and getting wasted every night. He got worse. He started coming home smelling like the slut he had slept with earlier that evening, and I put up with it. He'd tell me, 'we weren't married so he could do what he wanted'. In February, he went into town for some Mexican weed. He never came back. Farmer told me he's over in Newton Landing now. Max said he's never coming back."

The trail ended on Main Street. Half a block further, she led him by his hand onto Fox Street. Light from the full moon lit up their walk along the roadway. Leanne spontaneously pulled on Ken's hand and started running with him in tow. They ran down the road, past the fragrant lavender field, and into the open door of the hay barn. The single light bulb dimly lit the far end of the stacked bales of hay. She grabbed one of the horse blankets from the pile and spread it onto a row of bales.

"Come sit beside me. I've been doing all the talking. Tell me about what you do in the army."

"Well, I don't know. There isn't much to say about my service. I liked the Philippines, but living on a base is kind of like camping in your backyard. You're away from home but it's still America. I liked travelling to Australia and New Zealand. I really liked visiting Singapore; the city is probably my favorite."

Her bronzed skin on her exposed shoulders was smooth on his hand as she draped his arm around her head and pushed herself close against him. His eyes couldn't resist the view down her loose peasant blouse.

"Did you miss me?"

"Yeah, I did. I often wondered where you went."

Her long fingers traced his mouth moving up to his cheekbones. Repositioning herself, she straddled his legs while he remained sitting upright, keeping his back propped against the bales behind him. He didn't stop her from taking his face in her hands and kissing him. When she broke that kiss, she stroked his hair with her soft hands and kissed him again.

"What's wrong? Don't you miss me now?"

"Sure Leanne, I miss you."

"Why are holding back? I'm right here."

The light breeze blew in the marijuana smoke causing both of them to turn toward the door. Leanne rolled off him before an older man, with two young women, stumbled in the door. Each of them had a joint in their hand. The two girls were laughing as they held onto their man. The husky man stopped when he saw Ken in front of Leanne.

"Hey man, didn't know the place was being used," the intruder said as he eyed up Leanne. "You wanna join us, Leanne. It's good with the girls, right girls?" he said as he put an arm around each woman, women whose combined ages were less than his age.

The girls kissed the old geezer as their reply.

"We're leaving, man, you got the place to yourself," Ken replied on their behalf.

"Jesus Christ Andy, aren't you robbing the cradle," Leanne shot back at the threesome as Ken led her out the door.

A loud chorus of laughter was the reply from the stoned trio inside the barn.

"That jerk is one of Max's good buddies. Andy's grow op money gives him a free ride around here. An asshole like him should have to work for a living instead of making his cash the easy way," Leanne cursed as they walked toward her house.

* * *

It was late when Ken knocked on Farmer and May's front door and slowly opened the hand crafted cedar door to their house. Farmer was sitting in a leather recliner in the living room. The late night newscast was wrapping up on the upright radio set inside a gleaming hand polished oak cabinet.

"Anything new in the big world today," Ken asked, as he took in the sweet jasmine aroma wafting out of the trunk of the small brass elephant incense burner on the coffee table beside the radio.

"Not really, just another day in our life. The Russians are building more nukes and we have no idea where the hell they're storing them. Elvis played a wicked concert in Indianapolis tonight; he brought out *A Bridge over Troubled* Waters. . .. Our world needs more Elvis's," Farmer deduced as he bent down and turned off the radio.

Taking the chair across from Farmer, Ken slumped into the overstuffed suede chair, pulled out a Marlboro from his right pocket and lit up the smoke. "Want one?" he asked as he held the deck out towards Farmer.

"Sure one more won't hurt; May keeps telling me I should quit, she's probably right, as usual."

"You know, Farmer, this is a good place, man. I have to tell dad about what you've created here—he'll get it, he would probably fit right in here. This is a safe place for many people. I met a friend of mine from the past, and this is a good place for Leanne, this is where she needs to be. From what I've seen today, you've created a wilderness version of Mayberry."

"Yeah, well everyone works hard to make it click. Doc started the place and created a good base for the rest of us that came along after he had it up and running. It took a bit of politicking with the locals to give us our space. After they got to know Doc, and he was supported by some local friends, I guess they realized we weren't here to affect their lives. Then we got God on our side when Reverend Bob set-up here. No one ever questions that man's conviction to peace and harmony.

"The fact is that we don't bother anybody and most people accept that and leave us alone. That's what your dad and I fought for—for the freedom to be as who you are, at least that is what we thought we were fighting for."

"You know, I was too young to understand what dad meant when he spoke of peace, honor, and country, but now I know what he meant—I already feel that here. Thanks for inviting me into your home."

Butting out his smoke in the ceramic ashtray on the coffee table, Farmer turned to Ken, "It's all good. I have a busy week ahead, so why don't you hang out with me tomorrow. I'll show you around. It's getting late; let's carry on in the morning. May set out towels and water for you in the room."

"Okay. Thanks again for letting me stay with you in your house and showing me around. It's cool."

"I'm looking forward to spending some time with Shelby's son," Farmer said before he turned to walk through the kitchen toward his bedroom.

Ken turned off the light in the hallway after turning on the lamp in his room. He took off his boots and socks, setting them at on the floor at the end of the bed, and laid on top of the crocheted bedcover.

A light breeze blew in the sweet smell of ripening lavender from the fields through the open window helping to refresh and to cool the air in the room. Within minutes, he was asleep, with his mind replaying his walk with Leanne and reliving the haunts that he had carried with him these past years.

Chapter 3

Monday, June 27, 1977

While two coyotes communicated with each other via an exchange of howls cutting through the clear night air at New Pontiac, deep in his sleep Farmer had slipped back to recount another day of his old life. His mind had taken him back the beeping sirens inside the cockpit, flashing red lights, and the drastic flair of the Huey by the barely conscious pilot who had received the remainder of the enemy fire that had killed his co-pilot and taken out his transmission. The impact on the cratered clearing had bounced the helicopter twice, before rolling over to land upright again. Minutes of confusion, and then clearing of the live men, had been compounded by the deafening sound of mortars landing around their severely mangled helicopter. Farmer remained at the wreck, keeping his M-16 propped up within an arm's reach. Jet fuel fumes hung in the humid air, compounding the smoke from the mortars that they took in with each breathe.

His young radioman, who reminded him of Gilligan, had made it to the cover of a patch of surviving trees, sixty feet away from the wreck, lining a natural depression of a dry creek bed. Beside him, Sarge yelled into the handset working to determine the coordinates of the enemy. Once located, the 155mm big guns from Camp Carroll would take care of the VC.

Only the white of the medic's eyes confirmed he was still hanging on while Farmer and the engineer wedged the length of a severed landing skid under the collapsed transmission structure, which pinned the man's legs. The confined space was not allowing enough leverage for the two men to work together. As the engineer moved out the way, Farmer took the skid in his cut up hands and lifted the twisted metal as high as he could above the medic.

The medic's arms were too weak to move his body clear but the engineer had wrapped a canvas strap around his chest and armpits creating an improvised harness to pull the medic toward the door.

His awkward position, and the weight of the tower he was lifting, caused his biceps to burn as they were at their maximum. If he let the metal go back onto the medic now, the man would certainly die, from the new piercing of his body by the structure, since he had been able to move inches from his original location.

A vicious scream emanated from one of his men behind him as another soldier tied an improvised tree branch splint along a wounded leg and its grotesquely protruding femur.

The clear shrill of intense pain suffered by his man with the leg wound hit Farmer, sending his last shot of adrenaline through his body, charging his arms with the extra strength they needed to raise the metal off the medic's legs. The rescued medic was only inches clear of the entanglement when Farmer dropped the tower onto the deck and fell to the floor himself in exhaustion.

Still in the open area, there was little time to refresh, or regroup. Hoisting the injured man onto his back, he yelled at the engineer to get away from the carcass of the machine and run to the cover of the trees. Farmer's gait was impaired by some sharp bite to his left leg but he managed a hurried walk to the rest of the team. Two men hoisted the medic off his back and set the man down on the remnants of a stretcher. His rubbery legs forced him to drop to the ground.

They were now laying low in the dry creek bed. Sarge's directions had succeeded in moving friendly Howitzer fire to the VC's location. There was peace in the sky again. Sixteen eyes adjusted to the darkness, each set looking for enemy ground troops, praying the dust-off choppers would arrive first.

Farmer's heart was racing like a rabbit as he searched through his group of men to find Sarge. As he crawled his first length towards the sergeant, the next impediment to their survival occurred. A single rocket whistled in the air above them, making a direct hit on the crashed chopper. The remaining fuel in the tanks blew, sending a plume of flame well above the searing metal. Shrapnel went upward and outward from the combined rocket and fuel explosions. Miraculously none penetrated the imperfect barrier the men were laying within.

As Farmer resumed his crawl toward Sarge, his hand landed on something wet and warm.

"Gerry, wake up! Wake up!" a female voice said as he felt his shoulders being shaken. Cold water hit his face and his eyes opened to the bright lights in the room, with his wife May beside him and Ken pinning him by his shoulders.

His hands touched his hips and then he raised them above his stomach. They were clean, no blood was on them, and his engineer's left arm wasn't in his hand.

"You okay," Ken asked him.

"Yeah, was it a bad one?"

"Yes it was, Gerry. I tried to wake you but you fought too much. Ken held you on the bed while I got water."

"Oh Christ, I'm sorry, May. Thanks, Ken. I'll be okay now."

"Sure, no problem, man. Dad still gets them too."

* * *

"We're going to stop at the mill for a bit this morning," Farmer said to Ken as he drove out of his driveway in his Glenwood Green Chevy Blazer. "Usually the men can use extra bodies when they are starting a week. The shift doesn't start until nine and not many of the crew show up to help before then. We'll stop by and see how Fred is making out today."

The 9 o'clock start time intrigued Ken. "Does the mill start at 9:00 every day?"

"Yeah, we used to start earlier, but most of the crew wouldn't show up until later. By starting at nine, most of them get here on time," Farmer said as they drove past green fields of wheat and barley and the lavender patch with the barn Ken and Leanne had been to last night.

The hard gravel road continued past a number of metal sheds and farm buildings before they crossed the second bridge and turned into a parking lot.

The office of the Blue River Lumber Company consisted of a single story log building with a post and beam porch and a steep green metal roof to handle the heavy winter snow. Behind the front desk sat a middle-aged woman, with dark black hair tied into a ponytail, writing on a yellow document.

She looked up from her task, "Morning, Farmer. Hey, who's your friend?"

"Hi Mary, this is Ken. He's visiting us for a while and I'm showing him around the mill. Have you seen Fred today?"

"I heard him swearing out back so I imagine he's working on Puff."

Mary's eyes stayed focused on Ken, as she stood up from her desk. Ken took in the woman, taller than him, and apparently quite voluptuous beneath her denim skirt and bright flowered blouse. He recognized Mary as the woman who read the poem last night in church.

Walking to the front of the desk, she slowly looked Ken up and down, not even trying to hide the fact that she was obviously checking him out.

"Wow, you're a fine, young man, Ken. Now don't you worry, I know just how to watch out for you. Some of the women around here could take advantage of a handsome young man like you, but I'll handle them."

Farmer shook his head and grinned after witnessing another of Mary's flirting episodes. She had become an expert at playing the game.

Ken, however, damned himself once again for looking so young. He immediately got that it was good to have Mary on your side, but as for watching out for women, she was the one you had to watch. The other women likely never had a chance to meet any new man until Mary was done with them.

"It's great to meet you Mary. The poem you read last night in church was real deep."

The comment caught Mary off guard. The young fellow acknowledging her poetry actually made her blush, something she didn't do often.

"And thank you for the warning—I can see I am going to need your expertise around here," Ken replied, as Mary's eyes lit up while still staring into his own. He broke away from the gaze to rejoin his host.

He had to dodge around Mary to catch up with Farmer walking through the hallway to the back of the building. He stopped at an office where Leanne was at her desk writing in a ledger. Looking up from her work, she announced, "Hey Farmer, I just finished the interims and it's going to be a good month."

"Morning, Leanne," and with a smile he continued, "I think you've met Ken already. He's on tour this week to check out the place. Maybe we can convince him to stay for a while. Ken if you need any accounting advice, or need to know how to file taxes so 'The Man' doesn't take it all, then Leanne is the one to fix them for you. She's a wizard with the numbers."

She had added make-up today, but the powder did not conceal her blushing. "Oh Farmer, Eureka called. They're going to send up a bank draft with Jimmie. That'll bring them up to the end of May. They were very apologetic about falling behind. Apparently they had problems because one of their customers went broke."

"Good news then. I figured old Cliff would come through—he always has. Okay, well we better go find out what's being thrown at Fred today."

They met up with Fred at the beehive waste burner out behind the mill.

"Don't you just love fucking Mondays?" Fred said as Farmer approached. "Puff here decided to go out last night, but the brain surgeons on the clean-up crew ran the conveyor and never checked on how it was burning. Now I got a load of junk in there. Old Puff ain't burning any of it." Turning to his helper he continued, "Load her up with diesel."

The young helper pulled a hand pump handle a number of times, as Fred extended a long pipe through the access door at the bottom of the structure directing diesel oil over a large area of unburned bark and sawdust at the base of the waste burner.

"Okay man, stand back, and let's get this dragon breathing again." Fred started walking away from the burner, with the group following him behind the steel conveyer.

The helper used an acetylene torch and extended the flame. Remaining outside the access door, his torch ignited a section of diesel soaked bark. After securing the access door with the metal arm lock, he pulled his welding tanks set on its cart over to where Fred, Ken, and Farmer waited.

The debris pile was lit.

As more of the diesel soaked bark and sawdust burned, a thin column of smoke exited the top of the burner expanding into a thicker plume. When Fred threw the breaker to start the electric fans, they blasted air over the ignited fuel. A thick stream of black acrid smoke pumped out of the burner stack, fifty feet above the ground. Puff was alive again!

"Fred, are there any problems with the order for Eureka Builders? I want to ship her out this weekend," Farmer asked while watching the smoke flow out of the stack.

"Okay, if everyone shows up, we can complete the order. With just three days of running this week, she'll be tight. I'm bumping the Idaho order around to make fit her in. Yeah, man, we'll get her done somehow."

"Let me know if there are any problems," requested Farmer.

"Hey Ken, how's it hanging," Fred said as he tapped Ken's shoulder.

Intrigued with what he had witnessed this morning, Ken asked Fred more questions about the burner.

"Puff burns the sawdust, bark, trim and waste from the mill. The walls are lined with water-filled pipes that heat up and make steam. The steam turns the turbines in the electrical plant just over there," he said as he pointed to a building a hundred and fifty feet away.

"With the water wheel system on the river and the steam turbines here, we make most of our own electricity. We still need government electricity to give us power all the time though."

* * *

Today's order was for twenty-four foot long green fir beams. Sawdust, mixed with the odor of oil and grease, circulated inside the mill, floating around men and woman working at their machines or on the line. Workers wrestled with the large logs to align them before the circular saw blades while others cleared the waste slabs from the end of the line. There were no quiet spots inside the mill.

The tour, including Farmer's informal sourcing of information from the workers, had made the morning pass quickly. They were in Farmer's office when the lunchtime whistle blew. After opening the bamboo picnic basket in the middle of his desk, he handed Ken a cucumber sandwich on whole grain bread and a cup of green tea poured from the black metal thermos.

"May brings me lunch every day. God knows how she figures out where I'll be, but she always packs a great meal. I sometimes think she understands more about what goes on around here than I do."

"You're a lucky man. May is a special person. How did you meet her?"

"That, my friend, is a long story," Farmer said as he refilled their cups with more tea. "I met May in Vietnam when I went in on a civilian protection mission. You see, May is a princess of the old royal family; she is the niece of the last Emperor of Vietnam. He left for France in 1955, but many of his sisters and brothers stayed in Vietnam. Few Vietnamese knew that May's mother was related to the emperor, nor were they a concern of the South Vietnamese government, that is until the middle of the war. We came under orders to move them to prevent the risk of capture of the family by the North Vietnamese."

Farmer lit up a cigarette and continued, "My team was assigned to extract her family out of Hue in the winter of '69. We took them to a small village, north of Saigon. The location was fortified as a safe zone for them to stay until the war ended. Along the way though, I admired May from a distance. She was a beautiful and smart woman, who had studied finance and economics in Hong Kong and was fluent in English. I played the role of a good soldier and held back from doing anything. I couldn't compromise our mission by doing any more than talking to her during our move. Instead, I carried out my orders, delivering them safely to a residence under the protection of American soldiers."

He paused for a moment and reflected on the memory. "I found May again in April, 1972. I was in Saigon pulling out gear to take back to the States. A few of us were going to grab a beer and some food when I saw two MPs harassing a woman at the gate of our embassy. I heard her speaking to them in clear English. Apparently, she had shown up every day for the last week and every time they told her to leave. They didn't care who she said she was; she wasn't getting inside the embassy. Fortunately, something caught my eye about the woman; she was wearing a Yankees ball cap, with an American flag on the back. I gave the hat to May when I moved her to the safe house.

"I talked to the MPs and told them she was coming inside with me, and I walked her into our embassy grounds. She was shaking as I led her by her hand to the rear gardens."

Farmer shook his head before he continued, "May was a mess. She leaned into my shoulder and cried. Between her sobs, she told me about the rest of her family being slaughtered.

"She had been returning to her house from the river, when she heard shots. She stopped at the edge of the forest and waited. After another series of shots, a dozen ARVN soldiers left the house. When it was clear, she ran into the house, past the four dead American soldiers who had been guarding the residence.

"Her family had been rounded up into the kitchen. Each had been shot in the head, none survived. Her own people's army killed her family.

"She grabbed her papers, money, and the gold and jewelry her father kept hidden and walked to Saigon. I have no idea how she made the trip and lived. She travelled through some rough ground on that journey."

Farmer butted out his smoke in the green coffee tin filled with sand placed at the edge of his desk.

"Seeing her again, I knew I had to get her to safety. The only safety I knew of was to get her out of Vietnam. I met with the

Ambassador to get papers so she could go. Even after telling him about May's history, he wouldn't approve the visa."

Farmer lit another rolled cigarette, "I told him, this had become personal and I would accept all responsibility for her in the States. He didn't know me personally, but there were some tall tales about our crew floating around through the ranks. I figured he had heard some rumors, and you know, for one of the few times during my entire run in the service, I witnessed some compassion. I left with the papers and a visa for May to head to the States."

"How did you bring her back?"

"Getting the paperwork done up was one thing, but getting her out created a whole new set of problems. I worked with good loyal men, so I called in my helicopter to land on the roof of our embassy. I packed up a load of our files and got in with May heading directly for the Saigon airport. Our crew was pulling out of Vietnam. We had a loaded Herc ready to leave for the States.

"Our operations pilot was flying and I explained about May. Jim was a tough old bugger, an old-school pilot who started flying in the Second World War. I knew he would do whatever he had to in order to help us. I told him to take May right through to my mom's farm in Iowa."

Farmer put out his cigarette in the coffee can.

"I had flown many missions with Jim and he could pull it off. I gave him a second letter, signed by the Operations General, giving him complete military authority to get May to Iowa. With that piece of paper, he could do whatever he needed to do to deliver May safely to mom."

Farmer refilled the teacups and passed Ken a slice of plum cake.

"So dig this, Jim delivered May to the farm within a week. Uncle said he had never seen such a procession as when she arrived at home. Jim took on the assignment as seriously as I knew he would. He was protecting a princess so he had a jeep with two MPs leading the black Cadillac which May and he were riding in, plus an undercover agent in the front seat, too. Two more MPs tailed the Cadillac, securing the backdoor of the parade. Jim promised me a safe delivery and he wasn't taking any chances on messing the job up."

45

Taking a smoke out of his deck on the desk, Farmer looked out the window as he flicked his lighter. He continued with his history, "I went home in August of '73. Mom and May were getting along fine; they were like mother and daughter already. Yes, May fit right in with the family. We got married after a respectful courtship of three months. And Ken, my friend, she is the best thing that has ever happened to me."

Mary knocked on the door and entered the room with the natural authority inherent with her in the office.

"The Fuzz are at the gate. Your top-notch security guard Charlie is talking to them and keeping them at bay. You better get out there before he bores them to death."

"Okay, Mary," Farmer replied, while getting up out of his chair.

"Why don't you take a walk about this afternoon and join us at the house for dinner at six?"

Ken nodded, but Mary spoke up, "I could show him around. Be no problem. I'm a good tour guide."

"Thanks for the offer, Mary. How about another time. Right now, I need some time to look around on my own for a bit," Ken told her as he smartly followed Farmer out of the building.

* * *

On his walk back to Main Street, he found a path heading down the side of the wooden bridge following alongside the creek. It was a peaceful walk on the pathway, with the creek beside him. The clear water flowing over the gravel and rocks in the river gave him a sound feeling of peacefulness he hadn't enjoyed in a long time. The trail led him to a grassy opening, which was unique in that large flat rocks were set around the far edge of the opening, creating natural benches. The rocks were warm when he stretched out on the largest one, seizing the chance to reflect upon what he had learned about the farm since his arrival 24 hours ago.

The calming serenade of the water, led him to close his eyes and listen to nature around him. The cool water cascading over the rocks in the streambed was enhanced by birds chirping in the forest behind him and a chipmunk who took up the rock beside him. Its chattering to all other chipmunks was what he listened to as he dozed off in the hypnotizing Zen-like environment.

He had not been asleep long when something tickled his chin and then his left cheek. Not wanting to wake up, he tried brushing away the disturbance while keeping his eyes closed. Annoyingly, it persisted, forcing him to open his eyes to the bright sunlight and swat away whatever it was. Leanne stood above him with a bird feather in her hand.

"How did you find me stealing off to catch a nap?"

"Oh, Ken, it doesn't take me long to track you down." She reached down and took his head in her hands. Her smooth fingers rubbed ever so gently and seductively, while tracing the features of his handsome face.

He had not resolved the internal battle he was fighting on having her in his life again. The distant pain was milder now but not forgotten. Her distractions muddled the clarity he believed he had resolved, until yesterday.

Lying on the grass, she pulled him down beside her; she hadn't lost any of her strength over the years. Looking into her eyes, he saw her mischievous sparkle once again. She rolled him onto his back and sat on his knees. Her hands seductively reached for the fly on his GWG denim jeans and undid the button, then slowly unzipped his fly.

The voices of young children running on the pathway, toward them, prompted her to stop and for him to do up his pants. They were decent when the group ran past them in pursuit of a faster running dog with a teddy bear in its mouth.

Laughing at twice being foiled, Leanne settled for holding hands as they continued down the trail, like two young teenagers testing the waters, playfully walking and talking, oblivious to their surroundings.

* * *

It was just after five, when they returned to Main Street. Farmer and Doc were meeting at the end of the street, when he saw Ken enter the roadway from the trail. He rode up to Ken and Leanne on his Honda 175 motorbike.

"There you are. May has made a special dinner for you tonight. Why don't you join us, Leanne?"

Leanne looked at Ken who nodded his head towards her. "That sounds wonderful, but I have to go home and check if Anita can watch Christina tonight."

"That works out just fine. May will have dinner ready in half an hour."

Farmer put his leather boot on the kick-starter. The finely tuned dirt bike fired on the first attempt. He spun the Honda around and took off back towards his house.

* * *

"Ken, meet Anita," Leanne said as they entered into Leanne's A-frame cabin.

"Hey there," Anita smiled as she offered Ken her hand.

Anita appeared to be about their age. Her black hair hung down below her shoulders. She had deep brown eyes and a warm smile. She was shorter than Leanne.

"Nice to meet you, Anita," he responded with a handshake.

Little Christina walked into the room through the side door. Not surprising, she was a tiny duplicate of Leanne.

"And this is Christina," she said hugging the toddler wearing a bright yellow sunflower patterned dress.

"Christina, this is my friend, Ken."

Christina played shy and hid behind her mother. However, the shy act was brief.

"Come on sweetie, say hello to Ken."

Being Leanne's child, Ken should have anticipated her next action. The little brown haired girl did a curtsy and presented him with a beaming gap toothed smile."

"It is very nice to meet you, Christina."

"Kitties," Christina said as she took Ken's hand, pulling him toward the far end of the main room.

"Kitties," she proudly announced as they stood near a black and grey tabby mother with three little kittens sleeping against her inside a wood apple box, lined with a soft grey blanket. "Mommy kitty," she said pointing. Christina petted each kitten carefully. Her mother had taught her to be gentle with the small kittens.

Leanne rescued Ken from Christina repeating the show of pointing out the kittens and the mother cat.

On the walk to Farmer's house, Leanne explained that Anita needed a place to live after her old man brought another chick to Anita's house and then told her to leave. She had no place to go so she moved in with Christina and her. The arrangement worked since Anita looked after Christina while Leanne worked at the mill. She took in some other children during the day as well, helping her earn some extra money.

* * *

May arranged a magnificent table setting for the six of them. She had brought out bright, mandarin orange-colored china and silver cutlery, complete with hand-carved ivory handles. White jasmine scented candles burned in crystal lamps set in the center of the table.

Larry and his girlfriend joined them for dinner. Without the camouflage suit, the rifle, the brush sticking out of his clothes, and the helmet, he cleaned up well. He was over six feet tall with broad shoulders and bulging biceps. Larry fit the warning from Ken's father that Larry wasn't someone you'd care to mess with.

"Good to see you again. I'm glad you got up here to meet us. Your old man is great; I always liked working with him. He's a hell of a pilot. Farmer told me he's not doing well. Got tangled up with the cancer—that sucks man—he's one of the good ones."

"Dad has said great things about you Larry. He told me there was no one that flew a chopper like you," returned Ken.

The woman beside Larry put out her hand and introduced herself as Starr.

Larry's girlfriend, Starr, was a shapely woman with sharp blue eyes and long blonde hair. She couldn't have been more than thirty and stood a full head shorter than Larry. Ken thought she carried a New Zealand accent so he opened his introduction to Starr with the question, "Is that a Kiwi accent?"

Starr smiled, revealing perfect white teeth. "My god, imagine that, a Yank who can pick out a Kiwi's accent. You are the first American not to tell me that I had a British accent."

"Where did you grow up?"

"Ah, I'm from the city of Sails—Auckland. I'm a proud northern Sheila."

"New Zealand is a great place—I spent some time there last year. It is a very beautiful country. How did you wind up in Canada?"

"Well, in a word, *Larry*. Yeah, he's my knight in shining armor. I went to the States to meet up with my cousin. We were driving her car to her parent's home in Verona, cruising along the highway, when the motor in her Beetle quit. We opened the boot, but we had no idea what to do, so we waited for a lift. Instead of a car coming along, we heard this roaring motorcycle coming at us. The biker drove past us and stopped. He turned around and came back to us."

"I saw this beautiful woman so I just had to stop and meet her," Larry added as Starr jabbed him in the ribs.

"So this tough biker, dressed in his leather vest, over his white t-shirt, and with his long black beard and a ponytail, gets off his bike and walks up to us. He tells us his name and starts poking around the car engine. He pulled out this big knife from the side of his boot. My cousin was terrified, but I had a feeling we would be okay. Larry was very polite and well mannered. He even called us, *Ma'am*."

"He still calls you Ma'am," Farmer added.

"Yes, he does, and so he should. He used that big knife of his to do something with the wires and fixed the engine. We invited him home for dinner. My aunt and uncle were cool with Larry. He stayed in their guest room overnight. The next day, I rode away on the back of his Harley and we wound up visiting Farmer and May. We're still here." Starr grabbed Larry and kissed him, "My guardian angel."

"Okay you two, you have lots of time for that, come on and grab a chair." Farmer led the men into the living room. The women followed May into the kitchen. Farmer poured from a Czechoslovakian lead crystal decanter into three highball glasses, handing one to each of them.

"To another beautiful day," he said as they clicked their glasses together and then took a swig of the liquor.

Ken coughed on the bitter, but very sharp, drink.

"What is this?"

"Ah, it is a secret recipe. One of our friends makes this for us. Good old grain mash—just like back on the farm in Iowa."

"I guess it takes a bit of getting used to," Ken said as he coughed after another swig.

For the second time, he witnessed a smile on Larry's face, "Yeah, it takes a bit of getting used to alright; a man can get used to almost anything."

May led Leanne and Starr as they brought the cooked dishes to the decorated table. They were a perfect vision of three very different, and distinctly beautiful, ladies. With the dishes on the table, the men took up a chair beside their women.

Leanne tapped Ken on the leg and winked at him. She was happy and glowed with satisfaction. She had locked onto her man.

Farmer poured glasses of elderberry wine. May started by passing dishes around the table: the stir fried vegetables on noodles, the steamed rice, the Vietnamese beef stew, and the chicken mixed with green beans in a sauce made from curry and coconut milk. The food was delicious; the dinner was perfect. This dinner could have taken place in New York, San Francisco, or Los Angeles, but instead this dinner was taking place on a farm deep in the mountains of British Columbia, Canada. It was an unpretentious combination of the new world meeting the old world, with people from around the world.

After the feast, the women cleared the table and washed the dishes. The men wound up in the back yard starting a fire in a deep and wide old logging truck rim, serving as a steel encased fire pit. Ken smoked a cigarette, Farmer smoked a pipe, and Larry lit up a Black Cat cigar. Another round of grain mash went down as they sat on wooden chairs around the flames.

"Do you want to go flying with me tomorrow? I have to fly some gear up to fix our radio and TV system." Larry asked Ken.

Ken looked toward Farmer, who nodded back at him.

"That sounds cool. Where do you want me to meet you?"

"I'll pick you up about seven. The weather's calm in the morning; it is the best time to fly up there." Changing the subject, Larry turned to Farmer, "What did the Fuzz want today?"

"Oh, old Sergeant Cody had a few things to deal with today. He wanted to know about Max. Max stole a truck in town and drove over to Newton Landing. I told him that *shit for brains* Max doesn't live here anymore, and he won't be coming back either. What a fuck up. Ken, this dude is a real wacko. I don't know what Leanne saw in him, but the best thing that happened to her was him leaving town."

"Anything else?" quizzed Larry, as if he knew the answer already.

"Yeah, same old lecture. He said he'll be checking every vehicle driving into town on Wednesday and they all have to be licensed and driven by sober and legal drivers. Same old lecture."

"Nothing else?"

"Let me think," Farmer said as he poured himself another shot and passed the bottle to Ken. "Oh yeah, Larry, he also said you shouldn't be scaring the tourists around here."

"What the hell—I figured as much! He's too chicken shit to talk to me, is he? Well, I told you about those Albertans picking around in the river, 'looking for gold' they said. No way, those two punks were sneaking to the hot springs to catch some woman bathing. I just told them they were trespassing, and they had to leave."

"Uh huh," Farmer said as he tapped his pipe bowl on the side of the bench to loosen the ashes. "Say, Larry, were you carrying a gun when you jumped out from the bushes and scared the shit out of them?"

"Well, yeah, an M-60, I had been sighting in that morning."

"And were you in camo?"

"Well, I guess so. Hey, what the hell. Why is he so pissed off at me? He knows I wouldn't hurt them."

"Yeah, he knows that, Larry. Old Cody smiled, or at least the closest old Sergeant Cody would ever come to a smile, when he told me the men were still shaking as they wrote up their story for the report. When you shot the M-60 and knocked the top ten feet off the pine tree, they got a different message."

"I told you, I had sighted in the gun. I just wanted to make sure she was still good."

"Well, anyway, everything is okay again. Next time though, maybe you could just ask them to leave."

"Yeah, okay, but they shouldn't be poking around here anyway."

"You're right, and thank God you are here to help us out, man."

"Do the cops bother you much?" quizzed Ken.

"No, they leave us alone. If there is a problem, they talk to me, Larry or Fred and we deal with it in house. It's a lot easier on them, since they don't have to mix it up with any of our friends here. They don't want to come in here, anyway. There are stories about some of the residents. They just don't want to know if the rumors are true or not, so they stay away and let us deal with matters ourselves. It seems to work out okay."

Starr sat on Larry's lap and took his hand. "Honey, I'm tired. We should be going home."

Larry just stood up and did as instructed. He was Starr's man. When she said it was time to go, then it was time to go. A thousand other people could tell Larry what they wanted him to do and he wouldn't do it, but he did what Starr told him.

Leanne walked behind Ken, put her hands onto his shoulders, and started massaging his shoulders. "It is late for me, too. I have to get to work early tomorrow. I don't want Mary to think I am slacking off these days. Will you walk me home?"

Just like a couple, Ken mimicked Larry, got up, and stood beside Leanne.

Looking at May and Farmer, Leanne sincerely said, "Thank you for the lovely evening. I had a very special time tonight."

May thanked her for joining them.

They walked away from Farmer's house and down the side street in the bright moonlight. Before she ascended the steps to her house, he pulled her close and whispered, "Good night, my sweet Leanne. Be safe." They kissed in the moonlight while two eyes watched them from the shadows of the side window.

Chapter 4

Tuesday, June 28, 1977

Ken emptied his mug of thick black coffee just as Larry turned into Farmer's driveway in his immaculately clean, bright yellow, 1968 GMC pickup.

Larry didn't say much in the truck. As they headed toward the mill, the radio played the Canadian Broadcasting Company news report out of Vancouver. The crisp morning air, flowing through the open windows, cooled Ken's face. The aroma of fresh sawdust, lavender flowers, and freshly cut canola stalks woke up his sense of smell.

Before the mill office, he turned left onto a gravel road. The compacted black shale surface had been stabilized with used motor oil, thereby creating a strong and smooth road. Two tall buildings, each with a peaked blue metal roof to protect the structure from the heavy winter snowfall, were at the end of the road. They parked beside the first white building.

Opening the right door of the tall double doors on the larger building, Larry pushed the steel lock pin into a pipe fitting in the concrete driveway. The building served as both a workshop and a helicopter hangar. The sterile white walls appeared as clean as a hospital operating room. The solid, concrete floor was painted in Battleship grey; extra navy surplus paint in five-gallon pails lined one wall. A workbench ran down the entire fifty-foot length of the left wall. Tool chests, a welder, acetylene torches, and everything you'd expect in a full service garage, outfitted this hangar.

However, the everyman's dream pristine workshop was not the highlight of the building. No, the pearl white helicopter was the centerpiece of the shop. As the fluorescent lights lit up the shop, the waxed paint on the helicopter reflected the light off its polished finish and highlighted the lime green accent strip running down the length of the body. The long grey rotor blades, with their yellow tips, were aligned with the length of the machine and secured to its tail. Affixed to the front skids was a small gasoline-powered pull cart.

A wide grin lit up Larry's face when he said, "Ain't she a beauty?"

"Wow, what a cool place. Man, that's one great looking machine."

"Yeah, this is a Bell 206B. This one tangled with a rock bluff. I bought it as a wreck. It was a mess so I found an Army surplus OH-58 parts machine. She came together nicely, didn't she? She even has the Jet Ranger II motor, pumping out over 400 horses."

"You built this helicopter from two wrecks; cool man, recycling helicopters."

"Yes, I spent almost a year building her. This is one tight machine. Let me show you my other baby," Larry said as he walked toward the smaller hangar.

Inside the second white painted shop, with the accompanying grey floor, another helicopter was parked.

"Wow, cool man. A MASH helicopter," Ken said looking into the other immaculate shop. This smaller helicopter featured a protruding glass bubble around the cockpit—just like the choppers used in the popular television show. The helicopter resembled a big bubble-headed dragonfly.

"She's a 47G with the supercharged 280 Lycoming."

"Did you build this one, too?"

"No," Larry paused, "a buddy had her down on his farm in Texas. He had a good gig going, rounding up cattle and checking power lines. Then he was drafted and got shot up. You can't fly when you're paralyzed from the neck down, so he asked me to take his baby. She's a special machine. When I need to get away, I take her up into the mountains and tell myself this is where Chester would want her to fly."

As he closed the door to the hangar, a brown four-door Ford Falcon drove up, parking beside Larry's pickup. A short, thin man got out of the car. After adjusting his black plastic-framed glasses back upon his nose, he lifted open the trunk of the Falcon and unloaded three metal toolboxes.

"Ken, meet Elton. He's our chief electrician around here."

"Hey Elton," Ken said as they shook hands.

Larry returned to the 206 helicopter's hangar. As he had done a thousand times before, he methodically ran through his visual inspection, including checking the immaculate concrete floor for any leaked fluid spots.

Satisfied with the pre-flight review, Larry walked backwards out of the hangar while operating a gas powered pulling machine that resembled a large lawnmower. The machine pulled the Jet Ranger along the concrete roadway. He stopped in the middle of the yellow circle at the end of the concrete driveway, fifty feet away from the hangar and proceeded to remove the rotor straps and set them inside a small compartment on the left side of the helicopter.

Ken and Elton carried the toolboxes to the helicopter where Larry told them his rules: no walking behind the storage doors, close the cockpit doors very gently, no erratic movements getting into or out of the machine, and always crouch low when approaching it.

Elton sat on the forward facing bench seat in the rear of the helicopter cabin. Ken climbed in the left front door allowing Larry to push the door closed until the latch caught. They fixed their seatbelts and put on their headphones.

Larry's hands ran through a series of pre-ignition checks. Satisfied, he turned the throttle open, then closed, flicked more switches, locked the throttle at about 12%, and then pushed the starter button with his middle finger. The whir of the turbine spinning, followed by the engine ignition, echoed in spite of the headphones. Larry's eyes scanned the gauges using his finger to tap some of them to ensure they weren't stuck. While monitoring his fuel pressure, he throttled up the jet engine and the rotor blades increased in speed. He made the start-up process appear far easier than it was.

Larry surveyed around the machine one more time to make sure they were clear and focused on his gauges again. Slowly the helicopter lifted off the ground. They flew higher and accelerated east of the mill and over the vegetable fields, already at an elevation of 200 feet. Larry maintained the habits he picked up flying in the jungle and flew forward and fast, clearing what he needed to, but getting on with the trip.

They soon were over the glacier fed water of the Blue Ridge River. The gentle sloping colorful fields and mixed deciduous and coniferous forest were now behind them. Rising up from the deep green and lush forests along the river the trees thinned out as the trio flew up the mountainside. The trees grew right to the peak of the first set of mountaintops, but as they got farther up the valley, the mountains got steeper, and rockier, and fewer trees grew on the inhospitable rock faces.

The main road into the valley followed the river up the right side of the valley, with branch roads taking off up other parts of the mountain. The branch roads zigzagged back and forth across the face of the mountain, resulting in steep switchbacks on their route up to the top.

The river below churned white water as it flowed through a narrow canyon. Old trails and roads snaked up the side of some of the mountains, most of them were overgrown with new trees, but a few of them were being used to deliver logs and shed dust as vehicles traversed their inclines.

After twenty minutes of flying time, they arrived at the first tower. The radio tower consisted of a wooden base that looked like an old trapper's cabin, with a tall metal antennae extending from the roof. Larry flew around the site twice before landing on the rock pad with a yellow circle painted on it.

On Larry's instructions, Ken and Elton remained inside as he shut down the motor. The shutdown process took a few minutes so they waited until Larry unbuckled and got out. He pulled a 12-gauge shotgun out from a pouch in the rear seat and walked toward the building. The tower door was still secure. He held the shotgun in his left hand and opened the door with his right hand. There were no signs of bear visits. After emerging from the building, Elton and Ken got out to join him.

Larry returned from the helicopter with a thermos and three metal cups. "Starr makes this stuff a bit strong, but it'll keep you awake."

Ken and Larry drank their thick black coffee in the warm sun as Elton did the necessary repairs to the equipment inside the tower. Larry explained that this tower was one of three repeaters set up to receive radio, and television signals, while running their VHF radio system for the mill, logging and mining operations of the farm. Elton, who used to repair radar units on aircraft carriers, designed and built the system from military surplus equipment.

This tower was the furthest one in the set of three. The tower received television and radio signals from a tower in Northern Idaho, near the Canadian border. The signals were redirected back down the river valley toward the farm to a repeater tower, just above the orange bridge. The second tower directed the signals to a unit on the hill above the farm. The farm's tower rebroadcast the signals allowing them to receive television and radio signals almost anywhere on the townsite.

Elton had also run the telephone landlines to the mill and to Farmer's town office. For the rest of the residents, he set up his own pay phone in front of the bakery. Elton made about twenty-five bucks a month from his phone business.

"Yup, it was fuses again," Elton announced as he emerged from the tower building. "Damn things! I put in some slow blows so they will last longer. I'm done. How's the coffee?"

"Good stuff. A batch of Starr's best."

"Ah, well you got a good woman there; one who makes coffee in the morning. This is great java," Elton announced after he took his first drink. "Yeah, well Sunflower wasn't getting up to make me breakfast this morning," Elton laughed. In fact, Sunflower never got up to make coffee, or much else, around their house. Sunflower was a painter and sculptor. She didn't care much for household chores. She usually woke about noon, had her tea, sometimes worked on a painting in the afternoon, went for a walk, or meditated. Sunflower was a Canadian who met Elton in LA. When her acting career didn't work out for her, Elton followed her to Canada. She was the opposite of the structured and organized Elton, so they fit together well.

Back in the air again, they hovered along the ridge and then the tall mountain fell away from them as they left the ridgeline.

Ken's stomach sank as the earth disappeared below them and Larry continued the sightseeing part of the trip. Dropping the 206 down to the left, he took them up the river again flying at 2,000 feet above the river. The mountaintops were still above them. They continued climbing in elevation. When they cleared the tallest mountain, Ken was awestruck at the enormous white glacier planted on the top of the mountain. The glacier stretched for miles and miles. They flew above the enormous slab of snow and ice with its sharp blue crevices at the edges. At the end of the glacier, a small outflow of water ran down a completely different mountain range.

"The Blue Ridge Glacier melt flows down into our river on the south end and on the north side it feeds the Gold River system," tour guide Larry explained to Ken through his radio headset.

The glacial scenery in front of them was truly spectacular. The Blue Ridge Glacier stretched across the flat, cone-shaped mountaintop, with the closest exposed face over 400 feet deep.

Elton announced though the headset, "This is about where the farm starts. Some survey markers are dropped down into the glacier, but you'll never find them. Everything we are flying over is part of the property."

The farm's acreage was incomprehensible—so much larger than Ken had imagined.

Running back along the right side of the valley the mountains were not as steep as the other side and they were richer in vegetation with the tall straight spruce and hemlock forests growing to the ridge tops. Larry flared the helicopter to slow down and hover over a clearing at the top of one of the ridges.

"This used to be a gold mine. In the early 1900s, the camp had over a hundred men working in the underground mine. Mules hauled the ore down trails cut into the mountainside. You can see the line of the old trail along the side of this hill down to near the river," Larry said as he flew them down beside the trail towards the Blue Ridge River.

There were over fifty mines in this area in the last eighty years. We found some of the old maps. They sent their ore down to the concentrator in New Pontiac and boats took it to the railhead. The concentrator used to be about where the mill is now, but the old building burned down sometime in the '40s."

An empty yellow and green logging truck worked its way along the twisting road toward the orange metal bridge as they flew past it and continued down the river.

With the farm now in view, Elton spoke, "See our power house just at the back here where the Pontiac River flows into the Blue Ridge River. Water runs down along this hillside in a flume from the lake at the top. The flume takes the water right into the turbine of the powerhouse. They built it to run the concentrator. She was mothballed for years, but Doc brought up some friends about ten years ago and they rebuilt the turbine and the generator. With the electricity generated by the mill burner, we make enough to run the mill and power a few homes, too. We still buy from the government since we need an uninterrupted supply of electricity."

They flew back to the hangar in a direct line over the farm, from the powerhouse to the hangar. Just after noon, they were out of the helicopter and had loaded Elton's tools into his Ford Falcon.

Larry was working a pail of soap and water mixture and a handful of white towels to clean the glass and the front of the helicopter from bug guts and dirt stains. Ken asked if he could help, but Larry declined his offer as he cleaned the surfaces to his definition of a shine.

Taking his cue, Ken sat on the tailgate of the GMC and had a smoke. He finished his third by the time Larry parked the chopper inside the hangar. Carrying his thermos with him, Larry came out of the hangar and closed the doors. "Do you want to come with me to look at some logging? We won't be long."

"Sure."

Larry stopped the truck at the bakery. Starr met him at the door, handing him a large brown bag, after which she reached into the cab and kissed him after she stretched put her arms around him.

"Lunch is served," he announced, as he set the bag onto the seat of the truck. Today's lunch consisted of cheese and cucumber sandwiches, washed down with iced tea from a mason jar.

The steep and narrow roads demanded radio control for traffic. Pullouts off the road allowed for trucks to pass each other and the radio was the only way to prevent head-on collisions in the areas between the pullouts. Past the two-mile marker sign, they awaited the approach of a loaded logging truck. An oversized, grey and blue, Pacific logging truck pulled its load past them, clouding them in dust from the dry gravel roadbed. The large cedar load was destined for the mill.

Before the faded orange bridge, they turned onto a branch road. The logging crew was working by the 14-mile marker.

From beside the pickup, Ken watched as the huge Caterpillar loader struggled at placing a large cedar log onto the logging truck's trailer.

Larry met with a scruffy looking hippie, beside a black Chevrolet crew cab. The meeting was short, within minutes they were off again.

"I rebuilt the transmission on the skidder, and I wanted to make sure they changed the oil. They did and she was clear and clean. No problems with it."

On the drive back, Larry asked Ken about his life. Ken told him about university, the reserves, his service in Military Intelligence at Clark Air Force Base in the Philippines and some teaching he had done to fill in his buy-out time. Larry wasn't easy to talk to, he didn't talk much, or at least until now.

Parking downhill of the one-mile marker, he said, "I better check on the water for the boss."

The short trial from the road took them to a concrete water tank. Larry's inspection was brief; he opened a check panel to verify the water level and opened a small tap on the pipe leading from the tank. Water flowed confirming the outlet was clear.

"This is our backup reservoir. If we have a bad fire at the mill, or a home, we can draw on this 10,000 gallon tank. Our main reservoir draws from the Blue Ridge River, so we pull water from two different sources."

"Good idea," Ken replied.

"Sure was, Farmer's paranoia about safety is a good thing for us. The guy won't scrimp a dime when it comes to being safe. He's been that way as long as I've known him, he's steady eddy and he's always looking out for others."

Inside the truck, Ken was feeling more confident in talking to Larry. "Can I ask you how come you call Farmer 'boss'? Dad let it slip sometimes too."

A guttural laugh came from Larry. "He's a natural. Even in the toughest firefight, he can keep his men focused and going forward. I've seen him take green draftees and lead them into a lion's den. He never shucked being responsible for his men and we all saw that. The Major was usually first in and last out. From the time I met him, I saw that in him. Yeah, he'd tell you we all had a job to do, but we couldn't have done it without Farmer leading us. I got no problem calling him boss; he's earned that from me. It also pisses him off a bit, I think," he chuckled on the last words.

Ken's impression of both men just changed beyond the pedestal they were on already. Hearing Larry laugh but explain something with so much respect was not expected on this ride in the forest.

They arrived at the mill just after the 3:30 whistle and the workers were leaving for the day.

Larry parked beside Farmer's Blazer as Leanne walked out. "I've got some things to do here, why don't you walk Leanne home," he suggested to Ken, accented by a grin.

Leanne had already made her way to Ken and had taken his hand as he stood beside the truck.

* * *

In contrast to the sparse conversation of the day thus far, Leanne was brimming with it. Almost recounting minute by minute, she spoke of her day on their walk into town.

The wonderful and bright, but unpredictable, Leanne was there to highlight his day again. Instead of stopping at her house, they continued further along Fox Street. The fresh water smell of the Blue Ridge River became noticeable.

"Christina was sure impressed with you. She told me that I should be your friend. Isn't that cute! She is a sharp kid, with years of wisdom in her and not yet even three years old. I told her I also thought you were a nice man, and you would be a good friend, too. Well, Ken, do you want to be my friend," she said as she stopped their walk and kissed him on the lips. Her hand reached down and rubbed the front of his jeans.

Damn she was making it harder for him to find a reason to remember five years ago.

Just as quickly as she had prompted the kiss, she grabbed his hand, and began pulling him along with her. They ran along a trail through the trees until it ended at a large sandy beach off the main river. Going for broke, she taunted him by undressing on the beach, and setting her blouse and dress on top of her sandals.

"If you catch me, you can have me," she called to him as she ran to the water.

He was finally a broken man, giving into lust, burying deep his resentment, and did in fact want to pursue again the naked beauty in the water. She was already swimming in the quiet bay when he got to the edge. He waded into the cool water until he was waist deep and then dove in to catch up with her.

She was standing waist deep on the right side of the bay, when he caught her. Skin against skin felt right again. Lifting her out of the water, he carried her to the grassy shore. Their hands roamed over each other, pushing droplets of water off their skin as the warm sun dried their bodies.

Whether it was the tranquility of the colorful bay, or the ambiance of the setting, their re-union sex was a soft and gentle dance of sensation; so very different from their earlier times together, when rampant lust and quickies had too often been their relationship.

The past had been good, but this was better. Their old lives seemed a million miles away. It was as if they were meeting anew, with a clean slate and a lifetime of chalk to write upon it.

They didn't return to Leanne's house until after dinner. Anita brought out a large green salad with bean sprouts and smoked fish for them to eat at the outside table. Christina told them how Momma kitty carried a kitten by its head today. For added emphasis of the importance of this event, Christina sat beside Ken and repeated what the mother cat had done.

Christina brought Ken her Dr. Seuss book, *The Cat in the Hat.* She climbed onto his lap as he began reading the book. He created cartoon voices for each of the characters and soon Christina was laughing at the voices he used for each character. When the story ended, Anita took Christina into the house to get ready for bed.

Tomorrow is 'Welfare Wednesday'," Leanne explained, "so most of our people will be leaving to go to Riverbend to collect their monthly payment from the government."

Those that went in collected a check from the government of British Columbia after they proved their need for the money to buy food, clothes, and pay their rent. Since Anita didn't have a job, welfare was her only source of money. Leanne was in a different situation. When Max split he took all of Leanne's savings with him. He even ran up accounts in town under her name. Leanne needed help to get back on her feet. Her salary from her accounting job couldn't repair the damage that Max had done.

Therefore, Welfare Wednesday, a monthly event, promised to be a big day for many of the residents of the farm. Leanne offered Ken a ride into Riverbend, to see the town, but he held off on accepting the offer until he found out what Farmer had planned for tomorrow.

Chapter 5

Wednesday, June 29, 1977

By eight in the morning, the farm was alive with activity. Vehicles merged onto Main Street from every corner of New Pontiac. Those who could take on extra passengers congregated in front of the Pontiac Hall. Men, women, children, and even dogs were in the mix. Loaded vehicles drove past the hall and left on their own trip to the Government Welfare Office in Riverbend.

Over the years, the people had learned how to deal with the agents at the Welfare Office. The better you dressed, the longer it took to get through the line. Instead, the longer the time since your last bath, or the smellier your old clothes were, the faster you got through the agent's challenges. Therefore, they left their Sunday best at home and skipped last Saturday night's bath.

Gender also played a factor in the interview process. Men were not hassled as much as women, so a man was always in line behind a woman, passively intimidating the agent. Two single people received more than a married couple, since they each received a separate housing allowance, so no one was married. The monthly adventure to Riverbend had become a well-orchestrated handling of people for maximum return.

Farmer and Ken walked down to check on the process. A mud coated green Volkswagen Micro Bus passed them. A man with a thick curly black beard drove the bus while another heavily bearded hippie slept in the passenger seat. Four young children pressed their faces to the window, ensuring they caught sight of all the activity on their monthly trip to the big town.

The third vehicle in the line was a 1970 white and turquois Ford pickup. Leanne drove, with Christina in the middle, and Anita leaned against the passenger door, apparently expecting to nap on the drive. Even in a worn and tattered cotton blouse, Leanne could not look normal; she could not hide her natural beauty.

"Morning ladies," Ken said to the girls in the same voice he had created for the Cat while reading the *Cat in the Hat* the previous evening.

Christina laughed at hearing the voice again, followed by the woman unable to restrain from joining her laughing.

When they were out of earshot, Farmer commented, "You've made quite the impression on those women, Ken. They are good people."

"Yeah, or they have made quite an impression on me?" he replied. Realizing what he had just said aloud, he quickly recovered by asking, "What's up with the dogs?"

"Yeah, well, about the dogs. If you have a dog, you have to feed him, and that costs money, for which the government gives you a dog allowance. You have to prove you have a dog, so the dogs go into town to be shown to the agent. I've heard the same dog sometimes gets shown a few times, by different families, but who knows. That's probably not a bad deal for the dog."

"But don't some of these people also work in the mill?" Ken asked.

"A few of them do, but they don't show up enough to make much at the mill. Their families suffer if they don't get some extra money. The regular mill workers and loggers get the day off too, and some go into town anyway. Others will take her cool for the day and hang out here."

A loud backfire caused a reactionary turn to the location, where an old yellow school bus was on its way out of town, spewing a stream of blue exhaust from a much worn out engine behind it.

"I stay out of what goes on this day. I don't need to know anything. Everyone does what they need to do to get by. This day ensures the children get food, and for that I can accept whatever else happens."

* * *

Inside Farmer's main office, the Mr. Coffee machine sputtered, draining its last brew into the carafe below. Another fresh pot of coffee was ready.

"Looks like Starr came by and made us some Joe. Larry should be along in a while. Handing Ken a metal cup of coffee, Farmer continued, "It'll be a quiet day around here today. They'll start drifting back late this afternoon. Some will spend time in the bar and return tomorrow."

"Morning, men," Larry stated as he entered the office.

He poured himself a cup of java as Farmer continued, "What do you think about the place so far?"

"This is the most peaceful place I have ever visited. No sirens at four in the morning, no traffic jams, no buzz of the city, and no smell of the city. The air is pure here, the people are kind and friendly, and the place is real, man."

"I think he's been spending too much time with Leanne," Larry laughed.

Farmer interjected, "Leanne's a fine woman, Ken. She deserves for someone to be good to her. . . Yeah, we have a good family here. We all wound up for our own reasons. Some will leave, but most will hang around for a while yet.

"We've got time this morning to talk more about your visit here. Your dad's a good man. I see a lot of him in you Ken. What has he told you about Vietnam?"

"Dad didn't talk much about Vietnam, until recently. As he got sicker, he told me more about the war. He was short on details though. After he received the letter in the mail from his army friend, he stopped talking about the war and whatever he was up to over in Vietnam."

"Did he ever talk about a man named Colonel Henry or Harley?"

"A couple of times. He didn't really say much about him though.

Sitting in one of the big leather chairs to the left of Farmer's desk, Ken lit up a Marlboro. Larry turned away from the window where he had been reflecting on a life he had lived in what felt like so long ago.

"Did Shelby say much about Birdman?" Farmer asked Ken.

"Yes, he called him Baxter sometimes too."

"Birdman was quite a character. Your dad gave him the name, too. I think he liked Shelby for that moniker."

"What do you mean?"

"Well," Farmer started, "when we first met the chief he was a straight-laced, no nonsense agent. On a break from training, we were in a bar in Vegas. Baxter walks into the bar with a blonde under one arm and a brunette under the other. The man is strutting as if he is the rooster of the coop.

"He sees us, comes over, and sits at our table, leaving the two pretty ladies standing behind him, like trophies. Bragging to us, he says something like, 'Look at these two lovely birds I have found.' They were young and pretty; the kind of girls that stick in your mind. The brunette was tall with long legs coming out of a mighty fine tight white skirt. The blonde wore a tight yellow tank top. I still have a clear memory of the top she was wearing.

"Me, too", added Larry.

"Being the polite guy I was, and since he didn't need both of the ladies, I thought I'd see which one would take me on. I asked him 'What the hell is a guy like you doing with two beautiful chicks?'"

Farmer paused as he lit a smoke.

"Baxter replied the ladies were not 'chicks' they were 'birds'—and these lovely English birds came over here to the good old US of A to meet men like him. The next day, Shelby called Baxter, 'Birdman', and it stuck."

"Birdman, he was the real deal, man. The chief was one of a kind. Did your dad say much about him?" asked Larry.

"He said Birdman kept a lot of stuff to himself. He told me Birdman had been hurt in the Korean War. It doesn't make sense that he would then sign up for Vietnam."

"Yeah, Birdman came home a hero from Korea. He was an engineer, sitting pretty in a great job at Ford, and then like some other dumb fucks we know, he linked up with the army to help Uncle Sam—he went to Vietnam. Being a seasoned veteran, and a sharp guy, he didn't stand a chance in 'The Man's' new army. Sometime in the early '60s, he wound up in the CIA and got into special assignments. Birdman had real pull; he could damn near do anything he wanted. I still have no idea what his real title was, but whatever it was, it worked. He was different, but okay. He watched out for his men," Larry offered.

"I once asked him what his real job was and he said something like he was part of a team that was trying to figure out how to leave a war that could not be won and save our own soldiers while doing it. You know, that probably was his real job," Farmer said as the reflection ran through him.

Larry changed gears by describing the history of the town while pointing to markers on the old yellowed map on the office wall. He showed Ken where they had flown yesterday, including the locations of the towers.

Farmer grabbed three documents on his desk and set them inside a manila envelope.

"I'm heading up to the mill to drop off this paper. You coming along?" he asked Ken.

* * *

By lunchtime, they were sitting at May's table with a bowl of piping hot spicy beef Hue noodle soup for lunch. It was spicier than Ken was used to eating, but the glass of milk that May gave him tempered the burning in his mouth.

May had developed a trust with Ken, in such a short time. She questioned him about his travels in Southern Asia, and fondly reflected on her own visits to New Zealand and Australia during her breaks in her studies. She had taken up sailing while in Australia, which culminated in an eight person crew sail from Melbourne to Auckland. Unfortunately, the trip confirmed the open waters were not for her.

Her trip to meet with family members in France had been her only trip to Europe. Letting down her guard, she was able to egg Farmer on about how romantic it would be to walk out over the Seine in Paris or visit the Loire Valley.

Farmer did not take the bait, other than to admit, "Every day is a romantic journey with you, May.

Unexpectedly May did not shy away from the flirting, causing Ken to feel like the third cog in the system at that time.

* * *

Larry pushed the cyclic forward on the Bell 47G as the 280 Lycoming engine took the bubble-faced helicopter toward the alpine and treeless landscape at the top of Sugar Mountain.

Starr, his passenger, wasn't fond of flying, but Larry loved to take to the sky and he just needed to fly. She loved her man, so she would suffer through the flight for him.

In spite of not enjoying the flying, she loved where they were going. He set the ton and a half machine down on the flat meadow above the tree line. Out the bubble of their window, they looked directly at Starr Lake. The lake probably had another name, but to them, it was Starr Lake.

Without access by helicopter, not many people had ever been to Starr Lake. Starr Lake's crystal clean emerald colored waters shimmered like an oasis. When the rotors stopped turning, Starr reached across to kiss her man. She truly loved him; he was one of a kind. Walking from the helicopter, across the soft moss and stunted grass, they were absorbed in each other in their own Shangri-La.

As they approached the water, Starr took her hand from him and started undressing to go for a swim. With her dress and top nicely folded on top of a flat rock, she ran naked towards the glistening water. Larry was slower in undressing. He was a good minute behind her. He left a wool blanket at the edge of the shore and ran into the water. She was a stone's throw from the shore when Larry caught up with her. Carrying her on his back, he swam her to a spot where they could touch the sandy bottom of the lake.

Larry took Starr in his thick arms and held her tight to him. Her bare breasts pushed on his chest as he held her close—one of those perfect moments that happen so seldom in life. It was just their senses; there was no need to exchange words. Arms clamped the two tight together in the cool water; the moment would be lost when they parted.

Back on the grassy shoreline, lying on the blanket, Starr ran her hands along his hard muscles. She felt the scarred hole in his left bicep and the scar running across the front of his right shoulder. He did not feel her soft fingertips rub the marked skin across his back; the tissue had died a long time ago. This soldier had taken many wounds over his years of service.

His calloused and rough fingers felt each vertebra down her spine. As gently as he could, he massaged her from the top of her glistening bottom to the peaks of her smooth shoulders. She was a complete contrast to Larry; he was rough and marked, she was smooth and unmarred by foreign shrapnel—as different as sandpaper and silk.

They laid on the blanket, absorbing the warm rays of the summer sun. Her head rested on his hairy chest. He moved up from her shoulders to her neck with his massaging hand. She closed her eyes as she ran her left hand across his face. The scar above his left eye and the bump above his left ear were familiar to her fingers, as was the scar from a bullet wound in his left thigh that she felt as her hand playfully ran down his leg.

There was not much to say, it was a time for just being. Resting at the edge of the lake, surrounded by the sweet alpine grass, enjoying each other in Mother Nature's gifts, released concerns of anything outside of where they were. Days like this should never end.

* * *

The afternoon was warm in Pontiac, too. The large, green cedar trees surrounding Farmer's house shaded the back yard making it comfortable in the warm afternoon. Ken and Farmer each grabbed an aluminum framed recliner lawn chair to relax in while they drank green tea and smoked cigarettes in the shade.

"Ken, what do you think about hanging on here for a time? It's a good place to be, you'll fit in fine. I have a spot in the mill, if you want to give it a shot."

Ken butted out his smoke under his boot on the moist green grass.

"I've been thinking about it. I like the town. Leanne has become an unexpected, but pleasant, surprise for me. I still have six months to decide if I want to return to teaching."

"What's your status with the army?"

"Good, I'm clear with Uncle Sam. I've finished my service obligation. I can sign up again or go teach. If I did stay here, I'd have some time to think about what to do next," Ken paused, "Yeah, man, I'd like to hang around here for a while."

"Good, it'll be cool having you around. You remind me so much of your father.

The thumping from the helicopter rotors overhead meant Larry and Starr were returning. Then they heard the first of the vehicles returning from Riverbend.

"Let's head down and learn about what happened in town today," Farmer said as he got up and began walking down the driveway. They walked to Main Street to witness the residents returning from their adventure in Riverbend.

A rusted white Econoline van lead the convoy, carrying groceries, tobacco, liquor, clothes, and whatever money they still had left over from the monthly assistance. Farmer flagged down the van and found out that Sergeant Cody had parked on the side of the road, just at the town's entrance, but he was patient and left them alone. He hadn't pulled anyone over.

The truth was that Sergeant Cody didn't want to deal with the farm residents, but he had to put up a good presence for the Riverbend folks so they knew he was protecting them, too. He had to appease the grandmas and busybodies of the town, but avoided creating any reason to deal with anybody from the farm. It was a challenge to keep busy while not affecting anyone, but Sergeant Cody had grown quite proficient at the balancing act.

It was after five o'clock when the next convoy of vehicles returned. The lead 1961 GMC pickup had one man driving with his woman and three children sitting in the cab. Two skinny dogs and three longhaired men sat in the bed of truck surrounded by boxes of food and supplies. Every shape and size of vehicle, person, and dog was returning to New Pontiac.

Leanne was next in the convoy. Both her passengers were asleep in the cab, after a busy day of shopping in town. A young man and a young woman sat in amongst the boxes of supplies in the truck box. She saluted Ken as she drove past.

After ensuring Leanne had returned safely, Ken walked back to Farmer's house. Angler Fred and his girlfriend Chelsea were already there. Fred had a successful day of fishing and had brought an eight-pound Rainbow trout over as the main course for the night's dinner.

Another fantastic dinner had been prepared in May's kitchen and consumed in her elaborately decorated dining room. The difference tonight was that after dinner, May ignored the kitchen cleanup and joined in conversation with her guests. She literally dominated the depth of dialogue as she confirmed she was very well read and was acutely familiar with current and historical events throughout the world.

Following Fred and Chelsea's early departure for an early bedtime, due to the Chelsea's farming crew deciding to work from sunlight until noon and avoid the hot afternoon sun, Farmer and Ken returned to the old fire pit in the back yard to mix two fine Honduran cigars that Fred had left them with some of Farmer's mash liquor.

As soon as they set up around the smoking fire, a family of squirrels interrupted the peaceful setting by broadcasting that humans were in the backyard. A trio of ravens squawked at them to hurry up and leave so they could pick the area clean again. The smoke from the fire was not keeping the mosquitos away.

The snapping of crisp, dried, branches in the forest behind the house was accommodated by crying. A young girl was soon visible on the infrequently used shortcut through the forest separating neighbor's backyards. She ran through the meandering stream straight for Farmer at the fire pit.

"Mr. Farmer, Jed is real drunk and he's hitting mom. She needs help," the crying twelve year old pleaded with Farmer.

"Come with me, Ken," Farmer said as he bolted into the forest with the young girl following him through the trees.

By the time Ken had caught up with the two of them, they were beside a woman older than Ken, who was holding two younger children by their hands while she huddled behind the rusted carcass of an old Ford station wagon. Blood flowed from a cut on her arm dropping onto the gravel. Her cheek was swollen but the blood had dried.

"Farmer, I told Annie not to bother you. Jed will pass out soon. He'll be okay tomorrow."

"No, Betty, he won't be okay tomorrow. You can't hide the fact that he has hit you. Think of yourself and your children. You can't live like this."

"But he always apologizes the next day and he's real nice for a while after."

That statement was the fuse that lit Farmer. "Where is Dave?" referring to her boyfriend's brother.

"He's in there too."

Actions speak louder than words and Farmer bolted to the front door, thirty feet away. Closing the door behind him, he found the two brothers arguing in the kitchen. Each had a butcher knife in their hands.

"Jed, this is it. You're done around here. Dave, take your brother to your house, and find him a place in town tomorrow. He's not living here anymore."

"Oh shit Farmer, he's okay. They just had a little mix up," his brother Dave defended.

However, Jed was not as smart, and held the butcher knife out at Farmer. Slurring most of his words he said, "You think you're so much better than us, and you can just tell me what I can do to my woman. Well see this knife; I say I can do what I want."

"Wrong answer," Farmer said as he hit the knife out of his hand with a cast iron frying pan, sending the knife onto the table. A right, followed by a left, punch to the 250 pound man's stomach sent Jed to the floor, causing him to also throw up his insides, forming a pool beside him on the linoleum floor. *Further treatment would be wasted on the drunk*, Farmer thought, as he did have much more he wanted to do to the woman beater.

"Hey Farmer, I'll take him home," the smarter brother said as he made a deliberately careful move with his knife to set it on the countertop beside him. There was no way he was going to give Farmer any reason to take him on too.

"I mean it Dave; he's out of here tomorrow. You set him up somewhere, anywhere. Betty and her children will be fine here. They don't need a freeloading drifter shacking up in their home. I'll have a couple boys from the mill come over tomorrow and fix up the broken window and the other damage."

Ken was standing in the doorway where he had witnessed Farmer's actions. He turned and walked out ahead of Farmer, meeting Larry and Starr who were with Betty and her kids, behind the car.

"Is it okay?" Larry asked Farmer.

"Yeah," he replied with a nod.

"You know what kids, I have a new pail of chocolate ice-cream down at the bakery, and I was on my way to make a cone. Do you and your mom want to come with me?" Starr asked the children, winking at Betty as well.

"Yes," was echoed by all three children. Betty replied with a painful smile on her very sore looking face. The three children shot off running for the bakery while Betty and Starr walked behind.

"His brother's taking him out of here tomorrow. He's not coming back here anyway," He's just been mooching from Betty since he showed up here this spring. Farmer summarized the event for Larry, with Ken standing beside him.

"Can you ask Starr to find Betty a place in the bakery? She'll need some help, so the women over there will be able to sort it out. . . Oh, and we're going to install telephones in town. I want every house to have one. No little child should ever have to go running for help," Farmer said as they witnessed the two brothers stagger out of the house and stumble up the road to Dave's place.

* * *

On his walk to Leanne's, Ken thought the evening through and what he had witnessed Farmer do, who had been completely at ease the whole time. The man was full of surprises and Larry's comments of yesterday played through his mind, *"he's a natural. . ."*, in reference to Farmer's leadership. *"He never shucked being responsible for his men. . .."*

Leanne was waiting in the wooden swing chair. He took her face into his hands to give her a long kiss. She pushed her body against his. The fire burning in the pit in front of them gave enough light to show the special bottle of champagne she had set in a yellow plastic pail—the bucket shimmered with condensation from the ice inside. The new champagne bottle, and the two glasses on the table, took Ken's mind back so many years, to the years they spent together, and dreams and desires they had once held so dear.

Chapter 6

Thursday, June 30, 1977

Lenard Popoff, Sawmill Manager, had lived all of his life just down the road from the townsite of New Pontiac.

A twist of fate brought the local country boy to connect with the farm and its inhabitants. When Doctor Ray arrived in New Pontiac in 1966, his Jeep quit a mile before the townsite. Len met him at the roadside and fixed the Jeep with parts from an old one he had mothballed in his back yard. He refused to let Doc pay him for his help.

That chance meeting was the beginning of their longtime friendship. Len became the mill's first employee when Doc bought the mill components at an auction and moved them onto the farm. When Farmer arrived and took over, he and Len hit it off right away.

Doc and Len were completely different people, from two different worlds, but that seemed to be their bond. Len looked past Doc's hippie views and Doc had no fear from a man who lived a hard, honest, life.

Len treated the mill, and every piece of it, like it was his own. He had also learned to get along with the variety of people working in the mill. Those that worked hard, he liked. Those that didn't work hard, he tolerated. He didn't get involved in any of the politics of the residents of the farm. For a local country boy, Len had somehow found a refuge of peace within himself at the sawmill, and on the farm.

The early mornings were Len's 'walk around time'; time to be alone and check out wear on the conveyor chain, or the number of sharpened band saw blades, or the next load of logs to be run through the mill. This was what managing the mill was to Len; knowing the shape and size of everything in the mill to make sure it was ready to go and it would keep on going.

Len relished the morning walk around. Interrupting this special time would bother Len, but what had to be done, had to be done. Farmer met up with him as he was inspecting the conveyor.

"Len, you got a few minutes to walk with me?"

"Sure, she's looking good for start-up."

They walked down the long corridor, alongside the conveyor, and out the side door of the building. Len brought Farmer up to speed on the log supply in the yard, the finished orders, and the orders they were still working on.

Sitting in his office chair, behind his desk, Farmer began, "Len, a friend of mine's son is up here for a bit. His dad and I go back a long way. I've been showing him around, he's okay. He is sharp and he isn't afraid to get his hands dirty. What I am thinking is for you to take him on and show him the ropes around here. You work too damn hard. Ken can help free-up some of your time. What do you think?"

Len sat back in the leather chair and lit up his pipe. Len would say what he thought about the idea in his own time. He always spoke his mind. After another puff on his pipe, he started. "I've seen the young fella around, and Fred says he's good. I don't know about working with a new guy, though—I'm getting old, Gerry. These young people don't think like you and me. You know I'll take him if I have to, but I've got a different plan."

"Let's hear it. What's on your mind?"

"I know Fred could damn near run anything around here. He's a good man. I'm thinking Fred could take the new guy on and show him how to look after shipping, everything from the paperwork right through to the truck leaving the yard. God knows we ain't got the sharpest knives in the drawer working over there. If he could get the men to set up the yard properly, load the trucks, and get the office to have the paperwork done up right for each load, maybe Fred would have the time to run the forty other things he does around here. I tell you what, if it works, I'll take that week you are always telling me to take off and go fishing."

Farmer had what he needed. He knew better than to push Len for anything more. This was now Len's idea so he would make it work.

"It's a deal then. You talk to Fred and lay down your plan."

"Will do!"

"Also Len, I've been watching your son, Gord, around the yard and on the logging trucks. He's a good kid, a real chip off the old block."

Len smiled for one of the few times he would during the day. He was proud of his son. Gord showed up most of the people in the mill; he showed them what it was like to work hard. He could do twice the work of a hippie on any given day.

"I've been thinking that Larry should get right off the trucks. He does a lot around here, and hell, man, we aren't getting any younger. Gord should run the highway truck full time. You know how Larry is with those trucks; he won't let just anyone drive them. He complains the least about Gord, so I figure Gord must be onto something. If Gord wants to stay driving a logging truck in the bush he can, but if he wants to do the highway hauling, he can take over Larry's truck. How do you think that will rub him?"

For the second time in this day, Len smiled. His left hand rubbed his chin as he chuckled.

"Do you know how much the kid has talked about highway hauling? The kid will work his ass into the ground for you if you give him this one. I'll miss him around here, but he's twenty-five. Life on the road could do him some good. He needs to get out of here for a bit."

Farmer had hit Len where it mattered.

"Let Larry tell him the news. If Larry tells him he can drive his polished chrome 18-wheeler, then Gord won't ever let it get dirty."

"Yeah, that'll do it for him."

"Just to make it smooth, Larry is going with him on his next trip. He wants to hand his baby over properly. So he can head out with Larry tomorrow on the run to Eureka."

"The kid ain't going to sleep a bit tonight. Thanks, Gerry. He won't let you down, he's damn good."

"I know he is, Len. Now I have one more thing to talk to you about."

* * *

Ken woke to the chatter of the Whiskey Jack who determined no one needed to sleep any longer. He held Leanne close as they remained under the warmth of the quilt covering them as they lay on the soft sofa on Leanne's front porch. Ken looked at her face and brushed her brown hair away from her forehead. He held her tight in one final squeeze for this morning. She looked into his blue eyes, *it was going to work out*, she thought.

"I can't be late for my first day of work," Ken exclaimed as he sat up and rolled the quilt around Leanne.

They were both fully clothed. Ken set his left foot into his hiking boot and wrestled with the laces.

"Ken I have to talk to you. Until last night, I wasn't sure where we were going. When you said you were starting at the mill, I knew that was a sign that I needed to do everything I could to keep you with me.

"This is my second chance! People like me don't get that very often. I'm not going to wreck it. I want to make the best of this that I can."

"Hey, Leanne, it's alright. I like being with you, more than ever. I never saw it coming, but it's real for me too. You have a great life here. You're doing well. Are you sure that you want to try this again?"

"Yes, yes, I do. I want you to come and live here with us. We'll go day-by-day and see where that takes us. I know it'll work out."

Ken finished tying his right boot. Leanne rose with him.

"Okay, let's do it. Let's play house, and see where we get to," he said as he kissed her on her forehead. "I've got to get to the mill, before 'The Man' cans me on my first day," he announced smiling, and took off running to the mill.

Mary was at her front desk when Ken walked into the office to sign his employment paperwork.

"I hear we get to keep you. We need a handsome young man like you around here to keep us women interesting. Since you're going to stay, I want you over to my house for dinner. I cook a mean venison

82

pot roast. I have a special one for you. How about tonight? Do you want to come over and have the best damn meal you will ever get around here? I even got a plan for dessert," Mary reached out and rubbed her hands over Ken's week old beard. "Yeah, I got a real good plan for dessert."

"Is Ken bothering you again, Mary," Fred said as he walked into the office from the hallway.

"Hell no. He could never bother me."

"Okay man, well, come with me; let's talk about your new job. I'm thinking I need help in the shipping department. We have a mix of men that don't get it right too often. They can really screw up our shipments, sometimes. I figure you should start there and get it to run smooth. You need to make sure the trucks are loaded on time, with the right loads, with all the papers and permit money ready to go. Hell, getting them there on time would be a bonus, too. How's that hang with you? Do you want to try it?"

"Sure. I don't know what I am getting into, but why not. Learning will be a trip. How are the guys going to handle the scene with me slipping into this job?"

"Man, they'll love you. They'll be happy that you'll be there to take the shit when they fuck up. We got a real mix of people over there, some want to do it right, and some just want to show up so they get their electricity, water, and land for their house, covered. That's the only reason they show up; they got to put in if they want to take from the town, too."

"Okay. What's the crew like?"

"Well, the best man over there is Reno. He's the leader of the ones who want to do a good job. He was banged up when he rolled a logging truck a few years ago, but still he's the best loader and operator around here. He puts up with the slackers, but he doesn't like them."

Fred paused as he lit up a hand-rolled smoke he had been rolling while talking. After a long drag, he continued.

"Then you got Stoner. The space cadet lives up to his name. He knows not to smoke up on the job, but I know he can't go the whole day without it. He has a couple of followers, only here to earn their keep.

"They drive Reno up the fucking wall. Last week I caught Reno chasing the three of them around the yard with the forklift. Three of them took naps, while Reno was loading a trailer, and the back end of the mill got jammed up. Reno was pissed. His Italian temper doesn't show up often, but when it does, the guys know to get out of his way, man."

"Who looks after planning the orders to cut and when the loads are ready?"

"Yeah, that's kind of a problem, too. Stan Wearing, we call him Slick, is our salesman. He's on the road most of the time selling orders. Every Friday he comes back here with his week's work. I go over the orders with him and get all the delivery dates set up. See, Slick drinks a bit and sometimes he forgets things about a sale, so we got a routine now that gets the stuff straight when he is straight. It's working better now."

"Anyone else?"

"Oh, you'll like this gig. Mary does up all the paper for customs at the border, and she writes up the shipping bills.

"Most of our orders go to California, Nevada or Oregon so we need to get all the export papers done up properly. Mary gets the permit money from Leanne and puts the paperwork in a Zip bag for each load leaving here. She does a good job, but she has poor communications with the yard crew. Mary's pissed at Stoner and his friends, so she doesn't talk to them. I think they do it on purpose, but when they decide to load a different order than was planned, they don't tell her. Then she has prepared the wrong papers for the truck and the truck is held up until the proper paperwork is done. This is a big deal. You'll need to work with her and the rest of the crew to get that working right."

"Is Mary for real, man? I mean, today she organized a dinner for me at her house. Judging by her suggestions, I think she had an all-nighter planned for dessert."

"Mary is a real one of a kind. She's tough and gruff, but she has a good heart. She likes to jive with you. Most of it is just for fun. Mary lives in her own house but she and Reverend Bob hook up now and then. Loosen up and play along with her and you'll do fine. I don't know what she could do to you if she was given the chance, but hey man that's your deal. Work it out."

Fred led Ken over to meet Reno and the shipping crew. The 9:00 o'clock whistle blew as they sat down with the men at the two picnic benches beside the forklifts and the loader. Stoner welcomed Ken by stating, "An extra man around here would help them out so they wouldn't have to work as hard."

Reno said something in Italian, as he glared at Stoner, and then in English he told him that maybe Stoner didn't need to work there at all. Maybe he should be out in the bush hooking chokers or bucking on the landing instead.

Stoner wouldn't last an hour doing those jobs. He had a good show here and right then he knew he had better clean up some, so the new boss would keep him.

The clanking of the heavy metal chain conveyors started inside the mill. The primary saw powered up and the whining of the large electric motors flowed outside. Reno waved off the six men of the crew who headed off in different directions to begin their workday. Fred and Ken stayed to talk with Reno.

* * *

Farmer, Larry, Doc, and May left New Pontiac in Farmer's Chevy Blazer an hour before their 11 o'clock meeting in the town of Riverbend.

They rode without speaking. Each was deep into their own space. The howling of the hard rubber tires on the asphalt highway hadn't competed with the radio. The CBC's commentators were discussing current events. The discussion was about Perry Jansen, a British rock star, who hadn't shown up at a Toronto courtroom to face his charge of heroin possession this past spring.

He had also missed his June court appearance. A new date was now set in July. The female voice, a graduate student in Sociology, brought forward the discussion of the philosophy of the courts being wrong, whereby those charged are guilty until proven innocent. She proclaimed the law demands you to appear before a judge to prove you are innocent of the alleged crime. She argued, in this case, in fact, the ownership of the heroin could not be proven. Her basic premise was that being with something does not mean you have the care, custody, and control of the item. Meeting one criterion does not automatically presume the other two.

The male counterpoint, Dr. Grant Richardson, a professor of Criminal Justice, had remained cool and collected while the preposterous suggestion of innocence was being discussed. He had done well until Ms. Truss brought up one last point. Then he lost it. "How the hell could he be anything but guilty since he had the heroin in his hand when the police arrested him?"

The outburst caused a station break.

While the exciting discourse had been exchanged on the radio, no one in the truck heard it.

May's eyes were locked on the mountains across the lake but her mind didn't see the picturesque landscape. She was deep in her thoughts of the crisis facing Gerry and her. She had resolved that she couldn't blame him though.

Farmer was driving on autopilot as he thought about a land 15,000 miles away.

Larry did what he never did on the road; he fell asleep. Larry never slept in a vehicle, because he did not trust anyone else to deliver him to Fate. Yet today, he dozed on the forty-five minute drive.

Doc was reading a new book he had obtained from the Riverbend Library, the hardcover version of the new book, *Coma*, by Robin Cook.

The focus on their present task returned to all as they entered the town of Riverbend and drove past the hospital. Parking in the shade of the old Maple tree, in front of the single story green building on First Street, would keep the truck cool.

Entering the office, they were met by a pleasant secretary, sitting in front of the etched stainless steel sign identifying the office as *Berry and Associates, Barristers and Solicitors*. "Good day, Mr. Field, Mrs. Field, Mr. Johnson, and Dr. Miller. Mr. Berry will be with you in a moment. Can I get you a coffee, tea, or water?"

Their black coffee was served to them in the conference room. The room's side window gave a clear view of the lake and the snowtopped mountains on the other side of the valley. Mahogany paneling adorned the walls. Green linoleum flooring was under their high-backed black leather chairs. The centerpiece of the room was a lacquer coated conference table, made from laminated cedar planks cut at the sawmill in New Pontiac.

Jeffrey Berry joined his four clients. A veteran litigator, Berry had left the big city of Vancouver when he turned fifty and found himself divorced and damn tired of the day-to-day grind. He loaded up his new Corvette convertible with all the personal goods he wanted to take with him and headed east. He wound up in Riverbend and became the only resident lawyer.

Being the small town's only lawyer had its pros and cons. Most of the people who needed help had no money to pay him, while those who did have money often tried to weasel out of their bills.

Gerry Field—Farmer to those who knew him—was not like others and he always paid his bills on time. Farmer did interesting things, too, keeping the lawyer's mind active when working on his files.

Jeffrey was an unassuming lawyer. A short man, he was blessed with the baldness from his father and his mother's heavy frame. However, he did know the law, and had an accomplished record of success in the courtroom, in spite of taking on a significant amount of pro bono work for the residents of the area.

Jeffrey shook hands with each client and welcomed them back.

The secretary entered the meeting room, placing seven white file folders beside Counselor Berry. She removed four silver Parkers from the center console on the table, setting the shiny pens, each embossed with the firm's name and address in gold, in front of each person. She sat in the vacant chair to the right of her boss.

"Now Mr. Field, in reference to your Last Will and Testament, I have written a codicil whereby you leave your estate to your wife May. In the event that she is not able to accept it then your estate will go to Mr. Larry Johnson. In a reciprocal manner, I have prepared the codicil for Mrs. May Field to leave her estate to her husband Gerry Field, and in the event he is not able to accept it then her estate will go to Mr. Larry Johnson. Farmer and May were each given their documents to review.

The lawyer turned his attention to the codicil prepared for Larry, who now left half of his estate to Ms. Starr Harris and the other half to Mr. Frederick Hanson. Leaving half of his estate to Fred back at the mill was a surprise, yet it was no one's place to ask about why he would leave such a significant inheritance to the young man.

The secretary witnessed the signatures, before stamping the law firm's seal on each of the single page codicils.

The next document modified the corporate structure of the New Pontiac Corporation and its subsidiaries, including the Blue River Lumber Company, the New Pontiac Lands Company, and the lucrative New Pontiac Mines Company, which let out two major leases to a large mining company. Mr. Gerald Field, as majority shareholder and President, confirmed Mr. Larry Johnson as the Chief Operating Officer, Doctor Raymond Miller as the Vice-President, and Mrs. May Field as the Corporate Secretary. The motion was signed by Farmer and accepted by Larry, May, and Doctor Miller. The firm's seal was stamped on each copy of the motion.

The next matter should have been called, *Giving Away the Farm*. Farmer, as President of the New Pontiac Corporation, signed a document that issued 3,000 shares to Larry. Larry was now a one-third owner in the Corporation sharing equal status with Farmer or May, who owned the other two thirds of the voting shares.

However, it was the second part of the document that affected those in the room immediately. Through a distribution of non-voting preferred shares, in the same amounts as the voting shares, plus the addition of Dr. Miller's 1,000 shares, the four preferred shareholders were to be paid annual dividends of $15.00 per share. One hundred and fifty thousand dollars a year would flow to the four people in the room—$45,000 each to Farmer, May and Larry and $15,000 to Dr. Miller. Farmer didn't hesitate signing the document effectively diluting his personal wealth and his Corporation's healthy retained earnings.

The safeguard for all was that the lucrative 25-year mining lease contract that Farmer had negotiated with the international mining company would easily cover these annual dividends, as well as add serious cash to the accounts of the company, every year.

The next executed authorization was a *Letter of Instruction*, which in the event of a temporary absence of the President of the Corporation, the Corporate Secretary, Mrs. May Field, would assume the role of the President. The voting shares rights of the absentee were to be transferred in trust to Mrs. May Field during his absence. However, since May would be responsible for all operations of the large corporation, it was stated that Jeffrey, the lawyer, was to fill the vacant position of Corporate Secretary, but without voting share privileges. He'd serve in an advisory role to the acting President, May. The accounting firm of Gilles and Associates would also provide corporate direction during that time.

As if enough changes had not been made thus far, Jeffrey continued with the remaining paperwork he had been instructed to prepare. Turning to Larry, he set down three file folders in front of him. "Mr. Johnson, I have prepared Incorporation documents for Starr Enterprises, with the two subsidiaries, Starr Aviation and Starr Trucks and Equipment.

"Your helicopters have been transferred into Starr Aviation.

"Two International trucks and four Peerless trailers, along with one 14G grader, one 966 loader, and one D6 tractor, have been transferred into Starr Trucks and Equipment from the New Pontiac Corporation.

"I have also drafted up a contract to retain Starr Enterprises as the primary equipment contractor for New Pontiac Corporation. Furthermore, I drafted up an employment contract for you as the Operations Manager of New Pontiac Corporation, with the salary provided by Mr. Field and the term."

The lawyer paused as he shuffled through the stack of papers in front of him.

"I am missing one document, now where is it? Ah yes, here it is. I might add that this is a rather unusual request, Larry, but at the request of Gerry, your term is 'until you decide you don't want to do it anymore'.

Looking at Farmer first and then Larry, the lawyer asked, "Do these two orders satisfy your requirements at this time, gentlemen?"

"Yes, they do." Farmer said.

Larry shook Farmer's hand and turned to the lawyer with a nod to agree.

The agreement was completed with their signatures. The documents had just made Larry a millionaire, at least on paper anyway.

Doc Miller had been content to watch the ebb and flow of the exchanges, surprisingly with little emotion until it was his turn, at which time he suddenly felt like a glassy eyed kid in a candy shop.

Jeffrey took his last file from the stack of documents and set it in front of Doc Miller. "Dr. Miller, I have completed your contract with the New Pontiac Corporation. In addition to your role and salary as Vice President of the Corporation, this is a contract for medical services to be provided to the New Pontiac Corporation and the permanent residents of the town of New Pontiac. The salary is set at $5,000 per month, indexed to inflation for annual adjustments. If you have no concerns, would you please sign here and here and Gerry you will need to sign the one spot indicated with the yellow marker."

Doc Miller saluted Farmer after he signed the document and then gave his twisted lip smile that summed up the series of gracious gifts he had just received from Farmer.

The execution of all documents was complete!

The lawyer stayed with them for a lunch delivered by the secretary, providing him another chance to get to know his clients on a more personal level.

He was impressed with the quality of the characters in the room.

Mrs. May Field literally shocked him. She was quiet, unassuming, and reserved, but definitely, a strong and intelligent woman, who clearly understood detailed matters of law and business. Given the chance, she might reasonably challenge the lawyer on successfully running a corporation.

While the lawyer was curious about the communal farm and its inhabitants, he was smart enough to mind his own business. The New Pontiac Corporation was his largest client. It was one large and complicated organization.

Riverbend locals greatly underestimated the size and value of the Corporation. Since they used a number of banks, located in four towns in Canada, and three in the United States, the local people did not know enough to develop factual gossip. Instead, the locals had irrationally jumped to the conclusion that the farm was just a bunch of hippies living an immoral lifestyle—all of whom likely had no regard for the last four of the Ten Commandments.

The secretary returned with copies of the documents in a black leather satchel. After they finished lunch, Doc, Larry and May left for the truck. Farmer stayed behind a minute longer. He closed the door and spoke.

"Thanks for getting this together on such short notice, Jeff."

"Oh, no problem. We got it done," the lawyer replied. Although Gerry was a nice person, and they had done much business together these last few years, he still could not read him and was never completely at ease with Farmer.

Farmer put out his hand to shake. As Farmer closed his hand around the lawyer's, he felt the strong grip—not a painful grip—just a confident one. Then his eyes met Farmer's glare. The look carried a very clear, meaning. Whatever it was about Farmer, or his friends, he would forever be careful to do what was right for his clients, above all other interests, including his own.

* * *

May required some groceries, and the four of them walked the block to the store. Doc and Larry took a detour before the Safeway and went into the liquor store for their supplies.

May located the spices she was looking for and proceeded to the checkout. Farmer remained in the aisle talking with the store manager about the status of their account. May was in the checkout line, behind two '50s styled, greaser type, men in their mid-twenties. While reading the National Enquirer in line for the cashier, one of the men in front of her made the comment, "Look the Chink thinks she can read. Why don't you go back to your own country, we don't need you polluting our town." His associate laughed as May turned and walked away to avoid the obnoxious racists in front of her.

Farmer and the store manager approached the end of the aisle, talking while walking, and Farmer caught the slurs directed at his wife, who was now two aisles away. She did not hear the men further taunt Farmer by calling him a *useless hippie*. She also did not witness Farmer punching the talker in his stomach, hard enough that he doubled over, out of breathe, before he received a second punch to his right kidney.

The second one tried to hit Farmer with a glass bottle of milk, but Farmer blocked the bottle from hitting his face by angling his arm so the bottle glanced past him. The second man fell to the floor, as he was knocked unconscious by Farmer's right hook to his face. He had taken less than fifteen seconds to incapacitate the two men.

The store manager's mouth remained open in shock as his mind tried to comprehend the fight that was over as fast as it started, resulting in two men knocked out cold that were now lying on the floor of his store.

Farmer handed the manager 2 twenties to pay for the few spice bottles that May had intended to purchase. When he found her in the far aisle, he walked out the store with his princess's hand intertwined in his own. He didn't feel any discomfort as she held his swelling knuckles tight on their walk back to the truck.

* * *

Farmer drove the speed limit on the trip back to the farm. It was no surprise to him when he saw the cop car's flashing red and blue lights in his rear view mirror. He pulled over to the side of the road to let the black and white catch up to him. His three passengers looked in bewilderment at Sergeant Cody's car as he locked up his wheels to slide to a stop behind their truck.

"Were you speeding?" asked Larry.

"Something like that I guess," Farmer said as he left the truck to meet the cop in his car.

"What can I do for you today, Cody?" asked Farmer as he sat down in the cop car's front passenger seat.

"Farmer, you know what this is about. I don't know what those thugs said to you, but you can't just beat up two people like that. There are laws, you know."

"I see, and what is it that supposedly happened?"

"Well I am not sure. Sam isn't much help; he says all hippies look the same to him. He couldn't identify who took on the two men in his store."

"Yeah, well, I heard someone once say that about white people too."

"And Farmer, apparently the two men that got the other end of this hippie's fist describe him as being about seven feet tall, a monster of a guy, strong enough to withstand the blow of a full milk bottle to his face."

"Wow that is some hippie—seven feet tall, and strong. Must be one of those red meat eating hippies, cause the granola crunching ones couldn't be that strong or big. Well I'll keep my eyes open for such a man. What do you want me to do with him if I run into him?"

"For Christ's sake, understand there are a bunch of idiots in town. You can't be busting heads like that. This time no one can remember anything. They said there was some Chinese woman there too, but no one knows who she was either; apparently they all look the same too." Cody shook his head, and then commented, "Thank Christ it wasn't Larry. Who knows what paperwork I'd have to do on a double homicide?"

"Okay, I got the drift, Cody. I'll let you know if I meet a red meat eating, seven foot tall, hippie, with a Chinese lady friend. I'll keep my eyes open and my ear to the ground."

"Yeah right, Farmer. . . Oh what the hell, just get on your way."

"Well you have a safe trip, Cody," Farmer said as he left the cop car and walked to the truck.

"Did you talk your way out of the ticket," asked a curious Larry, a man who had many interactions with cops over the years about such matters.

"Matter of fact, I did. I promised old Cody that I'd drive the speed limit from now on."

"Yeah, that's what I always tell them too," rebutted Larry as he looked at Farmer's swollen red knuckles on his hand gripping the steering wheel.

They turned into Farmer's driveway as the afternoon whistle at the mill signaled the end of the day and the end of the week for the workers. The mill would be shut down for the Canadian celebration of the July 1st holiday tomorrow, a Friday, and in respect of those from across the border, the mill would not run on the Monday of July 4th, so anyone who wanted to celebrate the United States of America's Independence Day could do so.

Farmer put the black satchel, containing the documents from today's visit to the lawyer's office, into his tall black safe in the corner of his den. Recovered from the New Pontiac Mine Office on Main Street, as a birthday present to Farmer, Larry had rebuilt the lock and refinished the old steel safe, right down to the detail of putting on an original Diebold Safe & Lock Co. faceplate on the door. It was the most secure storage place in New Pontiac.

* * *

Reverend Bob was preparing for his Thursday evening sermon. New candles were set into the shining brass candleholders along the sidewalls. The magnificent inlaid stones under the chandelier were polished to a reflective shine. Now that the incense was burning in the pots at the front of the church, he was ready to receive his parishioners.

Ken and his new family were the first to arrive at the church, ahead of the five o'clock start time. Leanne was aglow in happiness. The reverend immediately noted the interesting change in her. It was proper. He welcomed Ken to their community.

Parishioners entering the yellow church were greeted by either the reverend or his Mary. A young woman collected the children and took them outside for their own gathering.

Dressed in a full purple robe of silk, tied around his waist with the golden cord as a sash belt, Reverend Bob stretched his arms high into the air to begin his sermon. "Welcome, brothers and sisters. Let us join hands and start tonight with a moment of prayer to the guiding path in your life."

The parishioners joined hands and bowed their heads while each person prayed, or simply meditated.

After one minute of prayer, Reverend Bob spoke on. "Please be seated. Thank you for meeting with us this evening. We have had a very busy week.

"On Monday, we were blessed with the arrival of dear little Rosemary Silver, the daughter of Jim and Teresa. Peace to you, young Rosemary."

Reverend Bob introduced the tall bearded man at the side of the stage as Charlie. Charlie began strumming his acoustic guitar while Mary's solid voice joined in to sing the words to Bob Dylan's *Blowing in the Wind*. By the second verse, the whole congregation was singing along with Mary and Charlie.

"Thank you, Charlie and Mary, for leading us through such an uplifting song," he exclaimed, and then looked up to the ceiling in silence. Bringing his eyes back to the parishioners, he began his short sermon.

"I have had my own experience with changes in my journey and I have a personal story to share with you.

"When I was a younger man, I became lost in a world that I did not understand, confused about right and wrong. I strayed from the path. Only eighteen years old, I was in front of a frightening and mean looking judge, expecting a jail sentence for the next decade of my life. I had given up on any chance of reprieve in a society that didn't want my kind roaming the streets. However, I was wrong. The Lord was watching.

"For a reason unknown by me, the pastor of my parish sat through my hearing. He approached the judge and made an offer different from a jail term. The pastor offered to take me under his care and teach me a more productive way.

"To this day, I have no idea why he chose to save me, nor why the judge agreed with him, but I must believe that he saw inside me something I did not."

Reverend Bob stopped his sermon to take a drink of water from a cup.

"For the next four years, I repeated a promise each day that I would repay my debt to society by learning how to be a strong reverend, one that could help others.

"After that period of training, I chose the best way that I thought I could help others. I believe I was able to help many others in the role I served."

He bowed his head and when again composed, started anew. "I tell you this to remind you that we are all vulnerable; we are all just one decision away from being free or enslaved. To get through these troubles you have to believe there is indeed a force, an indescribable guidance system, which will help you do what needs to be done.

"Yes, my friends, I have seen the force that can help us get through these challenges. I ask you to keep faith in your guiding force strong; it will give you the strength you need to get through times of challenge. Amen!"

The parishioners replied with a loud, "Amen."

"Now we shall enjoy a special treat," he said as he gave a nod to the man standing at the back of the aisle. The short man with a long black beard, and black hair hanging well below his cowboy hat, strolled up the aisle and sat at the organ. Charlie remained at the side of the stage, tightening the E-sting on his guitar, getting ready with his now tuned guitar.

A third man followed and plugged in a Fender five-string bass into a small amplifier set on the side of the stage. Finally, the fourth musician ambled onto the stage dressed in a brown leather jacket with white leather fringes on the arms, who slung his acoustic guitar over his head to rest by the strap on his shoulder. He gave the guitar a few strums to check that it was still tuned.

"Please welcome a traveler from afar that has chosen to stop by with his friends for a visit and to share a song or two with us tonight. My friends welcome Mr. Bobby Clayton."

"Thank you, Reverend. It's a treat for me and the boys to be with you tonight. You've got the real deal here; this is a cool town. I think I'd like to live here sometime. Well, how about a song?"

"Yeah," the parishioners replied in unison, followed by a round of applause.

"Okay then. A great man, Gordon Lightfoot, wrote this song a few years back, *Early Morning Rain*. Boys, let's do her—three, two, one."

The audience burst into applause when the song ended. Clayton strummed on his guitar and the band followed him as he played another familiar song, *Lodi* as written by John Fogerty.

The third song was a long rock ballad, written by Clayton. *Dancing Around your Circle of Fire* had reached gold record status in Canada and was heading upward on the charts in the US as well. Witnessing his deep voice pound out the song was a unique bonus for tonight's parishioners.

When they had finished playing, Reverend Bob led the audience in a standing ovation. Clayton took the microphone. "It's good to be here. It's good to see my old friend Charlie and play a bit with him. When we used to hang out in Toronto, we had all these plans about where we were going, and about seeing the country, and meeting people. Well, here I am, just older, greyer, and maybe a little bit wiser. Life's been a cool ride and she ain't done yet.

"Tomorrow we play a gig in Cedar Falls, but for tonight, we get to hang out in this great place. Yeah, my mother must be grinning ear to ear, as she looks down and sees me back inside a church. Keep it real, man!"

"Thank you, Bobby Clayton, for giving to us what you have. We are thankful that you will be able to spend another day with us. May your guiding light burn bright on your path in life," Reverend Bob offered as Clayton and his friends walked back to the last pew to listen to the end of the sermon.

The service ended promptly at 6 o'clock as Reverend Bob asked them to go in Peace and to Respect their fellow men and women.

The crowd moved along toward the New Pontiac hall and the evening's dinner.

Tonight was Spaghetti Thursday and huge pots of savory tomato sauce made from fresh green peppers, ripe tomatoes, field onions, and zucchini squash were set out on the central tables behind tubs of cooked durum wheat spaghetti.

The wheat was from the local fields. Volunteers used an antique stone grist-wheel to grind the wheat for the spaghetti. Fresh baked garlic bread was in baskets at the end of each table. Tonight's volunteer cooks had assembled an incomparable feast for 120 people.

Leanne and Ken joined Fred and Chelsea at an outdoor table away from the hall. The air was still warm from the afternoon.

After spending just one day in the mill, Ken and Fred had work talk that kept them occupied.

Chelsea and Leanne took the dishes back into the kitchen once they were finished eating, returning with black coffee. The coffee and a puff of one of Chelsea's homegrown joints gave a peaceful buzz to end the day.

Tonight life was again calm on the farm, in New Pontiac.

Chapter 7

Friday, July 1, 1977

Since becoming a country on July 1, 1867, annual celebrations we held in most Canadian towns. In Riverbend, the celebration kicked off with a traditional parade at noon.

Leanne, Ken, and Christina left new Pontiac in Ken's Mach 1 an hour early, to get to town before the procession started. Christina and Leanne loved the annual parade.

This was the family day plan many residents with young children. It was the only day of the year that the carnival came to Riverbend. Kids could drive in the small bumper cars, revolve on the merry-go-round, go for a horse ride, or try their luck in the arcade section of the carnival. The old fishing pond always promised a good toy as a catch.

Adults had their own entertainment in the beer gardens with live music. There were the typical games of chance, poker, blackjack, and roulette, ready to take their money.

Other residents of New Pontiac drove across the US border in advance of the Independence Day celebrations in Spokane. The Spokane fireworks were famous—an exceptional performance in the Wild West. People travelled miles to witness the grand show. The travelers from New Pontiac would stay for the late night fireworks on Monday and return to the farm at their leisure on the 5th day of July.

* * *

The hard reality of life continued in spite of the special day and the places other people were going. Starr drove Larry in his polished yellow GMC pickup down to the mill. The metallic green International 4300 was set to pull a forty-foot open trailer with dried cedar lumber. Starr held Larry's hand and looked into his eyes.

Larry held Starr close. "I have to do this, Starr."

"I know you do, because you are you, and that is why I love you. Please remember me and come back soon. I'll be waiting for you," she said before he stepped out of the pickup.

Starr's eyes started tearing up as she put the truck into reverse and turned around to drive home.

Larry opened the door to the truck tractor and put his canvas bag inside the sleeper. Gord, the soon-to-be regular driver was checking the straps on the trailer as he worked through his pre-trip walk around.

"Morning, Larry."

"Hey, Gord."

"The boys in the yard did a good job on the load. She's loaded tight. Every strap is secure. There's a first time for everything."

"Yeah, I guess so."

Gord lifted the hood of the truck tractor to check the fluid levels. Satisfied the oils were good he carefully let the fiberglass hood drop back into its mounts and locked it down with the rubber locking straps.

The asphalt surface was already warm as he crawled under the trailer to set up the brakes. After rolling out from under the trailer, and ensuring the airline gladhands and electrical pigtail connection were tight, he stowed his coveralls back inside the driver's side storage compartment along with his gloves, hardhat, and tools. The truck was ready to go.

When he fired up the Cummins diesel motor, two clouds of white exhaust blew out of the twin chrome stacks. The engine knocking sound calmed down as the diesel engine warmed.

Gord kept busy by checking the paperwork in the black document bag. The permit and expense money was in a series of separate envelopes inside the leather folder; all $1,100 in US bills was present, along with the proper documents.

Jimmy Smith rode up to the sawmill yard on his shovelhead Harley Davidson, rumbling past the men and straight into the shop. Toting his canvas bag over his shoulder, his thick arms displayed colorful tattoos extending up under his sleeveless leather vest.

The burgundy International 4300 was his truck. He had been driving the rig for the last two years. He was a skilled driver and a great operator. The two-year-old truck stayed in excellent shape under Jimmy's care. He and Larry saw eye-to-eye on this matter. They got along well.

Jimmy quickly worked through his pre-trip inspection, since he had just returned with the truck yesterday and had changed the oil and gone over the truck in the shop. Blue exhaust smoke shot out of the twin chrome pipes after he started the Detroit 350 horsepower engine.

While the engine warmed up, he looked through the document pouch for the load of fir beams loaded on his attached forty-foot highboy trailer. The paperwork and permit money was all in order so he hopped out to light a smoke and talk to Gord.

While Jimmy walked over to Gord's truck, Farmer walked his dedicated pace into the sawmill yard holding a green kit bag over his shoulder.

"Hey," Farmer greeted Gord and Larry as he made his way to Jimmy. "Need to catch a ride with you today, Jimmy."

"Great! It'll be good to have someone to talk to for a change," Jimmy replied, "I've wore out most of my eight tracks and the ones that still work have been played so many times I can sing every word to every song. You don't ever want to hear me sing."

Jimmy led the convoy of the two trucks out onto the highway by running through his 13-Speed Road Ranger transmission. Gord followed him, double clutching while working on the gears of the 15-Speed Fuller.

"You on this one?" Jimmy called through his CB radio back to Gord.

"Yep, you have me to talk to for the next few days," was Gord's reply on channel nineteen.

Larry was even less talkative than usual as he rode with Gord. He didn't comment on anything Gord did, which of course made Gord more nervous, and he was forced to focus on driving well. He was on his big test run. He wasn't going to screw up.

Jimmy didn't have the same pressure on him. Although Farmer was a good truck driver, he seldom drove anymore. Farmer was not testing him; Jimmy had earned his stripes too many miles ago.

It was a three-hour drive to the border crossing at Frontier, Washington. Entering the United States was always a challenge, since the Customs officers, with their .38 sticking up in their hip holsters, seemed to thrive on making the drivers as uncomfortable as possible. Many had an authoritarian streak that made the whole experience more painful for the truckers than the crossing had to be.

Crossing the border, and dealing with the bullshit from the officers, was simply part of the job. Jimmy drove onto the weigh scale at the US Customs and Border Security office. The red light told him to pull ahead into one of the truck parking lanes on the side and to bring in his identification and papers for his truck and load.

Knowing the drill, and the crap he would have to deal with once again inside, Jimmy prepared himself while he walked across the parking lot carrying his document pouch. He entered the flat brown brick US Customs Office building through the bullet proof glass main entry door, as Gord pulled onto the scales.

He met the young pimple-faced officer standing on the other side of the elbow high counter, sporting the regulation crew cut of his ginger hair, set on top of the regulation square head.

"Well lookie here, we got one of those Deep Fried trucks wanting to enter our country."

The phrase, 'Deep Fried', was typical of the officer's limited ability at humor, by attempting to categorize the pot-smoking hippies who worked at the Blue River Lumber Company.

Jimmy knew better than to antagonize the agent. Some officers were okay, but others were simply assholes with guns. This officer was one of the latter.

"Good afternoon, Officer. Here's my license and the export documents for this load," he said as he extracted the papers from the pouch and set them on the counter.

"So let's see what you got here today," the officer sneered as he held up the forms. "You don't have any of that wacky tobacky y'all smoke up there, do you?"

"No sir."

"How about some of those women that I hear run around naked all over that place? You got any of them naked ladies inside your truck?" the smart mouthed officer said as he tried egging Jimmy on.

Beyond the counter, and this exchange with Jimmy, two things happened at the same time.

Farmer entered the building, but the rookie officer had not yet noticed him. After hearing this kid talking to Jimmy, Farmer stepped forward to confront the rookie. At the same time as Farmer moved ahead, a grey-haired, and muscularly built, officer walked around the corner of the office behind the counter. The stocky officer had heard the end of his trainee's question and immediately saw Farmer walk toward Jimmy at the counter. He moved to cut off Farmer's charge toward the rookie.

Before Farmer could say anything to the young agent, the older officer put his thick left hand on the left shoulder of his officer, increasing the pressure of his grip until the training rookie yelled out in pain and exclaimed that he was hurting him.

The veteran glared into the back of the redhead.

"What the hell are you doing? You don't ask dumb questions of our guests. Get your shit together and apologize to this man. Now!"

"Sorry," the humiliated trainee said, as he stared down at the floor.

"Now get over and run the window, the elder ordered. The apologetic rookie walked away from the counter.

"Sorry about that, Jimmy. I still don't know what the hell to do with my damn nephew." He looked across at Farmer and said, "It won't happen again, Gerry."

"Okay, Clive, you got your hands full with the kid—good luck. I won't have anyone talking to my men like that, ever," Farmer said in his distinctly clear and authoritative voice.

Clive nodded back at Farmer.

"Okay, let's finish this up here so you can be on your way."

Clive quickly looked at the papers, reached for his big black stamp, and stamped the approval on each of the four documents.

"Going to Eureka, are you? Good place to be for the 4th. They do up quite the fireworks show."

"Yes, Eureka's a good place to be," Jimmy acknowledged.

Clive skimmed the completed fuel tax form and said, "That'll be $220.00 for fuel taxes, Jimmy."

Jimmy pulled out the first envelope inside his permit pouch, which was an envelope with $220.00 in US funds. Mary was on the top of her game, once again.

Clive took the cash, but for some reason, he glanced out the side window and saw his second man talking to Gord in the parking lot. The officer was looking inside the cab. Then Clive saw exactly who he did not need to see right now. Larry appeared at the front of the truck, walking straight toward the officer.

"Jesus Christ! I'll be right back," Clive said as he hit the security lock button allowing him to exit the building quickly by the side door. He ran over to Gord's truck, arriving in time to hear the second young officer remark, "Hey there, I heard you Deep Frieds like your marijuana. You got any marijuana in here, boy?"

Larry and the out of breathe Clive arrived beside the officer simultaneously. Clive stepped in between Larry and his officer.

"Sorry Larry about the ignorance of my man here. He is going to apologize to your driver and let him know this will never happen again," Clive said as he wrapped his large fingers around the back of the officer's neck. Clive was a strong man and his officer understood that when Clive had him by the back of the neck, there were no options left for him.

"Sorry about hassling y'all."

"Good, now let's go inside and get your paperwork done so you can head out with Jimmy," Clive let out as he turned his second disruptive employee, while still firmly holding him by the neck.

Larry walked up to the grabbed officer, stopping when he was right in front of him. He stared down at him. Then, Larry turned to Clive.

"Clive, this is Gord Popoff, my new driver, and he's driving my truck for me from now on." Larry shook his head. "You know, man, life is too fucking short for this bullshit. Go get the paperwork done. This is over; she's done! Never again, man," he said as his own glare swiveled from Clive to the younger officer.

Gord felt ten feet tall as he walked behind the retreating officers into their den of subjectivity.

Larry sat on a rock beside the truck and lit a Player's Plain cigarette.

Back inside the office, Clive recounted the cash from Jimmy and quickly stamped the documents for the load. He accepted Gord's money from his envelope marked as Washington Fuel Taxes and just as fast stamped the entry permit. Both were good to go.

Farmer felt a mixture of frustration, at what had happened, but also satisfaction that the message had gotten to Clive. He also took note of the paperwork and the permit money being correct. Ken, Mary, and Reno's boys were doing all right, at least for their first day as a team.

Back in the sanctuary of his truck, Jimmy fired up his Detroit diesel. He didn't waste any time getting onto the comfort of the highway and was soon cruising at the double nickel, south on 25.

Gord was right behind him. Jimmy picked up his CB microphone and told him they'd stop for a bite to eat a few miles ahead at the Gulf Truck Stop, this side of Northport, Washington. Gord was in complete agreement; his stomach had been growling since they left the mill.

* * *

Back at the Border Office, Clive was smoking mad. Unlike his two co-workers, he knew what a major screw up was, and this had been one of the worst kind.

After his nephew had completed his thorough interrogation of the seventy-five year-old driver of the Datsun pickup, Clive yelled at him to close the window and put up the sign telling the next traveler to wait for the next available officer. He called his two morons to the counter.

"Well, you two are the dumbest people I have ever met," he began. To his nephew, he asked, "Do you recognize who you were dealing with there?"

"Jimmy the tattooed biker. He's just a trucker from the Deep Fried hippie farm!"

Clive punched him in the stomach. "You're an idiot, numb nuts. Yeah, Jimmy is the driver all right, and from what I see in him, I don't think you ever want to take him on, even with your .38. He could probably break your neck faster than you could draw your pistol.

"No dickhead! You are dealing with Farmer, also known as Major Gerry Field! That is Major Gerry Field of the Green Berets. That man saw more action in Vietnam than we will ever know.

"A good friend heard he had four Silver Stars, three Purple Hearts, and a Medal of Valor. Who knows what else the man has for his service over there."

"Oh good, he has some medals," is all his nephew got out before Clive punched him in the stomach again.

"And you, dumber fuck," he said as he glared at the second offender, "You were about to piss off Captain Larry Johnson, one of the best helicopter pilots and Special Forces men in Vietnam. He was a legend flying his gunship in and out of hot-zones while saving thousands of our soldiers. He flew through the toughest fire to save our men. He has a box of medals, too.

"My buddy also said he could break your neck before you even saw him coming. You just do not want to fuck with him."

"Oh, here goes another Viet-fucking-Nam story from you, Clive. Haven't we heard all of them by now?" his nephew piped up. "It was a loser war, it's long over."

Clive punched him again; this time into his solar plexus—the redhead rolled on the floor trying to catch his breath. "You fucking idiot. You are too stupid to understand what we went through over there. We did what our country wanted us to do. I lost a cousin and some of the best friends I've ever had.

"I tell you, all it would take is for either of those men to make one phone call, and you'd be gone—vanished. If you were real lucky, maybe you'd only be relocated to some post on the Mexican border.

"One call and you'd be down there hawking burritos. You'd be running in the fields to catch Mexicans as they run into Texas to pop out a kid on American soil. Do you want to be a Taco Head and spend your days chasing pregnant Mexicans in the desert heat, you dumb shit?"

"No Sir," both officers replied in unison.

"Okay then, so when one of their trucks come through here, you talk to them real nice, you treat them real good, and you get them on their way. This is real, you two idiots. If either of you ever try any of that bullshit on those drivers again, I'll recommend a transfer down to the Taco Land border. Hell, I'll even drive you down there just to get rid of you. You got it?"

"Yes Sir," the pair sang together once more.

"Now, get out of my sight. Go hassle some old woman driving down to buy knitting wool. You should be real good at picking on old ladies."

Clive walked into his office and slammed the door. From his lower right drawer he pulled out a forty-pounder of Jimmy Beam. With a shaking hand, he poured a three finger shot into his coffee cup.

He rubbed the scars on his neck and left shoulder. He still could not think about the war without reliving the nightmares of his own two tours. The only time he ever drank was when he thought about the war. Lately, he'd been drinking a lot more; days like this didn't help matters.

* * *

The Northport Truck Stop advertised the orange and blue colors of the Gulf Oil Company. The inside decor resembled a battered 1950's diner, including tables with chrome frames placed between orange leather padded wooden benches.

Recognizing Jimmy and his friends when they entered, the bleach-blonde waitress gave her best walk as she approached them dressed in her tight white blouse and pink mini skirt—her tip earning uniform. She had become a lifer at the truck stop. At thirty-five, she had to move faster to earn merely a portion of the tips that used to flow so much easier.

"Men, today is our lucky day," Jimmy announced as she arrived at their booth.

"We have the sexiest woman in all of Washington right here. Nice to see you, Montana. You are even more beautiful than you were in my dreams last night."

Montana rubbed Jimmy's long hair to tussle it out of shape. "And this tough guy is the heartbreaker of Route 25," she smiled as she massaged his right shoulder, wishing she could do more.

"Here are your menus, gentlemen. Today's special is a steak sandwich, on garlic bread, with our homemade fries and coleslaw," she paused to look at each of the four men, "What can I get you to drink?"

"A Coke," was the reply from each.

Gord was itching to get the story on the pretty waitress from Jimmy. "So she's quite the babe, Jimmy, a real hot one. How well do *you* know her? She seems to know you real well."

"Man, you know, she's a good lady."

"Yeah, yeah, a good lady, but how is she really? Are you with her now, or is she open season for me, too?"

"You know, Gord, here's the deal, she's a lady, she needs to be treated like a lady, and she's way more than you can handle. You need to ease yourself into the game, man."

"See here, young fellow, you can't just move in on a lady like her. She's been spoiled by Jimmy," Larry chimed in adding to the regular truck stop conversation.

"You have to appreciate a woman like Montana. She's like Jimmy's '68 shovelhead; a classic, dependable, smooth ride, and he has made it one of a kind.

"Now you take the shovelhead and compare that machine to a Honda 750, which there are thousands of out there, and that is the difference. Sure, the Honda will get you home, but the ride will never be the same as riding the Harley. Montana is like the Harley, one of a kind, the one you want. You get it?"

Gord just shook his head. Being the youngest one in the group meant he would have to take the ribbing from the others.

"Wow, good one, Larry. I think young Gordy understands now. Gord, I figure instead that you might want to talk to Annie. She's a real nice girl for a nice boy like you," Jimmy offered. "See the waitress over at the till, that's Annie. I'll give you a good introduction if you wash my truck when we get home.

"Yeah, right! I don't think so. I can do just fine without your help," Gord said as he eyed up Annie, while she was standing at the cash register making change for another driver. The girl had a cute face and her straight brown locks cascaded down the length of her back.

Montana returned to the table to take their orders. Jimmy and Farmer ordered the Northport Clubhouse and Larry and Gord picked the steak sandwich.

"Another Coke, guys?" Montana asked.

"Yes, and young Gord here would like to meet Annie, too," Jimmy added as Gord punched him in the shoulder.

Gord's face blushed as Montana looked at him.

"Oh, I see. Well, young man, you best show me your manners here today. If you are very good, I just might introduce you to my beautiful cousin, Annie. I'm going to keep my eye on you," Montana laughed.

Truckers came, ate, and left 24/7 at the Northport truck stop. Jimmy, with the trucker's expense account, paid the lunch bill in cash from his money pouch. Larry dropped two five spots on the table for Montana. He had met too many Montanas in his time—every one of them could always use the tip money.

While the men used the can, Jimmy was with Montana out the side door of the restaurant. They parted with a big kiss and a commitment to get together soon.

"Why don't you ride with Gord? I'll drive your truck. You can take Gord through Spokane and show him the route down to Portland along 325 and 97," Larry said to Jim. "We can meet up down at Grimm's, this side of Portland. We'll be there about midnight."

"Sure, man, I could use the sleep. Gord here will have to take her easy on the gears while I get some rest. Right, Gord."

Gord replied with his middle finger pointed at Jimmy.

109

"See you down at Grimm's, then. You can buy me the buck ninety nine breakfast."

Gord followed Larry through the half circle exit to get out of the parking lot and enter onto Highway 25 South. Running through the gears, in eighth direct he hit 55 so he dumped it into eighth over, remaining at the speed limit on the flat road.

* * *

Back in New Pontiac, Starr and May sat in the sitting room, drinking green tea. Though they did not need to say much to each other, they needed to be together.

Starr broke down first.

"May, I love Larry. I didn't want him to go on this trip, I didn't want him to leave me, and yet no matter how hard I try and think about how could he do this to me, I know that it is also the reason that makes me love him so much. It's just not fair! How much does a person have to sacrifice? How much is enough?"

May took Starr's hand between her two small hands.

"Starr, all will be fine. Soon he'll be back, and life will go ahead once again. We trust them and they know what they are doing. It is not our place to tell them they can't do it. We would be taking from them the very existence that makes us love them so much."

They collapsed beside each other on the leather couch with May's arms around Starr, pulling her tight to her.

"They are who they are. This is difficult for them, but they have found peace here and they will find it again when they return. We'll all be together again soon," May said assuredly, as she stroked Starr's head.

Chapter 8

Saturday, July 2, 1977

Just past midnight, Larry parked in the open spot beside Gord's truck and trailer. Grimm's Truck Stop was outside of Portland, at the junction of highway 84 and highway 205; the bypass route truckers drove to avoid the traffic congestion in Portland.

Farmer joined the men inside the cafe, while Larry stayed in the cab and entered his trip into the truck's logbook. As soon as the diesel engine's turbocharger had cooled, he shut down the engine and locked the truck for the night.

Jimmy and Gord had finished their Midnight Trucker's breakfast as Farmer met up with them. He ordered one for him and one for Larry, along with two black coffees. They ate while Jim recounted Gord's attempt at hitting on the young waitress back at the Union 66 truck stop outside of Spokane.

Gord bragged about getting her phone number, pointing out that was all that mattered.

"Bet it's not her real number. Bet it's her parents, or maybe the cops," Jimmy retorted.

Gord and Jimmy were anxious to get over to the bar for a few beers. The girls only danced for another hour. Farmer noticed them looking across the road at the bar. "Why don't you head over for a beer before closing time?

"You two are doing a great job. Larry and I are getting off here, to visit a friend. Take the loads through to Eureka and return to New Pontiac. We'll meet you at home."

"Sounds good. I'll make sure the young fellow gets home okay. Have a safe trip and we'll catch up with you back at the farm."

An hour later, they were draining their third coffee when a gangly man, with a long grey beard and a long ponytail under his green jungle hat, approached their booth. His faded army jacket hung open, exposing the Grateful Dead's 'skull and roses' logo on his white t-shirt.

"Evening, Gerry, it's been a few years. Evening, Larry, ditto I say," the stranger said as he grabbed the hand of Farmer. Their hands met by locking thumbs. The same shake went to Larry.

"Damn good to see you again, my friends!"

"It's been a while, Professor, but it's good to see you again, too," Farmer said as he stood beside the man who had six inches on him in height. "How are you?"

"Well, you know. . .okay, I guess! Man, when you called to say you were coming down, Christ the day just got a hell of a lot better. I don't get many visitors anymore."

When they sat into the booth, he continued, "I miss you guys and the others. Do you know Skipper died last year?"

"He was a good man. What happened?" asked Larry.

"Last July 4th he had just finished driving the Battalion float, when a group of young jackoffs met up with him. Still dressed in his uniform, they started mouthing off about him being a loser, a baby killer. You know the shit they say. Then he lost control. Skipper cracked and took on all six of them on the street. He beat them up real bad.

"One of the punk's old man made the Sheriff arrest Skipper and put him in jail.

"This shit just never ends," commented Larry.

"You got her right there, man. One of the officers refused to keep a war hero caged on Independence Day. He drove Skipper home and told him to come back to the jail in the morning. Skipper must have been torn up bad inside, because he took his first drink in over a year. He finished off the bottle. Then he blew his brains out with a shotgun, right in his own house, the poor bugger."

The professor rubbed his eyes, "Skipper, man he was one of the few friends I used to visit, and now he's gone." He looked up at the ceiling, "Hey old Skipper, we'll meet again."

Larry's head nodded in respect of another dead fellow soldier.

When the professor returned from wherever his mind had gone, he was ready. "Well, men, let's get you back to my house."

In minutes, they were at the professor's acreage south of Gresham, Oregon. The modest 1950's log home, and the assortment of outbuildings, was part of the former 1,200-acre dairy farm and rangeland.

Inside the house, Larry, Farmer, and Professor clanked cold bottles of Budweiser together as their host announced the toast.

"To Skipper, and a simpler time—when things worked."

$$* * *$$

The simpler time was six years earlier, in 1971. Farmer and Larry first met the man they called Professor, as a member of the 191st Military Intelligence Company.

Only a year earlier, he had been a professor of Fine Arts at Portland State University. Although extremely talented in graphic arts and geography, he had earned the reputation as a lone wolf amongst the clutches of the Democrats who ran his faculty and, in fact, controlled most of the university.

In contrast, he was a hard, conservative man, a Nixon supporter, a diehard Republican—with well-known views. He often spoke at public events in support of the troops in Vietnam.

In 1970, the dean, and his fellow liberal Democrats, convinced three young students to file sexual harassment charges against him. They were fictitious charges, but the three women would do anything to get rid of a man who so strongly supported the Vietnam War.

After submitting his resignation, the women dropped the charges.

Out of a job, the professor walked into the recruitment center and enlisted.

Three months later, he was on the ground in Vietnam working with Military Intelligence on special assignments. His background filled a valuable role in Military Intelligence. He could draw maps, read maps, and possessed total recall of the minutest detail on the maps. He also had the experience and education to make small cameras for security and night photography. Yes, he quickly became a skilled and desired asset of the MI team.

Because of his special talents, Professor received his famous assignment, cataloguing and mapping mineral deposits in Vietnam and Laos; an operation determined to be of vital intelligence for the security of the United States of America.

Stay or leave, the United States of America would know the location of all mineral deposits. An ally of today could become an enemy tomorrow. They wanted to know what and where these resources were, particularly uranium deposits. When the United States military exited this part of Southeast Asia, they would know what they were leaving behind and where it was located.

To accomplish this task in a compressed timeframe, a hundred 'Prospectors', drawn from Special Forces, CIA and the army, scoured the villages in search of information on the location of minerals.

Professor extracted information from monastery records, the Hmong people, and cooperative French advisors who remained in the country. He excelled at assembling this data onto paper maps and writing detailed reports on each deposit. Soon the mapping project became known as the 'Professor's Maps'.

It was because of this mapping of minerals that, in 1971, Professor met Larry and Farmer when they arrived to support the project. From March to September, they worked closely with the professor to learn the latest intelligence on the vast network of trails, supply lines, tunnels and the remaining infrastructure of South Vietnam and eastern Laos. Using Professor's network of Prospectors, they were able to field prove the information. The field verification gave them the most current and detailed records of this critical information. During their work together, Professor didn't ask why Larry and Farmer needed to be there, and how they had slipped in the side door on this operation, he knew they were there for a reason, and that was all right with him.

* * *

On the professor's acreage, the bright daylight shone in the eastside window of Farmer's bedroom. If he had been asleep, the bright sunlight might have been annoying, but it didn't affect him, as he had only been able to sleep for two hours during the night. Although his eyes were looking at the fir beams forming the vaulted ceiling, his mind was laying out what he had to do in the days to come.

He ran through the plan again, and again, until despite the sunlight, he fell asleep. Eggs frying in the kitchen woke him.

Joining Larry and the eccentric professor at the large wooden table, Farmer poured a cup of coffee from the glass carafe in the center of the table. The pair had been talking before he entered.

"So I figure this fiberglass composite material is going to lighten up everything we make. Just imagine, it will mean lighter airplanes, lighter trucks, and lighter buildings. When you make them lighter you need less jet fuel, less diesel, less electricity in the factories, and so on. I figure, this means a big drop in the demand for oil.

"Since I am up 300% on my oil shares in the last couple of years, I am taking profits by selling half of my oil shares. Guess what I am buying instead.

"No, what are you going to make your next million on, Professor?" Larry revealed a light-and thin-smile.

"Michigan Near Metals, it's called. The company holds the patent on the material. Hell, when Boeing wants to use the stuff on their planes, they pay royalties to MNM. She's a cash cow. Here's a tip you can take to the bank, buy Michigan Near Metals stock and you'll be set."

"You never cease to amaze me, Professor," Farmer said as he poured himself a cup of coffee.

"You have to be looking ahead, Farmer. You don't know when 'The Man' is going to hit you again. Live together, live proud, but protect your ass. That's what I say."

"What's this about *live together?*" You own half the county just so you can be alone?"

"No, I mean help those who need help. Yeah, what a thing for an old Republican to say, but I have seen enough destruction, and that doesn't work at all, so I say live together and help those who need it. By the way, I voted for the President. Can you dig it, me voting for a Democrat? Even I can see the light."

"I hope you haven't changed too much. We need your help; help from the old professor," Farmer said as he looked at the eccentric man.

After an hour of laying down what had to be done, Professor took Farmer and Larry out to the third barn in the row of six. Inside was a grey 1969 Pontiac GTO Judge with its hood, trunk, and rear spoiler painted black.

"Keys are in her. I renewed the insurance yesterday and dropped the oil. She's a beautiful car, Farmer. No one has been around her since you left her here a few years ago. I've been starting her up every month just to keep the fluids flowing."

"Professor, you're a good man. We'll be back around dinnertime. How about if I pick up some of the Colonel's chicken for dinner," Farmer offered as he opened the passenger's door. "Want to drive Larry?"

Larry's eyes lit up like a small child's on Christmas morning. He jumped into the driver's seat and turned the key. The 400 cubic inches of pure V-8 power, pushing out over 360 horses, came to life, rocking the car while Larry balanced the rough idle by feathering in the choke. He loved muscle cars and this one had the complete package.

Once they hit the pavement, Larry punched her, burning rubber in every gear.

Thirty minutes later, they walked inside the historic Bank of America building. The 120-year-old stone structure had been restored recently. Its wood floors shone brightly with the new wax finish. Polished brown handrails displayed their superb fir grain structure. The tellers stood behind a solid wood counter with open metal framed windows through which they served the customers. A wooden bench, finished with green velour was located to the left of the teller's window cages. Larry plunked himself onto the bench while Farmer went to the right side of the teller windows to the Customer Service counter and spoke to the clerk.

A male employee escorted Farmer around his wood desk down the narrow hallway to the vault containing the safety deposit boxes. To verify his identity, Farmer produced his Oregon Driver's License, with the name of Mr. Gerald Archer on the license, but with Farmer's picture. The banker accepted the identification.

Farmer set out his key for Box 402 on the table when the banker pulled out the sign-in card. Farmer noted he had also last signed as Gerald Archer in 1975.

The teller used the two keys to open the grey metal door for the slot and extracted the long green security box. Carrying the box under his arm, Farmer entered the secure room, locking the door from inside.

Inside the deep box was only one item—a soft brown leather satchel he had placed in the box in the summer of 1975 after Colonel Henry, aka Harley, had given it to him.

Harley had not said anything about the contents, other than he asked them not to open the bag unless they knew they needed to open it. Today was that day!

Until last week, he had not given much thought to the contents. Using the key, which was also in the box, he unlocked the top flap of the leather case and extracted four brown envelopes, simply identified as 1, 2, 3, and 4. Breaking the wax seal on the first envelope, he removed the single piece of paper. The typed note from Harley was on plain white stationary.

July 1, 1975

Men:

I prayed you would never have reason to read this letter, nor need these materials, but unfortunately that is now not the case. You are on your way to clean up. Despite Robin's attempts to sanitize the operation, he couldn't get it done. They wouldn't support his plans; no one had the guts to touch it! However, this is no time for sentimental history; it is time for tomorrow.

In the second envelope is $50,000, in mixed bills, and a key to a safety deposit box, under your same aliases, at the First City Bank on First Avenue and Main Street in Portland. Open that box today, as well.

In the third envelope is a document that I wrote detailing Operation Quiet Thunder. You may have a need for that report someday.

After we last met, a sniper shot missed me while I was having coffee in a cafe in the middle of the afternoon in West Portland. Soon after, I spoke with Birdman. He also had some unusual events occur around him in Langley. The coincidence was too odd so I assembled this package for you. There are no other documents of our mission's history.

In the fourth envelope are clean blank passports—six each from Canada, United States and England. Most importantly, there are also three letters signed by President Huntington, one for each of you, reinstating you as operatives of the Agency, to carry out operation TS White Bear's Paw under your command and with absolute authority to conduct the operation.

The Presidential Executive Order is classified as a Top Secret National Security Operation. It cannot be revoked by any future president. The document gives you the capacity that you need to finish Quiet Thunder.

There is no trail to you from Quiet Thunder. You have only been identified by knowing the Executive Order name of which the implementation will begin by providing the passkey—the eight-digit code which we all learned for Operation Quiet Thunder.

May no man be asked again to do what we were asked to do for our country,
Harley

The letter was definitely a Colonel Henry brainchild.

Harley was a diligent man, one who left no loose ends. He built this recovery plan because he knew it would be needed. Again, his intuition had been correct. Farmer looked quickly at the document Harley had written about Operation Quiet Thunder. The report included details of orders to the colonel from the CIA agents, men with no names, but avoided identifying the team. The document wouldn't have been overly helpful in a situation necessitating its use, except for the fact that it included four photographs of two CIA men meeting with the colonel.

Judging by the basic decor, the four photographs were taken in a hotel room. The pictures were labeled as 'September 13, 1971, Austin Hilton, Agents Simpson and Dickson'. The pictures captured the three of them in the room. Two photos showed a briefcase with money and papers beside it on the bedspread. The twins in the black suits had to be CIA.

There was no time to read the entire document now. Farmer took the package of envelopes and returned them to the leather pouch.

After placing the case into the black leather briefcase that he had brought in with him, he closed the empty safety deposit box and exited the secure room. He closed the account for the safety deposit box.

Within five minutes, Mr. Gerald Archer was opening Box 175 at the First City Bank, merely two blocks from the Bank of America. In the secure room, he opened another safety deposit box and removed a second brown leather pouch. Two manila envelopes were inside. The first contained another note from Harley.

> Your mission may become expensive. Enclosed are twenty US $10,000 dollar Bearer Bonds. I have also deposited $800,000 with the Bank of Switzerland in Vienna. The bank account number is on the white card attached to this note. The identification password for access to this account is our eight-digit code.
>
> Harley

Farmer extracted the contents of Box 175 and put them in his black briefcase. He locked the box with the female clerk concluding the security process by using her key to secure the box's slot.

Larry fired up the Judge before Farmer slipped into the car. He drove them to the Portland Military Cemetery, Center Road, parking spot number four. In the vacant parking lot, Farmer told him about the notes, the boxes, and Harley's instructions. When he had finished, they secured the briefcase in the truck of the car, locking the trunk before they left.

Cobblestone walkways lead through the rows of headstones. With only a few quick strides, they stopped at Harley's white marble headstone.

Colonel Arthur Gerald Henry
May 1, 1935 - October 19, 1975.
A man who took the road less travelled.

Larry rested his hand on the conical top of the headstone and closed his eyes. Farmer also said his respects to Harley through his own silent prayer. Before returning to the GTO, they each saluted the gravestone.

* * *

It was 3:30 when Larry parked the Judge under the large maple tree at the far end of Professor's house. Farmer carried the bucket of Kentucky Fried Chicken, with homemade fries, gravy, coleslaw and six white bread buns. Larry grabbed a two-four of Bud off the back seat. The professor was at the wooden picnic table under another maple tree, so the food and beer was set down in front of him at the table.

This type of challenging work excited the professor, confirmed by the wide grin he offered as he announced that he had a successful day. He lifted the top page of the file folder and gave a Canadian passport to Larry and one to Farmer. In the bright daylight, they each scrutinized the forged passports in the names of Mr. Gerald Brightman and Mr. Larry Brown.

"My friends, you're now journalists with the Canadian Broadcasting Company. I made a call to a friend at the CBC in Montreal; he has officially hired you as freelance reporters. Your registration with them was backdated to March. All is clean.

"As for equipment, I brought out some old gear. You'll be familiar with the stuff. The video camera has been cleaned, so has the Leica SLR 35mm camera. The cases are scuffed already—I did not need to distress them. The gear is typical of a freelance CBC reporter's gear— rough, tough and not the newest stuff on the market.

"I also gave you two new cassette recorders. You have to take advantage of the latest Japanese gear in that part of the world."

Comparing the new passports to the three original Canadian documents that the professor used as models, Farmer confirmed Professor still excelled at his forgery work.

"Now, the travel visas are a bit more difficult. The one I prepared for Hong Kong uses the British Commonwealth format. Burma and Thailand have not changed their forms recently. We are okay there as well. I used an Underwood typewriter, which is a familiar typewriter in use in the consulates."

Professor paused as he re-examined two of the visas.

"Laos is a bit of a challenge. The government is not stable, and the documentation standards vary. Visas are not a high priority over there these days. They really don't want foreigners in the county while they convert it to communism. However, I was fortunate to meet with a friend of mine, a foreign aid worker for UNICEF, and prepared these papers from his six-month-old document. I expect the worse that can happen is you may have to pass some cash to the officer who challenges the visa. No one really knows what is in effect in Laos, so everyone expects a bribe with whatever travel documents you have in your possession anyway. Did I miss anything?

They examined each visa letter, noted the particular folding, creasing, and even the weathering of the different papers. The documents looked like they had been travelling with two ragged reporters through the backcountry. Another fine set of forgeries had been prepared by the talented enigma.

"Professor, you have outdone yourself this time. You are a genius! Thank God you're on our side. Man, this is real cool work," Farmer said as he shook Professor's hand.

With the documents safe in their envelopes, Larry dug into the chicken bucket, grabbing a deep-fried thigh. The paper plates with the chicken, gravy on the fries, green coleslaw and butter on the white buns made for the best fast food dinners ever created.

Cold Budweiser continued being served late into the night, while they sat around the fire pit telling stories about friends, those still here, and those that had already gone.

* * *

The night back in New Pontiac was a good one, too.

Leanne, Christina, Anita, and Ken went to the family hot springs pool. The residents had built the pool west of the first bridge. The concrete pond filled with the natural hot water from a spring that came out of the ground about 600 yards up the draw from the pool. Cold water from the Pontiac River mixed with the hot water to keep the pool temperature around 98 degrees, since the natural hot spring's water came out of the ground at 135 degrees. The pungent smell of sulfur clung to the cool evening air, bringing it back to the pool area.

The swim was a fine family event since other children and parents were in the pool, too. Christina played with a girl a year older than her. Ken and Leanne sat on one of the concrete benches inside the pool.

Ken was in his blue Speedo. Of course, a Californian would have a tight fitting Speedo. Sitting on the bench, soaking in the relaxing warm water, immersed from the neck down, Leanne squirmed on Ken's lap. He would not be able to exit the pool anytime soon.

A second sulfur water pool was located further up the trail. That pool was for adults only, clothing optional. The party at the adult pool was in full swing already, sending intermittent rambunctious outbursts downstream to the family pool.

The mosquitoes and horseflies were getting thick around the pool, confirming that it was time to take little Christina home. As Leanne got out of the water, her form-fitting bikini clung to her tight body. She walked over to the fire to collect Christina and wrap a blanket around her for the walk home. Ken stayed in the water still having to wait until he could get out while wearing his taut bathing suit.

Stoner and two of his friends walked over to the fire, drunk and stoned, as usual. They'd been kicked out of the adult pool area since they weren't swimming; they were just watching the women.

Stoner watched Anita as she climbed out of the pool. Her lime green bikini accented her thin and shapely body. "Wow, Anita, your body looks great," he said as his friends laughed at his brilliance.

"Piss off, Stoner! Go jerk off somewhere else. This area is for families; can't you see the kids around here? They don't need to hear any crap from you," Anita shot back.

"Hey, you're quite the firecracker, aren't you? I think you need to be lit up."

Leanne left Christina at the table, moving instead over to Stoner. "Don't be such a prick Stoner. Get out of here. We don't need you mouthing off around here."

"Hey, you got quite the body too. I'd like to see more of it," Stoner said to Leanne.

Leanne swiftly lifted her left foot and kicked him in the crotch. He groaned in agony before falling to the hard packed soil. Ken arrived behind her, witnessing her assault. He watched her walk past him back to the table, knowing Leanne well enough not to say anything to her at this time. When she was pissed off, it was best to let her be.

Stoner was still crying on the ground as Leanne led the procession home. Ken carried little Christina so they could keep up with her.

The walk back to the house almost calmed Leanne down.

Christina fell asleep in Ken's arms. Leanne removed her sleeping child's bathing suit, dressed her in cotton sleepers, and set her into her small bed. Her brown teddy bear slept under her arm.

Leanne joined Anita and Ken for a joint around the fire pit in the front yard. No one mentioned the incident; it was over.

Chapter 9

Farmer woke to the smell of cooked bacon and eggs. Larry and Professor were in the kitchen with a bowl of scrambled eggs, a plate of bacon, and a stack of toast in the middle of the table, along with a pitcher of grape juice.

The professor was immersed in the middle of a dissertation on investments with Larry.

"Morning, Farmer. Grab what you want. There are still a few beers in the fridge, if you need to chase last night with some hair of the dog." He turned back to Larry and continued, "I bought myself a computer two years ago. The machine came as a box of pieces that I had to assemble myself. The computer was cool, and it made me think about the utility of the device. I figure someday, every big office might have a need for one of these machines.

"Think about how many offices there are and if every office buys a computer, well that would create enough demand for a few million. This is huge, man. I looked into who controlled these computers and found four companies, but you can only buy into three of them now.

"International Business Machines have their foot in the office door with most companies, since they had been building the big machines for accounting work already. They have a great future.

"Hewlett Packard has been building machines of a different sort for engineers. I think they will bite at this new smaller computer market too.

"Then a company called Intel makes the brains for these machines. Every computer needs a brain to run, and they will probably be the main supplier for all computers. The more computers out there, the more money the company will make. In only three years, I've tripled the value of my initial investment of their stocks.

"Then there's Victory Computers. Dig this. Until this year, people like me could buy kits to build our own computer. However, they were odd machines and didn't do much more than a good calculator could. Then two young men built a unit in their garage, and it worked better than any other one. They put them out to the market and they sold out fast. Other companies are getting into this 'ready to go computer market' too. These home computers are heating up and I can feel some good money can be made if you bet on the right company. Who knows, if these companies get it right, maybe one in a hundred homes will buy one, too. Hey, that is another million computers. Yeah, if they crack it right, the market could be huge. If you ever hear of Victory going public, buy their shares."

"Man, your head's going to explode someday, Professor. You need to get out more to clear your busy brain," Larry joked.

It was after ten o'clock, when Larry secured the black briefcase in the trunk storage shelf he'd built in the Judge years ago. He had also added hidden compartments throughout the car.

The briefcase sat inside a tray cut into the top of the gas tank, where there was enough room to build the steel compartment above the tank, hide it with the lid, and cover the whole set-up with the trunk carpet. The extra papers and passports fit inside a compartment built on the inside of the rear side panel. The leather upholstery seams set right back into place perfectly with the documents behind the panel. The camera gear and their bags were stowed on the trunk floor.

An hour later, they were driving south on the I-5 freeway. Larry held the Judge tight at the speed limit. By mid-afternoon, Larry poked Farmer to wake him up.

"Looks like the boys are heading home," he said as he pointed to the two northbound trucks on the other side of the meridian. Jimmy was leading with a black Model A coupe on his trailer. Gord was pulling a small John Deere Tractor on his highboy.

"Jimmy finally got the Ford loaded and is taking her back home. It'll be a cool project for him."

"I bet they don't get past Northport until Tuesday. What the hell, spending the fourth in Northport with good women won't hurt them," Farmer said.

* * *

Reverend Bob was working on his sermon when Mary arrived at his garden table behind the church. She had been picking Huckleberries with her friends. Their favorite berry patch in the forest was just a short walk up the logging road. Mary handed him a dish of fresh wild berries, topped with thick cream.

Over their meal of berries, Mary forced the conversation to discuss their arrangement. Tired of skirting around the issue, Mary just came out with her point. "Bob, it's time we made a commitment. You need to move into my house and be with me each day. I don't mean that we have to get married, but I think we need to be together."

Reverend Bob looked at Mary, "Okay."

Mary took his right hand in her two hands and said, "Good, then that's done. Now do you need any help tonight's sermon?"

"No. Thanks though. I have just decided to talk about friendship. Yeah, you must have good friends—you need to have a good special friend—this is a good idea," he said as he put his pencil to his notepad and started writing.

Reverend Bob's heart was in full force in the evening's rip-roaring sermon. He was hot. His words rang true to his sisters and brothers in New Pontiac. Mary sat in the front row, to the right of the pulpit and took in the performance with an enlightened heart and a feeling of contentment that she had never experienced before.

After the sermon, ninety people were served at the potluck dinner. They enjoyed the special offering of fresh Huckleberry pie. The women in the kitchen had been picking too. They pooled the succulent berries, making the haul into juicy pies. Thick, chilled cream was in the pitchers to pour onto the slices of pie.

Leanne and Ken sat in the rear garden area watching the fire, while listening to Charlie and his musicians play songs into the starlit night. Tonight a violinist joined the group. The sweet music, combined with some good elderberry wine, reminded Ken of when they were together years ago, and they used to travel to the Haight-Ashbury area in San Francisco to sit on the grass in the park and listen to the musicians perform their music—so similar, but yet so different—and so long ago.

A tap on his shoulder caused Ken's mind to return to the garden behind the New Pontiac Hall. Mary was behind him. She needed to talk to him, 'in private'. Looking at Leanne with a confused expression on his face, he followed Mary away from their bench.

"I must tell you that Bob is moving in with me, so we have to cool it down. I am off the market now. Sorry, but it has to be that way. I won't be able to have you over, unless Bob is at home. I'm sorry to disappoint you."

Ken knew better than to mess around with this one.

"Oh, I'm glad to hear you and Reverend Bob are doing this. You deserve a good man like him and you two will do well together. He is one lucky fellow. I'll respect your decision and thank you for being so upfront about this."

"I had to tell you in person. I am sorry, but it has to be this way."

"Mary, I got it. And thanks for being honest with me." Ken said as he hugged her.

When he returned to Leanne, she questioned him about his private conversation with Mary.

"It was very important, very personal, something just between Mary and me."

"Come on, cough up the goods, what did she want?"

"Mary had to inform me that she is off the market now. Reverend Bob and she are shacking up together, which means I'm out of luck."

"Oh, that was nice of her to tell you in person. I guess that's so you don't sneak out from our house and go knocking on her door in the middle of the night," Leanne said as she pushed on Ken's shoulder.

Working with Mary had helped her understand the woman; she had run many fantasies in her mind over the years. This one had now ended.

* * *

At 7:30, Farmer turned into the Red Lion Inn parking lot in Redding, California. Their plan was to spend the night in Redding and head into San Francisco tomorrow. After paying for the two rooms, he parked the car in front of his room.

He need not be too concerned about the security of the car. Another set of modifications that Larry had made included modifying the locks on the Judge so the lock barrels couldn't be popped. He added a motion alarm, and the immobilizer, which prevented hot wiring of the car. The car could not be hotwired, because Larry's system required a secondary circuit to be turned on at the same time in order to start the engine. The car and gear were safe.

As the steaks were cooking in the Lion's Den, Farmer made the call he had been thinking about the whole trip. He put five dollars in quarters into the pay phone and dialed the number. While the telephone was ringing, the haunting concerns ran through his mind. Would he still be alive? Would he be able to recognize them? Would he want to see them? On the fifth ring, Carol answered.

"Hello."

"Oh, hello, Carol, this is Gerry Field. I'm calling to see how James is doing?"

"Oh, Gerry, I am so glad that you called. It's good to talk to you again. When you called last Thursday, James was so excited to hear from you that he had a great day. He is still in the hospital. His blood count is not good and they are giving him transfusions to bring up his levels."

"Would it be alright if we stopped in to visit him tomorrow?"

"Oh, by all means. Yes. Who is with you?"

"Larry came with me."

"James will be so happy to meet with you two. He talks about you every day, but I do not always know if it's him, or the morphine, talking. Is Ken with you, too?"

"No, Ken is in New Pontiac helping out while we are away."

Carol's voiced dropped a tone with her disappointment after learning her son was still in New Pontiac.

"Gerry, it's great to hear from you. When can you get here?"

"We are in Redding. I figure we'll be at the hospital by noon."

"Noon it is, I won't say anything to James. It'll be his Independence Day surprise."

"Okay Carol, we'll see you tomorrow."

"Goodbye, Gerry. Thanks for coming down."

The steaks and the second Bud had arrived at the table when Farmer returned.

"Green light, boss?" asked Larry.

"Yes, he's in the hospital. He's not doing well, but Carol is happy we are going to visit him. Who'd have ever thought that cancer would take him down? Life just isn't fair. It makes you wonder if there is a god?" questioned Farmer.

Farmer was deep in thought, thoughts of frustration, thoughts of his good friend dying from within, and thoughts of where they were going. His distraction was broken when the bubbly young waitress returned and asked, "Can I get you another couple of Buds."

"You betcha, and bring double Jimmy Beams on the rocks too."

The bouncy waitress returned with the beers and whiskeys, feeling good in knowing that the more liquor these two men drank, the bigger her tip would be. It had been a good tip weekend so far.

"Here's to those that we have met along the way, wherever they are now."

"Right on," Farmer replied.

They clanked the whiskey glasses together. After draining the double shots, they washed them down with the fresh Buds.

Larry finished first and slammed his beer bottle onto the table. "I'm still the champ," he bragged.

Chapter 10

Monday, July 4, 1977

The engine oil deposits on the hot asphalt parking lot steamed from the baking daytime heat. It was noon when Farmer and Larry walked into the air-conditioned entrance of the Veterans' Hospital dressed in the clean uniforms they had retrieved from the professor's house yesterday.

A mix of odors permeated the airspace. Bleach, floor wax, and sick people's musk, met them after entering through the electric doors of the hospital.

God I hate this smell, thought Farmer as they proceeded to the front desk.

A perky receptionist greeted them at the reception desk, obviously immune to the hospital smell.

"Hello, where can we find Captain James Schmidt?"

"Good afternoon. Now Captain Schmidt. . .let me check," she replied as she flipped through the pages in her aluminum binder.

"Ah, yes, here he is. Captain Schmidt is in the oncology wing. He is on the fourth floor, room 4431. Sirs, I will have one of our attendants escort you to his room. You are welcome to sit in this waiting area until the attendant arrives," she said as she pointed to the two silver sofas to the left of her desk.

"Thank you ma'am," Farmer replied.

He did not sit on the sofa because as he turned toward the waiting area he caught his reflection in the polished glass of a darkened room beside the sofas. The glass acted as a mirror. In the mirror was the image of a weary, old soldier, one who had been in fighting for too long. His polished brass buttons, white shirt, black tie and clean service strips, provided a flashy contrast against the somber dark grey-green of his uniform.

He had dressed in many different uniforms over his years. Each one served the role of the time. He liked this one the best, especially for today's visit. This uniform was the one that the three of them wore for public events, it was most recognizable, caused the fewest questions, and brought them together again as a unit.

In contrast, Larry looked crisp in his uniform. He shaved ten years off his age when he dressed in full uniform; the sharp fit took away the edge he forever carried with him.

The male attendant, wearing a blue smock, arrived at the desk and saluted. They returned a salute.

"Please, sirs, would you sign in," he said as he held out the ledger for Farmer, who took the pen and signed the paper before passing it to Larry.

"Very well, sirs, this way," the orderly said as he led them through the right wing hallway. Two hallway security guards eyed up Farmer and Larry as they approached. They saluted them and buzzed the locked entrance, so they could continue through the security door. A nurse in a white uniform sat on a collapsible metal chair outside the closed door of room 4431.

"Major Field and Captain Johnson are here for Captain Schmidt," the attendant announced to the nurse.

The broad nurse stood up from her chair, which had been propped against the wall. In a Scottish accent she said, "Ah, gentlemen, Mrs. Schmidt is in with the captain now. She told me you'd be arriving shortly. Let me check on him to make sure he is ready to receive you."

Within a minute, she returned and opened the door. "Captain Schmidt, you have visitors," she announced as Farmer and Larry walked into the room.

Muted sunlight lit up the private room and a rainbow of colored flowers in decorative vases lined the windowsill. The room resembled a command center with all the machines trailing wires and hoses surrounding the bed. Larry and Farmer both felt a guilty sadness as they witnessed their friend lying in his bed. Dressed in his uniform, it was obvious that he was now a much smaller man. His uniform appeared to be at least two sizes too large. He had lost his hair. His skin resembled yellow leather, his eyes were dull, and his face had shrunk inward.

Both raised their arms and saluted. Shelby somehow found the strength to raise his right arm and wave due to the hoses and wires around his arms.

"Hello Shelby, my old friend, it is good to see you again," Farmer announced. "And Carol, how do you continue to get younger each time I meet you? You look great," he said as he gave her a hug.

Carol returned a warm smile, and hugged him back.

Shelby lifted his left hand to shake Larry's. His right hand was intravenously restrained so he couldn't lift it far off the bed. Larry took Shelby's hand between his hands.

"Hey, man, it's been too long." He held his hand until Shelby's arm went limp from the exertion of lifting his arm.

Shelby couldn't speak much, but a faint smile never left his face. Two orderlies lifted Shelby out of bed and set him in a wheel chair so the three of them could tour the hospital grounds. He asked them to talk since it was painful for him; he wanted to know all about New Pontiac. He wanted to hear about May and Starr. Farmer told him Ken was working at the mill, and he had met up with Leanne. Shelby liked Leanne—she was full of life, and she knew how to enjoy living it.

Shelby insisted on seeing the Judge. Being a car fanatic, the legendary muscle cars were his favorite. Larry pushed him around the car so he could inspect every detail from his wheel chair. Since he was not strong enough to climb into the car, Larry picked up his friend and set him into the driver's seat. A wide smile went across Shelby's narrowed face as he stared through the windshield. It wasn't his 1965 Shelby Mustang, but every muscle car buff had respect for this car.

For the rest of the afternoon, they toured the meticulously maintained grounds. At 3 o'clock, a nurse caught up with them and changed the IV bag hanging from the chrome post on the wheel chair. She also pushed a needle into the line adding the morphine into the cocktail of pharmaceuticals.

"Now Captain, we are meeting for our special dinner today at five. We will be starting the parade in the patio area at 4:30, so don't you and your friends arrive late."

The morphine affected Shelby quickly, allowing him to talk to them again, albeit in a soft and quiet voice. In the garden area, shaded by a cluster of oak trees, Shelby spoke. "I wish I could be with you on this trip. You don't need to tell me anything. . .but is it going to work?"

"I think so. We have a few loose ends to work on, but they can be worked out on the way. We still have to acquire some assets, but I figure Billy Bob can help us and then we can get this over with."

Shelby closed his eyes for a nap break. They sat on the bench and watched the nurses in their starched, white, uniforms walk by as they moved around the ground to attend to their patient's needs.

The PA system announced the parade would begin in fifteen minutes, requesting all participants to assemble in the patio area. The announcement woke Shelby. The morphine had done its job and numbed the pain so he could speak with them again. He spoke about his concern for Carol after he was gone.

He said that Carol could return to teaching school. She had taken a one-year leave to care for him. She would receive a military widow pension and should be okay for money. They had no debt, other than a bit over the ten grand in unpaid medical bills. They had hired a lawyer to fight against paying those costs, since Veteran Affairs should have treated him when he first went in with the symptoms, instead of him having to pay his own doctors to get the diagnosis.

The parade consisted of veterans that were mobile, in some manner, following the marching band from a local military academy. Over a hundred veterans followed the band, as they circled the grounds. Some were on crutches, some hobbled on prosthetic legs, some were in wheel chairs, and others just put one foot in front of the other while they existed wherever their minds thought they were at the time.

All the men wore their uniforms, and for just a small part of the day, they were able to leave their cares, worries, and frustrations somewhere else. This was their parade; they were again in a unit. The uniform was the unification of their group and not much else mattered.

For most of the veterans, this was the closest feeling to a family that they had for some years.

The parade ended outside the cafeteria.

The band members removed their musical instruments and formed two honorary guard lines. As the veterans passed down the line to enter the cafeteria, they saluted them.

The tables had been set with red, white, and blue cloths. Those without families had nurses or other staff sit around them. A group of hospital volunteers delivered dinner plates of ham, turkey, creamed corn and mashed potatoes to each person. Beer was served to those who asked for it. Shelby ordered three beers and a red wine for Carol. The three former team members shared a beer together, one more time.

By 7:30, Shelby fell asleep in his bed. Carol noted he had not been awake for this many hours since Easter. He'd be out for the night now. They each shook Shelby's left hand and saluted him for what might be the last time they would see him alive.

* * *

Life back in New Pontiac had been an eventful day.

The Americans were celebrating July 4th at a house party. They had beer, drugs, and the barbeque flowing with the joys of a good old American celebration.

The rest of the townsfolk enjoyed a sunny and quiet day. Fred went fly-fishing on the Blue Ridge River. Ken had little Christina at the beach with the other children while Leanne was reading a book at home. May and Starr were out on a walk around the fields, watching a herd of mule deer with their fawns travel through the cover of the young corn fields to get down to the river. It was a peaceful summer day of rest.

At 2:00, May noticed a man on a motorcycle ride past the mill and down the road toward them as they stood at the edge of the cornfields. She did not recognize the rider but since Charlie had let him in the sawmill gate he must know him.

"Who is that?" May asked Starr as the biker approached them.

"Oh Christ, that's Max. We have to find Leanne," replied Starr.

"Go find her and take her to my house. I'll find Fred. Don't let Max get anywhere near Leanne!"

Starr ran down the shortcut through the cornfield towards Leanne's house in an attempt to get there ahead of Max.

Max was just turning onto Fox Street.

On the trail through the cornfield, she met Jerome and his family returning from the beach. The 6 foot 3 inch tall carpenter joined Starr in the race to Leanne's house. His boy ran off to find Fred.

When Jerome and Starr got to Leanne's cabin, Max's bike was already parked in front. Leanne screamed from inside the house.

Max was yelling at her, "You fucking bitch, you're mine. You will do what I tell you to do. I'm the man here."

The sharp sound of a slap came from inside the house as Jerome jumped up the steps and forced open the locked door.

"Get out of here, Jerome, this ain't none of your business," Max said as he held Leanne in front of him. Leanne's left cheek was already bright pink and swollen and her lower lip was bleeding. Her shirt had been torn open.

"Can't do that man. Let her go and get out of here. I tell you Max, I'll rip you apart," Jerome said, just as Ken barged into the house and stood in front of Jerome.

"Who the fuck is this? Is this your new man? Well he don't look like shit to me. Hey bud, get the fuck out of here. She needs a real man, not some little kid. What is it; do you need Jerome to do your fighting?"

Ken was staring, glaring.

"Let her go. Now! Take me on and show me how tough you."

Max held Leanne a good four feet away from Ken.

"Okay, asshole, now you got me mad." Max said as he pushed Leanne out of the way and went for Ken. He jumped at Ken, but his fist glanced off Ken's left shoulder, causing Max to lose his footing and fall to the floor.

"Jerome, take Leanne out of here. Now, Jerome!" Ken ordered.

Max climbed up off the floor and back on his feet as Leanne and Jerome went out the front door.

"Now, asshole, you will never touch Leanne again, you will never hit another woman," Ken said as he sent a chop kick into Max's stomach, knocking the wind out of him and causing him to double over. Ken's locked arms went down on Max's back.

Out of breath, Max staggered as he threw a limp swing at Ken. Ken grabbed his arm and with a chop from his right hand, Max's arm snapped. Max's face took the next hit, removing his front teeth from their sockets.

Max had no idea what was going on now. He was in so much pain, nothing registered. Ken locked his arm around Max's neck and walked him toward the door, keeping him contained with the chokehold.

"Is Leanne gone?" Ken asked through the closed doorway to whoever might be outside.

"Yes, she's gone. Just Jerome and me are out here," answered Fred. "The cops will be here in an hour."

"Well, okay then, I'll take this piece of shit out to the gate so they can take him away," Ken said as he opened the door and walked the barely conscious Max down the steps.

Fred and Jerome exchanged startled looks when they saw the bloodied face of Max and the beating that Max had received.

"Does he need anything," Fred asked.

"No, he's fine. How is Leanne?"

"She's okay. I'll walk with you to the gate," said Fred.

"If you want. Old Max here won't be hitting anyone again, will you Max?"

Max shook his head side to side.

A few spectators had gathered along the roadside to watch Max being walked out of town. Fred remained beside them, to keep the situation calm and to prevent Max from getting hurt anymore, should Max be dumb enough to rile Ken in any manner.

Charlie met them at the gate. After Fred spoke to him, he swung the gate open.

"Get me some rope, Fred," commanded Ken. His military training had taken over Ken. He was operating on instinct.

Fred handed a coil of hemp rope to Ken who took the rope and walked Max over to a cedar tree on the highway side of the gate. He stood Max against the tree and tied his arm that was not broken around behind the cedar and looped the rope around to wrap around Max's body and the tree. He would be secure until the cops untied him.

Ken said his last words to Max, "If you ever touch Leanne again, you'll be going home in a pine box."

Fred overheard the fact being stated to Max.

"Give him some water and splint up his arm. Stay with him until the cops come," Fred said to Charlie as he and Ken started their walk back into town. Not a single word was spoken on their walk.

By the time Ken arrived at May's house, May had attended to Leanne's injuries. Her lip was swollen, but the bleeding had stopped. Her face was puffed up around her cheek and eye, from one of the hits she had received from Max. Doc had left her a bottle of valium to help her sleep and rest. She had taken two pills already, and was calm when Ken held her hand and hugged her. She didn't ask about Max. She knew that he would never bother her again.

"Christina is staying with Starr tonight. She already picked up her teddy bear and pajamas. Later we are making pizza and then going to pick flowers in the garden," said May. "Why don't you two go home so Leanne can rest?"

When they had left, May turned to Fred.

"Is he going to be okay?"

"Who. . .Max or Ken?"

"Ken."

"Yeah, he'll be fine. May, I have to tell you that I knew Ken was a different dude, but I did not know how different. May, I know his type; Farmer and Larry are like him, too. Those men are able to manage themselves just fine. He did what he had to do. Now it is over, he has returned from that place, and he will be okay. A friend used to call them 'Gate Keepers'. You wanted those guys in your unit."

"And Max?"

"Oh yeah, he'll be okay. Max won't ever hurt Leanne again."

"Then this is good," May said as she nodded at Fred.

Fred's distant stare in his eyes meant that there was nothing more to discuss about this incident. The situation had been neutralized.

Chapter 11

Tuesday, July 5, 1977

In New Pontiac, the mill started up on time without Farmer or Larry on site. May arrived at the office at 7:00 setting up at her husband's desk.

Since Leanne would be away this week, recovering, May had arranged for Fred's girlfriend, Chelsea, to help in the office.

Mary, the veteran of the office, was concerned about how these changes in the office would affect her status; however, the concern was short-lived. Instead, she had the opportunity to witness May in action.

By 8:30, May had met individually with George, the mill manager, and with both Fred and Ken. Mary had not seen this effective side of May, but she liked it. She especially enjoyed seeing May's charms work on these men. They had all underestimated May's direct, hands on, management style that she had so clearly demonstrated during her first two hours on the job.

At 9:30, May invited Mary and Chelsea into her office. She explained how she would be taking over some of her husband's responsibilities for the next while. In this interim re-organization, George, Fred, and Ken were assigned more responsibilities to cover Farmer and Larry's mill duties.

She also made a direct point to recognize Mary's experience and identified that she would be relying on Mary's knowledge to help the whole operation run effectively. May knew of Mary's influence on the people in the mill and was encouraged when Mary jumped on board by endorsing the changes. As the result of May's ability to coerce the men, and cajole the women, there was a seamless transition to a powerful and functioning management team to continue the diverse operations.

* * *

May's next test occurred less than one hour after the organizational meetings had concluded.

In the shipping yard, Stoner and his two friends had heard about Ken beating up Max so they were scared shitless of screwing up in front of Ken, especially since they knew they had pissed him off on Sunday night by commenting on Leanne at the hot springs pool.

Therefore, Stoner's solution was simple. Since Ken was in the office working with Mary, it was the perfect time to toke up so they could relax from the stress of having Ken around them the rest of the day. That meant they had to get away from the rest of the crew and the way to do that was to load the long trailer with fir beams while the other men handled the back end of the mill. Since the fir beams and the trailer were located at the far side of the yard, they'd be away from everyone else, no one would bother them, and they would be able to have a carefree morning.

Stoner put his plan into action by sitting on the cool pavement behind the empty lowboy trailer and smoking some of his Mexican bud.

The medicinal properties of the weed hit the three of them fast. After a confused babbling of jokes, it was time to do up this load. They could celebrate with another joint after they finished loading. Yeah, life was good.

When Stoner got to the forklift, he couldn't believe that May, dressed in jeans, a denim work shirt, and steel-toed work boots, was sitting in the driver's seat.

"Stoner, you have been smoking marijuana. You can't drive this forklift, and you can't be working while under the influence of drugs. Today you and your two friends will leave the sawmill property. Tomorrow, if you are drug-free, you can return here. If you can't do that, then don't come back.

"Brenda and Susan will take over your jobs here today. They will be loading this trailer. We are fortunate to have people so eager to help us at this time."

May climbed down out of the forklift and Brenda drove the machine away to get a fir beam to set on the empty deck of the trailer.

Stoner and his two friends were dumbfounded. The only reaction they could manage was to stand in place, with their minds reeling on what had transpired and watch May walk away from them, and back to her office.

Susan, a six-footer, wearing blue work coveralls that covered her big-boned body, turned to Stoner and lifted her left leg in a strong kick upward off the ground. The action mimicked what Leanne had done to him on Saturday. Stoner wasn't going to let this Amazon have a chance to kick him. The trio ran away from the mill yard.

They would be sober for tomorrow! They would change and work hard to ensure that Brenda and Susan didn't replace them.

* * *

The end of the day whistle blew, signaling the conclusion of a nonstop workday for May. She had survived her first day in this new environment. In her new role, most of the workers had been quite accepting. She had taken on difficult matters and handled them well. Mary praised her for her strength. Fred had no complaints either; the mill had run smooth today.

When May sent Stoner home, and put Brenda and Susan into the shipping yard for the day, all the slackers took note. The women working in the mill admired her for taking on Stoner and replacing him and his friends with two women. There was no question, in Fred's mind, that she would follow through on her ultimatum with Stoner. Stoner would be drug-free at work from now on, or he wouldn't be there.

* * *

In San Francisco, at 10 o'clock on May's first day, Farmer, now Mr. Gerald Brightman walked into the Midland bank in Union Square and met with a Mr. Pointer, primary business manager. Dressed in a blue, pinstriped suit, Farmer looked the part of an import/export mogul.

Mr. Pointer arranged to deposit $200,000 of the US Treasury bonds into a new account for Mr. Gerald Brightman and his partner, Mr. Larry Brown.

Mr. Pointer, ever anxious to attract new money to his branch, acted promptly on Farmer's request.

The paperwork to set up the banking requirements took merely minutes. After the initial deposit into the new bank account, Farmer requested that $160,000 be transferred to one of their associate banks, the Hong Kong and Shanghai Bank of Commerce, in Hong Kong.

A male clerk delivered the wire transfer confirmation to Mr. Pointer.

Everything had gone through without a problem; Mr. Pointer was a very proficient business account manager. He even took it upon himself to increase the interest rate on this new account by another percentage point as a bonus for the new clients.

Farmer and Larry received silver Parker pens and calendars, each of which were nicely embossed with the Midland Bank's logo. They departed the bank on the finest of terms with the banker, who offered them his personal assistance with all of their banking needs in the future.

A crisp, gentle breeze blew in from the bay as they walked the two blocks to their next stop at the Western Union office. The salty air, mixed with a fishy element, was unfamiliar. Farmer actually missed the wood smoke smell, mixed with lavender and the smell of fresh cut hay, back home.

A cheerful strawberry blonde met them at the Western Union counter. Farmer explained that he needed to wire $30,000 to Bangkok and keep the funds in a wire transfer account until he arrived in Thailand later in the month.

To avoid the trigger of suspicion of a potentially illicit activity, because of such a large amount of money being transferred to one of the larger exporters of illegal drugs to the United States, Farmer laid out the story of doing a photo journal of modern Thailand. By showing the teller his CBC identification, and his Canadian passport, he quelled any concerns about the money transfer.

The young Western Union teller became very interested in Farmer's adventure, and the man himself. Upon returning with the proper documents, one more button on her lilac polyester blouse had been undone. Farmer stood in the enviable spot of enjoying the view of her expanding cleavage.

Confirmation of the funds transfer arrived within ten minutes. The teller took it upon herself to locate Farmer next door and bring him back to the office to conclude the transaction.

Following the teller's hips, confined within her high pencil skirt, Farmer watched her second best asset. Inside the Western Union building, the teller assembled the transfer documents, slipping them into an envelope, and passed the envelope and a note to Farmer.

"Phone number?" Larry asked when Farmer opened and read the teller's note during their walk back to the parking lot.

"Yes, a good one too, from what I saw. A different lifetime ago for me though," he said as he tossed the paper with the teller's phone number into the garbage can.

The next storefront stop was at the American Express Travel Agency.

The receptionist had acted on Farmer's call from Portland on Saturday and had the tickets ready for processing.

Out of his back pocket, Farmer pulled out $1,850.00 for the two tickets and gave the cash to the travel agent. The transaction was straightforward; two tickets from San Francisco to Hong Kong, via Vancouver, on Canadian Pacific Airlines, for tomorrow.

After re-counting the cash, the agent wrote the authorization code on the three-part ticket voucher and recorded the identification numbers of the baggage tags on the cover of each of the ticket folders.

* * *

Fifteen minutes later, they arrived at the grey storage building off Webster Avenue in the Marina district. Farmer opened the heavy steel security doors and closed them after Larry parked the car inside.

During the Second World War, the United States Navy built sixty of these identical warehouse buildings for the collection, and distribution, of supplies and equipment for the war in the Pacific.

For the Korean War, they were activated again for preparing heavy equipment prior to shipping overseas.

After sitting vacant for a decade, they were again put into service for operational support for the shipment of cargo to Vietnam. When the United States involvement in the Vietnam War wound down, so did the need for the military to keep these old WW II buildings.

In 1974, the Treasury was digging deep to extract money from every department in government, to reduce the financial impact of the Vietnam War. The Department of Defense sold all sixty of the warehouses at a public auction.

Farmer purchased this 50-foot wide by 200-foot long, two-story warehouse for $5,000 at the auction.

This warehouse had been a machine shop and pieces of metalworking and automotive machinery were left in the building when he took possession. The second floor mezzanine used to be offices. The largest windowed office still had a handwritten sign printed onto the door announcing it as, 'Camp Lifer'.

He had converted two of the offices into bedrooms. A good-sized central bathroom had been added. In the large open room, he had included a kitchen along the far wall, complete with a stove, fridge, and a double-sink. The result was a very spacious apartment.

In the first bedroom, Farmer changed into his t-shirt and blue jeans he'd left in the closet this morning before the trip to the bank. From the other bedroom, Larry emerged wearing jeans, cowboy boots, and his black baseball shirt, looking every bit like an ordinary American traveler.

Farmer went to work preparing his gear. Although he trusted Professor and his diligent work, Farmer re-checked the gear to ensure it was clean. He emptied the contents of the camera gear bag onto one of the two long tables in the large room. Starting with the camera case, he removed the cardboard separators in the case and the base of the case to ensure it was clean inside. There could be no remnants of left over joints, powder—or anything else—hidden inside the case which could attract the unnecessary attention of a checkpoint or border agent.

Satisfied the case was clean; he cleaned the camera, installed a fresh roll of film, and placed the gear into the black box.

The final piece of equipment was the cassette tape recorder. To prepare it, he removed the cassette tape, the four C batteries, and the seven Phillips screws used to hold the case together. He put four of the five-hundred dollar bills in the base of the case, underneath the circuit board. After reassembling the recorder, he dabbed two of the screws with white hobby paint to replicate the factory finish of the case. If the paint wasn't there, then the unit had been opened, which from the manufacturer's point of view would void the warranty claim on the recorder. Farmer took the precaution to minimize the potential that a sharp border agent might check such a detail. The illegal drug trade in Southeast Asia required all travelers to be extra diligent when packing their bags.

Packing of the gear bag continued with the addition of pencils, notepads, twelve rolls of film, a lens-cleaning towel and a small tool kit for the camera along with eight additional batteries, wrapped tight within his socks. The bag was now what a travelling reporter would carry on assignment.

Satisfied he had packed the camera gear safely, Farmer went over the contents of his personal canvas bag. He rolled up some t-shirts and added them to the soft bag. Two pairs of jeans went inside along with underwear, hiking boots, wool socks, and the rest of his bathroom items.

Reporters travel light.

The last items to pack were the documents that he would take with him on this trip. He laid out his passport and visa papers, which Professor had made, at the end of the table. His CBC credentials, with a set of fifty business cards, were set with the papers. Each visa letter was again reviewed. Document by document, he scrutinized each piece of paper to verify the details. Satisfied of their accuracy, he collected all of them and set them into a brown manila envelope inside his gear bag.

The bank account paperwork was rolled into a cylinder and slipped inside the telephoto lens case. He rolled 10 one-hundred dollar bills inside two pairs of socks and stocked his money belt with $2,000 in fifties. Another thousand went into his wallet.

He did not concern himself with how Harley had obtained the money; too many actions in Vietnam had not made sense and this likely was the result of another one. The fact was that it had been done in the past. How, or whatever had been done, did not affect their current mission.

Larry was just as diligent in his packing. All gear was inspected, documents were reviewed, and $10,000 of Harley's money was stashed within his camera and personal gear.

His clothing consisted of t-shirts and denim jeans, suitable for the world-travelling reporter—simple, light and worn. They could only pack what they could carry.

At 3:30, they had completed their packing and left the warehouse.

They drove to the Travel Lodge hotel beside the San Francisco International airport and checked into two rooms for the night.

The ground floor rooms meant they did not have far to carry their travel gear. They met for dinner after settling into their rooms.

After ordering, Farmer made one call from the restaurant pay phone and then returned with perfect timing to a large steak meal. The salad bar he would visit later.

After dinner, one of Pedro's Moving and Storage rigs stopped in front of the hotel. For $225, Pedro was taking the Judge to Professor's acreage on the back of his Peterbilt cabover.

After Larry drove the car onto the auto hauler trailer and chained the car down, he handed the keys to Pedro and said, "She's like a baby to me, get it!"

"Yes, sir," the tattooed trucker, Pedro, replied while looking up at Larry, with the keys in his hand and Larry's bigger hand firmly wrapped around his hand and the keys.

The car would arrive unharmed.

Chapter 12

Wednesday, July 6 & Thursday, July 7, 1977

The fifteen hour flight in the Boeing 707 took them across the International Date Line bumping them ahead a day. It was midafternoon on July 7, 1977 when the wheels hit the tarmac at Hong Kong's Kai Tak airport. Travelling with their Canadian passports accelerated Farmer and Larry through Hong Kong Customs—British Commonwealth member countries still enjoyed the favoritism of British Customs service.

The Western Union office was easy to locate in the bustling airport. Farmer sent Billy Bob a telegraph confirming their arrival plans:

> Billy:
> Meet at Joe's tomorrow at noon.
> Farmer

Within the Kai Tak Airport, they purchased two tickets to fly to Bangkok after dinner.

* * *

The Thai International Airlines Avro twin prop was noisy. Only half of the four dozen seats were occupied. The cabin filled with blue cigarette smoke from the Thai and Laos nationals on the plane, each of which seemed to chain smoke their sharp Asian cigarettes.

The flight crossed the Sea of China and returned to the mainland at Vietnam. Through his window, Farmer saw the green landscapes of Vietnam, the land he had left behind, four years ago.

The mind proves to be selective in its recall. After seeing the Vietnamese landscape below, Farmer's mind flashed back to a night operation on that land now far below him. In the darkness, he was looking out over the fenced encampment from his position behind a rock pile. It was a crudely constructed holding camp for American POWs. In this vivid replay, there had been no movement within the perimeter of the camp since the guard in one of the two watchtowers had lit a cigarette an hour ago.

His watch showed 0500 hours. Turning to the row of eight men on his right, all dressed in black striped fatigues, and laying along the small ditch, he tapped the first man's shoulder with his right hand. This signal transferred down the line. He signaled to the four men on his left as well.

The four on his left used their M67 recoilless rifles to send rockets into each of the two guard towers. The direct hits blew the towers off their stands. Two more rockets hit the two guard huts at the road gate, leveling them.

With the towers demolished, he led the team through the opening in the fence at the rear of the camp, the opposite end of the camp from the service road entrance.

Inside the perimeter of the fence, the men dispersed to throw grenades into the remaining four bamboo huts. The remaining four men setup inside the camp with their rockets loaded and ready to be fired.

Two North Vietnamese prison guards ran out of their hut with their AK-47 machineguns in hand. They did not have time to use them, as Farmer used his M-16 and sprayed a burst of shots. The dead guards dropped to the porch floor of their hut at the same time as the walls of their hut exploded and erupted in flames from grenades.

Six guards tried to escape the burning huts by running out the door. They were summarily leveled by machine gun fire.

Then the men began shooting off the locks of the underground cages. Farmer ran to the first cage and asked, "Where's Martin?"

"Don't know," came back as the reply from the American prisoner being pulled out from the hole.

Farmer ran to the next cage while two of his men pulled out the four remaining prisoners in the hole.

Shots were fired at him from a North Vietnamese guard who had hidden behind the truck at the gate. Instinctively, he rolled to the ground and took aim at the truck. He shot off a quick burst at the base of the truck—enough to hit the gunner in the ankles and shins, dropping him to the ground. The next burst of shots from his M-16 machine gun cut through the guard's chest and head.

"I found him, I've got the Aussie," came the call from one of the men pulling the Australian prisoner, Captain Martin, out from the third holding cell buried in the ground.

"Where the fuck are they? The VC are on their way from the other camp," exclaimed one of the American commandos.

"They'll be here. Get everyone together at the front gate. They'll land on the road."

The Special Forces team herded the group of American prisoners and the Australian prisoner through the camp to the main entrance.

As they huddled around the gate, the familiar sound of the rotor wash of a group of helicopters pulsed through the darkness. In the faint daylight, they couldn't determine the direction of their approach.

Shots rang out a few miles down the road as the reinforcements from the other camp also heard the choppers flying overhead. The North Vietnamese began firing at helicopters cloaked in darkness in an attempt to draw them out of the dark sky. Their blind shots in the air worked because one of the escorting gunships set off a barrage of missiles at the men on the ground. Larry Johnson's gunship took a direct run over the enemy soldiers while his co-pilot sprayed lead at them from their side-mounted M-60 machine guns.

Back at the POW holding camp, the first chopper landed and loaded on ten of the prisoners, including Martin and a CIA field agent, the primary targets of this mission. The second chopper came in right behind and loaded the remaining four POWs and six of the rescue team.

Down the road, Larry's helicopter had drawn more ground fire, but had made its return to deal with the advancing North Vietnamese soldiers by launching missiles into the enemy troops.

A large fireball rose into the twilight, confirming a truck had been taken out by the gunship. When the third helicopter had been loaded with team members, the helicopter lifted off as soon as Farmer's foot was on the landing skid, forcing him to roll into the airborne helicopter. His team, and all POWs, had been retrieved.

In the dawn's light, he saw the North Vietnamese soldiers arrive at the camp behind them. As the last to leave, their helicopter took ground fire. The co-pilot was hit but remained in place by leaning against the door secured by his seat belt harness. A shot bullet from the ground penetrated the belly of the helicopter and hit one of his men in the stomach, spilling the soldier's blood across the floor of the chopper.

Through the open side door, he watched the gunship make one final pass over the enemy soldiers.

"Hey, Farmer, shake it off, wake up," Larry said as he shook Farmer by the shoulder.

Farmer came back out of his daydream.

"Another bad one, man. Shake it off. We are landing in a few minutes. You were starting to mumble something. No one needed to hear it."

Farmer shook his head realizing he was still in the airplane, descending into Bangkok. He lifted his hands to check that they did not have any blood on them. They were clean, just another bad memory. He rubbed the sweat of his forehead with his hand and stared out the window to witness the landscape drawing nearer to the plane.

* * *

The nine-month reign of the military installed Prime Minister of Thailand rested heavily on all government employees. They worked under the duress that the next coup could send them to wherever the communist sympathizers and left wing ideologues had been sent after this last change in government. Therefore, Immigration agents at the

Bangkok International airport were serious and focused on exceeding expectations. To ensure nothing slipped past them, the security forces expressed no friendliness toward Americans, which is what all white, English-speaking visitors were presumed to be, until proven otherwise.

Eight guards with machine guns hanging on their shoulders took up stations in the arrivals section of the airport. The intimidation factor was enhanced by the pistol that each one wore on their hip. They would not risk an unfavorable review by their superiors.

A single agent directed the arriving passengers to one of the six booths designated for inspection of the arrivals. To the left of the booths were four rooms with large windows facing the security area— the interrogation rooms, perhaps left from the previous administration.

Larry noted that all *Americans* were directed to either booth 5 or booth 6. The inspectors at these booths took their time in intimidating the arriving Americans. Adding to the intimidation was the positioning of four of the guards with eyes locked on the queue. They were looking for suspicious travelers, drug mules, rebel rousers, libertarians, or anyone else who looked like they should be detained for investigation.

Farmer was behind Larry in the main queue. Ahead of Larry now were just two people, a slightly intoxicated blonde haired man, in his early 20's, and his equally intoxicated girlfriend. Each had metal-framed backpacks they held onto as they stood in line laughing and joking with each other. They were inexperienced travelers to show up drunk or high at immigration.

The sharp-tongued Thai agent at the head of the line directed the man to booth 6. The agent directed his girlfriend to booth 5.

Only a few feet away from the booth, the drunken young woman stumbled and fell onto the concrete floor. Her backpack spilled onto the floor, including what appeared to be a dime bag of marijuana.

Immediately, a guard broke from his post, swiftly lifting her off the floor by grabbing her left arm. With his other arm, he grabbed her pack and pulled her to booth 5. The inspector barked out an order to the guard, who re-gripped the arm to drag the wailing woman into the first interview room. A second guard carried the evidence to the room.

The woman's boyfriend complained to the agent in front of him about the treatment of his girlfriend, hoping to remind him that they were citizens of the United States of America and that they could not treat Americans like this. Two guards summarily arrived at his booth. One guard led the boyfriend to the same interrogation room, as the second guard walked behind the man.

The line agent directed Larry to booth 6. While he was walking the fifteen feet to the booth, he listened to the guards yelling at the two shattered travelers in the interrogation room. The male was appealing to the guards while the female was crying. A thick scar-faced sergeant joined them in the interrogation room. The door closed behind him.

The rush of anticipatory adrenaline cursed through Larry's body as his volatile anger grew within him. He knew what these guards were capable of and how they preyed on young travelers. The drugs were simply a convenient reason for detention.

He was once more in the land of corruption, payoffs, and unwritten conventions—creating a country in which an error, or a belief, could cost you your freedom, or your life. Clearing his mind of all these thoughts, he focused his attention on the agent in front of him.

The agent looked at his Canadian passport and visa. In broken English, he asked him the reason for his trip and Larry used today's cover story on how he was a reporter following the work of the Universal Child immunization program, a program that Canadians had contributed medicine and doctors to help the good work continue to serve the people of Thailand.

The inspecting agent was a middle-aged man, with dark, sharp eyes. He held up Larry's passport and visa for review. After slapping the documents on his other hand, he began reading the visa document.

A new burst of crying emanated from the woman in the interrogation room. Her screaming got louder, until they heard a thudding sound. Laughter from the guards inside the room followed.

The inspector noted the curtains had been drawn closed.

Larry's instinct put him on the ready. If he needed to, he could snap the inspector's neck and get the machine gun from the guard behind him within seconds. The little man lifted his stamp, stamped the passport and the visa with the date and the entry seal of Thailand.

"You go, now," Inspector 6 barked to Larry.

Larry met Farmer at the exit of the inspection section.

"No!" Farmer said to Larry as they passed beside each other.

They rode in the taxi in silence on the drive to their hotel. These regime changes caused anxiety for all. The Prime Minister was surrounded by three dominoes that had fallen, leaving behind communist regimes on the other side of three of his borders. He would not tolerate any radicalism on his watch. It was safest not to say anything that the taxi driver could report to the local police.

The Siam City Hotel reception desk was crisp, clean, and polished. The clerk collected one hundred dollars for one double room for the night, a rate that was at least four times the going rate. Farmer paid the exorbitant rate anyway. He would not risk their mission over an excessive room charge.

They were not much for conversation tonight, choosing to eat Tom Yum soup and prawn noodle plates in their room. The lack of a television, radio, or even a magazine left little to do before bed. Knowing their days of deep sleep were behind them, they each lay on their bed, staring at the ceiling while waiting for their bodies to accept the uncertainty of the night and allow them at least a short nap.

* * *

In New Pontiac, Leanne's recovery was progressing well, with the exception of her black eye, which was taking longer to go away than she would like. With a coat of bronzer, she tried to cover the bruised eye. Christina accepted her explanation that her mom tripped on the step and fell against the railing. Christina became her nursemaid, bringing her glasses of water and cookies.

Leanne enjoyed evening walks with Ken. It was her private time to reconnect with the man she had fallen in love with for a second time. New Pontiac, with only a few minor distractions, was the perfect place to work on their newly found relationship.

Ken worked hard to adapt to the ways of rural life on the farm. He hadn't shaved for three weeks, which gave him an itchy beard, but Leanne liked the change. The new look made him appear older and perhaps added a rugged edge.

The manual work at the shipping department and the chores around Leanne's house worked his muscles. His new domestic tasks, including splitting firewood, were different from calisthenics and running through the training fields, but the activity gave him the same results. However, now he felt like the exercise served a purpose since work was being accomplished.

Ken's arrival proved to be timely for Anita. She expected Ken would be around for a while, at least if Leanne had her way, which she likely would. Anita moved things ahead in her relationship with her new man. She announced she was moving in with him, which left Ken, Leanne, and Christina alone at the house. They would have a real chance to practice not just playing house, but living like a family.

In their first night minus Anita, Leanne and Ken received a gift of half a large rainbow trout from Fred. The fish, however, presented a challenge for Ken. He didn't know how to cook anything, never mind complicating the task by cooking over an open fire pit. Nevertheless, he recognized his shortcoming in the cooking department. When Leanne asked if she could help him get the fire set for baking the fish on the coals, he did not object.

When she hugged him, Ken felt the new energy within Leanne. Still the happy-go-lucky, energetic woman of their past, now she was also the provider, the mother and the most beautiful girl he had ever known. People spend their entire lives looking for such a person, yet she was right here.

The reflection of the firelight accented her bruised eye. The wound was another sign to him, one that clarified his future. He could never leave this woman he had again fallen for; they would be together as long as she allowed. It was one of his few decisions, which made sense and gave purpose to building his personal foundation. That foundation would lead to a better life for the three of them.

When Christina had fallen asleep, Leanne curled up to Ken in their bed, her naked body spooned against his, and asked if he could just hold her tight; neither had the need for their driven sexual past.

Perhaps this is was what happens when shacking up changed into creating a home, Ken thought. They were certainly entering uncharted territory for both of them.

Chapter 13

Larry and Farmer returned to the airport at 0800.

The departures terminal was crowded at this time of the morning allowing them to be absorbed into the crowd of people trying to work their way through the airport facilities.

After purchasing their tickets, they proceeded to Laos' immigration and security checkpoint. Three officers were on duty, one of which handled the English American travelers. The young man spoke English well.

After reviewing his Canadian passport and his Laotian visa, the officer questioned Farmer regarding his travels to Laos. Farmer explained about the documentary they were working on following the humanitarian work that UNICEF was doing in cooperation with the Laotian government for the orphans of central Laos.

The orphanage located on the outskirts of Muang Phin, sixty-five miles east of Savannakhet, had become well known in Laos. Many of the children of Laotian women and American soldiers arrived at this orphanage after the father went back to the United States. International organizations provided funds to keep the important facility functioning, while locals and Buddhist monks worked within the school and the orphanage to make it work for all.

The Laotian Communists continued to struggle with the role of the Buddhist monks and the purpose the schools and orphanages played in the greater goal of converting Laos to communism. For the present, they left the religion and associated activities alone, but had strongly suggested to the monks to remain moderate and peaceful.

In reality, the Laotian government needed the money that these facilities received in donations from foreign countries. The donations, always in US dollars, were exchanged for supplies from the government, which had been collected from the communal farms, and thereby the government obtained the hard currency needed to purchase military equipment in the international market. The Laotian government had reluctantly accepted these facilities as necessary, at this time, to advance their greater goal of communism for the country.

Larry showed his documents to the same officer and moved through the checkpoint in minutes.

The plane was a Caribou C-4, built in the mid '60's. The de Havilland airship continued as a workhorse in Laos. It could land on the poorest gravel landing strips in the rugged mountains of Laos. This particular plane had been modified to carry twenty passengers with the rear section as an open cargo area for freight.

Although the reality had hit them last night when they arrived at Thailand immigration, climbing into the Caribou plane clearly cemented the fact they had returned to the war torn lands they had left behind years ago. As if a switch had been turned on, their survival instincts returned and their civilian demeanor departed.

Both men took note of every movement, heard every noise, and looked for anything out of place. The humming of the twin 1450 horsepower Pratt and Whitney served to reinforce the change by being such a familiar drone, taking them back to a life they had escaped from for the past four years.

After landing in Savannakhet International Airport in Laos, at 1020 hours, they walked past five Lao People's Revolutionary Party's soldiers standing beside the concrete walkway leading to the terminal.

Their passports had been reviewed at the Laos departure line in Thailand, but they were interviewed again on their arrival at the airport. One inspector processed the twenty-two people on this plane. Larry, first of the two of them to meet the inspector, explained about the documentary they were producing about the orphanage and school, while the inspector perused his visa and looked at his passport. When

Larry finished his description of their documentary, the inspector exclaimed, "You from Canada. You make good movie, okay?"

"Yes, sir, I will," Larry replied clearly indicating his respect for the important man.

The inspector stamped the visa and his passport.

When Farmer arrived, his passport and visa were summarily stamped while the officer also told him to make a good movie.

If the soldiers were not around the airport, the inspector would have expected a payment of $20.00 for such a service, but the governing communist Lao People's Revolutionary Party (LPRP) hit such payoffs hard and the inspector was no fool; he would not risk becoming one of 'the lost'; one who had crossed the new regime. The inspector's income this year had dropped dramatically, following the stationing of the Lao People's Army (LPA) at the airport.

Outside of the building, they were exposed again to all Savannakhet had to offer. Their bodies first registered the variety of smells. The smell of gasoline fumes hit them from the blue exhaust clouds left behind the small, motorized three wheel carts, known as tuk-tuks. The strange mix of spices and smoking pots from the street vendors outside the airport building, drifted to them as a break in between the gasoline fume flows.

The air was heavy from the high humidity caused by the pounding rains the day before. They were not acclimatized to this humidity and their bodies reacted by sweating profusely in the muggy, suffocating, air.

They recognized the feeling of fear that gripped the people they passed. People walked with their eyes looking to the ground avoiding eye-to-eye contact with others. They walked fast to prevent being stopped or detained by the police, or the soldiers, either of which would demand to see their papers and have them answer many questions regarding where and why they were going to their purported destination.

A mud caked brown taxi was parked across the roadway. Noting the taxi was empty, they quickly crossed the road to catch the driver before he drove away. The old driver saw the Americans coming and was onto Farmer right away. Americans paid their fares in US dollars, which he could trade the dollars at a premium, likely exceeding what he would make on the fare.

"The Sala Savanh," Farmer said to the driver as they started away from the airport.

"Very good, sir," the driver replied in quick but broken English—a smile stretched across his toothless mouth. He knew this would be a lucrative fare for him. An American staying at the great Sala Savanh might tip five dollars, equivalent to his whole week's pay.

The ride to the hotel on a street paralleling the Mekong River gave a glimpse of life in this new Laos. The streets were not busy, they were only populated with some tuk-tuks, and the odd motorcycle with one, two, or three people seated on the small machine. Tired old men and woman pulled carts loaded with goods to sell at the market or supplies they had bought at the market already. Locals walked in lines along the streets. Poverty showed itself everywhere. The fear of the civil war kept everyone wary.

When the cab turned left onto the waterfront street, Farmer saw the checkpoint three blocks ahead.

"Stop here," he said to the driver as he held up a twenty.

The taxi pulled over immediately.

He gave him another ten for the fare as he collected his gear from the trunk. The taxi accelerated away from them, leaving behind a blue cloud of oil and gas exhaust. Realizing the taxi driver would run into the blockade three blocks ahead, and be questioned about the passengers he did not have with him, they hurried back to the end of the block, away from the Sala Savanh, crossed the street, and got into an old green Toyota sedan taxi.

"Lucky Joe's," Farmer told the driver. "And twenty American dollars if you get us there quickly."

"Okay Joe," the driver exclaimed before he accelerated the dented taxi to meet the instruction that meant to avoid all checkpoints.

Lucky Joe's was a brothel on Highway 9, 2 miles outside of Savannakhet, built by the Laotian government in 1967. Located close to the Air America operations base for Middle Laos, the brothel became a convenient hangout for the pilots and employees of the unofficial air corps.

In its heyday, over two hundred men worked at the supply base. In addition, pilots came and left each day. All these men needed the attention of the girls working at Lucky Joe's. If they did not need the comfort of a woman, then the gambling tables on the lower floor took care of the rest of their money. Either way, the Laotian government got the hard currency it needed, and that was all that mattered to the government.

The taxi driver received thirty dollars from his American customers, who he assumed were anxious to visit with a girl at Lucky Joe's. The elated taxi driver returned to Savannakhet with an amount of money he'd not seen for many years.

Minutes after the taxi left, a brown Land Cruiser locked its brakes as it slide to a stop beside them. Instinctively, Larry looked for a piece of pipe, wood, or any other weapon-like material, to use instead of destroying his camera case by using it as his weapon. From the open window of the Toyota, the driver announced, "Hello to Laos, we go now. Billy Bob waiting."

The men felt a lift of relief as they recognized young Quan. He was now a young man, twenty-one going on fifty. His wide grin, exposing his two missing eyeteeth, gave civility back to the two strained travelers.

The short drive to Billy Bob's airfield and warehouses lasted only five minutes, but during the entire trip, Quan did not stop asking them about their lives in North America. He told him of his dream to go to California. Billy Bob said they would make the trip, someday.

* * *

Billy Bob had taken Quan under his care in 1970, when he was only a young teenager, orphaned as the result of brutal North Vietnamese retaliation strikes on his village near the Vietnam border.

Flying for the CIA's Air America, Billy Bob had been sent in to rescue a downed pilot and his observer after their Cessna had been shot down while doing damage assessments on the villages.

Quan rescued the two men out of their plane and walked them out to a large dry field. When Billy Bob landed, the rescued pilot lifted the young boy into the helicopter and insisted that Quan would also go with them back to the Savannakhet base.

Quan was a quick learner and worked as a houseboy on the base. Billy Bob taught him English, and he soon became the trusted translator for the camp.

When Air America pulled out of Laos, Billy Bob stayed. He just never figured out where to go instead of remaining in the region he so much despised. The capacity to lead a structured life in a civil society had left him long ago. For better or for worse, he was in Laos for the duration.

In February of 1976, his decision to remain in Laos became written in stone.

The Lao People's Revolutionary Party (LPRP) had advanced on its mandate to expand the communist doctrine to collective ownership of lands and enterprises. A small unit of advance soldiers led the party of government educators into Savannakhet.

When the educators reached the old warehouse area which Billy Bob and Quan used as their own airport and storage facility, Quan took on the lead role, explaining the critical role that they played by flying supplies to the remote work camps for the miners and flying supplies for the LPRP army.

The senior government educator, in charge of re-educating the Laotian people to understand the way of communism, questioned the need for the American, Billy Bob, to stay in Laos.

Quan discussed with the important official, and his armed support group, the value of Billy Bob's flying experience and knowledge of the dispersed landing strips located throughout Laos. In spite of his best efforts, he could not convince the educator of the need for the American.

Quan turned to the sergeant and explained the value of their operation to the government. The sergeant listened, and then asked again for his papers. The sergeant walked away to speak with the lead educator and his corporal. Their private conversation was not good for Billy Bob.

The sergeant commanded Quan to walk with him away from the group. Billy Bob remained with the soldiers and the government officials. The young sergeant asked him what village he came from, the name of his mother and father, and when he left his village. Quan answered the questions and added that Billy Bob had raised him like his own son. He owed his life to him. Oddly, this argument appeased the sergeant. The party of government officials left, but Billy Bob warned Quan that they would return.

His instincts were correct, because the next day the party returned along with armed trucks and a tank. Billy Bob grabbed an M-16 machine gun and thanked Quan for trying to help him.

Quan told him to go back into the office and stay put, he would deal with these men. Only nineteen years old at the time, he stood in front of the hangar as the army convoy came to a stop ahead of him. Two soldiers, with their AK-47's slung around their shoulders, opened the rear door of the black sedan. A man in a green uniform climbed out of the sedan. As the man spoke, Quan found his voice familiar and his dialect gave him a clear voice and sharp script. The man, who did not identify himself, asked for Quan's papers and for details about his family and his former village. He repeated the answers he had given the day before. He asked questions about the American and Quan repeated how Billy Bob had raised him, and they worked together.

The official walked around the front of the hangar and returned to Quan. "Quan, I am Kowan, your father's oldest brother. I last saw you when you were four years old, when I left the village to help our country. I can now help our country of Laos. The sergeant that you met yesterday also came from our village. His family was killed in the extinction of our town. He also remembered you as a small boy in the village."

Quan did not ask anything of his uncle, but his uncle knew what Quan's life would have been like if he had not been rescued by the American. He would have been forced to be a child soldier—he would have been dead within months. Uncle Kowan knew that the American had saved his nephew's life.

Kowan understood the life he wanted for his country of Laos and his fellow residents, and under the communist doctrine, he would need better access to the remaining remote villages. He offered Billy Bob a series of contracts for the government to deliver supplies from the collective farms in the lowlands to the mountain villages.

Billy Bob became an asset, under order of this General. They did not receive a blank check to unearned riches. No, instead they obtained a promissory note to a more secure life. If they did the work, they would be looked after. They agreed to his offer. They never met the general again.

* * *

Quan honked the horn on the old Land Cruiser as the brakes squealed to a halt in front of the first building. Billy Bob walked out of the hangar to meet his old friends.

Billy Bob, at forty-five, had put on a bit of weight, but had all of his hair—still black as coal—not a gray strand in it. Dressed in his blue coveralls, his company uniform, he reached out his hand to Farmer and then grabbed him with his big arms and pulled Farmer tight to him.

"You old son of a bitch, good to see y'all again, the place hasn't been the same since you left," and he laughed, a deep belly laugh.

Billy Bob grabbed Larry's arm next and squeezed his hand. Larry squeezed harder until Billy Bob hollered.

"Jeez, man, you're still strong as an ox. What have they been feeding you over there in the States?"

The re-union began, inside the first building. The huge metal structure was a former airplane hangar. They'd added a corner office, complete with leather-padded chairs. Quan handed each of them a cold beer from the antique soda pop machine.

"Where is Shelby? Where is my friend who pulled me out of the jungle when I got shot down? The guy who also fixed my Cayuse chopper with his Swiss Army Knife," he asked.

Shelby had been the first of the team to meet up with Billy Bob. They became good friends through a series of adventures, beginning with Shelby evacuating him from a crash that Billy Bob had when some small arms fire took out his transmission. Billy Bob then flew as co-pilot for Shelby while they took a man named Birdman to many remote sites as they delivered or picked up 'Prospectors' and their burlap bags of rock samples. During these exercises, he met fellow pilot, Larry. Farmer he knew as the man that ran a special group of Prospectors through the mountains of eastern Laos.

"Well, Shelby isn't doing so well these days. He has cancer. We visited him on Monday. I don't think he has much longer. For a person who had nine lives over here, he just could not pull an extra one for this disease, man. When he got your telegram, he sent his son up to give it to me in Canada.

"Canada, what the hell are you doing up there, Farmer?"

"Just some things, I have a quiet life now. Yes, I even got married. She is a beautiful woman. I am damn lucky that she'd take on a guy like me."

"And you Larry. Are you building things or destroying them?

"Bit of both, I guess. I get by. I got myself a real special girl. See here she is," Larry pulled out a photograph of Starr and passed the Polaroid along to Billy Bob.

"Wow, where'd you buy her? Christ I know you couldn't find her any other way."

"You are still a screwball, aren't you? She found me, and not a day goes by that I don't realize how lucky I am."

The conversation had taken a dangerous change in direction. "What's up around here? Do the communists, or their soldiers, give you much trouble?" quizzed Farmer as he purposely changed the subject.

"No, it's just another fucking war. This time it's Laos fighting itself. You never know which way the wind is going to blow. Today the wind blows well for us. Quan's uncle likes us, and we do as we are told.

"I make some money flying for him; it's kind of how it used to be flying for Uncle Sam. Christ, all my gear came from them when they ran out of here. They left behind some good machines. I have a C-4 Caribou, a Huey, and a Cayuse. I got a yard full of spare parts, too. We do okay here.

"Quan has been flying the Cayuse. He's a good pilot and he's been working on these machines forever. I use a few of the local boys for flying, but we can handle most of the stuff ourselves," replied Billy Bob.

"I'm not surprised the CIA left behind such prize gear, they were in a hurry to get out of here in 1975," commented Larry.

After lighting a thin, brown cigar, Billy Bob continued. "Yes they did get out of here quick. It was a strange time while they were leaving. I don't think most of us believed they would really pull out."

Billy Bob continued, after his pause, "I don't know much about what you guys worked on around here. I sent the telegram to Shelby because he gave me his address and told me to get a hold of him if anything changed at Elephant Mountain."

He lit his ivory pipe with a Zippo lighter and continued, "Quan delivers supplies to the monastery, and this spring he noticed some white men talking to the monks. Quan knows this one monk real good and he told Quan that the men were Russian miners. The Russians told the monks to leave the east side of the mountain, since they were going to be pushing in a shaft and start mining operations.

"The monks refused to leave the area. They told the Russians about the sacred Elephant Mountain and pleaded not to mine in their place of worship. They warned them bad things would come to them if they tried to do any mining in the mountain. That didn't mean anything to the Russians who said they'd be back in a week and the monks had better clear off the side of the mountain."

Billy Bob took a long inhale off his pipe. The pungent smell of local tobacco filled the room. He then downed the beer before Quan gave him another one.

"So how does this mountain tie back to Shelby?" Farmer asked, as a rhetorical question.

"See, Quan is liked by these monks. His friend asked him for help. He said an American had been there over six years ago. His Sangharaja told him to help the American into the mine from the entrance at the monastery."

Billy Bob took a chug of his beer.

"The monks have been mining for copper, lead and silver for centuries. They make candleholders and boxes from the lead, and use the silver to make jewelry, which they leave for those that provide for them with alms. Quan's friend told him that the American returned to the monastery less than a year later with a big problem. He needed to leave something inside the mountain, forever.

"This posed a problem for the Sangharaja and his monks since the mine was sacred and it had only been used by the monastery for their sacred workings. Somehow, Shelby got approval from the Sangharaja to do what he needed. Quan's friend was told to help Shelby and his two men into the mine. The mountain is riddled with miles of tunnels. Shelby and his friends loaded a wood crate onto a pushcart and rolled the crate into the mine."

"What happened to the men?" asked Farmer

"Shelby and his two friends took hours inside the mine. The monk, who remained at the entrance, thought they had got lost and he had given up on them returning from the mine. Other monks had died the same way. However, Shelby and his two friends returned, without the cart, the crate, or any of their tools. Shelby asked to speak with the Sangharaja and the monk took him. The monk remembers Shelby giving the Sangharaja an envelope."

"Does Quan's friend know what happened to the wood crate?" Farmer asked.

"Box still in mountain," Quan replied.

"How do we find this box in the mountain? You said there are miles of tunnels in the mine, and how do we get into a mine controlled by the monks?"

"Quan's friend told him the old monk was shot by a group of LPA soldiers who attacked the monastery two years ago. He suffered with his wound for only a few days before he died.

"See, here is the thing, the old monk called for Quan's friend before he died. He gave the young monk a small lead box and told him to hide it in the mine. He wasn't to ever bring it out again unless an American came back and asked to go get the box from the mine."

"Can your friend show us this lead box?" Farmer asked Quan.

"Yes. He doesn't want the Russians to find the box and doesn't want any trouble or for them to kill anyone. He wants the big wooden box out of the mine. I will bring him here tomorrow to show you what the Sangharaja gave him. He will help you," replied Quan in his clear, quick English.

"How long do we have until the Russians start mining?" Larry asked.

"The soldiers told the Russians they can't mine in the mountain. The Russians are in Vientiane trying to get approval. If they mine, they will break up the mountain. My friend asks me to help take away whatever was put into the mountain. Will you help us?"

"I believe we can. However, we need to start with the basics. We are Canadians news reporters, only here to examine the work that Canada is doing with UNICEF to help the Laotians. This is very important! We need to keep our reasons clear for being here.

Both Quan and Billy Bob nodded.

Farmer sat back in his chair and lit up a Thai cigarette from his pack. He gave one to Larry, who took the light from the match and puffed in the sharp Thai tobacco.

Farmer ran the thoughts through his mind. What Billy Bob and Quan said was the same as what Shelby had told him about the aborted operation.

Back in '72, Shelby wound up with two corporals during his part of the operation. They stayed with him for the trip. Those two soldiers were the two men with Shelby that day. Shelby and his two draftees put the wooden crate into the monk's lead mine.

This was the right spot and the two stories matched in details.

In a normal world this storage plan could have worked. In a normal world, a wooden box could sit in all those miles of underground tunnels and never be found. In a normal world, there was not a war bombing the hell out of a country—over and over— sacrificing forever the chance of a peaceful life for the innocent people. This was not a normal world. No, now it was up to them to fix this half of one screwed up operation that had to end, and they were going to have to end it. The problem was how to bring something so deadly, so critical to the stability of the world, back out of miles of tunnels and end this ill-conceived plan once and forever. The next step was theirs to make.

* * *

Billy Bob landed the Bell 205 at the end of the village road at 1730 hours. Larry stepped out of the helicopter onto the orange soil on the narrow roadway to retrieve the camera and gear out of the side storage compartments. This was the *reporter* part of their trip: the detail that had to be performed to validate their reason for being here.

Quan was their interpreter. The greeting committee consisted of the mayor of nearby Phin, the hospital doctor, a Buddhist monk from the local temple, the schoolmaster, and a woman from UNICEF.

They exchanged greetings. Quan translated the conversations during their walk to the hospital. The charming middle-aged Australian woman from UNICEF spoke Laotian well.

Only the previous Monday, she'd received notice of the $10,000 donation from Canada. The trucks loaded with the purchased supplies left Savannakhet on Wednesday and arrived this morning. This explained why the villagers bowed, or said thank you to the group as they walked about the grounds.

Larry continued shooting video throughout the tour.

After three rolls of film, he switched cameras and shot stills with Farmer's 35 mm Leica. There would not be a shortage of proof of their tour of the property. The pictures would be the authentication of their purpose for visiting Laos. The records fit the alibi.

The hospital had been constructed with bamboo walls separating the two operating rooms and a US Army hospital tent for the rest of the hospital—more refuse from Uncle Sam. One of the four-wheel drive, 2½-ton trucks was parked in front of the hospital, loaded with the new hospital supplies. The second truck contained the new school supplies. Larry took more pictures of people around the trucks and supplies.

The doctor, born in middle Laos, but educated in Australia, explained that before these precious donations had arrived, they were down to just a small cupboard of medical supplies.

He showed them the empty cupboards, which soon would be restocked with vaccines, penicillin, bandages, ether, and pain medicines.

In addition to new instruments, the doctor was very excited about obtaining a generator and lights for emergency night surgeries.

The doctor had worked with so little for so long, he was looking forward to saving lives instead of only being able to offer comfort to the dying patients. Farmer took out his note pad and wrote some notes about the supplies. Larry continued interviews with the Australian doctor, the UNICEF woman, and a very cute Laotian nurse.

During their tour of the recovery area in the hospital, the effect of the abandoned ordnances was obvious. So many people, skewed toward young children, were missing legs or arms. Yet, even the children with missing limbs smiled at the visitors. These innocent people, maimed and crippled for life, found the capacity to show their appreciation of these gifts for the hospital.

The doctor left the tour so he could administer the newly received medicines to his patients. The UNICEF woman completed the tour by showing the group the old water well and explained how, for three hundred dollars, they would be able to drill a deeper well to supply clean and safe drinking water.

Continuing the tour, they entered the school hut where the children sat on benches with crudely made desks in front of them. Pencils, paper, and books were now available to the children.

At the end of their tour of the school, a group of young children met them. The students started singing a song in Laotian. The song was a 'Thank You Song to Buddha' for the gifts.

The last stop was the orphanage.

The orphanage stuck a particular soft spot with Quan. He had three younger brothers and two sisters when his village was destroyed. He prayed for at least one of his siblings to make it to the orphanage. Over the years, no one from his village had arrived at the orphanage.

Many of the children in the orphanage were Amerasian, the result of too many Americans in the area for too long. Those children were destined to be foreigners for life in their own country.

By 2130 hours, they had completed their tour of the hospital, school, and orphanage. Billy Bob lit up the Huey 205 with Larry seated as his the co-pilot. He still flew with the habits of being shot at too many times; take-offs were fast, climbing above the tree tops quick and getting away from Highway 9 fast.

Remnants of the war, anti-aircraft installations, remained along Highway 9. Billy Bob habitually avoided flying anywhere near them, even though they were not likely to shoot at his blue and white machine. In this land, one could never anticipate an operator error. Avoiding the sites was the safest way to live a longer life.

While flying over the flat farmland, Billy Bob asked Larry through his radio headset, "You want to take her over?"

"Sure, man."

"Roger. Tell me when you got her."

"Got it," Larry replied over the intercom after his hand had taken over the cyclic and his feet were on the pedals.

Even sitting in the co-pilot seat, it came back to him quickly. He liked the 205. It was lighter than the military UH-1s, more responsive, and faster. Billy Bob observed how Larry had been able to take over the machine and fly in a straight line, without tail wiggle. Larry still lived up to his reputation amongst pilots.

Farmer followed their flight on a map. Long ago, it seemed, he knew every landmark on this route. However, he had travelled too much of the country. He felt he was starting over in familiarization with the Savannakhet province, prejudiced by the fact that his passion for travelling across the flat fields below him had left him long ago.

Larry flew like Billy Bob, fast and at 5,000 feet. He brought the machine in fast for a landing and flared the 205 up quickly to slow down and softly set her down on the middle of the concrete pad at Billy Bob's airport. Pilots that had put in many thousands of hours in machines could pull off those fast landings; or pilots that had landed in hot landing zones far too many times.

Larry's soft landing was flat on the skids, proving he knew how to use the machine's capability, without abusing the machine through sloppy habits.

They made the sixty-five mile flight from the UNICEF facility to Billy Bob's airport in just over half an hour. Flying northeast to the monastery at Elephant Mountain would be less than an hour and half each way. Billy Bob said they wouldn't have to refuel during the trip.

Late into the night, they reviewed the maps of the area to confirm safe flight routes. This time the ground wouldn't be covered in VC transporting supplies through their labyrinth of trails cut through the hills and forests beyond the flat plains east of Savannakhet. In its day, the land east of Highway 23, running north to south, hid more Viet Cong and North Vietnamese Army, NVA, enemy forces than were on the South Vietnamese side of the border beyond the Annamite mountains. The extensive trail system was the key to the success of the NVA; there was always an alternative route to use while repairs were being made to the most recent American target of the day. By 1970, the area north of Tchepone, Laos, through to the four northern Vietnam mountain passes, was like a large ant farm, with the VC ants constantly on the move, overcoming every hurdle they encountered in their work to move supplies to the south and back into Vietnam to fight the Americans.

While the forests wouldn't be hiding NVA anti-aircraft guns, or hiding thousands of VC with rockets ready to take down any of the American airships that came within range, the challenge now would be to fly unnoticed by a nervous and reactive new communist controlled military in Laos.

Farmer knew that Billy Bob and Quan were essential to the work they had to do, but it was a gut wrenching acceptance to bring them into this operation at this stage. He believed they should not have to bear the burden of this dangerous past for a country that long ago left them behind, but there was no alternative to doing so.

Chapter 14

They were only able to salvage short power naps through the night, as they remained ever alert to all sounds, necessary survival instincts for this part of the world.

Larry heard Quan fire up the Hughes Cayuse for his trip to pick up the monk. He watched Quan lift the helicopter off the pad, quickly moving forward and up at the same time. Billy Bob taught him how to fly to survive in this country. He cleared the trees and gained altitude as fast as the chopper could.

By 0900, Quan returned with his friend. The monk, with his shaved head and wearing his orange saffron robe, bowed when he met Larry and Farmer. From under his robe, the monk pulled out a small lead box, a case with very detailed etchings on its outside surface.

Quan led the meeting as the translator into English and back to Laotian, suspecting that Farmer and Larry might be rusty in their language skills. The monk did understand, and could speak, some English.

"This is for you; I don't want it in our mountain. I don't want the big box. You will take it?" begged the monk in Laotian.

"Does anyone else know of this big box, or the trip into the mine by the Americans?" Larry asked after which Quan translated the question.

"No. I tell no one. Only the Sangharaja, but he is dead. Sangharaja told me the American was a good man; he gave us money to buy food for the village people and orphans. We can buy food for many years.

171

No one knows where the money came from. That is good," was Quan's translation of the monk's reply.

"Yes, that is good," Farmer commented as he removed the lid off the metal case and extracted the folded yellow paper that Shelby had put into the box five years ago.

Larry compared the monk's map to the map that Shelby had given him when they visited him in the hospital. Both maps were drawn on yellow paper, written with exactly the same directions, line by line, turn by turn. Since Shelby wrote these directions, the distances between each marked point would be accurate. Larry's nod to Farmer confirmed they had correct directions to get the box out of the mine.

The monk informed them that the other monks were leaving the Elephant Mountain monastery tomorrow to go down to serve the village below the mountain and conduct lessons.

This was also the only day when the current Sangharaja left the monastery to spend the day in the village. They agreed that tomorrow at 0800 they'd meet the monk at the monastery. The monk would take them into the mine.

The entry plan was set.

Chapter 15

Sunday, July 10, 1977

At 0630 hours, Billy Bob and Larry walked around the helipad working through the pre-flight checklist. To maintain normalcy, in an abnormal world, Billy Bob and Quan would be in the pilot and co-pilot seats, flying the 205 as if they were on just a regular delivery to the monastery.

Quan refueled the helicopter using the electric pump. If he was nervous about the operation today, he didn't show it. Another survival skill he had learned from living his entire life in a war zone.

Farmer and Larry each pushed a wheeled cart to the left side of the helicopter. They loaded four canvas bags into compartments from the first handcart along with rice and dry rations for the monastery from the second handcart. Billy Bob stowed a rope sling in the starboard storage compartment.

After opening the throttle, Billy Bob pushed the starter button with his middle finger. The turbine spun and the jet engine fired. He methodically ran through his gauges and flipped switches to test circuits. Satisfied, he pulled up on the collective lifting the helicopter into the air.

If he had kept a logbook, the entries would have listed over 14,000 hours of flying history. Since he stopped recording his hours after losing his last logbook years ago, his skill of coaxing the 1,100 horsepower engine to pump out available lift, while accelerating forward, was his testament of hours in the pilot's seat.

Farmer took the ride in silence as he monitored their route on the 1:50,000 maps. The pot-marked landscape below soon reminded of what the notation 'abandoned' or 'destroyed' below a village's name meant. While looking at the bombed out clearings that remained he cursed to himself that *too many innocent people had paid the toll for the Secret War in Laos.*

At the monastery on Elephant Mountain, the 205 landed behind the long hut, fifty yards from the cathedral entrance to the mine. Parked in this location, the helicopter was partially hidden and only observable from the air, due to the multi-layered canopy of mangrove trees. The steep face of Elephant Mountain on the north prevented anyone from looking up into the monastery from the valley below.

Quan's friend stayed at the doorway to the housing hut until the helicopter rotors stopped spinning. When Quan met up with him, he confirmed no one else remained behind and accordingly he was alone on the site. He had volunteered to stay and await Quan's delivery of supplies.

Farmer tossed one of the green canvas bags over his shoulder. Larry grabbed the second one. The slight monk pulled open the tall wooden doors of the main mineshaft. Inside the entrance oil lamps, matches, helmets, and old army gas masks were stocked on a wooden shelf. They dressed quickly, hanging around their necks the new gas detectors donated by Billy Bob this morning.

Farmer handed Billy Bob a small cloth bag containing their passports, papers and other documents. If they did not return, Billy Bob would take care of their affairs.

Larry slung an M-16 machine gun over his shoulder. He started filling his backpack with the rope, water, day rations, flairs, and two extra flashlights. Farmer did the same. They were ready to walk the map.

Billy Bob tried one last time to join them inside the mine, but the request was denied. They needed the outside to look as normal as possible. He and Quan would slowly unload the rations, making the visit appear as a regular delivery to the monastery.

They had no idea how long they would be inside the mountain. When Shelby stashed the target, he had to learn the route, find a secret hiding spot, and map the route on duplicate documents. His three-man team completed the work in three and a half hours.

With the benefit of a detailed map, Farmer expected they would not take as long to locate the target and bring the box out of the mine. Today, they had to complete this extraction before the monks returned this evening. No one else needed to witness this mission.

The cool air inside the mine made walking comfortable. They spoke little as they followed the map's directions. Larry had the Shelby's map and Farmer had the map that the monk had given him yesterday. At each junction, they confirmed their turn and Larry lit a flare, and jammed the glowing flare in the center of the outward tunnel. The flares would light their return route, providing for a quick return.

The mineshafts narrowed as they progressed deeper into the mountain. The tunnels also became shallower so they had to duck their heads under the wooden cross members used to support the tunnels. The walls reflected the colors of minerals and ore they contained. Most were dark green or grey and black with shiny silver sprinkled throughout. Some sections however, were colored in a burnt red color, indicating where the iron ore wept down the tunnel walls.

"Did you ever think there could be a worse place than the elephant grass, bamboo, snakes, leaches, and spiders? This long hole in the ground beats the jungle," said Farmer, as they stopped and verified the sixth junction in their fifteen-minute walk thus far. They were making good time.

"Hell, this ain't so bad. It's a lesson, man. Once you thought you knew where hell was, and now you know it wasn't there at all," Larry joked as he lit the seventh flair.

One hour inside and they arrived at the critical juncture of the mine trip. If they had followed the map correctly, just ahead would be a water crossing, draining water from the underground spring into a ditch system. The tunnel would end just past the crossing. However, the tunnel did not end. They did not cross a channel of spring water.

"Hey man, we fucked up. Where are we? Where is the box?" Farmer barked to Larry. The dark, damp, claustrophobic confines of the tunnels did not help Farmer's temperament.

"Whoa, slow down there cowboy. We are where we are supposed to be. We didn't fuck up. Let's have a smoke and clear our heads for a minute."

Farmer sat down on his haunches to light a smoke, passing the lit match to Larry to light his thin, brown hand-rolled.

"I knew the trip was going too good. Not one phase of this operation ever went well nor turned out the way we expected. Why would this salvage mission be any different?" a frustrated Farmer exclaimed.

Larry smoked while he looked at his map. "Let me look at your map."

Farmer handed him his copy of the map.

Larry butted out his smoke, got up, and shone his light across the left wall of the end of the tunnel. He poked at the rocks until a pile of them fell to the rock floor, dislodging a metal container from the wall.

The metal can was a slightly rusted first aid kit. Inside the airtight container, a waterproof match cylinder contained a handwritten note.

"What's the note say?"

"It's a note from Shelby. He had a 289 in his Mustang, right?"

"What the hell kind of trivia is he asking us?"

"Yeah, yeah, so what was the engine? A 289, right?"

"Yeah, a 289."

"Okay then, let's go get the goods," Larry said as he got up and started pacing back along the tunnel. He waved his arm at Farmer. "Do as the man says, 'Back up the size of the best Mustang motor'."

"How the hell did you know to look for the can and the note?"

"Remember when we were pushing Shelby around at the hospital and he started muttering before he went to sleep?"

"Not really, he mumbled a lot."

"Yeah, well he repeated 'look on the wall, look on the wall'. When I looked at both maps, I realized the line didn't end straight at a spot; it had a line taking off to the left, like a small hook. I thought of everything Shelby said to us and then his phrase came to me. He was right; I just had to look on the wall for the final clue. You need to remember the team we were; we trusted few and gave it all for our country and our team. Shelby designed a burial plan that could be figured out only by the few of us that thought the same, and maybe were a bit odd to begin with."

Satisfied with his philosophical lecture of the day, Larry backtracked, pacing 280 feet in distance. Walking beside the small water flow down the ditch, he poked at the tunnel walls with his metal rod. At 285 feet, he hit the tunnel sidewall and realized in the dim light that it was a mildew coated canvas tarp. He continued hitting the false wall with the metal rod causing the ore that had been placed in the folds of the tarp to fall to the ground. After pulling the tarp off the sidewall, a new tunnel was exposed, including the steel wheel cart with the target intact on it.

The wood crating around the metal case had become coated in black mildew. Faint weathered red crosses were visible on the wood slats.

Farmer shook his head in bewilderment. They had found the target. Now the real work could begin to get the incriminating evidence out of the mine.

Not hesitating at their success, Larry used a tube of axle grease from his pack to grease the open bearings on the metal axles of the loaded cart. He once again became impressed at the ingenuity of the locals to recycle pieces of blown up machines and use them to build a functional cart. The metal wheels on the cart rolled with ease after being lubricated again. Their cart design was good, since despite the target weighing the high side of 250 pounds, the loaded cart rolled easily on the hard rock base of the mine floor. Larry tied a rope around the front of the cart and hooked the other end to his belt sling. He was the puller; Farmer was the pusher.

Two hours after entering the dark mine, they were on their way back with the target.

Larry only got out the first line of *I've been working on the Railroad* before Farmer cut him off. They continued the trip to the music of the metal wheels rolling on the rocky road of the mineshaft.

The cart rolled easily on the slight grade of the tunnels. Since each junction had been marked with a burning flare, the endeavor went well. At 1015 hours, they were back at the mine entrance.

Larry hesitated on opening the doors because he had a strange premonition that something had changed outside. Two green canvas bags, which should have still been in the helicopter, were inside the mine. The bags contained the two large caliber M-60 machine guns and ammunition. Larry, still at the front of the cart, raised his hand to tell Farmer to stop.

After cautiously prying the heavy wooden doors open, he could see across the grounds to the Huey. He backed up from the entrance and motioned for Farmer follow him back into the mine.

"Bad news, boss. Two white no-necked men in green have their pistols drawn. Billy Bob, Quan, and the monk are on their knees. They are barking something out at Billy Bob. Damn it, they're the Russians."

"How far away are they?"

"Forty yards."

"We have to take them out."

"You got her," Larry said as he checked his M-16. "They're five feet apart; I'll take the one on the right. We have a clear shot at both of them."

"Got it, I'll do the one on the left."

When they returned to the heavy doors, and propped them open enough to shoot through, nothing had changed in the visitor's locations. The Russians were still spaced apart, but now one threatened the monk and the other was on Quan. Billy Bob pleaded with the occupiers, "We don't know! We don't know!"

The small birds resting on the layers of the mangrove trees were still making their warning calls to each other when the 5.56 mm copper-tipped 62-grain bullet went through the back of the head of the Russian standing on the left. The dead Russian fell forward forcing the quick reflexes of the monk to roll out of the way before the corpse landed on top of him. The other Russian heard the sharp whistle of a monkey squeal before the bullet blew apart the left ventricle of his heart. His body folded at his waist, then rolled into a ball on the ground beside Billy Bob, who was still kneeling on the ground.

Farmer and Larry remained in position, with Larry on the ground and Farmer above him securing his M-16 against the tall door. There was no other movement on the grounds. No one else came out from the huts. Billy Bob got up off his knees and waved for them to come out, but signaled to be quiet with his finger on his lips.

"There's another one around here. Last time I saw him, he was walking into the temple," whispered Billy Bob.

Larry handed Billy Bob his Smith and Wesson .45 from his hip holster before he took off running to the right side of the monastery's main building, M-16 ready in his right hand. Farmer took off to the left side of the temple.

There was a good chance that the two earlier shots were muffled, since they had been shot from inside the mine. The third Russian may not have heard the shots, Larry hoped.

He signaled to Farmer before he entered the temple.

Farmer took the instruction and moved to the door to provide cover.

Slipping inside the temple, Larry located the squarely built Russian holding a gold cup in his hands at the side of the building.

The Russian decided to pocket the large cup, which confirmed his pistol remained in his holster since both hands were visible. Larry didn't want to risk the attention from an open M-16 shot sounding down the valley, so he stalked silently through the building to get closer to the intruding thief.

The birds and the monkeys were on Larry's side and continued their chatter outside the open windows. He rushed the last ten feet and ran the razor sharp blade of his twelve-inch knife across the Russian's throat, severing his jugular vein. The gold cup fell to the ground as he let the corpse slide down onto the floor. Larry had not lost his edge, his agility, or even a single step.

Quan met them at the door. "They said they had to kill us to teach the monks a lesson. They want the monks to leave the mountain."

"They came up the trail to the south. The three of them were talking, as if it was a walk in the park for them. The monk heard them first and told me, so I took out the last two bags and put them in the mine, hoping you would be able to figure out something was up. Thank Christ you got here when you did. They would have killed us. Man, this fucking war just won't end," added Billy Bob.

Farmer resumed control of the situation. "Let's get out of here as fast and clean as we can. We'll start with loading the box into the chopper."

They each took a corner and lifted the wooden crate off the cart. The four of them easily carried the crate to the helicopter. The crate slid in with ease and rested in the cargo bay, with the bench seat removed for today's trip. The tie-downs from under the fold-up seat secured the crate to the pop-up floor hooks.

Grabbing the heavy bags with ease, Larry carried two of the canvas bags from the mine to the chopper and took off his pack and harness while keeping his M-16 slung over his shoulder.

Meanwhile, Farmer carried the other two gear bags from the mine and set them along the top storage netting on the left side of the cargo area.

Quan efficiently gathered up the remaining gear from the mine entrance, setting it inside the cage in the cargo area, under the folding seats.

Finally, to clear the evidence of the expedition, Larry returned to push the steel wheel cart back inside the mine, leaving it at the first junction on the left.

The monk swept the khaki sand with a broom to remove footprints and other evidence of his guests and his intruders.

Normalcy had returned as confirmed by the whistling and squeals from the Colobus monkeys, high above in the mangrove tree.

As a man to get the job done, Farmer opened a green tarp beside each of the Russian bodies. Larry lifted the first corpse by the shoulders and Farmer lifted the feet to set the body on the tarp, Larry used a quick wrap of rope to secure the rolled Russians inside each of their tarps. The three wrapped corpses were stacked like cord wood beside the target, inside the cargo hold of the helicopter, and secured in place by tying them to the floor mounts.

On his hands and knees, the monk scraped up all bloody soil in a large bowl. Surprisingly, very little blood had been spilled. He poured the contaminated soil around the red-hot coals of the cooking fire he had prepared before the Russians arrived. The monk continued with his cleansing work as he went inside the temple with a bottle of liquid and a cloth to clean up the blood on the floor.

After verifying no evidence had been left behind, Larry tossed his mine map into the fire. Farmer did the same. They did not need memoirs of this mission.

The monk pointed out that the Russians must have come to the site in a truck. Quan seized the moment, taking off down the south trail to find the vehicle.

The Mutt M151 was parked at the road, 350 yards down the trail. Quan drove the truck as fast as possible along the rough trail to get to the logged area below the mountain. Three miles down the road, he turned the truck toward the sharp edge of the rock cliff and climbed out over the passenger's seat. Reaching across from the passenger side, he jammed the stick shift into second gear. The truck lurched ahead, almost stalling, but by then the front wheels had crossed the edge. Gravity took over as the truck rolled off the road, flipped, and somersaulted its way down the rock-faced canyon into the creek below.

Quan ran along the rest of the canyon roadway to a suitable landing site. He was gasping for breath, at the side of the road, when Billy Bob landed on the grassy opening. After climbing over the collective arm, and taking his co-pilot seat, the machine was airborne again.

The flight back to Savannakhet was quiet. Feelings of anxiety had replaced the brief elation, which had replaced sheer nervousness. Farmer stared out the window, watching the earth below. Quan closed his eyes and prayed for the karma of the three dead Russians. An hour and a quarter later, Billy Bob landed the helicopter at his base. He shut down the 205 with his solemn crew on board.

Farmer had the haunting feelings return. He had to force them out of his mind. Killing was never easy to accept, no matter how many times you have done it. Your inner humanity still reels from the finality of the action.

However, they had rescued the last component of the mission. Once they disposed of it, there could be no ties to the American Government or the American people. The Russians and the Chinese could not use this damaged endeavor against them in the international court of opinion.

Two issues had yet to be resolved. One was disposing of the three Russian bodies. Larry and Billy Bob worked on that matter. On site was the large industrial incinerator, which had been built to burn the air base garbage, back when over 200 people occupied the base. In seven hours, it would be dark. In the evening, an easterly flow of wind came off the Mekong River across the town of Savannakhet and over the incinerator. The smoke and fumes would disperse across the open plain fields and the sparse forest to the east of the base. They resurrected the incinerator by connecting the twin fan forced air system to increase the combustion efficiency of the burner. Quan and Larry loaded the incinerator with the three dead Russians, pails of used engine oil, a couple of tires, and rotten upholstery from one of the old parts airplanes in the back forty. The incinerator would take care of the dead Russians.

The question of how to get rid of the target package became a more difficult challenge.

Billy Bob and Farmer went over the alternatives. While Billy Bob had a good idea what was in the crate, he did not ask. It was not important to the task. It was also better for him to remain in doubt than to have confirmation of what his country of birth had thought they would do to end another war.

They concluded there really was only one method of disposal, the one that should have occurred five years ago. The package could only be dumped into very deep water, to rust to a slow death and never to be found again. However, two potential graveyards were available—the Sea of China or the Bay of Bengal. Since they did not have a regular transcontinental aircraft at their disposal, they would have to design their disposal around using the Caribou airplane to dump the package.

If they chose to move it west, they would have to fly through Thailand, which was fighting a civil war, across Burma, which was even less friendly, and then drop it into the Bay of Bengal, ending their flight in India. They would be landing in an unfamiliar land. Leaving the area, without raising suspicion, would be difficult.

The second option was to move it east. They could cross Laos, fly through Vietnam to Da Nang, and then southeast across the Sea of China to the Philippines. The strength of this plan was that Billy Bob often hauled freight from the Philippines to Laos and Vietnam. Since the Vietnamese couldn't fly into the Philippines, they used Billy Bob's services. He just had to develop a credible story. Ideas floated through his mind on how he could explain how he had picked up the two Canadians. Damn he hated making up lies; he was a pilot, not an agent.

The Philippines was chosen as their destination. They'd drop the package in a mile of salt water and then land the airplane in the Philippines, where they would deal with the matter of two hitchhikers.

Their simple dinner of fried water buffalo steaks washed down well with the local beer. They relished in a sense of satisfaction that they had indeed retrieved the target and they had a disposal plan ready. Billy Bob passed around hand rolled cigars, which he reserved for special events; no event could exceed this one.

Billy Bob first spotted the lights on the lead truck as the cumbersome unit weaved its way onto the compound road. "We got trouble, coming," he said as the others saw the lights of the second truck turn onto the entrance road, still half a mile away from them. "Why would the army come for a visit at this time of the day? This can't be good Farmer," Billy Bob said.

Farmer and Larry had already moved over to the canvas bags and were pulling out the guns and grabbing ammo.

The first LPA green army truck screeched to a stop, just ahead of the hangar. It could have been comical, in another circumstance, as the second truck smashed into the back of the parked lead truck, pushing it ahead another 5 feet. However, tonight no one recognized the humor in the event.

The soldier driving the first truck began screaming at the driver of the second truck as he waved his pistol at the other driver. His swagger confirmed he was drunk. The shot he fired at the second truck, over the top of the cab, confirmed he was also a loose cannon.

Farmer had made his way to the far side of the hangar and slipped out the side door. His machine gun was loaded as he sighted in the group of six men. The failing daylight still allowed him to determine the two white men were Russians. The taller targets would be his first, since they appeared sober. Their pistols remained in their hip holsters.

The four drunken Laotian soldiers continued an intense argument amongst themselves.

After one of the Russians barked a command, the four soldiers lead the two men toward the main hanger's office door.

Quan met the group thirty feet away from the building, halting their progress toward the hanger. He did not recognize the soldiers.

Slurring in Laotian, the lead drunk soldier demanded money from Quan for his safety.

Billy Bob listened from inside the hangar as Quan replied to the soldier that they had none. He started to explain about the work they did for the LPRP when the second driver shot his machine gun in the air and commanded, 'silence'. They were there to find the two white men who were seen at the hangar yesterday by one of their comrades.

"There are three friends of these men who are missing," he got out in his slurred speech. "Where is the American pilot," he continued in a reference to Billy Bob, "he will tell us what we need to know."

For added emphasis, he recklessly let out a burst of machine gun fire, but fell to the ground while still releasing the shots. His errant shots hit one of his own men, causing him to collapse on the concrete. Another shot cut through Quan's leg, forcing a scream from Quan as dropped to the concrete. The shooter was too drunk to stand again.

The confrontation ended as Larry emerged from the open space between the two hangar doors. With the big M-60 in his thick arms, fed by an ammo belt hanging loosely from his left arm, he walked toward the gathering, firing single shots spaced in a rhythm to the recoil of the machine gun. One by one, the men fell to the ground as they received the impact of a 7.62 metal jacket slug. At this close range, every shot mangled the body it hit. When he saw an injured Russian lying on the ground, trying to pull out his handgun from his holster, he added certainty with headshots on all six of the trespassers. In twelve seconds, Larry, the man on his focused mission, had neutralized the situation.

Farmer caught up with him after he had eliminated the last soldier. He dropped onto his knees to deal with the injured Quan. One AK-47 shot had entered and exited his leg. However, he couldn't stand on the injured leg. He couldn't put weigh on it. Farmer carried Quan on his back the thirty feet inside the hangar to the office chairs.

Billy Bob was in his office, still holding Larry's .45.

"Better clear the gun before you shoot someone," Farmer commanded. "We're bumping up our plans, we're leaving at first light."

Outside, Larry loaded the six additional dead men inside the industrial sized incinerator. Once it was loaded, with all bodies and debris, he flipped the ignition and burn switch on the control panel and the stream of ignited kerosene got on with destroying evidence.

Soon black smoke from the oil and the tires spewed into the atmosphere. The smell of burning rubber masked the cremation of human flesh and bone as the large burner consumed its charge. Convinced the burner was doing its job well, Larry left to help Billy Bob ready the Caribou plane for their advanced departure.

Indochina Operations

1970 – 1972

Chapter 16

Spring of 1970 – Seven years earlier
March 25, 1970

Waiting proved to be the personal challenge of night operations. Waiting for the action to start was a test of patience, waiting for extraction at the end of a mission was a test of nerves. Being good at waiting was a skill that Major Arthur Henry had yet to master. He did, however, thrive on the doing part of every operation.

Major Henry was proof of how some men do not make sensible career choices. The West Point graduate did well at his desk job as a statistician for the Pentagon, but through a series of fast track promotions, he made Captain in the Quartermaster Corps. Most would be content at observing the emerging war from the safety of a base camp in Thailand. However, after witnessing the buildup of forces on the ground in Vietnam, he transferred into field operations. Through a series of his own requests, he wound up working men on search and destroy missions in Vietnam. How far he had gone or maybe how far he had fallen? He sometimes questioned how he had allowed this patriotism thing to get so deep down into his gut.

Tonight, though, none of these thoughts ran through his mind as he lay in position. He was working another search and destroy mission to disrupt the flow of North Vietnamese supplies through the roads and trails from the north to the south in another attempt to prevent the NVA from resupplying their operations south of the DMZ and behind the American forces in South Vietnam. Every successful mission his men had against the NVA meant that more Americans would live to die another day.

He looked at his watch one more time. As of 2215, they had been in place for 4 hours. He had advanced another 240 minutes closer to completing his second tour of duty.

Intelligence had learned that a NVA convoy of trucks was to be moving through a reconstructed river crossing, only 250 yards from the hill they were waiting on. The strategic position proved least accessible from the crossing side, due to the sheer rock face, but it provided a quick retreat down the hillside back to the helicopter landing site for their retrieval. Their forest trail had been cleared of mines by South Vietnamese engineers yesterday.

The ARVN, Army of the Republic of Vietnam, Major running this operation had his South Vietnamese soldiers placed on only the south side of the river, so that their klick and a half retreat from Laos back to Vietnam could be done immediately after hitting the expected eight-truck convoy and a squad of NVA.

After the attack, returning to Vietnam for extraction was critical. Major Henry, and an American private, had been instructed to stay with the South Vietnamese field squad to observe how they operated. The South Vietnamese patrols had been unsuccessful in too many missions this year. They had incurred significant losses in their battles with the NVA soldiers on these supply trails. Strategic information was being leaked to the VC; the VC often knew of the mission and prepared for the South Vietnamese to begin their assault and then the tipped off VC slaughtered them. While Henry and his fellow American were contravening the "no American boots on the soil in Laos" edict, it was a risk that his American Commanding Officer and the ARVN Major had decided to take today to try to isolate the leak or succeed in at least one mission.

At 2300, with the aid of the clear sky and bright moonlight, the NVA convoy was spotted, slowly moving toward the narrow crossing of the slow moving river. The convoy slowed as the first truck dropped down the steep bank into the river. The South Vietnamese Major had positioned his men with their 72 mm Light Anti-Armor Weapons, LAWs, in an ordered arrangement along the crest of the hilltop. The infantryman's orders were to hit the first truck after it had crossed the river, and take out the others while they were still in the river, thereby effectively blocking the crossing. Henry knew that the disruption of the crossing would be short lived since the diligent VC would reconstruct another crossing. However, for a short time, the flow of goods along the trail would be affected. Such was warfare against a determined enemy.

The first truck approached the target zone when Major Henry heard the blade wash of the Russian built Mil helicopters coming at them fast from behind him and the men. Once again, the details of their operation tonight had been gifted to the NVA, despite the extra planning that had been put into this mission to prevent such a leak.

The South Vietnamese soldiers poised to launch their rockets at the convoy were killed first by the machine gun fire from above. More than one LAW exploded because they sent their explosion and shrapnel into the men behind them. It became a turkey shoot for the helicopters as they fired at the men trapped on top of ridge, aided by their bright spotlights.

Henry and the American private were furthest from the first explosions and closest to the exit trail. After the helicopter's first rocket hit the hillside, he felt a sharp bite in his left thigh. A second bullet grazed his ribcage as he fell forward into a hole in the rock hill and rolled into the crevice. Before he could think of what to do next, the helicopters departed, leaving him face down in his trench.

He looked down toward the river and watched the convoy of trucks continue along the old goat trail of a road, with its cargo on its way to be used against Americans, somewhere in southern Vietnam.

Burning brush and trees yielded sufficient light as he pulled himself out of the hole and crawled from man to man on the hill. The men that he could find were dead. Parts of soldiers littered the hillside.

He did locate the American private, unconscious, but still breathing. A glass vial of ammonia under the soldier's nose caused him to open his eyes and shake his head away from the vile smell. Private Jones had been stunned from a rocket blast, but otherwise, was unharmed.

Major Henry ordered Jones to check the last three men to the right side of the group. The major tied a compress bandage around the bullet entry in his thigh.

Jones could not find any other survivors, and he confirmed the Vietnamese Major was dead. He collected the radio off the dead radioman's back and strapped it onto his back. Henry was able to walk, albeit in significant pain, with the aid of a stick for a crutch. Their immediate priority however, was to get off the hill, since the NVA soldiers from the convoy would be making their way up to the site to take care of any survivors.

They had only made it two hundred yards when they heard the voices in the dark forest as the soldiers moved up the hillside. Major Henry and Private Jones froze in their spot, hidden by the cover of night and a thick mangrove tree. Not one shot was fired back on the hillside, confirming they had not left any survivors.

Under the cover of the forest at night, they had to get as far away from the area as possible before dawn. Since the mission had been compromised, Henry searched through his memory for an alternative landing site. The original location would be lined with NVA snipers expecting to deal with the helicopters coming in to retrieve the returning soldiers. Fortunately, his leg had not suffered much damage. Using his tree limb crutch, the major moved at a reasonable pace through the thick jungle. He took the lead since he had been on these trails many times in his career.

They did not have time to consider the horrors of the jungle at night; they had to focus on getting across the next hill and back into Vietnam, an irony not lost on Henry. For their safety, they had to get back into Vietnam.

Perseverance paid off and by 0500, they crossed the walking bridge, strung across the small river, as the rising sun's rays broke through openings in the forest canopy. Back in Vietnam again, they now had to locate an alternative pick up location since they were no longer near the original extraction point. It was Henry's move to get them out.

Still dark inside the dense forest cover, Major Henry risked using his flashlight to look at his compass and map to locate their position and plot a course for the opening that he remembered which should be less than a kilometer from them.

Voices were heard on the trail beside the wide river. The two men withdrew and dropped into a small depression, just up the slope from the patrol's trail. Below, two NVA soldiers followed behind a line of American prisoners, each of which wore leg shackles with their arms bound behind them.

The marching group of prisoners stopped after one of the NVA soldiers barked out an order. The American POW's were in bad shape. Most had blood-soaked bandages covering wounds. The first NVA soldier moved to the side of the second to light up a cigarette. The Major understood enough Vietnamese to understand their boasting about the food and drink, and maybe even a nice girl, they would receive as a reward for capturing these prisoners. They continued to talk, but the major no longer listened to their conversation.

As the 5.56 mm slug passed through the right ear of the closest soldier, the left side of his head exploded onto the face of the second soldier. The second shot hit his ribcage, sending bone shards into his pulsing heart, thereby shredding the heart muscle. He fell to the ground exposing the remaining enemy soldier. The next four shots from the Major's M-16 went through the second soldier's head and chest before he could remove the blinding splatter of blood and skull fragments from his eyes. In just eight seconds, both enemies had been taken out.

Private Jones instinctively darted around the trees and ran toward the American prisoners. Cutting the rope away from around the closest pair of hands, allowed the prisoner to grab the leg shackle keys out of the dead Vietnamese soldier's pocket and unlock his leg shackles. Passing the keys to the second freed man, he returned to the dead Vietnamese soldier to take his knife and rifle. A second American cleaned out the other Vietnamese soldier's knife and ammunition clips and took his captured rifle in his hands.

Major Henry cautiously got up from his hiding spot, remaining ever alert for additional enemy soldiers.

The freed men scrambled up the slope to join Major Henry. Jones ran back to the Vietnamese soldiers and placed a grenade under the back of one of the dead soldiers. He pulled the pin leaving the weight of the dead body to hold the lever in place.

No words needed to be exchanged. The injured men awkwardly moved across the slope of the hill. They walked for twenty minutes along the rocky forest trail until they arrived at the edge of the bomb-made clearing. Multiple bombings had created a reasonable landing site. Remaining within the cover offered by the mangrove and jackfruit trees, the two American prisoners with captured rifles took positions ahead and behind the men, as the group rested on the dry grass. Major Henry took Jones with his radio fifteen yards away from the former prisoners to listen to the radio traffic. He picked up a conversation between two Medevac helicopters and broke into their conversation.

A Medevac pilot relayed his request for the extraction of the 18 men. After confirming his identity and answering the security check for the base, he was informed that the Slicks were on their way. On this news, Major Henry slumped on the ground. Waiting for an operation to start was hard, but waiting for an extraction was the closest thing to hell a man could go through. Fifteen minutes felt like fifteen hours. Every strange noise meant another risk of not getting out.

The rescued American soldiers had been trained well. Not one of them moved or made a noise. They sat and waited, not knowing why, but they knew these two soldiers had saved their lives and they had no reason to doubt their command now.

Captain Larry Junior Johnson's Bell UH-1D Huey gunship broke over the ridge to the south of the group at full throttle over the rough terrain. The machine dipped and swayed as it passed above the treetops and entered and exited the shadows of the hillside. A second Huey flew in behind at almost the same speed, followed by another Slick. When the gunship got closer, Henry threw an orange smoke flair into the opening.

Johnson's Huey gunship passed by the smoke and continued on to survey the dense forest canopy and the natural rock outcroppings around the landing site. After confirming Charlie wasn't in the vicinity, he returned to position and hovered 400 yards above ground, surveying the land for the enemy. His co-pilot was ready with twenty-four 2.75-

inch rockets at his disposal. Both were prepared to use their side-mounted machine guns.

The second helicopter, a Huey UH-1D, a Slick, had gunners standing on each side of the open cargo doors. The door gunners trained their M-60 machine guns on the forest around the men. The first Slick landed roughly on the uneven crater. Eight men scrambled inside as the helicopter lifted off. The second Slick landed at the same spot, also arriving with a bump on the rocky ground. Eight more Americans scrambled inside. The pilot pulled off the ground as soon as the eighth man had been pulled inside and onto the floor of the cargo bay.

Only Henry and Jones remained on the ground.

Johnson dropped his gunship and flew into the edge of the tree line. He set down on the rocks, waiting merely seconds as his crew chief grabbed for arms and pulled in the pair of heroes around his side gun equipment, which hung outside and blocked part of the cargo bay entrance. By the time Henry sat up on the cargo bay floor, the gunship had lifted high above the trees and was following the ridges again as they left the area. They passed by the first helicopter and took their position in the front of the line.

It had been a flawless evacuation of 16 American POWs and two survivors of a failed mission, all in the enemy's backyard and within the confinement of his highway of trails along the border, south of Highway 9. When Johnson's Huey dropped down the last ridge, he could see the Yorkton Base on the cleared plain, straight ahead, home of his Special Forces unit and segregated units of marines, and the 101st airborne.

What he also saw ahead was not good news. Three Russian built Hound helicopters were dropping NVA troops on the far side of the hill 317, 8 miles north of the camp.

Seeing his new mission in front of him, Johnson veered his gunship to the right to cross over the ridge, north of the base. The two Slicks continued into the camp. Johnson accelerated, closing in the gap, before the enemy pilot saw him.

While keeping his machine level, Johnson's co-pilot fired five of his rockets at the closest Hound.

The North Vietnamese pilot only caught a flash of reflection of the sunlight off the approaching rocket just before it hit his door and blew his cockpit away from the carcass of the rest of the helicopter. Machine parts fell onto the offloading troops. The second machine did not escape the flying shrapnel and the transmission started emitting smoke as he tried to leave the area. One of Johnson's next three rockets hit the damaged machine's fuel tank and that helicopter exploded in the air, killing all inside.

Johnson was only a mile away when the third NVA helicopter cleared out of the smoke while turning his ship to direct his side-mounted machine guns on Johnson's gunship.

That turned out to be a fatal mistake, since five, made in the USA rockets, slammed into the exposed cockpit of the NVA helicopter, only seconds after his guns had begun firing. Johnson swung to the right and upward to protect him and his ship from the resulting explosion.

A tight circle brought Johnson back above the landing site so his starboard gunner could fire on the soldiers that had offloaded onto the ground. On his second tight circle turn, Johnson received a radio call from a pilot bringing in an F-105 Thunderchief fighter-bomber. Two F-105's were coming in fast and Johnson was instructed to return to the Yorkton base.

The supersonic F-105s each carried 12,000 pounds of explosive death, while moving at 500 miles per hour. The F-105s carpeted the drop zone with high explosives, leveling it and eliminating anyone who had survived Johnson's attack on the disrupted drop of field troops.

Johnson's two passengers had witnessed an extraordinary gunship operation. This crew was a finely tuned death squad.

As Larry Johnson flared his helicopter, Major Henry's eyes remained wide open, he wasn't blinking, and he was in complete awe. After the speedy landing, he received help from two medics. His damaged leg was too painful now to stand on, since his adrenaline no longer masked the pain.

When an orderly arrived with a wheel chair, he sat down without trying to hide his agony. Major Henry asked the man to wait then proceeded to shake the hand of each of the helicopter crew, thanking them for their work of saving their lives. Finally, the tall lanky pilot climbed out of the helicopter. Major Henry shook his hand and asked his name. Larry Johnson replied, and then turned back to his helicopter.

"Those fucking commies got me," Johnson exclaimed in anger as he rubbed his hand over four bullet holes in his door. After all Johnson had just done, he was pissed they had hit him.

Major Henry asked the orderly to wheel him to the Officer's Club for a stiff drink, which the man politely ignored. During the one hour operation, the bullet lodged in his femur was removed. Two hours later, he woke up from the ether-induced sleep. An injection of morphine put him back to medicated rest.

The next day he met the CO and a 'Suit' from some branch of Intelligence to whom he gave his debriefing. The general had already interviewed the prisoners and Jones so the major didn't yield any new information.

Private Jones had been thorough in his debriefing; despite being a field grunt, he admitted that Major Henry had been remarkable in their trip back for extraction. Not often, a short timer field grunt would commend an officer, but Jones had done just that.

"Jones was impressed with your shooting ability. Where did you learn to shoot an M-16 so well? Have you been through marksman training?" the CO asked Henry.

In a calm voice he replied, "No sir. I grew up in Oregon. Back home we grow up with guns for the gophers in the fields and the grouse in the forest. The VC are bigger targets than a gopher on a stump or a grouse in a cedar tree."

Major Henry impressed the general with his frank replies.

Three days later Major Henry received the Silver Star for his rescue of the American prisoners and the Purple Heart for his wound, his second of each. In addition to his promotion to the rank of lieutenant colonel, his new assignment was to return to the States and help the Pentagon get on with ending this war.

Chapter 17

One year later

September 28, 1971

On a rainy Monday morning, the two-tour veteran of the Vietnam War, 36-year-old Colonel Henry, was working in his office in the Pentagon. At 1000 hours, he received a call from General Whiteman's chief of staff at the Department of Defense, requiring him to attend a meeting at the Hilton Hotel in Austin, Texas, at 1800 today. He was booked on a 1315 hours flight on Transcontinental.

This type of urgent and non-descriptive meeting notice was not out of the ordinary in a day in his life. He was at the beck and call of General Whiteman. Someone would brief him before he arrived at the meeting.

At 1800 precisely, he knocked on the door of room 212 in the Austin Hilton, still uninformed of the purpose of the meeting. Only once before had he been sent to one of these urgent rendezvous without a briefing.

A tall man answered the door, inviting him inside.

Inside Room 212, a second man met him. Both men were clean-shaven, had identical haircuts, wore dark glasses, and wore dark black suits. Government men of some sort, likely CIA or FBI. Defense employees did not dress like twins.

"Colonel Henry, you can call me Simpson, and this is Dickson."

"Gentlemen," he said as he shook their hands.

"Colonel, this will be a short meeting. We are here to brief you on your new assignment."

"A new assignment. Why isn't General Whiteman here?"

"The General has been informed of your departure from his staff. This order will clear up any questions you may have," Simpson said as he handed him a white envelope.

The Colonel read his name typed on the front of the envelope and the office of the Central Intelligence Agency embossed on the closing flap on the back of the envelope.

September 14, 1971

Colonel Arthur Gerald Henry, this accommodation is to notify you of your transfer to the Office of the Central Intelligence Agency. Upon completion of this assignment, you will be re-instated in the Office of the Pentagon.

This is a Top Secret Security Level operation. Accordingly, you will be out of communication with your personal contacts during this mission.

The two agents with you now will deliver your instructions.

Eldon Cross, Director of Southeast Asia Division,
Central Intelligence Agency

The letter might have appeared suspect, had not General Whiteman's handwritten note been included below Director Cross' signature.

Henry:
The Director requested I offer my best operational man to this work and I selected you. I respectively offer you to take on this work with the same quality and care you have given to my work.

Sincerely,
General Alfred George Whiteman

The comments from General Whiteman confirmed the legitimacy of this new assignment, since they were in the General's words and in his own writing. Henry turned his attention back to agents Simpson and Dickson.

"The letter, sir," Simpson said as he put his hand out for the letter and the envelope.

Henry returned the document and envelope to Simpson, who folded the letter and reinserted the letter into the envelope and then into his left side interior lapel pocket in his suit jacket.

Simpson led the meeting. "Now that we are finished with the formalities, take a seat."

He took the lounging chair with its back to the wall, facing the center of the room.

"Now," Simpson began, "let's be clear, you do accept this assignment, am I correct?"

"Well I don't know what the assignment is and I don't know if I even have a choice in this decision. I believe my decision has been made for me."

"Yes, you are correct. Do you have any family who must be contacted prior to your absence for the next six months?"

"You know the answer to that question: Parent's deceased, divorced, no children, one distant sister. Come on now, you obviously know that I can disappear for six months and only my cat will miss me."

"Very well, we will place your cat with one of our families to await your return. Agent Dickson will now fill you in on tonight's details."

Agent Dickson handed Colonel Henry a five-page document, extracted from a brown manila envelope. "I will leave this report for you to review. We will return to this room tomorrow at 1300 hours. You are not to leave this room; you are not to make any telephone calls. You are welcome to order the service to your room for your meals. We will meet tomorrow with the rest of the information. Any questions?"

Henry wasn't shocked, nor surprised, by these instructions. This was reminiscent of many of his assignments and the motto for those assignments: "Do as you're told, ask not why, and don't screw up".

He turned his attention back to Simpson, "Do I have a team? Where are they, and where are we going?"

"Read the document, sir, and this will become clear." Simpson and Dickson stood up in unison turned toward the door. "Tomorrow at 1300 hours, then," Simpson said as they left the room.

Colonel Henry walked around his room, tapping the document against his other hand. Knowing how the CIA operated, the room would be bugged, perhaps even filmed. He couldn't leave the room without them knowing about it. Accepting his confinement to the room for the night, he sat on the padded wooden chair in front of the oak desk, and started reading the document.

The document was incomplete since it lacked specific details of the ground operation. Apparently, he had been selected to command a small team of former Special Forces men in an operation at an undisclosed location, in Vietnam.

Apparently, another member of this team had also been volunteered, but the other members had been preparing for this assignment for some time in Laos and Vietnam. This second man had selected the other members of the team after working with them in field operations.

The timeline was condensed. The mission had to be completed by the end of February, giving him less than five months to train and execute the mission. The tight timeline was unusual, based on his experience. However, what appeared to be as most unusual about this mission was that there would be no progress reporting, and no communications with anyone in the CIA, or anyone else. He, and this second leader, were in charge of the mission and they had complete freedom to complete the mission. The document went on to further detail the significance and the security of the mission. On the last page of the document, almost as an afterthought, the operation had been given the name *Quiet Thunder*.

It was too early to turn in, and it was unlikely with so many unanswered details rumbling through his mind that he would be able to relax enough to get to sleep anyway, so he re-read the document.

At 2300 hours, still unable to sleep, he called room service for a Texan Clubhouse and a house salad. Food was a welcomed break from the documents and the mission. The local television news moved his mind to other issues in the world, including a brief recount of the

American troop withdrawals from Vietnam proposed for this year. A couple of double Ballantine, on the rocks, also gave his mind the relaxation it needed to put a perspective on this new chapter in his life. The scotch provided three hours of sleep.

By 0600 hours, he was wide-awake with his room-serviced bowl of bran cereal and cup of black coffee at his desk. He reviewed the document for the third time. It still seemed surrealistic.

This was a mission without reporting, without controls, and for which the success would only be known to those who needed to know. Moreover, the operation was back in the land of Vietnam, via Laos. He was sure he had left the place behind, forever.

He could not shake the haunting feeling of this being a set-up; he was to be taken as a fall guy for a mission doomed to fail, or perhaps one that had already failed. The instructions did not add up. Why would the CIA want him to perform a mission that they did not want to take credit for in any way, even upon its success? Why would the CIA pick him and this other, unnamed person, to lead this mission? Did he know this other operative? Could he trust another handpicked man, or his handpicked crew? His mind rolled all of these thoughts through, and he came up with a resolution; Quiet Thunder was an operation that the government would not admit to unless it succeeded, and only then they would focus on the result and not on how the operation had been carried out.

He would be an instrument in the mission but not acknowledged for the success of the operation. If the mission failed, they would deny involvement. They were purposely detached from any reporting to ensure there would be no consequence to the Administration of the Government of the United States of America. Quite likely it was a 'lose/lose situation' for him and the team.

Was he capable of carrying out a mission that could not yield the support of the CIA, the Army, or the Administration, regardless of success or failure? Essentially, the question became: *Could he conduct his own war in Vietnam?* During the next hour, he focused on this question.

Gazing out the window of his room, at the intersection below him, his thought process was interrupted by a commotion on the edge of the curb across the road. In his blank stare at the street, he witnessed a taxicab hit a young woman who had been jogging across the intersection. The woman had been thrown to the ground as the cab drove over her lower body. A group already gathered around the injured, and probably dead, woman. The taxi driver kneeled beside the downed woman, yelling and waving his arms at the growing crowd of people. The effect of hitting the woman's body unhinged the driver. He was being encircled by a growing mob of concerned citizens. This was not going to turn out well for the driver.

Hell, war was everywhere, thought Henry. *What difference did it make if he fought it here or over in Vietnam?*

* * *

At 1300 hours, Colonel Henry, showered, shaved and dressed in a clean, pressed shirt, let Dickson and Simpson into the room. Simpson held a wide leather case in his left hand.

"Colonel, after reviewing the document, do you have any questions?" Simpson asked.

"Yes, I do. Oh Christ, I can't remember who is who? Which one are you?"

"Simpson."

"Ah, yes, okay Simpson, now how exactly do I go about performing a mission in Vietnam with no reporting and no organized command structure? Without recognized authority, how do I work with the team, acquire assets, and do whatever I am supposed to do. Who is going to source my operational requirements?"

"Fair enough, but again do you accept the mission, and then we will get into the details and address your questions?"

"Okay, Simpson, I'll do it. Now how do I do it?"

Once Henry accepted the mission, Dickson took over. "Very well, Colonel, yes, this might appear confusing, but it will work well for you. We have brought together you and a unique chief from our special operations department. Chief Baxter will break down these hurdles and facilitate the operation. He is somewhat of a legend in our Agency.

"He's fought in two wars. He knows how to get things done, on paper or in the field; he's a real CIA man. In addition, about reporting and your authority, after this meeting, you will not meet with us, or anyone else from the Agency, other than Chief Baxter. You know your mission. You will receive the necessary resources to do your work, but you will do this mission on your own under the authority of Operation Quiet Thunder. Quiet Thunder is a Top Secret operation."

Simpson took over, "You will be meeting Baxter soon. However, let's review the assets we will provide to you."

Simpson opened the thick briefcase and set the thick case on the desk. He handed Henry a two-page document from the case. "Here are the details of Quiet Thunder. The objective is very clear; you are to deposit a *mechanical device* at a location in Vietnam. Then you and your team will return to the United States."

"A mechanical device?"

"Yes, Colonel, a new device that has been developed to encourage a successful end to this conflict in Vietnam."

"Agent Dickson, can you be more specific about this 'mechanical device'? Is it a new type of bomb or is it a machine?"

"You will soon learn those details. All you need to know now is you have a package to deliver. Think of yourself as a person delivering freight, a *Roadman*." Agent Dickson smirked as he came up with the name on the spot.

Henry felt a cold chill in his spine as he said, "Am I clear on this, the objective of Operation Quiet Thunder is to drop a nuclear bomb in Vietnam."

"No, Colonel, your mission is deposit a mechanical device on the ground, leave Vietnam, and return to your civil duties at the Pentagon. Should this mechanical device be utilized, or not, is not your concern, and nor is it part of Quiet Thunder. Your objective is only to deliver the device."

He lit a cigarette and took two long drags. The thought of being involved in the use of a nuclear bomb in Vietnam sent chills through his body. Yet, by the third drag on his cigarette and the deliberate silence by Dickson and Simpson, his logic returned. The reason he had been selected for this job was because there could be no errors, there could be no mistakes, and the operation had to be completed. To allow any miscalculations in this mission could lead to significant fallout for the President, the CIA and for the entire United States of America.

As he took his third drag, he had formed the answers in his mind. He could not afford to have anyone else do this mission, because failing would certainly yield far worse repercussions for his country than succeeding.

After slowly exhaling the smoke he stated, "Agent Dickson, I will need assets and your man, this Chief Baxter, had better be the best you have."

Agent Dickson's poker face did not even offer a slight smile or sign of emotion. No, in keeping with the non-persona that his mirrored black sunglasses and black suit portrayed, Dickson continued, "Chief Baxter can fill in those details. Rest assured, you will secure all assets required for this operation.

"Let me start you off then. You now have access to a Swiss bank account with one million dollars in it; here is the account number and password. Memorize them both and destroy this document. In this package is $600,000 in $10,000 bearer bonds," he said as he pulled out a brown paper envelope containing the bonds. "Finally, you also have $500,000 in non-sequential numbered one hundred dollar bills. You will take this money to fund Operation Quiet Thunder—it is not traceable. I do believe these funds will help you overcome any barriers you might encounter during your execution of this mission," Dickson conceded with a painful smile.

Henry added up the funds, as he looked at them spread onto the bed cover. "Why would I need $2.1 million dollars to perform this task?" still completely shocked by the amount of money given to him for this operation.

"Well, Colonel, you do not directly have the backing of assets you are used to relying on from Uncle Sam. You will need to buy or hire them. Chief Baxter can get through many of the hurdles, but at the end of the day, in the corrupt world of Vietnam, money talks. Operation Quiet Thunder will not be handicapped in any way by a lack of assets."

That comment confirmed that Dickson had never been to Vietnam, nor fought in the war. Corruption was very low on the list of how the war was being fought on the ground. Maybe that was the perception in the offices of Langley, but in Vietnam, the war was a hell of a lot more brutal in the rice paddies stocked with landmines, and treetops hiding snipers, than whatever corruption these men imagined happened in a land as foreign to them as the surface of the moon.

"You will meet our man Chief Baxter in the lobby in 15 minutes. You will not meet us again. Do not try to contact us. We will not be there. We have unlimited resources at our end to dispel anything related to this mission. Colonel, this operation is yours to take forward, in silence."

Agent Simpson had his hand on the door and awaited Dickson to finish his statements to Colonel Henry.

"Good luck, Colonel," Simpson said before he walked out of the room.

Henry lit another Lucky Strike and opened the thick briefcase again. Yes, the money was real. Smoking his cigarette, he unfolded a shirt on his nightstand and took out the small pen camera that he had put inside the shirt. The camera had been pointed at the desk and had been set to take a take a picture every three minutes. In the Pentagon, or the CIA, or even in the jungles of Vietnam, one never knew what resources might help one to see another day.

* * *

Sitting in the brown leather chair in the lobby of the Hilton was a very average-looking man, dressed in pressed navy blue slacks with a white turtleneck poking up from under his blue shell of a blazer. He rose the minute Henry got off the elevator.

"Henry? Pleased to meet you again," Special Operations Chief Robin Baxter said as he extended his hand.

"Again? Have we met before?" Henry replied as he looked at the man and tried to remember if or where he might have met this curiously odd man.

"Ah, yes, we can discuss our history as we head out of here. My car is parked by a fire hydrant so perhaps we should leave before I get towed." Baxter turned and led the way.

He drove a non-descript 1970 Plymouth Valiant, black wall tires, round hubcaps, a government car, which might also serve as a police car, a detective's car, or a government accountant's car. They all used these dependable automobiles.

Henry put his luggage on the back seat and settled down into the passenger's side of the bench seat. Baxter lit up a Marlboro and offered the same to Henry. Henry took the cigarette as Baxter pulled away from the curb.

"I believe we are in a predicament chosen by others. We have been put together to complete this mission. I trust we can make the best of this and succeed in our orders. Earlier, you asked, 'where had we met before'? Well, we have met twice. Once was in late March in 1970 at Yorkton Base in Vietnam. You had taken a shot in the leg and one in your ribs. Your surviving private had much to say about you. He praised your rescue of our POWs on your way back to base. Those POWs were my men. You saved our country a significant amount of intelligence by bringing those men back."

"I know you. You were the 'the Suit' who led the debriefing. You did that to make sure your men hadn't told me anything."

"Yes, you are correct; I did wear a nice suit in those days. You made a favorable impression on me, and of course on my men. It is important to remember the good ones you meet in life. As for the second time, well, quite innocently we both attended General Whiteman's Christmas Party. I spoke with the general about your career. He was supportive of you and your accomplishments, and didn't mention any black marks on your career. Now that too is a rarity for those of us who have done our time by serving our country. Therefore, based on his comments, you became recognized for a second time."

"I see, so you're the one that I should punch in the face for getting me involved in this new operation."

Baxter took his last drag on his smoke before flicking the butt out his window onto the street. "There are days that I would like to do the same as you. We are puppets of a much larger master and but I'll be damned if I can narrow it down to what puppet master is pulling these strings. Instead, I look ahead and do what needs to be done. That,

Henry, is our common bond, regardless of how we got here. We are now on our way to complete an assignment for the benefit of our country and that is all we can look forward to from now on."

Baxter was right. How they got there did not matter now, the operation demanded their absolute focus.

"Okay Baxter, what do you bring to this operation? They gave me some assets, but what resources have you accumulated?"

"I will get to all of that soon. We have a plane ride to catch first. Shall we continue the reunion on the plane?"

Baxter wheeled the Plymouth into a parking stall at the far end of the Austin Airport, the private plane section of the airport. Airplanes arrived and departed unattended, and uninspected.

Henry followed Baxter through the gate, which he opened with a key, to a white Cessna 414. The co-pilot waited at the entry ramp. Henry carried his bag and case into the plane with him, after declining the advice of the pilot to stow them in the luggage compartment. The co-pilot closed the outside door after Baxter and Henry sat in the plush, white leather seats in the second row. The plane had six seats, with the first row facing to the back and the second row facing the front. This arrangement provided more legroom and space for the passengers when only two of those four seats were being used. Henry set his luggage on the third row of seats. The plane received immediate clearance and they were airborne within minutes.

Baxter, always on the watch for matters out of the ordinary, advised Henry that perhaps they should have a drink and a sandwich on the flight. There would be time to go over the details on the ground, where they could avoid any ears that might be listening.

Henry was starting to realize how this sharp veteran of two wars, now carrying the respected rank of Chief of some form of Special Operations, was so acutely aware of his environment. He was beginning to understand why Baxter was selected for this mission, yet he was still not certain why he had been chosen to work on this assignment.

After Henry had consumed two scotches, a tuna fish sandwich, and had a quick read of the most recent issue of Time magazine, the Cessna made its approach into the North Las Vegas Airport, six miles north of McCarran International Airport. The airport provided private planes with quick landings and departures, while passengers avoided the usual time lost in larger airports.

A black car pulled up to the front door and Baxter and Henry got in the back seat of the Lincoln Continental. They still had not said much to each other, at least about their assignment.

During the flight, Baxter learned that Henry favored the 49'ers and the Los Angeles Kings for sports teams. Henry learned that Baxter liked European Football, but conceded the fact that Green Bay was okay for an American Football team. He did not follow hockey.

The drive took them an hour northwest of Las Vegas. At 2230 hours, they arrived at the security gate of Area 51. Baxter led the way through the security building and produced documents for himself and Henry. Henry received a security tag for Baxter's paperwork. After finger printing, they departed in a nondescript beige Suburban, with two monster-sized MPs as their escorts.

The MPs dropped off Baxter and Henry at a new modular home with a small module attached to serve as their office. The five-bedroom bungalow still smelled of fresh paint. This would be the new home and office for Baxter and Henry and their men while they trained for Operation Quiet Thunder.

Chapter 18

Area 51, Nevada, USA
September 30, 1971

Colonel Henry shaved in his private bathroom as the scent of cooking eggs and sausages wafted through the large bungalow. His stomach started to growl as he realized he hadn't eaten much yesterday, his day of indoctrination into this new role.

On the corner of the oak table in the dining room, four newspapers had been set out: The Washington Post, The New York Times, The Los Angeles Times, and The Wall Street Journal.

Henry accepted the breakfast plate as Baxter offered it to him.

"We'll have our meals delivered here from the base's mess hall, but I have some basics here, in addition to C-rations. I have been informed our lunch will be here on time. We won't miss any more meals."

"C-rations. Another thing I thought I was rid of when I got back to the States. Sure I'll take mess hall food any day over C-rations."

"No disagreement here, I don't think I've ever eaten another fruitcake since I ate my first one out of those damned tins."

"Henry, before we get into today's planning, I have some paperwork for you to sign to take your leave from the Pentagon and accept the temporary post with the Agency. I also have an agreement for you to return to the Department of Defense after our work is done here, and your pension and benefits will continue to accrue, regardless. This last blue form is to accept your new pay—double your old rate—since you are again in the field. I did that one myself."

"Thanks Baxter," Henry said as he signed the documents and returned them. CIA Chief Baxter knew his way around the bureaucratic paperwork required of the government.

After breakfast, work began in earnest. They reviewed the operational plan that had been fed to Baxter in pieces and he had filled in the holes in the plan. No one would know the details of Operation Quiet Thunder, other than this team.

The mechanical device consisted of two components. One was the detonator; the other was the chassis assembly—the guts of the device. For the security of the operation, and to prevent anything useful from falling into the enemy's hands, the two parts were to work their way to the mating site separately to be assembled just prior to depositing the armed device at its destination.

As Baxter went on with the logistics and details of the mission, Henry wondered what purpose he served; Baxter had mapped out the whole plan.

Henry soon had the answer. He was to oversee the logistics of the operation, meaning he would be on the ground for the operation. Baxter's focus would be to tie in with other operations, borrowing their firepower, and most importantly, to ensure the Vietnamese, Russian and Chinese intelligence organizations did not learn of any part of the operation. The team would not see much of Baxter after they left Nevada, but he would be around and ready to return as the mission required.

By lunchtime, Baxter had taken Henry through the entire plan for Quiet Thunder.

Their designated private arrived with the pair's lunch— cheeseburgers and French Fries, which they ate on the small deck under the sunshade.

"Don't you miss this great food," Henry said to Baxter as he guzzled his Coors to wash down the greasy bite of his burger.

"No, I must admit, mess hall food is not one of the things I miss."

After lunch, Baxter produced the files of the men he had selected for this operation. As a secret mission, he had to choose people he trusted to maintain confidentiality for a lifetime.

Baxter had worked with the men since February. The three were capable men with a broad range of skills. He had no doubt in their capacity to complete the assignment. Two of his three were considered to be in the top quartile of helicopter pilots. The third man was a proven leader amongst the men of the Special Forces. Each had been in country for three years. Baxter knew these men's conviction to their country would also lead them to carry the burden of the secrecy of this operation to their own graves.

The first file immediately confirmed Baxter had good judgment and had chosen well. Henry was looking at a picture of Captain Larry Junior Johnson, the pilot who had rescued him not so long ago. Reading further into the file, he learned that this man not only flew helicopters exceptionally, but the man was a one man wrecking crew. Intrigued by the background and skill set of the pilot, he wrote out his own summary of the man in his coiled notebook. Henry would have picked this man himself.

The next file showed the picture of Captain James Robert Schmidt, another highly educated member and a helicopter pilot of notoriety in Vietnam. Henry's notes on him filled the next page in his notebook.

Another good pick by Baxter.

The third file on Major Gerald Field was thicker than the first two. Major Field was the nucleus of this operation. He knew the ground, he knew the assets in the area, and he could easily learn how to work the damn mechanical device they had to deliver. Henry used two pages in his notebook to describe this man's talents and abilities of which one did not normally associate with such an academic man. He underlined one of Baxter's handwritten notes as he copied it into his notebook, 'he can command Johnson; together those two are a force to be reckoned with. You want these two on your side'. Major Field was proof that you can take the boy off the farm but you can't take the country out of a farm boy.

Common to all three of these men was the fact they were enlisted men who accepted commissioned ranks. Not one of them would have been drafted. Yet each of them had an unusual set of personal choices for entering the war in 1968, especially since they were in the United

States witnessing the protests against the Vietnam War. All three of them graduated as Special Forces in August of 1969. Baxter recruited them in 1971 from the Forces, after which they thrived as operatives for Baxter. They were decorated men; that is, decorated with some of the highest honors a service man would ever obtain. Each of them had extended their tours of duty and apparently were staying on for the duration. Baxter might have just found the right men to pull off this mission.

* * *

Henry's chance to confirm Baxter's assessment came the next day.

At 1000 hours, a beige GMC Suburban arrived at the house. A muscular dark-haired man, with a developing full beard, climbed out of the driver's rear passenger door. He was followed by an older man, clean-shaven, and slightly shorter than the corporal. Around from the passenger's rear side walked a man with a determined stride, head looking straight at Baxter and Henry. All three wore new green fatigues.

Carrying their bags slung over their shoulder, they walked up to Baxter, who was sitting on a chair on the covered deck. He rose to greet them.

"Good to see you, men. Colonel Henry, this is Captain Johnson, Captain Schmidt, and Major Field."

They raised their right arm to salute, which Henry returned and dismissed the salute.

Colonel Henry then put out his hand to shake the hand of each of the men. "Men, you have now given the last salute of this operation. We are part of a team, each with our own role. Military protocol does not fit into this assignment."

Baxter watched for reactions to Henry's stand down of military protocol. Field's slight smile confirmed what he needed to see.

The men had just finished two weeks of R&R, most of which had been in Bangkok, Thailand. Schmidt cut short his time to visit his family in San Francisco. Field and Johnson arrived in Las Vegas two days ago.

It was time to return to the order of the military once again. The new beards and long hair were cleaned up as each of them set up in their own room, returning their minds to the secret world of another mission.

During a dinner of meatloaf and Coors beer, formalities ended. The beers made the conversation lighter and took them on an evening vacation away from their preparations that would begin in earnest tomorrow.

Schmidt introduced Henry and Baxter to the working names of the three of them. He was known as Shelby, Major Field was called Farmer, and Captain Johnson was, and would always be, Larry. Shelby warned Henry that it was only a matter of time before he earned his own nickname.

The first week of training focused on the detailed review of the land of south central Laos. They knew they would start from the Royal Thai Air Force Base, only 9 miles outside of Nakhon Phanom, on the west side of the Mekong. Where, or how far east, they would travel had not been finalized by Baxter. The terrain started as flatland, but changed as you travelled east across central Laos to the mountains of the Annamite Cordillera, which extended into Vietnam. The area south of the 19th parallel and east to the South China Sea was a large tract of some of the most inhospitable terrain any American soldier could encounter in late 1971.

The ill-fated Lam Son 719 action on the VC and NVA on the Ho Chi Minh Trail east of Tcephone, Laos, had been a huge set back to the South Vietnamese forces, and the diminishing US air support forces this past spring. The action lit a new fire inside the NVA working the supply trails, collectively called the Ho Chi Minh trail. The assault had been like stomping on an anthill. More angry enemy soldiers poured into Laos to reinforce the stronghold they had earned. East of Highway 23, in Laos, became an ever-adjusting landscape with supply routes shifting as fast as the American airstrikes tried in vain to sever the active supply trails.

The fluid motion of the NVA troops in Laos made the logistics of the operation more difficult, and dramatically increased the risk of failure and exposure of the operation. Therefore, Baxter had not determined the final delivery point yet.

Farmer and Larry knew the land. They lead the crew over the entire area, based on their recent reconnaissance maps, and satellite photographs, ground proven by them this year. The team worked through the information until they learned the ground conditions as well as anyone could from 13,000 miles away.

By the second week, Henry was formally accepted as part of the team when Shelby gave him the nickname Harley—after Henry's disclosure of his collection of motorcycles back home. They were now a field functional four-man team.

Baxter led the discussion on the device they would be delivering. The mechanical device was a new type of static fission bomb developed at this military base, Area 51. The bomb was one of a new family of efficient, but compact, bombs identified as *Candles*.

Candles used the combination of nuclear warhead technology, for weight reduction, and stationary fission bomb technology for effectiveness. Candle plutonium bombs were designed to be placed at a target location and then later detonated remotely. This afforded the bombs to be smaller and lighter since they did not have the rigid body structure required by other implosion-based nuclear bombs—bombs which were armed and had to remain stable through transport. The Candle was instead created from two separate components that were only brought together at the detonation site.

The Candle's plutonium bomb body was the *Chassis*. The detonator for the bomb was the second component and it was called *the Engine*. When the Engine mated into the Chassis, and the arming code was entered, the live Candle bomb could be detonated by a radio signal sent from a location far out of harm's way of the resulting blast and the subsequent radioactive release.

For Operation Quiet Thunder, Farmer and Larry became Alpha Team, responsible for the safe handling of the Engine. Bravo team, Shelby and Harley, were responsible for transporting the Chassis.

Farmer would be responsible for assembling the Engine into the Chassis and arming the weapon so it could be set at the target location.

The destination still had not been confirmed. This uncertainty did play on the member's minds. Baxter wanted to confirm the delivery site, but his associates overseas were feeding him information that there was too much noise around the DMZ (Demilitarized Zone) in Vietnam and even more in the Laotian side in the Annamite mountains. He would not be able to finalize the delivery location until their field reconnaissance confirmed the appropriate site at a date much closer to the delivery date. This uncertainty rode heavy on his shoulders. He made the call to offer up one potential site, to direct their focus on orchestrating the operation, even if the theatre did have to change.

His preferred destination was the beach at Mui Lay, north of the DMZ, and in North Vietnam. Farmer and Larry would place the loaded bomb inside the hull of the beached destroyer, the USS Jackson, still resting on the sandy beachhead.

He reminded them that after the placement, some commander, on some ship far away from the beachhead, would detonate it, when it was time. That matter was not the concern of Quiet Thunder's deliverymen.

However, Baxter, and his men, knew that the success of detonating a nuclear bomb in North Vietnam was like sending a warning shot over the bow of a destroyer. Its intention was to send the message that the President of the United State of America was prepared to end this war in a milder form of what had been used in Hiroshima and Nagasaki. The message would be clear to the Chinese and the Russians that the United States of America was willing to risk the use of nuclear weapons to end this conflict. The President accepted the risk of a nuclear retaliatory strike, but realized the likeliness of such was minimal. Instead, what affected him personally was the realization that the international press, and sovereign government condemnation, would do more damage to his political memoirs than the nuclear explosion would. However, if he was to save his men still in Vietnam, his advisors had convinced him he must take this risk.

Once the team knew the destination, they had an actual piece of real estate to focus on. When the two helicopters arrived on site during the second week, the mission really felt closer to fruition and operational field training began.

The Hueys were painted in green and black. They were clean of any identification, save that a number 1 or 2 had been painted on the pilot's door. Baxter's invisible workers had already modified the machines. Each of the helicopters had over 500 hours on them, confirming the machine had been tested and used sufficiently to confirm its airworthiness. They had the latest night vision technology and a new form of Kevlar material had been affixed to the metal panels to blunt the damage from shrapnel or bullets. The machines weren't bulletproof, but they were an improvement over other Hueys.

Strapped inside were two M-60 door machine guns that could be mounted on doorposts if needed. Four M-16s were strapped to the sides of the helicopter's cargo bay. Each had a M158 seven-tube rocket launcher and M134 7.62mm machine guns in a fixed mount position on both sides of the machine. Either the pilot or co-pilot could fire each of the systems.

An aluminum lift table had been installed into the cargo bay. The design of the lift allowed the impotent Chassis to be secured to the lift and to be raised, by a hand crank, into the cargo area. The lift was designed to fold into itself, such that the bomb remained secure on the platform inside the cargo hold. The lift also enabled the armed Candle bomb to be unloaded just as effortlessly and set outside the helicopter at its destination.

While Larry and Shelby worked on their helicopters in the morning, Farmer and Harley developed the troubleshooting procedures, and the testing procedure, for the Engine. Their test unit, without the charge, became the model for the development of the protocol affectionately known as *How to Light a Candle*.

The Engine was a perfectly polished silver cylinder, with a small keypad, an LED display, and a row of toggle switches on the top, with a set of protruding titanium cogs at the bottom. The electronics had redundant circuits and could be bench tested without firing. The Engine measured twelve inches in diameter and thirty-six inches in length. The Kevlar-coated steel carrying case for the detonator resembled a black golf bag.

An inert Chassis, the bomb body, had also been delivered to the site. Weighing in at 220 pounds, the delivery driver and two of the crew easily carried the crate into the workshop.

The unification assembly was straightforward, but the mating process had to be sequenced for the security lock to engage to complete the assembly procedure. Otherwise, the assembly was designed to be executed in field conditions.

Farmer developed a system testing technique to test the redundant circuitry of the detonator prior to installing it into the body. Working with Farmer, Harley developed the unpacking and base installation technique for the body and ultimately for the assembled and armed device, including working with Shelby on modifying the secure points for stability while in transport.

The delivery plan had not changed. Alpha team, Farmer and Larry, would transport the assembled Candle to the destination. Bravo Team, Shelby and Harley, would fly as the gunship for protection. At the landing on the deck of the USS Jackson, Farmer would use the lift to lower their package, in its crate, onto the deck of the beached ship. Farmer would then enter the activation code into the keypad, close the crate, and nail it shut. Larry's Huey would short line the device to set it inside the shallow cargo hull of the USS Jackson. The container would appear as normal wasted cargo as it awaited detonation inside the damaged ship's hull in the South China Sea.

At the end of the third week, Baxter ordered a four-day break in the training program. He sprung for them to stay at the Dunes Hotel and Casino in Vegas. On the second night, Shelby won big at roulette. They celebrated by going out for a steak and lobster dinner, and then caught Elvis playing at the Royal Casino, all on Uncle Sam's dime.

Baxter disappeared after the show, the rest of them stayed in the bar to make sure they got their money's worth. About midnight, Baxter walked in with the blonde and the brunette and became forever after that, the man known as Birdman.

By the end of the fourth day, they had run up a good bill for Uncle Sam, which Harley paid without blinking an eye at the tab. When the limo driver dropped the five of them off at the security checkpoint at Area 51, they wanted to get on with Quiet Thunder.

Birdman and Harley were determined to include as few people as possible in the operation and thereby minimize the risk of a security breach. Additional men involved meant more potential loose lips. They had decided from the start not to include co-pilots, nor extra crew, on this mission. While the decision reduced the size of the team, it introduced another level of risk into Quiet Thunder.

Harley and Farmer were not pilots, but they had logged many hours inside helicopters. In the fourth week of their stay at Area 51, Harley and Farmer began an intensive helicopter flight program, taught by Larry and Shelby. The intent was not to train them to fly helicopters for a living; no instead, they would be able to do what had to be done for this mission. During the next twenty-eight days, they flew in the machines for six hours a day, in three-hour shifts. This aggressive training program taught them the weapon system and the basics that they needed to fire up, take off, take over, and land the machine. By the end of their training period, Shelby and Larry were confident of their new co-pilots ability to keep the helicopters in the mission.

During the ninth week at Area 51, Farmer led the team through the entire protocol for the delivery of the Candle. Every man knew how to unpack, system check, and then insert and lock the Engine into the Chassis. Each member of Operation Quiet Thunder memorized the eight-digit arming code and entry sequence. They all knew how to arm it, and how to repack the complete unit inside the container again and lock in the antennae.

The final stage of the stateside operational training was to bring it all together. They ran practice runs bringing the two machines with their cargo to a rendezvous point, assembling and arming the device and then short lining their practice Candle to deliver it. After the eight complete trial runs, which included switching team members and responsibilities, Harley declared they were ready.

Chapter 19

Winter of 1971 and the return to Indochina

December 15, 1971

During breakfast at the training facility in Nevada, Birdman informed the men that their Hercules was ready to move them to Thailand tomorrow.

Technical problems in Laos delayed their deployment to Nakhon Phanom. Birdman remedied the situation by finding them a place to stay for two weeks of R&R. The wait would give their stomachs a chance to adjust again to the spices in the local cuisine. In the New Year, they could begin their field reconnaissance work.

They were only in Bangkok for two days when Birdman left them. The team had become accustomed to his unexplained departures and surmised he likely had to tackle another technical problem in Laos.

Birdman caught up with the men on December 25, 1971. He was in a somber mood, but worked hard to hide it and celebrate Christmas Day in Bangkok. The next day, he passed along the bad news. Boxing Day marked the beginning of a new air offensive against NVA military targets in Laos. The sky was loaded with F-4s, B-57s, and AC-130s; a myriad of heavy fighter-bombers focused on destroying the SAM (surface to air missile) sites, anti-aircraft artillery sites, and North Vietnamese radar sites. This new war was to be fought up to fifty miles north of the DMZ, but within Laos. They would not be able to run Quiet Thunder in the middle of such crowded airspace, and in the midst of the heavy anti-aircraft artillery fire being thrown at them from the NVA.

Birdman and Harley left for the day and returned in the evening with a brand new plan. Rather than fly through the heart of the NVA strong hold, along route 9, and through the Lao Bao mountain pass, and then risk the significant challenge of crossing the DMZ and dropping of the Candle in North Vietnam's Mui Lay, they would change the destination. Instead of fighting the crowded airspace, they would use it to their advantage. Their new location would be a mountain top in North Vietnam, just southeast of the Ban Raving pass—the most southern North Vietnamese pass used by the NVA to supply the Ho Chi Minh trail in Laos. The new destination would yield an even more dramatic explosion, when the Candle was set off at night from the 4,500-foot high mountain. The light up would be seen by the NVA in both Laos and North Vietnam, maybe even north of Vinh. The message would give a dramatic effect on all those that witnessed it, and the stories of the force of the nuclear bomb would be transferred along the trail to other VC and NVA. This new location was a better detonation site than the original beachhead.

* * *

The protective reaction strikes of the United States Air Force against the North Vietnamese active anti-aircraft targets in Laos and North Vietnam continued for four days. Over a thousand strikes had been made by the air force on NVA targets. Then the limited duration strikes stopped. The calm air space on New Year's Eve marked the start of the rebuilding process by the persistent NVA.

The Roadman had to regroup and modify their operational plans for the new delivery location. On the second day of 1972, they moved to the Air America section of the Nakhon Phanom Royal Thai Air Force Base in Nakhon Phanom, Thailand, a fifteen-minute flight west of Thakhek, Laos. The sizable base was the largest northeastern base in Thailand and proved to be strategically important for all forms of American Air Force operations in the Secret War in Laos. The numerous military and Air America flights in and out of the site meant two additional Hueys would not be noticed.

The Roadmen took over two hangars at the end of the field with two empty buildings separating them from the regulars. However Birdman did these things, he did them with absolute perfection. Their gear had already been loaded into the furthest hangar. Two identical back up helicopters were stored in the second hangar. The back-up helicopters had also been equipped with the cargo lifts. Birdman's security force made an impermeable barrier to their location.

Their plan called for the Candle to be moved over two days. On the first day, each team would source its component and fly to their secure location in Laos for the first night. On the second day, they would rendezvous at a secure landing site, near Vietnam, prepare their helicopters for the final leg, and fly off to deliver the loaded Candle.

Since the destination had changed, the tentative landing sites selected back in Nevada were no longer relevant. Farmer and Larry combed over new maps and identified new landing sites—a preferred and alternative site for each team, and a main and a backup rendezvous location.

By the next night, Birdman had photographs of all proposed landing sites. His anonymous miracle workers, this time Air America pilots, visited each location during the day and then prepared a report on the condition of the landing site. The team agreed that all the sites were viable. The confirmation was all Birdman needed. He left to negotiate with the Royal Lao Army, and discharge a team of men to clear the landing sites, transfer fuel to the locations, and move in Hmong units to keep them secure prior to, and during, their use.

The surge in air force activity, against the response by the NVA in Laos, dramatically increased the risk for this mission. There was a lot of big metal flying around now, which meant the small Huey's would need to fly within a formation if they expected to get through to their landing site, and then deposit the armed Candle. It proved to be too much of a risk for the team to run naked practice runs to the landing sites. Instead, they would learn the flight routes from maps and aerial photographs and observe their landing sites from the comfort of an American Air Force airplane.

Three days later, Alpha team was looking through binoculars at their two landing sites, 5,000 feet below their seats in an AC-130 gunship. This was not a preferred way to learn the lay of the land, or the positions of the NVA. However, Charlie continued to be quick on the move and tomorrow the enemy would be in a different location, armed, and ready to fire at any American or South Vietnamese aircraft flying overhead. Therefore, the real run would be the only run. There would be no practice drill for this game.

While waiting for Birdman to make the call on the date for the operation to commence, they fought off boredom in the hanger by reviewing the latest photographs and reading the bombing reports following each day of protective reaction strikes. They got into the air at least twice a week on an Air Force airplane, but the days of action were sporadic. Too many Charlies had infiltrated the Royal Lao Army and the South Vietnamese Army. The decision to fly, or not, was now being made on a daily basis, to minimize the readiness of North Vietnamese forces and their SAM installations.

Waiting was demoralizing for a team ready to go. They could only review their equipment and the flight plans so many times before they started to lose interest in the repetitive process. This was dangerous to their readiness, but they knew Birdman and Harley would have to return soon with orders to proceed.

* * *

Harley and Birdman kept busy during the month of January working out of their offices in an Air America building at the other end of the Nakhon Phanom Air Base (NKP).

On their second day, an unexpected contact arrived at Birdman's temporary office. After an abbreviated update, Birdman left NKP in an Air America Bell 205 helicopter. He did not tell Harley his destination.

Harley spent the first two weeks working with Birdman's friends to coordinate protective reaction strikes that the Huey's could slip into for their two days. Birdman must have called in some huge debts to open up these doors for Harley. Similarly, Birdman knew where Harley had to go to grease the palms of the Thai and Laotian commands to look the other way while the plans were made, within their jurisdiction, without their involvement. He finally secured the timetable, but only he, and the air commander of the US Air Force in Nakhon Phanom, knew the two consecutive dates.

Harley also opened his briefcase for another of Birdman's friends who took charge of orchestrating the security of the landing sites by the Hmong fighters. The Hmong were to remain out of sight as they guarded the ground perimeter of each landing site. Birdman had recommended the Hmong units as utility guards, since they were the least likely to leak intelligence information to their historic enemy, the North Vietnamese.

On January 30, 1972, Harley returned by himself and briefed the team on the new developments. Birdman had spent the last two weeks working through documents that had been captured with a VC messenger on one of the trails. As expected, the NVA and VC were gathering significant forces on the trail in Laos and North of the DMZ for what was anticipated to be a run at the south before the summer. However, the rate of movement of men, machinery, and the collection of aircraft was surging. He expected an offensive would come sooner, rather than later.

Two days later, Birdman arrived at the hangar on the Thailand base. He confirmed that the mission was a go for tomorrow, February 2, 1972. Birdman announced the green light. "May we be successful in what we have been asked to do by our country and may God help decide an end to this war," he said after his salute to the men.

Harley moved on to unveil the final details of Operation Quiet Thunder.

Alpha team's Engine package would be delivered by an ambulance to this hangar at 1400 hours of tomorrow.

Also at 1400 hours, Bravo Team, Shelby and Harley, were to pick up their Chassis package at the rear of the Hospital heliport on the base, from the back of a disabled ambulance.

Although most of the protective reaction missions had been flown at night, for the next two days, daytime flights were authorized to cover the Hueys on their mission. They anticipated that excessive bombings during the preceding nights should draw the NVA away from being prepared for afternoon flights too, and for those two days, the element of surprise should favor the Hueys.

Harley arranged for two separate runs to be made by an AC-130 gunship, covered by an F-4 Phantom and a B-57, during the afternoon, as support for each Huey in Operation Quiet Thunder. The big boys would clear the flight path for the helicopters. One of the B-57's targets was the top of the mountain in North Vietnam, to create the landing site for the placement of the armed Candle bomb on the second day. A large squad of Hmong guerillas was responsible for securing the mountain between the creation of the destination and the placement of the armed Candle. Inquisitive VC would be dealt with by these men. No one asked about what would happen to the squad when the Candle was set off.

All the training and planning would culminate in placing the armed Candle bomb by 1800 hours on February 3, 1972.

Birdman also gave the men new radios with a scrambled frequency for their use only. Birdman would monitor the channel at all times and be ready to coordinate whatever had to be done. The enemy, or the civilized world, would not know about Quiet Thunder.

* * *

At 1200 hours on February 2, the four shook hands and made their pledge to meet again in Bangkok after this mission. Harley said he'd buy the drinks, knowing they'd hold him to his promise. Harley handed each team member an envelope containing $5,000 to use as needed, to do what had to be done.

Larry checked over the Huey on the landing pad as he waited for the delivery of the Engine. Farmer did the final check of the hangar to ensure it was clean. Birdman's men would do the same after they left. No traces of the Roadmen would be left in this hangar.

Precisely at 1400 hours, an ambulance drove up the helicopter. Two paramedics set a stretcher inside the helicopter, resting the stretcher in the cradle of the lift. The men left almost as fast as they had arrived. Anyone observing could only imagine a body on the stretcher inside the waiting helicopter.

At 5,000 feet, they crossed the Mekong River flying south of Thakhek, Laos, still above the flatlands and west of the VC controlled areas. Staying south of Highway 12, flying at 7,000 feet, a Phantom F-4 fighter flew past them at such a speed it created the illusion that they were flying backwards. Soon after the ground below began exploding in fire as the F-4's bombs ripped up the earth below.

After entering the lowland hills that the F-4 had just bombed, an AC-130 gunship passed below them. The airplane did a 90-degree pivot and let off its large 105 mm cannon at the reflection of sunlight on metal that had flashed at them through the thin forest below. Whatever it had been, the explosion sent off a tall column of fire followed by dense black smoke.

Larry had also seen the flash of sunlight reflection from the ground. He reacted by turning 90 degrees, and then back 45 degrees, to make a zigzag in his flight path. Larry never took anything for granted. Farmer monitored the hillsides looking for any more flashes of metal or other unusual signals from below.

The gunship had done its job well by peppering the earth below the flight line with its 20mm and 40mm cannons. Not a single shot came near Larry and Farmer, resulting in successful flight to their overnight landing site, *Cowboy 1*.

Cowboy 1 was Alpha team's name for the recovered landing site, formerly used by Air America. Abandoned a few years ago, an old metal hangar remained. From the outside, the building looked like a weathered, rusting hulk. Inside, Birdman's men had cleaned the hangar, brought in fresh Jet B fuel for the helicopter, and stocked it with new C-rations and fresh water. The team would overnight at Cowboy 1 and then meet up with Shelby and Harley tomorrow at landing site Union 1.

* * *

At the Nakhon Phanom base hospital, the Chassis package waited for Bravo team in the disabled ambulance at the last helipad. Harley brought the cargo bay lift to waist level to enable them to load on the crated Chassis body of the Candle.

On time, the second ambulance arrived and parked beside them. Two corporals got out.

With a quick salute to Harley and Shelby, they opened up the door and pulled out a metal roller frame, just as a stretcher would roll out on its own wheels. On this roller frame was the wrapped wooden crate. Red crosses had been painted on the wood, suggesting the crate contained medical supplies.

Grabbing the front end of the frame, the corporals pulled the crate out so Shelby and Harley could lift the rear of it. The crate was set onto the lift and secured, exactly as practiced. Harley cranked the lift while he watched it collapse back into the cargo bay of the helicopter. *Quite an ingenious design*, he thought.

After the crate had been secured, Harley swung under the tail section of the helicopter and thereafter yelled, "Sniper".

All four of them crouched down low to hide behind the chopper and the two ambulances. Blood flowed out of Harley's right arm. The closest corporal took off his belt and pulled it tight around Harley's arm.

The sniper's single shot changed their circumstances.

For a moment, everything seemed to move in slow motion as Shelby sought a solution. He had to get his machine into the air. Shelby pulled out his .38 automatic pistol from his shoulder holster and pointed the gun at the head of the closest corporal.

"Who sent you here?"

"I don't know the man's name. He was your height, brown hair, older than you."

The young soldier started shaking from the fear of having the loaded gun pointed at his head. Shelby would receive the truth from this soldier.

"He told us that you would question us. We were to tell you that 'Birdman says hello'. I don't know what the hell that means."

"It means you are getting inside and coming with us. Now help my man inside and let's get out of here."

The two soldiers had to have been Birdman's men since they did as they were told. Shelby lit up the Huey, ignoring the normal check procedures. At forty feet, he spun the helicopter, clearing the ambulances. Believing the sniper had to be in the trees away from the hospital, he flew southeast.

He lifted the lock on the triggers for the side-mounted M-60s and the rockets. He settled at 7,500 feet, staying south of Highway 12 as he flew over the panhandle below. When he glimpsed over at Harley, Harley clenched his teeth but nodded back at Shelby.

One of the corporals prepared a dressing to cover the bullet hole in Harley's arm. Harley arm was useless so Shelby's two new recruits would need to stay on to do the heavy lifting of the Chassis package. Right now Shelby could not think past the rendezvous destination. He'd deal with collateral damage as it happened.

It soon became apparent that the first wave of the bombing and fighter flight had been through. Columns of smoke rose from the ground below. As the landform changed to low hills and forest, a Phantom F-4 passed high above him, nearing Mach 1 in speed. The fighter held off until he got into the higher mountains ahead and then set down a line of fire on the forest below. The AC-130 gunship following him made a northeast run, paralleling a widened section of the Ho Chi Minh trail. A wrath of 20mm and 40mm shells hit the trail. Explosions confirmed that something had been hiding in the trees until the gunship had found the asset.

Shelby turned north. His landing site was ten miles ahead. Tracer shots from the ground flew past the front of his helicopter followed by a mortar explosion close enough to rock the helicopter. He barked out to the corporals to look for the source, but they were too late. The gunship had made a 180-degree sharp turn and fired its 105mm cannon into the mortar location. A direct hit caused the stockpile of mortars to explode, sending a thick black cloud of smoke into the air behind Shelby.

In five minutes, they circled their overnight landing site carved out of the forest on a bench on the mountainside. The site extended well into the jungle foliage. C-rations, fuel, and camo nets awaited their arrival.

The landing sequence was to fly low over and wait for a Hmong tribesman to flare orange smoke. No orange smoke came from the first pass. No orange smoke showed after the second pass. Shelby abandoned the site and flew west to the backup overnight site, one mountain to the north.

The second site, *Redneck 2*, had also been carved into the forest. Redneck 2 was approached over a dry riverbed leading into the cleared landing area, allowing the Huey to park under the cover of the tall mangrove trees. Hmong tribesmen were supposed to be in the forest around the site for security of the site, but Shelby didn't see any of them on his approach. Instead, an Air American Cayuse helicopter was parked at the landing site. The AA helicopter was supposed to have checked the location in the morning, but he should have left hours ago.

Shelby did a fly over Redneck 2, keeping his index finger ready on the M-60 machine gun's pilot trigger.

On the fly past, the Air America pilot, from the back of his chopper, waved for Shelby to land beside him. This felt like a bad deal, but he had to park this helicopter soon. He had to get it out of the sky, since the morning mist had burned off hours before, revealing a clear and sunny day, and thereby making his chopper more vulnerable.

He edged the Huey closer into the mangrove trees, to the left of the Cayuse helicopter. Shelby found there was enough room to set down, but it was a tight fit.

"Keep your guns ready, men, I don't know what the fuck we have here," he barked. Harley was still awake, but barely, he had lost a lot of blood. He would have to hang on for them to get to the rendezvous point tomorrow. *Keep him alive another two days,* Shelby prayed to himself.

Keeping the engine running, Shelby had one of the hijacked corporals go and ask the Air America pilot why he was still there. Seconds seemed like minutes. Shelby stayed armed, on alert, and ready to lift off if anything changed.

"He says his chopper won't start and figures it's some wiring problem. He asked if you know anything about the battery and charger on these things. It's a new machine for him."

Of course, he needs my help, why not? Why not today, of all days? Lord, what kind of tests are you putting me through today? Shelby thought to himself as he shut down his machine.

"Hey, Shelby, what the hell, you're rescuing my sorry ass again," said the Air America pilot.

"I should have guessed, only Billy Bob would leave his Swiss Army knife at home when flying a new one. Let's get you out of here."

"Sure thing, Shelby."

Shelby lifted the battery panel and twisted on the battery cable. The cable broke away from the electrical safety switch. "Some green boy work on this rig?" he said. "Get me my kit."

Billy Bob ran past the two corporals, standing watch with their M-16s ready. He ran past them again as he returned with a leather case of tools from the small cargo bay on the port side of Shelby's Huey.

Shelby stripped the coating of the copper wire with his knife and bolted on a new connector from his kit. The fix would probably outlast the predictable short life of the machine. "Hit her," he said to Billy Bob.

Billy Bob held the starter button as the whine of the turbine took over. He waved Shelby over as he ran the jet engine up in RPMs. He passed over a headset to Shelby explaining through it that his boy Quan went to find help, since they were told not to use the radio today. Quan would see him leave and return to the site. He asked Shelby to keep the boy with him overnight and tomorrow at 1400 hours, he'd be back to get him.

"This is exactly what I need today, to babysit one of your kids. Okay, man, then you're taking one back for me, too. This colonel is the best. Get him to NKP hospital, stay with him, and do not let him out of your sight until a man named Birdman tells you can leave him. Watch him and protect him."

The two corporals loaded Harley into the rear seat of the Air America Cayuse.

"Got it man and be safe," Billy Bob said as Shelby handed him back the headset.

Billy Bob backed his Cayuse out onto the dry riverbed, and hit her hard to pull out up above the canopy of the forest as he left. Ten minutes later, a corporal met the young Vietnamese man named Quan.

"Mr. American, I okay. I with Billy Bob."

"Let him in," Shelby barked.

Quan came to Shelby.

"Billy Bob will be back tomorrow at 1400 to get you. Help me refuel. Do you know how to run the pump?"

"Yes, sir. I put gas in helicopter," the young Laotian replied.

Shelby tied down the rotors and checked his load. It remained secure. Corporals one and two rolled out the camouflage drape over the helicopter, it wasn't important to Shelby to learn their names; he'd be finished with them tomorrow.

He grabbed an M-16 and four clips of ammunition and made his way into the bug tent at the side of the landing site. Bravo Team was now a one-man team with a boy and two corporals to babysit. Oh, and of course, half a nuclear bomb sitting in a helicopter in no man's land, which was in the middle of too many wars. Just two more days and he was done. It was time to pack her in and go home.

Shelby picked up Birdman's black radio.

"Birdman this is Shelby," he said and his message ended with a beep from the transmitter. Now he had to wait for Birdman to reply, assuming Birdman was as competent with this secure radio system as he had been with everything else so far.

Quan refueled as the two corporals took up posts ahead and behind the machine. As Shelby watched the men, his mind recounted today's mess. Harley was shot, he acquired two grunts to take with him, and they missed overnight Landing Site 1 and wound up at Site 2 only to find Billy Bob down. However, he made it to his safe site, and he would make it to LS Union tomorrow to offload his part of the Candle. Birdman's call on the radio interrupted his thoughts.

"Shelby, this is Birdman. Go!"

He picked up the black portable radio and set the mouthpiece to his face. "Status green at Redneck Two. Harley hit. Alpha India Romeo Alpha Mike bringing him in to you."

Baxter replied, "Do you know AIRAM?"

"Roger."

"Roger. Alpha team is green too. Your destination has been successfully created."

"Roger, green it is," Shelby ended the radio call. The Phantom fighter, or the B-57, had made its tactical bombing of the target mountain. Now they could deposit the Candle in the newly created opening. The mission was on track.

Tomorrow he would meet Farmer and Larry, offload his package for them, and then fly support for them to deliver the Candle. Then they could fly off into the sunset and drink up Harley's money in Bangkok.

Pilots are pilots; most of them feel closer to the machine they are flying than to anything else in the world. Pilots feel the same about their machines when they are parked. Larry slept inside his helicopter that night, with a loaded M-16 propped against the co-pilot's seat. No one was going to touch his machine.

Coincidently, Shelby did the same. He set some tarps on top of the Chassis and slept on the improvised wooden bed frame. As he fell asleep, he wondered how many people had been that close to something that could end this damn war.

Sleep did not come easy for any of the team. The continuous bombing northeast of them rattled their already strained nerves. US planes fiercely attacked the Ban Karai mountain pass, through to Dong Hoi in North Vietnam. The explosions continued until dawn, which offered only short naps for the men as they waited for the clock to tick away time until they could get on with this last leg of Operation Quiet Thunder.

* * *

By 1200 hours, Larry had completed his electronics check of the helicopter, still inside the hangar. Checking the machine guns and the rocket cradles, he walked his normal pre-flight inspection of the outside of the Huey. He was ready to go.

"Let's get this done today," he said to Farmer as he started pulling on the wheeled dolly to roll the helicopter outside. He parked the machine thirty yards away. As Farmer bumped the two doors together, closing the hangar, he heard the haunting drone of a plane coming from the south.

"The guys are early in their run. They aren't supposed to be flying over us for another hour," Farmer commented to Larry.

233

"It ain't our guys. That's a Puff coming this way," Larry said as he ducked inside the hangar's doorway.

A 'Puff' was a Douglas AC-47 Gunship. The plane had been nicknamed Puff because of the three Gatling guns mounted inside the cargo area. When those three guns let loose with their hundred rounds per second, per gun, the fire emitted from the barrels and the lights from the tracers and the noise from that much lead flying out of the plane made the haunting airplane appear to be spewing fire, like a dragon.

Having Puff fly past the hangar wasn't a good thing. The South Vietnamese Air Force, SVAF, now operated the AC-47s, and they flew them into Laos. Puffs had proven to be extremely effective at protecting villages, as well as supporting ground and air forces. They had become a versatile and dependable airship that had helped slow the flow of goods southward along the Ho Chi Minh Trail.

Farmer stood beside Larry as the Puff flew over their hangar. From the other side of the building, they looked out the window and watched as the airplane turned to circle them again. Larry knew they were trying to reach him on the radio. They only had Birdman's black portable radio in the hangar. The Huey's radio was the only way to communicate with the pilot. That meant disregarding their orders to maintain radio silence for this mission.

"I have to talk to him," Larry said as he started toward the Huey. He ran to the machine as Puff passed again. Farmer waved his arms to the pilot to ensure they saw him—the crew had to be able to identify them as Americans.

Inside the helicopter, Larry tried to find the radio frequency Puff was using.

He did hear some ground chatter from field grunts in the hills, but no call from the plane. Puff was coming closer again so he took the channel they had used to listen in on the support aircraft yesterday. He broke radio silence by calling for Spooky 72, the number on the tail of the airplane. There was no answer. Farmer continued waving his arms as he stood between the hangar and the Huey. It was obvious they were Americans and allies.

The comfort level changed when short bursts of gunfire came from Puff. Puff shot to the north of the hangar and across the landing strip into the building. Larry still couldn't find them on the radio. His only choice was to get the Huey out of there. Farmer jumped into the helicopter as the jet engine fired. Puff came back into sight, well behind the hangar.

They were no match in firepower, but they stood a much greater chance of surviving in the air than staying on the ground as sitting ducks. Larry had not reached maximum power, nor sufficient rotor rotation speed, when Puff let loose with all three guns. The bullets and tracers sprayed the ground from the hangar over to them sitting in the helicopter. The trail of lead cut across the tail section of the Huey, slicing the main beam off the engine frame.

When the rear rotor spun off and hit the ground, at almost full RPMs, the spinning rotor ran down the concrete pad, forward, past Farmer. Pieces of metal flew all around. The main blades had been hit badly. The transmission twisted as it tried to contain the unbalanced, but spinning, rotors.

Larry killed the motor immediately and locked out the electric power. "Run as fast as you can," he yelled to Farmer.

Holding the black radio in his right hand, Farmer ran away from the helicopter into the canopy of the surrounding forest. Larry took off in the opposite direction, back into the hangar.

Puff made its final flight over the destroyed helicopter. Content that the unmarked chopper had been destroyed, Puff turned to fly back to Vietnam.

Farmer made his way back to the hangar. He had taken shrapnel in his back and left arm, but he could feel no pain. Adrenaline still coursed through his body's systems.

Larry had the first aid kit beside him as he sat on the hammock while tying a tourniquet around his left leg. Shrapnel had cut into his leg, and he was bleeding badly. Farmer tied a compress bandage over the three entry points and offered Larry a vial of morphine. Larry shook his head, "Not today, man, I have to get out of here first."

Farmer's blood soaked his shirtsleeve. Larry cut open the sleeve, poured iodine into the long gash down the arm, and wrapped cotton gauze around it.

The cuts on their backs were not good either, but Farmer used pliers to pull a piece of metal out of Larry's shoulder. He also extracted a silver dollar-sized chunk of steel out of his own shoulder. Although pain began to settle into the pair, they were still mobile—no bones had been broken.

Once he was bandaged, Farmer ran to the helicopter to retrieve the Engine. The Engine case had two holes in it, and the backside had a long shrapnel tear. The case had been hit at the same height as his, now bloodied, back. The case must have taken the brunt of flying metal fragments. It likely saved his life. He unstrapped the detonator from the lift. Using all the strength his good arm could muster, he pulled the unit onto the ground, dragging it to the hanger. He entered the hangar as Larry woke up from his pain-induced blackout.

One of the two bullets entering the case hit the detonator electronics. The switches and keypad were now fragments of wire and plastic shards. The bullet impact also sheared off the battery compartment and the two charge wires going into the sealed cylinder. Now he had to figure out how to salvage the Engine.

Then he saw where the other bullet had hit.

A bullet had broken off one of the four cogs on the lock of the detonator. In this state, the Engine could not be inserted, or aligned, to set off the Candle; the precision impact needed from the Engine simply could not be aligned properly without the metal cog. How a bullet could rip off a titanium cog was beyond his comprehension, but it had.

The Engine was useless.

With pain searing through his body, being pushed back by his mind, he thought back to Nevada when he had asked Birdman for a back-up Engine. Birdman had been over this matter with the physicists who were adamant that he did not need one, since these parts were *bulletproof.* Birdman was convinced that no extra components needed to be taken overseas. Extra parts would only increase the risk of the discovery of their operation. Damn it, he wished he had been more aggressive and demanded a backup. Now, because of not allowing a backup detonator, the mission was off. February 3rd would not have a Candle light up the top of Candle Mountain in North Vietnam.

"It's fucked," Farmer said to Larry as he picked up the black radio. "Birdman this is Alpha."

Birdman responded immediately, "Go Alpha."

"Birdman, we have a red light. The Engine is dead. Alpha team is disabled."

Birdman's response arrived after a very pregnant pause, "Can you fix it?"

"Negative, negative. The Engine is gone. FUBAR. Red light for Alpha."

Another pause and then, "Are you mobile?"

"Negative. MARVIN drove a Puff over us," Farmer replied using the slang for the ARVN, or South Vietnamese army, as he watched Larry holding in the pain. "We need a cleaner and a medic."

"Roger, Alpha. A dust-off is on the way. Confirm landing site."

"Cowboy One"

"Roger, Farmer, hang in there."

"Roger. Over."

Farmer laid Larry down on the cot on his side and elevated his leg by placing his ankle on top of a wooden box. The wound in his leg had stopped bleeding, but the pain had gotten worse. He refused the second offer of morphine. Farmer couldn't take the morphine either; it was up to him to get them home.

He was certain that Puff would have radioed their location and the NVA or VC would have intercepted the information, resulting in them knowing the exact location of the destroyed helicopter. Birdman's hired, but hidden, Hmong guerillas had better be out there to hold off the men in black pajamas who were on their way to find out what was left of the assault. The race was on between Birdman and the VC.

The next hour seemed to last a full day for the damaged Alpha team. Every noise made Farmer clench the M-16 in his hand, ready to get anything coming through the door. He knew it would not end that way. They would burn out the hangar, or blow it with rockets and then come in to kill whatever survived.

Finally, he heard the rotor wash of a helicopter approaching their hangar. The green and black Huey helicopter landed close to the hangar. Two medics ran into the hangar. Two soldiers in green field camouflage dress jumped out and followed the medics. The pilots stayed in the helicopter, rotors spinning, and the turbine whistling.

The medics got onto Larry. The two soldiers asked what Farmer needed help with.

"What were you told?" Farmer asked.

"It's too hot around here to bring her back with a Jolly Green, so we are going to blow her up," said one of them. We'll time some C-4 charges. Two Phantoms are on their way too. In an hour, this place will just be a bunch of holes. As instructed by Farmer, the men carried the Candle's Engine and heaved the case into the carcass of the destroyed Huey. Two C-4 blocks were set on top of the case and two blocks went under the cradle.

The medics loaded Larry into the helicopter and Farmer walked into the back and sat on one of the fold-downs. After the soldiers climbed in, the co-pilot lifted his Huey off the gravel pad, taking the machine out of the trees and up to 7,000 feet flying onward to the NKP base hospital in Thailand. A Cobra gunship caught up with them as an escort.

Now in the air, Larry accepted a vial of morphine from the medic. The warm flush flowed through his body taking away some of the pain. For one of the few times in his life, Larry wasn't in control, and had resigned himself to that fact.

As they flew away from Cowboy 1, they did not witness the timed C-4 bombs light up the fuel in the damaged Huey ending the life of the Candle's Engine. Nor did they see 16,000 pounds of explosive fury being dropped on the burning chopper or the steel of the hangar of Cowboy 1. The landing site was transformed into another hammered piece of Laos when the Phantom F-4s turned back towards Thailand. No remnants of the Engine survived at this moonscape.

* * *

From Redneck 2, Shelby witnessed a Phantom fly south of him, laying down a destructive line of 500lb MK-82 bombs. The bombs kicked up a number of clouds of smoke from successful hits on the trail past the next mountain. They were clearing the way for the following AC-130 gunship, which was to run the flight line from Redneck 2 to landing site Union 1.

This was his signal to get into the air. Shelby and his two corporals lifted off at 1215 hours, right on time, on their way across the cleared mountainsides to meet up with Farmer and Larry at Union 1 within the hour.

Again, the effective fighter and the efficient gunship had cleared a clear route for Shelby. He did a fly over Union 1. The wide landing site, and the small adjacent hangar, looked exactly like the photo he had seen two days before. The windsock flew in the light wind. All looked fine. One of the drafted recruits mounted the door gun and was ready on the right side of the cargo bay. Shelby set down on the rocky soil. He had faith that Birdman's Hmong warriors were hidden around the site, but he would never know for sure. He had his life staked on Birdman's capacity.

Secure the hangar," he barked at his crew. One carried the large M-60 machine gun; the other took an M-16. They'd be good at clearing a building and working as a team, at least Shelby assumed. Birdman had picked the two men himself. Shelby thought every pilot should have two of these grunts with them for these missions; they made life safer for the pilots.

His hijacked corporals topped up his fuel. He was ready to go again. While waiting for Larry and Farmer, he laid on the hammock of the cool hangar while his men stayed armed and alert at the doors of the hanger.

By 1430, Alpha had not arrived. Shelby picked up his black radio. "Birdman, this is Shelby."

He had time for two smokes before Birdman replied.

"Shelby, Birdman. What's your status?"

Shelby walked to the other end of the hangar, away from the soldiers to take the call. "Bravo team secure at Union One. Status is a green light."

"Roger. Shelby." An eerie pause in the radio transmission occurred before Birdman continued, "Alpha is red light. Stay in position. Wait for further instructions."

"Roger, Birdman, over," Shelby replied.

Shelby's mind raced for an answer. Now what was wrong? Red light! Were Farmer and Larry down?

Birdman worked the mission from every angle he could.

Nothing had shown up on intelligence reports from the Russians, the North Vietnamese, or even his own people. This was good news.

No one expected anything from them, which meant everything remained an option. Birdman preferred to eliminate the Chassis of the Candle bomb as soon as possible, but the Russians or the Chinese would pick up the radioactivity in the air from a demolition. They had planes monitoring the air for just such an event.

If these North Vietnamese allies did measure the release of radioactive particles, from blowing up the nuclear Chassis of the Candle, accusations would reverberate around the world. The demolition could have more international attention than the original mission might have caused.

Therefore, Birdman had two plausible options: Dump the Candle Chassis in the ocean or bury it so damn deep that no one would ever find it.

He preferred the first option.

However, to get to water deep enough in the China Sea, they would have to cross Vietnam in a plane with half of a nuclear bomb as cargo—a huge risk. That would also mean the Chassis would have to be flown through the most fortified section of Laos, the area around Tchepone, and the NVA stood a good chance of dropping the helicopter with its stronghold of anti-aircraft stations, SAMs, and large mortars—many of the same reasons they had changed the destination to the Ban Raving Pass.

Furthermore, the Vietnamization program had caused a reduction in the number of American troops immediately south of the DMZ (Demilitarized Zone), which thereby decreased the strength of air power south of the 17th latitude. Although the South Vietnamese Air

Force existed, he did trust them, nor believe in their capacity to escort a plane, with the Chassis on board, out to sea.

If he persisted in a plan to dump the Chassis in the sea, then how could he contain the event? The crew of the plane would know about the operation. SVAF planes would need to be recruited. The Navy would have to be brought onboard, since he'd be flying over the sea and they'd track his plane and likely demand to support the airplane over their water. Flying over the China Sea was not an option.

He also considered disposal in the Andaman Sea of the Bay on Bengal. While Laos was still a daily confusion of control, Thailand was organizing, and his fellow Americans were helping them. Air America, the Army, and the Air Force were already established. Getting a plane across Thailand and through Burma would require others to join their very tight circle. Too many people in the know meant that someone could, or would, leak the attempt to set off a nuclear bomb in Vietnam. Disposal in the western waters was not possible.

* * *

Birdman continued strategizing while sitting in a lightly furnished office at the Nakhon Phanom hospital. His thoughts were interrupted by a knock on the door.

"Come in," he called to the armed soldier stationed outside his door.

The older lieutenant assigned to watch the door, entered the room, producing a quick salute. Birdman liked older soldiers; they didn't use, they understood orders the first time they were given, and they were soldiers. . .24/7. He returned the salute.

"A Mr. Cameron is here for you. He has an urgent matter to discuss with you."

Cameron was here. He wasn't expected. Cameron was the Assistant Deputy to the CIA Section Chief for Saigon—a career agent who took his work very seriously.

"Let him in, Captain."

Cameron entered the small room and did not speak until the door shut solidly.

"What's new, Cameron?"

"Well, sir, you requested that we monitor the movements of the North Vietnamese Air Force. I have personally taken on your request. For the last three days, I've determined a pattern of consolidation of air and ground forces. There's been a buildup of armored vehicles and T-54 tanks. We estimate at least seventy-five tanks are moving down from Dong Hoi.

"We've also noted artillery batteries moving down Highway 1, south to Vinh Linh. Normally, a dozen MiGs fly out of there, but now over fifty are on the ground.

"The tank build up is perplexing, because they'd need to cross the DMZ to get to the south. If they respected the DMZ as a barrier, the only way around was to travel through Laos, and keep on going south.

"This assembly of MiGs is troubling, too. They are conducting daily runs now into Central Laos. This does not feel right. My gut says they're setting up for a big run at us. We expect they are planning an offensive this year, but so far they have been very quiet, almost lulling us to think that they've accepted our troop withdrawals as reason to back down. I can't nail it exactly, but something is not right, sir."

Cameron was correct; the changes did not make sense. *Is this why the air had been so quiet this year? Was Cameron correct in his gut feeling?* "Any idea on when they would launch such an offensive?" he asked Cameron.

"No, sir. The Air Force says this is the largest collection the North has put together in some time. Estimates run as high as 40,000 VC and NVA in Laos already. They think an attack is imminent, and it is going to be real ugly. They know our Vietnamization plan has left the south undermanned. Even with all the gear we are giving them, they can't hold off a directed attack like this."

Birdman did not need to hear the term, *Imminent*. "Do you have any other intelligence reports?"

"No, sir, and honestly this is just my gut feeling. But the flyboys are thinking the same way."

"Very well, Cameron, I'll need you to keep on top of this!"

Cameron left Birdman to contemplate this latest information. A southern assault would involve the NVAF to use Laos's airspace and the North Vietnamese Army to use the Ho Chi Minh or Laos highways and trails. He also didn't believe the DMZ meant a damn thing to the NVA. They would plow right through it to the south if they had enough equipment. Tanks were good equipment to move across the line. They could be planning a three-pronged attack, from the north, west, and south. A three-flank attack would cripple the South Vietnamese forces.

Regardless of what might be coming at them, this information meant that Operation Quiet Thunder had just run out of time to organize any water disposal of Bravo team's Chassis. They would need to deal with damage control immediately, and stay within Laos.

Birdman had hit the wall. He had little time to hide a nuclear bomb inside a country that was being torn apart from all sides.

* * *

"Shelby, this is Birdman," the black radio squawked. Shelby grabbed the radio off his chest and sat up.

"Go, Birdman."

"Roger, Shelby, we have a red light. Confirm."

"Roger, Birdman, we have a red light."

"But you will move the Chassis."

"Roger, Birdman."

"When you worked with the professor, you worked an area and found orange. You found an orange elephant."

Shelby thought about what Birdman was trying to use the code words to mean. "Negative, Birdman."

"This is a heavy area. You found a big, heavy hole."

Shelby worked on the coded message in his head. *Heavy hole might mean a series of bomb craters or a decimated village. Hell no, he had been working as a Prospector so the hint had to be resource related. A heavy hole might be a mine of some type; it could maybe mean a lead mine. Elephant? Orange? Think, think. He did map out a huge old lead and silver mine that the monks used. That was it, Elephant Mountain, the monastery. The lead mine inside the mountain. Yes, that was it. Of course, hide a nuclear bomb inside a lead mine, the safest place to hide it. This must be a last resort plan to do this kind of dump.*

"Birdman that is a Roger," Shelby confirmed he understood where he was going with the Chassis.

"Okay. Leave the Chassis deep and return to base."

"Roger, Birdman."

"Shelby, good luck."

"Roger, Birdman."

Birdman clicked the mic twice to close. He had nothing more to say. At that moment, his mind wandered to thinking where Simpson and Dickson were now. They would be straight-faced, uptight and having fun turning the screws on someone, somewhere. They might learn that the Candle was not delivered. Nothing would stick to anyone, since there was no paperwork on this operation. Dickson and Simpson had only met with him and Harley.

No one owned Operation Quiet Thunder and no one had any paper on the mission.

Birdman also gave thought as to how many *one percenters* the CIA was using through the region. He knew other operations were in play. He also knew that it was understood to the highest ranks, including the President, not all of these one shot operations succeeded. They accepted the chance of one plan working out as a risk worth taking; no regrets would fall from this mission not succeeding, other than agents Simpson and Dickson might need to try again.

Such was the world of war, intelligence, and missions with the odds stacked against them. Fortunately, failed missions were thrown away and were not talked about; successful missions were bragged about to the right people.

* * *

Shelby and his two men flew at 5,500 feet, heading to the monastery on Elephant Mountain. Only last summer he had met the Sangharaja. He had left him a contribution of $500 to look in the mine.

The Sangharaja appeared to like Shelby. Today's request would be the real test to see if that was indeed the case. The monks had stayed out of the war, but the communists from North Vietnam were not so kind. They had been hard on the monks, giving Shelby a favorable edge—he hoped the edge would allow him to ask for a very difficult favor.

Shelby circled the monastery twice. He wanted to get out of the air quickly, so he landed at the edge of the clearing and inched the Huey into the cover offered by the huge mangrove trees on the grounds.

A young monk hesitantly walked over to the helicopter and watched as the rotors slowed their rotation to come to a stop. The monastery seemed to be deserted, or at least far quieter than his last visit. The monk led Shelby to the Sangharaja.

The Sangharaja, dressed in his vibrant orange robe tied with a silk sash cord, recognized Shelby as the man who had visited him before. They spoke by the mine entrance. After a long discussion with his American friend, the Sangharaja told the young monk these men would be entering the mine. He was to help them with their needs.

At 1530 hours, Shelby and his two soldiers set a large wooden crate on one of the track carts that ran on hard rock trails inside the mine.

This was also a fortuitous day for Bravo team, due to an odd set of concurrent events.

Only this morning, twelve American soldiers arrived at the monastery and asked for assistance to rescue the surviving children and women from a devastating VC night raid on a small village four miles away. The Americans anticipated the North Vietnamese would return tonight and kill the rest of villagers. They had to evacuate the survivors to keep them alive.

The Sangharaja had been reluctant to participate in the war, in any manner, but the orphans were a different matter. He would support the cause of orphans. He sent his monks with the soldiers to retrieve the children.

The young monk stayed at the big doors of the mine entrance. The three men pushed the wooden box on the cart into the tunnel illuminated by coal oil lamps. He closed the door and waited for a long time.

The monk suspected the three might be lost inside the miles of tunnels; monks had suffered the same fate over the years. Nevertheless,

Shelby and his two men returned, without the cart, tools, or tarps, they took in with them.

Shelby spoke again with the Sangharaja. Staying back at the doors, the young monk witnessed Shelby hand the Sangharaja an envelope and a folded piece of paper. The Sangharaja put the paper inside a shiny lead case.

* * *

Shelby wasted no time in radioing Birdman after he fired up his helicopter. The very tired corporals slumped into their jump seats, ever anxious to return to base. Birdman was relieved to know the Chassis had been safely deposited deep inside the mountain. One thing had gone right on this 3rd day of February. Once Shelby was back, they all could get out of Laos.

The Chassis was left for a cleaning crew to decommission. It was someone else's headache, now. They could extract the plutonium and take it back to Area 51, and destroy the empty carcass in country.

Shelby flew a zigzag flight path from the monastery, prior to turning west toward Mahaxay, Laos. The pattern confirmed no one had taken note of his flight. They were a half hour from the base when a ground-fired rocket severed the drive shaft to his tail rotor.

At 3,500 feet, he had time to pull up and start an auto rotation, but his tail rotor was too damaged. His partial flair-up did slow the impact into the treetops. The tree canopy buffered their fall to earth. They came to a quick halt in the tree limbs only to slide to the ground, crashing on the skids.

Shelby woke as a medic cut away his seat belt. A second medic ripped off the door to extract him from the mangled cage of the twisted cockpit. They rolled him out as he blacked out once more. He awoke in a dust-off chopper, lying on the stretcher beside his men, both of which had blankets covering their entire body. The medic working on Shelby's leg gave him an injection of morphine. He passed out.

* * *

When Shelby next awoke, Birdman was sitting beside his bed. The curtains in the Nakhon Phanom base hospital were closed, causing the dim lamps to cast an iridescent aura on the wall behind him. He turned his head groggily to see Larry sleeping in the bed across from him.

"This is the 'wounded leg' department," Birdman said as he got up. He put his arm on Shelby. "You did a great job Shelby. You broke your leg, but the surgeon said it'll heal fine. Larry is going to be okay too. He lost a lot of blood, but luckily the bullet missed his femur and he only needed some stitches in his hamstring.

"It's been a hell of a ride, but she's done. We did everything we could to make the mission work and only the five of us know what we did here. No one is waiting for a result from us. It's over! You know, for about the first time in my life, I am glad this one didn't succeed. I think we did a lot of people right by this one."

Shelby just nodded. "What about the trigger man, won't he be waiting for the word?"

Birdman held up his right thumb and flexed it as if he was pressing the button. "I already gave myself the bad news."

Shelby's lips formed a light smile as he closed his eyes. Too tired to talk he fell asleep again.

Over in the 'wounded arm' department, as Birdman referred to the next room, Farmer and Harley rested. They did not speak of the mission, but they recognized the cruel irony to this mission right from the start. Success would have led to an international event, but success might have also ended the war.

Their failed mission prevented a nuclear bomb detonation, which could have caused a retaliatory strike by China or Russia, both of which were very interested in the success of their North Vietnamese comrades in removing the Americans from their backyard. Quiet Thunder's termination might just have been the best resolution to the entire proposal.

* * *

Farmer, Harley, and Larry went off to Bangkok after three weeks in the hospital. Their wounds were healing fine. Shelby's leg was taking more time to set so he stayed behind in the hospital. Harley had money to spend, and Farmer and Larry volunteered to make up for Shelby's absence.

Two weeks later, when Birdman arrived in Bangkok, he informed them that their mission had gone unnoticed by any intelligence operation, even the CIA. Birdman viewed this as a great achievement. They had succeeded in silence.

Birdman offered Harley an assistant deputy chief position back in the States. Harley accepted. This corner of the world no longer needed Colonel "Harley" Henry.

Shelby took the desk job in aircraft parts procurement in San Francisco that somehow Birdman had been able to set up for him. He was back in service but this time inside an air-conditioned office, and home for dinner every night.

Birdman and the CIA still had one big problem in Vietnam. As part of the 'Vietnamization' program, South Vietnam was taking back the defense of their portion of the torn country. United States troops were leaving Vietnam in record numbers. Birdman expected by the end of the year there would be less than 20,000 advisors and soldiers in the country. From the Administration's political point of view the plan sounded fine, but from an intelligence gathering perspective, the plan was far from a good decision.

There were still too many assets remaining in Vietnam. The CIA needed to work fast to dismantle their networks and remove critical resources. Farmer and Larry were asked to stay for one final tour—to take down whatever assets Birdman wanted pulled back to the United States, including civilians, government officials, structures, equipment, and historical records. He needed men he could trust and men that could run operations autonomously. On March 5, 1972, Larry and Farmer agreed to help Birdman with this last assignment.

Savannakhet Laos

Five years later

Present Day

Monday July 11, 1977

Chapter 20

Monday, July 11, 1977

Working through the night, Larry and Billy Bob prepared the plane for its advanced escape from Laos. The aged Caribou, circa 1964, was in very good shape, having gone through a major rebuild in late 1973. Billy Bob bought the C-4 a year and a half later, at a salvage price. At the time, the Operations Manager of Air America was happy not to give another good airplane to the South Vietnamese Air Force.

The Caribou had a range of about 1,300 miles. The flight from Savannakhet to the American-occupied Wallace Airport in San Fernando City, Philippines, was about 1,050 miles. Depending on the winds and the air temperature over the ocean, they were pushing the limit on their range. Since no secure refueling points were on their flight path, they strapped in two fifty-five gallon barrels of av gas to refuel while in the air.

In addition, they loaded six pails of engine oil and five pails of hydraulic fluid for the trip. Even in good mechanical shape, the Caribou still consumed oil and topping up the engines during the flight would be necessary.

Securing aviation fuel and oils remained a challenge in Laos. The Caribou had been used to pick up fuel and oil from Thailand and the Philippines many times in the past. A fuel run was a normal pass through a country; all airplanes faced the same problems.

Farmer treated Quan's gunshot wound with iodine and a compress field dressing, wrapped with cotton gauze. A wrap of Duct tape secured the bandage in place. He forced Quan to drink some Cavalier brandy obtained from Billy Bob's well-stocked liquor cabinet. As an abstainer of alcohol, the 40% sedative proved effective. He fell asleep before he finished the glass of brandy.

Farmer finalized the route and identified the drop zone. They'd fly on dead reckoning and lock in on a Philippine radio station to get them to the Philippines. Billy Bob likely could fly this route without any navigation assistance anyway.

With an hour to go before daylight, Larry informed Farmer that the Chassis package had been secured in the cargo hold. The plane was ready.

The future for Billy Bob and Quan had become markedly limited following the killing of the four LPRP soldiers, and the two Russians with them, last night. Billy Bob could not return to Laos after this flight. He would be implicated in the deaths of the LPRP soldiers, or the Russian deaths, or possibly the clandestine operation associated with the retrieval of the Chassis package. The tide could quickly turn on him and his future life in Laos.

Farmer had a better offer for Billy Bob when he told him he could set-up Billy Bob in the Philippines, or the USA. At forty-five years of age, Billy Bob figured the Philippines would do just fine. A hut on the ocean, and a beautiful Philippine woman, would be a good life. Sure, count him in.

Quan, created another issue for Farmer. His immunity had been taken from him by last night's killing of his reckless comrades. His injury wasn't life threatening, but without proper medical attention it could become such. In Laos, a man on the run, needing medical help, had a survival expectancy that could be measured in days. Therefore, no difficult decision needed to be made after all. Quan was coming with them to the Philippines.

Quan had sobered up when Farmer told him he was leaving with them. Fighting past the throbbing pain from his wound, he nodded his head to confirm he understood. Quan had lived his entire life in a war zone, knowing that whatever gave him life today could change again tomorrow in the midst of a fickle civil war. He spoke the word 'Yes' after his mind realized that he would be thankful to leave Laos, his country of birth, his country of conflict.

Billy Bob didn't have much to pack. He travelled light by loading some memorabilia, including photographs and his favorite rifles, into the airplane. His golden retirement plan was in the false bottom of the navy locker in the corner of his office. It contained gold coins and jewelry that he had collected over the years in exchange for work performed. He manhandled the metal locker into the plane by himself.

Quan travelled even lighter. He took four pictures, two with his uncle, and two with Billy Bob. He had few clothes and a set of small animal carvings that he packed together in a small suitcase.

They were ready for the one-way trip across the South China Sea.

* * *

The sun just cleared the horizon as the wheels left the concrete at Billy Bob's airstrip. Finally in the air, Farmer closed his exhausted eyes for a moment. Unfortunately, the lapse in stress triggered his mind to flash back to 1971. Colonel Benson at Camp Apollo had called him in to his office. Within an hour, he, Larry and Shelby were working for Special Operations Chief Baxter, Birdman, on a new assignment. Their location training was to work on Professor's mapping project, in central Laos, and then return to the United States for the team mission training.

To the drone of the plane's engines, his recollections continued. Meeting Harley and getting to know Birdman. Arriving in Nevada and going through their training. That 1971 meeting with Birdman had led to their flight today and the chance to finally close the book on Operation Quiet Thunder.

* * *

Flight plans weren't filed in the disorganized airspace over Laos. They flew east from Savannakhet, near Highway 9, intending to enter Vietnam north of Da Nang. As they neared the Loa Boa pass into

Vietnam, they received their first call from Vietnam air control in Vinh. Billy Bob replied in Vietnamese requesting passage through Vietnam. The radio traffic noise increased as they approached the border. The commander wanted him to land in Dong Hoi for an inspection. Billy Bob told them his tanks were full of fuel, since he was headed for a run to the Philippines. His plane was too heavy to land. He would have to drop fuel over the sea to lighten up enough to land now. The commander insisted. The heated discussion continued as the Caribou entered Vietnam. Billy Bob could not land with this freight and his passengers. He wondered if they were already aware of the run-in with the LPA soldiers last night.

At 0700, two Vietnamese T-28 fighters approached him from the rear. Quan sat in the co-pilot seat, barely awake while fighting the throbbing pain from his injured leg. Larry and Farmer stayed in the windowless cargo area. The T-28s remained at Billy Bob's wing tips. *Something was wrong*, Billy Bob thought. *They no longer ran T-28s out of Vinh. Why were these two here? Had they already found out about the shootings or were the Vietnamese inventing a new game?*

Billy Bob had to pull out his last playing card. He asked to speak to General Phong. The radio went silent for a time. The hesitant reply came back stating the general was not there, he was busy. Billy Bob asked the air controller to find him and ask him if he needed anything in the Philippines, or else the next time he saw him, he would ask why the controller had not asked the question of him. The two T-28s and the Caribou were now flying near Da Nang, with China Beach ahead of them, on the shore of the South China Sea. Thirty seconds later, the controller called back to Billy Bob and said General Phong had three packages for him to pick up.

Clearance to continue the trip to the Philippines had been granted. The T-28s rolled away, leaving the Caribou's wings to glide over the sea toward San Fernando City on Luzon, the most northerly island of the Philippines.

"Greedy General Phong just raised the travel budget by two cases of Chivas double malt. Last time I needed his help he was happy with one case. Something is going on at Vinh. The general is always there, even at this time in the morning. He lives to make his men miserable, while flaunting his power in front of them. Why is he not there now? Something is going down since they never send up the old T-28s to shadow me. Their MiGs must be somewhere else. I wonder what war they are trying to create now? Well man, today is a good day to move to the Philippines," reasoned Billy Bob.

Two hours later, halfway to the Philippines, they reached the drop zone where the sea was a mile deep. Vietnamese radar did not cover this international water, but the Americans did from Clark in the Philippines. The Caribou would be a familiar blip on their radar screen.

Farmer and Larry were secure in their safety harnesses when Larry unlocked the ramp switch, causing the red interior droplights to flash as the rear gate lowered and the siren beeped to confirm the action. Once the ramp was level, Farmer pulled the pins off the Chassis package ties allowing the crate to glide down the rolling track on the floor. Billy Bob lifted the nose of the plane to help the Chassis package roll off the ramp, thereby throwing it out of the airplane. Farmer witnessed the splash of the package hitting the seawater after its fifty-foot drop. The mass of metal sunk immediately. A flyover the drop zone confirmed the Chassis package was on its way to the bottom of the sea. Operation Quiet Thunder was over.

* * *

The sight of Luzon was a relief for all. It was a complimenting shoreline at the end of a calm, blue sea. The landing at Wallace Air Station was never a problem for Billy Bob. He was one of the American pilots who just never went home. Dozens of his kind flew out of the Philippines. Even some of the airport employees were ex-Air American employees. The conflict had created a variety of wandering souls.

Billy Bob secured the plane at the temporary hangar he used for his trips to the Island. Whenever he chose to leave, the Caribou would be ready for him. He had good friends here. Quan remained in the plane, resting, while Billy Bob fed him another shot of brandy.

They entered the terminal with Farmer leading Larry over to the corporal stationed at the front desk. Farmer laid out his passport and told the young soldier he needed to see the Commanding Officer. The corporal looked at the stranger, with clear, green eyes, glaring with purpose.

"And why would a Canadian need to meet the Commanding Officer of this base?"

Farmer's eyes did not blink. "Get me to the CO."

The corporal hit the alarm button under his counter. Three soldiers, each with an M-16 hanging over their shoulders, came out from the poker game they were playing at the rear of the building. A massive sergeant rose slowly from the card table and followed.

Farmer knew the game that was to be played out. The sergeant strolled up and stood straight, hands on hips, behind his three men, who were now only four feet away from Larry and Farmer. Farmer and Larry stayed in place, arms at their sides, waiting.

The fifty-five-year-old sergeant was a career man. First sent to Guam in World War II, he stayed on for Korea, and did three tours in Vietnam. Next year he was going to retire to Hawaii. After thirty-two years in the Army, he'd developed an ability to read people well, since those who didn't learn, did not make it to the half-century mark while still in active service.

The sergeant found these two men very familiar. Not that he knew them personally, but he'd worked with men like these two. Men who could remain calm when they should be shitting bricks. These two had been in worse situations before and they had obviously survived.

"Stand down, men; I'm going to have a private talk with these gentlemen."

The men backed up three feet, while lowering their M-16s, pointing them to the ground.

Farmer and Larry walked with the sergeant.

"So what is it you are looking for?"

"The CO," Farmer said.

"And why do you two Canadians need to meet with our CO?"

"I would expect you will want the CO to decide the merit of our meeting. Sergeant, do yourself a favor and let him deal with this shit, you just don't need it."

The sergeant understood what this man was telling him. If he had not been in the Army for so many years, and fighting on the ground for too long, he would not have recognized what this man was telling him; but he'd been there and he did get it.

"I'll have to find him. Might take me some time. Why don't you wait here and I'll be back soon."

The sergeant returned with General Hanson and two MPs within fifteen minutes. General Hanson sized the pair up and concurred with his sergeant that it was highly unlikely that these two were reporters—Canadian or any other nationality. His curiosity led him to continue on though.

"Now what is this all about? I am not at the beck and call of every Canadian who asks for me."

"Yes, sir, I understand. We need to speak in private, sir."

"Whatever asinine thing you have to tell me, my men can hear it too. Get on with your story," he replied in an assertive and louder voice.

"Sir, it is for their benefit that I ask to speak to you in private," Farmer replied calmly.

The burly general had been sizing up Larry and Farmer. They were different, but there was something distinct about their command. He knew this first man from somewhere, he was sure, but not as a Canadian. Instead, from somewhere else, somewhere far removed from Canada.

"Come with me," he said as he motioned to the office across the entry area.

After the general closed the door to the meeting room, he asked, "Now what is this all about?"

"Sir, we need your co-operation to meet with the CIA's Chief of Station, here at your base."

"What the hell is this about? You drag me here to talk, and you ask for the CIA. I don't have time for bullshit games. No, I won't get the chief to come here."

"Sir, I am not sure what I would do in your position either. I do know, however, you don't want to learn any more about us or why we need to meet the Station Chief. General, some things are better left in few hands, and fewer minds."

The general was still working up these two men. They were military, maybe CIA, maybe both in the past. They had obviously been in country, but doing what he could not figure out. Farmer's words rang true. This was not double talk. The words came from someone trained to keep secrets for a living. Someone who had earned secrets to keep. Then it came to him. He did know this man, in fact, he knew both of these men, a long time ago, it seemed a lifetime ago.

Choosing his words, very carefully, he began, "I was at a Christmas party in Da Nang a few years ago and an Agency Chief of some kind introduced me to two men, I believe a captain and a major. He said the men, and maybe a few others, were going to be around for a while and I was to help them with any of their requests. For the next year, I remained in Da Nang, yet I never met these two again, but I suspected they were around, somewhere. Have you ever been to a Christmas party in Da Nang?"

"Been to a lot of Christmas parties, sir, and I expect to go to many more."

The general knew these men now. "Are you men hungry, our chow ain't half bad here. We have locals doing the cooking, so the food is edible. Men, I'll have my MPs get you some food and drink. I'll get the CIA chief over here as soon as I can."

"Thank you, sir," Farmer sighed. One more thing, "When we are done with the CIA, I will require the services of one of your very discrete doctors and an operating room."

"I don't want to know why, do I?"

"No sir."

"Very well, I'll have the facility and the doctor ready. Tell the sergeant when you are ready for him."

"Thank you sir," Farmer said as he saluted the General.

* * *

Over the next hour, they ate thin strips of beefsteak and slices of fried potatoes, washing the meal down with a couple Cokes. The general had left some Marlboros. They patiently waited while reacquainting themselves with tobacco from home.

General Hanson returned to the room followed by a tall man in a black suit. The CIA's Station Chief Mackhill, was a thin pale man. He looked like he hadn't spent a day on the ground in his forty-something years. However, he had made it to the Philippines and must have some useful skillset to be a CIA Station Chief in the comfortable environment afforded by his Manila offices.

"Now gentlemen, do you have real names or do we play the game of using these aliases," he flipped open a small black notepad, "Mr. Gerald Brightman and Mr. Larry Brown?"

"Those names will do for now. Sometimes it's better not to know more than you need to."

"Very well then, Mr. Brightman, the general said you are a serious man who needed my assistance. Therefore, against my better judgment I flew in here from Manila just to meet with you. What do you need from me?"

Farmer looked at General Hanson who took the hint and exited the room. Only the three of them remained.

Farmer began, "I need to secure US citizenship for one person and adjust the history of another to bring them into good standing for time served in country."

The arrogant chief flinched his shoulders. "Sure why not, what the hell type of genie do you think I am? I'm not going to spend the rest of my life doing paperwork for you. This will not happen," Mackhill was furious. He did nothing to hide his contempt for suggesting that he would be at the service of this stranger.

"And I need this done today. We have to leave soon," added Farmer.

"Are you deaf? I can't do this!" exclaimed the exasperated Station Chief.

"Yes you can, and you will, and we need this done now. You don't want to learn more than what we are dealing with here.

"You remember the Trang Bang incident in '72 and how well that one went for us. Man, that one is just a drop in the bucket in comparison. You don't want this one to get out of our little conversation here, so I suggest we get on with putting this to bed.

"Don't fuck around with me on this! I need this done and then we are gone. You can go back to your quiet job with the beautiful women and your cushy government-funded house on the beach," Farmer said as he put his arm on the chief's shoulder.

Mackhill replied, "Come on now, do you think the CIA can get an alien citizenship and give another person a service record, just like that? Hell, I don't know who you really are, or what your motive is, but the CIA doesn't issue passports nor do we falsify military records."

"You are right, Chief. You may not do these things, but you can get them done," Farmer said as he handed him the folded letter, from President Huntington, the document Harley had obtained for him and left in the safety deposit box in Oregon.

June 3, 1975

To whom it may concern.
Be advised that by Presidential Executive Order of Brian Alfred Huntington, the 38th President of the United States of America, the bearer of this Order has been commanded to operate in every manner he deems necessary to conduct the Presidential Executive Order of the operations associated with, or caused by, the Executive Order TS White Bear's Paw.
The bearer of this Order will provide you with the security key code to confirm his authority to execute this Presidential Executive Order.
This mission will be unobstructed from within. He shall have all available support, from all forces of the United States of America, to complete his objectives.

President Brian Alfred Huntington

The document appeared to be official. The Great Seal of the United States had been pressed beside his signature.

Farmer took the document back from the hand of Station Chief Mackhill and returned the letter to the rear pocket of his jeans. He had only used the order because his hand had been forced. He had to ensure attention to these matters in a timely and proper manner.

"Now, about the documents I need."

"Sir," Chief Mackhill, began, "with all due respect, you must admit this puts me in an awkward position. There are many things that I do not want to know about, that I do not need to know about, but anyone could have forged that letter. You must grant me at least that suspicion."

Farmer was losing interest in what this poor, fumbling bastard was struggling with.

"Listen, Mackhill, I've had a long run, and I am tired. Save us both some pain from here on. Call and have them confirm operation 'White Bear's Paw'. I will provide them with the security key and we can get on with what I need to have done."

The chief did not need to call anyone. As the Chief of Station for the Philippines, he knew the names of the three autonomous operations under Presidential Executive Order at this time in Southeast Asia through to his own Station. These were 'do not pursue, just get the buggers out of your area if they ever show up and forget they were there', orders.

One such order was indeed TS White Bear's Paw.

This man in front of him was running one of three Presidential Executive Orders in effect in his region. The man was not what he expected to see. Mackhill's view of intelligence and secret operations portrayed men in black suits, or at least casual business attire, not ragged jeans and a denim shirt. His assumption had been incorrect.

"Well, sir, in order to facilitate your requirements and allow you to move on, we should get on with the tasks. Now how do we proceed with this?"

"First, I need our passports stamped with our arrival date of four days ago, July 9th, and let's make them from the Clark Base.

"Second, a Mr. Quan will be issued a passport and naturalization papers. He has been an ally of the United States of America, fighting the war in Laos and Vietnam on our side, and in return, he shall be declared a naturalized citizen and receive a passport. Here are his papers from Laos."

The chief interrupted, "Are you suggesting through Section 1440," referring to the section on Naturalization through Active Duty service in the Armed Forces during Vietnam hostilities.

"Your decision, not mine, I just need it done. Third, one of our longest serving men in Air America, and many other operations, shall be granted active service credit for his last fifteen years of patriotic duty, and be offered the chance to retire in peace, with a comfortable pension. He will be retired at his former rank of captain, which he was before he joined Air America. His old papers are long gone in some jungle over here, so he'll need a new passport. Here's his information."

Chief Mackhill took no notes, he did not want any of this documented.

"Sir, would you like to do this here or would you like to come back to our office for me to have my people work on this."

"We will not be leaving here; you will do this work here. We don't want anyone else to carry the details of this task to their graves, do we?" Farmer said as he put his hand on CIA Station Chief Mackhill's shoulder and squeezed to reinforce the message.

"Err, no I guess not. Okay I will bring the staff here. I'll go make the calls."

"Make them here, be my guest," Farmer said as pointed to the phone on the desk.

Chief Mackhill picked up the telephone headset, demanding a clean line from the operator. He dialed a number and spoke with his assistant.

Ninety minutes later, a white Learjet landed on the tarmac and taxied up to the terminal. One man got off the plane and waddled toward the building, toting two steel cases on wheels rolling along beside him. The man was quite short, with a puffy face lined with burst blood vessels earned from years of drinking well-aged scotch. He was panting from the exercise of pulling the steel cases on wheels across the flat tarmac.

Chief Mackhill met him at the doorway and led him into the room. Perspiration began to flow from his forehead, as the elderly man opened his cases and laid out his materials on the desk.

Farmer thought that Mackhill had selected this agent as most likely to die soon, yet owning the skills needed to complete the unique task— a convenient way to minimize risk.

The administrative agent began his work by stamping the set of Canadian passports with the arrival date of Saturday, July 9 at Clark Military Air Force Base. This point of entry would raise the fewest questions for Farmer and Larry when they returned to the United States.

As for the naturalization papers, the man rolled the preprinted document into his typewriter and entered Quan's information onto the form. This man was efficient, and a good typist too. He peeled off the complete document, already signed, to verify his assistance to the United States of America during the conflict. The form already bore the ambassador's signature to attest to the accuracy of the document. Since ambassadors do not like being told by the CIA to sign incomplete documents, Station Chief Mackhill must actually have some pull.

A retired two star general, used by the CIA for such matters, had already signed the blank authorization, which was completed to attest to the reinstatement of Billy Bob as a captain. Attached behind was his retirement request to Veteran Affairs. Billy Bob officially retired as a captain of the United States of America's air force. His first pension check would arrive in two months.

Finally, two passports were prepared as authorized by the US Ambassador to the Philippines. The efficient CIA agent completed the piles of documents by stacking them, neatly.

"I'll need pictures of the two men," the agent said.

Larry left the room to get Billy Bob and Quan who were still in the hangar, lying low. Larry carried Quan to the office. For some odd reason, no one else was around the hangar or the pathway to the office. *The general must have cleared the field*, thought Larry.

Still somewhat sedated by the brandy, Quan had to be propped up by Larry holding him from behind. No one asked about his condition, they remained focused on the task.

The Polaroid shots were trimmed and glued to the passports, with an authorized stamp mark across the lower half of the picture and onto the passport. A second picture of Quan went on his application form for citizenship. Signatures from Quan and Billy Bob completed the process.

"Welcome to the United States of America, gentlemen," the CIA agent said as he handed Billy Bob his document and after trying to hand them to Quan, also handed Quan's documents to Billy Bob. He took no documents with him. It wasn't the red-face agent's first rodeo. He knew better than to round up any sort of evidence for the tasks he'd just completed.

The Naturalization form was sequentially numbered. Quan would have the original. The ambassador's copy would be declared as lost in filing, should it ever be called on for verification. Quan's original document would be the true record.

The passports were logged in the ambassador's books as replacements and the failure of his staff to record properly the names of the applicants would fall on some secretary in his office. A convenient denial of truth for the office.

The agent finished packing his equipment and then asked if Chief Mackhill was returning with him? Farmer walked with Mackhill toward the exit door to answer the question.

"Mackhill, sometimes things happen for reasons we don't need to understand. I urge you to treat this afternoon as such a time. I find that is the best way to live a long life and retire in peace."

He did not reply, but nodded his head as he left Farmer and climbed up the stairs into the jet. He did yearn for the safety of his plush air-conditioned office in Manila.

* * *

The general had indeed selected a discrete doctor. An Australian doctor, working on an American Air Force base, must have done something to earn such a unique arrangement. Farmer suspected whatever the circumstances got him there, would be beneficial to keeping the wraps on the operation he was to perform on Quan.

The doctor worked fast, knowing better than to ask any questions. Within forty minutes, he had sterilized the bullet wound entry and exit locations in Quan's leg, sewn up both cuts, and given him a booster shot of penicillin, a tetanus shot, and an injection of morphine. The bright white bandage wrap finalized the procedure.

The surgeon gave Farmer a bottle of penicillin pills to prevent an infection. He found a bottle of codeine painkillers to help get Quan through the next two weeks.

Sporting a new pair of dungarees, obtained from the PX, Quan, under the influence of the morphine, walked out of the operating room with the aid of a pair of crutches.

* * *

The evening was a celebration of sorts. Billy Bob, as the local tour guide, had checked them into his favorite set of huts next to the ocean. The owners of the sparse resort knew Billy Bob and Quan and treated them like family. To celebrate the events of this last week, Billy Bob asked the owner's family to prepare a feast and to keep the cold beer flowing. All members of the host family participated in cooking the meals, serving the meals and ensuring the guests had extra delicacies and cold beer to celebrate at their secluded section of the beach. One of the young girls made an extra effort to make Quan comfortable on the cot she had arranged for him, so he did not have to sit upright in a chair with his repaired leg.

It didn't take long for the last of their energy to be consumed-advanced by the consumption of a few beers. By 2200 hours, Farmer announced he was going to crash.

Tomorrow would be the start of a new life for all.

Chapter 21

Farmer tossed a rock into the receding tide. The crisp morning breeze off the water carried the salty seaweed odor. Fresh air, combined with the tranquility of lapping waves, gave him a clarity he had lost during the past two weeks. He'd made peace with himself. With each step on the walk back to the gazebo, he felt one step closer to the life he would now build for him and his wife.

The owners of the huts prepared eggs with ham, bread, and pineapple for breakfast with rich, black coffee and locally grown tea. A young girl set the plates and utensils on the table for these guests. Billy Bob and Larry were already eating their meal when Farmer returned from his seaside walk.

The injured Quan continued to absorb the attention of the young girl who insisted on helping him eat his food.

Billy Bob raised his glass of pineapple juice to Farmer and Larry and offered a toast. "To you, Farmer and Larry, I suspect our country owes you a debt they will never know about. And for what you have done for Quan and me, I thank you for our new start in life."

Farmer nodded back and grabbed for some eggs. He was not hungry after last night's feast, but he had to deal with the beer still in his system.

"I've got a bit more news for you, Billy Bob. You gave up a lot to leave Laos. God knows what future Quan gave up with his connection to the leadership. I can make some of that right for you. Your pension check won't arrive for a few months so you'll need money. I can help you out there

"You told me sometimes you rented a house not far from here. You said you could land a helicopter on the grounds. I can arrange for the property to be yours, if you want, but I'll need to wrap the deal up today."

Billy Bob choked on the smoked ham he was eating. He couldn't believe what Farmer was offering him, but his answer was clear. "Holy shit, you really mean this, don't you? This is a dream come true. Quan and I will do just fine here. The house is beyond anything I ever imagined."

"Okay then, arrange to meet the owner this morning to discuss the price. I don't know how these transactions and property transfers work here in the Philippines, but I'll need you to manage that part discreetly and quickly. We need to leave soon, so the sooner the better."

Billy Bob shook Farmer's hand and then ran up to the owner's residence. In thirty minutes, he returned to the breakfast at the gazebo.

"Sorry man, the guy is greedy. I guess too many foreigners are buying up land. Now the locals all think their properties are worth lots of money. I'll look somewhere else, if the offer still applies?"

"What does he want for the place?" queried Farmer.

"225 grand," Billy Bob exclaimed.

"Do you like the place?"

"Hell yeah, she's a beauty, but the price is way too high."

"Tell him you'll get the money this afternoon, and to bring his lawyer do up the paperwork."

"You serious, man?"

"Sure, let's do it. Next, can you register the Caribou here okay?"

Billy Bob was still flustered with the surprise that he was to be the owner of a five-acre estate in the Philippines.

"Yeah, sure, registering a plane is easy. There's so much ex-Air Force stuff flying around, they will register almost anything as long as you pay the fees.

"Good, now which helicopter do you need here? Who knows, you might want to gouge the hell out of tourists and fly them around just so you can get up into the air again. A military pension isn't all that great," stated Farmer.

"A helicopter, too. Have I died and this is heaven? Are you playing with me?"

"No."

"Wow, no shit, man. Well, I don't need to do the big stuff now. A Bell 206 JetRanger would do us just dandy. Quan can fly the machine too."

"Okay, where do you buy one and can you do it today?"

"I know a pilot here who has a great Ranger. He might sell it. Do you want me to call him and ask what he wants for it?"

"Sure, you call him and let me know the number; you can buy the helicopter when you want."

For $75,000, Billy Bob was getting a 1973 Bell 206B JetRanger, with 830 hours.

To conclude the deal, Billy Bob arranged with his friend, the one selling him the chopper, to fly Farmer and Larry sixty miles down island to Dagupan enabling Farmer to wrap up the financial transactions.

Using the services of Hong Kong and Shanghai Bank of Commerce in Dagupan, Farmer transferred in the balance of his deposit account in Hong Kong and used the $160,000 to purchase Bank of England US bearer bonds.

At the Western Union Building down the street, he had the $30,000 from his account in Bangkok brought into the Philippines. He purchased Australian bonds in US dollars with these funds.

The Bank of the Philippines was the final stop.

It was a straightforward transaction to transfer $210,000 from the Bank of Switzerland. However, due to the account number and security code structure of accessing accounts in Switzerland, designed to avoid personal identification, the process took almost an hour. $65,000 in Bank of England bearer bonds and $145,000 in Bank of Australia bearer bonds were purchased.

At noon, they returned from their money run. They met for a seafood lunch at the secluded gazebo on the beach where Farmer gave two envelopes to Billy Bob. The first envelope contained the $225,000 in bonds to purchase the estate. The second envelope contained $75,000 of Australian bonds to purchase the helicopter.

Farmer wasn't done yet and he pulled out two more white envelopes. Each envelope contained $50,000 in bearer bonds. One was for Billy Bob and one was for Quan. He handed both of them to Billy Bob.

"Help Quan to go to school and push him get on with life," Farmer told Billy Bob. "You will also need to remind the people you do business with to keep the transactions, and the form of payments, a secret. You have the resources, should they not listen. Well, my friend, you are now an estate owner in the Philippines. And thanks for everything you've done for us," commented Farmer as he extended his hand to shake Billy Bob's.

Billy Bob was speechless. Merely, two days ago, he left behind a shoestring operation, living under the constant pressure that any day might be the day some unfit soldier would come and shoot him. Today he became someone he'd never expected to be. Everything had happened so quickly and with such civility. Still numb with surprise, he uttered, "Thank you. Yesterday is gone, and I thank you for my tomorrows."

"Hey bud, it's been a surreal adventure. We couldn't have done it without you. You have a right to know that what you have been a part of here is for the greater good of all mankind." Larry replied as he shook Billy Bob's hand.

Quan returned from his exercise stroll with the young girl from the host family. He was able to use his crutches well enough to keep up with his pretty friend.

"Watch over Billy Bob, Quan. That's a big job, but you can do it. You are alright, man," Larry said as he patted Quan on the head and gave him a thumbs-up signal.

* * *

The wheels of the Boeing 747 screeched emitting blue smoke as the airplane landed in San Francisco. The fourteen-hour flight put them back in the United States at eight o'clock of the day they had left

Manila. Sleep had come easy on the aircraft. They were rested for the repeat day.

Customs and Immigration was straightforward, even if the ex-marine reviewing their documents and luggage had a chip on his shoulder directed at all passengers.

Quick on the spot, Farmer got him to shed the attitude by enquiring about his tattoo on his right arm. The ex-marine told him it was earned from his tour on the USS Washington. Farmer, the returning reporter, made the marine feel more important than he was. He scanned their passports one more time and after looking down the long line behind them, decided two Canadian reporters returning from an assignment were not the ones he needed to challenge today. Four young punks were back in the line. He could have more fun with them.

They left the airport in a yellow taxi destined for Fisherman's Wharf, precisely where two Canadians would go when in San Francisco. Another car took them within four blocks of the old warehouse.

The warehouse felt like home. They had the space to clean up after the flight, unpack their gear, collect the remaining money, and lay down on the old army cots. They were back.

By late in the afternoon they'd had enough of dozing. They would work through the jet lag over the next few days. Dressed in jeans and t-shirts they left to find some food and a telephone. Six blocks toward the wharf, they found the Lobster House and ordered dinner. Farmer used the pay phone in the entranceway and called Carol.

"Gerry, he is hanging on, God knows how. His kidneys shut down. He is back on dialysis. The doctor's say he will not be with us much longer. Are you planning to visit him?"

"Yes, Carol. We hoped to swing by tonight if you think he is strong enough for a visit."

"He'll always find the strength for you. I would like to meet up with you too. I'll pop by around seven."

"Sounds great, Carol, we'll catch up with you soon."

"Good bye, Gerry," Carol choked out the words.

It was difficult for Farmer to imagine what Carol had been through this year. She was a strong woman, but even a strong woman can only take such pressure for so long.

"What's up, boss?"

"Carol says he's hanging on. We'll meet her at the hospital tonight."

"Yeah man, I figured out how he got this god damn raw deal in life," Larry stated, before he took a bite of his seared T-bone steak.

"How's that?"

"Pilots are different from other people. Our machine is part of us. We know if we look after her, she will look after us. It is like we become one when we are in the air."

"I think you are like that with everything made out of metal, and maybe even things made in New Zealand," Farmer shot back.

"Yeah, well, being a pilot is different than that, Mr. Funny Guy. I've been thinking about the run and what Shelby had to do and what I had to do. When we were at Cowboy 1, I wouldn't leave my machine alone for the night. I slept inside her; she was under my control and the Engine for the Candle was my responsibility. See that is what we do; we live with the helicopter when we are with her. I remember talking to Shelby about our cargo while we were in the hospital."

"When you were in the 'wounded leg' department?"

"Yes, you are full of one-liners today. Yeah, anyway he slept on the Chassis crate on top of two canvas tarps that night too, inside his helicopter, protecting her and the load. Farmer, he slept right on top of the nuclear shit. Man, that can't be a good deal. No one said anything about radioactivity or 'don't sleep on the fucking nuclear bomb Chassis,' but I figure they should have. I think that night of sleep gave Shelby the cancer."

Farmer, the former nuclear physicist, thought about this revelation as he ate his well-done steak. "Whenever we worked on any models of nuclear bombs the plutonium was always coated with Tungsten, except at the rifle entry point. The casing was lined with lead to stop any radiation leakage. However, the Candles were a new form of a cheaper, lighter, atomic bomb. The documents I went over regarding the casing and structure, proved it was lined with Tungsten first, then encapsulated in lead. The diagrams and my inspection of the model were correct. There shouldn't have been any leakage. Christ they could have given us a Chassis that leaked, but I wasn't allowed to take a Geiger with me to Laos, for the political safety of mission."

"Hey, man, this isn't our fault," said Larry. "When people aren't affected, they just don't get how someone else is going to pay for their mistakes. If they messed up in Nevada, we wouldn't know."

"I don't know if that caused it or not, but I can tell you that I am not certain that it didn't. I've thought about the risk too. I just didn't want to believe it could, or would, happen. Until now, I didn't realize he slept on top of the Chassis.

"It's possible that radiation leakage could have hit his body though. Christ, this fucked up operation killed him," Farmer said before he emptied his bottle of cola.

"Hey man, let's go visit Shelby and tell him this is all finished now. I won't talk to him about this though," said Larry.

Larry left thirty dollars on the table for the meal.

Farmer didn't speak in the taxi. Guilt haunted his thoughts as he pictured the bomb diagrams and retraced every step of his limited involvement with the Chassis. They arrived at the hospital and made their way to Shelby's room with the guidance of a reservist.

"Hey, Shelby, bet you didn't expect to see us again so soon," Larry said as they walked in the room.

Shelby was even smaller than the last time they visited him, merely a couple of weeks ago. His skin was yellow in color. He looked like he was already dead. Shelby nodded his head and lifted his right arm slightly as his form of a wave.

Larry leaned closer to him and said, "Mission complete. It's over."

Shelby understood the message and straightened his lips into a thin smile. He tried to lift his hand to salute, but couldn't. Larry instead saluted Shelby.

Shelby opened his lips enough to say, "Thank you."

Carol entered the room and Shelby twisted his head at her. She gave Larry and Farmer quick hugs. When they looked back at Shelby, he had already closed his eyes and fallen asleep.

"Sometimes he needs a short nap and then he is back with us. Let's grab a coffee and let him rest a bit. The cafeteria is down one floor. It has a comfortable lounge," Carol said.

Sitting in the plush leather chair in the lounge, Carol looked so beautiful, with her sandy brown hair flowing down her back over her yellow dress. She didn't look like a woman who had been beside her dying husband for the past year, wondering if each day would be his last.

Larry, in his matter of fact way asked, "Carol, how are you doing?"

"Okay, I guess. It's been hard to watch James go through so much. The pain he has endured. The treatments he's been through and now this wait for the end. Ken and the girls have been great, they try to spell me off, but the disintegration of the man never leaves you. The girls have their own young families and jobs so they've got enough on their plates."

"Carol, how are you doing for money?" asked Larry.

Surprised that Larry would ask such a direct question, Carol hesitated, "Okay, I guess. The house is paid off, but this last year has used up most of our savings. Veteran Affairs tries to help, but they seem to forget about you after being discharged. I met a good girl in the VA, but they don't give out any money without a challenge."

"Yeah, bureaucracy is brutal. It's almost as if none of those people have seen what war does to families. That has to change. Yes, that has to change," quipped Larry.

After coffee, they returned to Shelby's room, but he was still asleep.

"Carol, do you want a lift home in the taxi?" Farmer asked as they walked out of the hospital.

"No, thank you, I've got the Pinto, here. Where are my manners? Can I give you a ride?"

"That's okay. We are going to walk a bit to clear our heads and go back to the motel."

Carol kissed Farmer on the cheek and then did the same to Larry.

"I don't need to know what you have been doing, or what you used to do. James was very good at letting me know just enough. I can live with that. I really do care for you two. You've been there all along.

Now you have Ken and Leanne at your home. I know you will take care of them. I know Ken will do just fine. Can you help him remember where I live? I want him to come and visit me."

"Carol, all is well now. We'll watch Ken and make sure he comes to see you. Shelby means a lot to us. So do you," Larry replied and then added, "Carol, we are leaving tomorrow but can we meet you at your house around eleven?"

"Sure, that'll be nice. Well, here is my car so I will see you tomorrow."

"Take care, Carol," Larry said as he closed the door when she was inside the Pinto. They continued walking toward the Wharf.

"What was that all about? I think you blew the tough guy image right here, Larry."

"No, it's a pilot thing; one pilot knowing about another."

Larry remained silent for the block as they walked toward the warehouse.

"You know what we have to do, don't you?" he said as he turned to Farmer.

Farmer nodded, "Yes I know what we have to do. You are right. Man, we've been together so damn long that just when I think I know you, you come up with another new angle."

"Yeah, living does that to a guy. I got a whole new bag of tricks you ain't seen yet."

Chapter 22

Wednesday, July 13, 1977

The old warehouse had character. It was built to serve, but it also held a feeling of sanctuary.

After a restful night of sleep, Farmer poured a cup of coffee from the black metal percolator. Larry had been up for a while. He had pages of paper strewn across the table. The man was laying out a plan.

As he drank his coffee, Farmer read the one page summary. He was impressed. Larry set his sights, and he would execute his plan.

At eight o'clock, they caught a taxi four blocks east of the warehouse to take them to visit Mr. Pointer, account manager, at the Midland Bank in Union Square. Mr. Pointer was most disappointed that Mr. Gerald Brightman was closing his account so soon. He urged him to stay with the bank, but Gerald informed him that he needed the funds for renovations to his house. Mr. Pointer arranged for the cashier's check, which included interest income. Farmer left the bank with a cashier's check for $40,250.

The next cab ride took them to Raymond's Gold and Currency Exchange, the largest gold bullion and coin dealer in the city.

Chalkboards lined the rear wall as workers wrote in current exchange rates of all the world's major currencies. The price of gold was indicated in dollars per ounce.

Larry advised the clerk at the entry door, skirted by two armed guards, that he wanted to meet with an account manager. While he was waiting, he noted the price of gold was $142.80 per ounce.

Mr. Hyder led them into his glass walled office, closing the door behind them. "Now what can I do for you gentlemen?"

Larry took the lead. "Mr. Hyder, my mother passed away and left me a small inheritance to manage. I've never been much of an investor, but mom always told me gold was a good investment. I always did what my mom told me. I'd like to buy some gold."

"I am sorry to hear of your loss, Mr. . . ."

"Brown, Larry Brown."

"Ah, yes, Mr. Brown. I am very sorry to hear of your loss. However, I must admit your mother was a wise woman to recommend gold as an investment. Are you looking for gold bars or coins?"

"I know she bought gold coins. I guess I should do the same."

"Well, in gold coins there are really two coins to consider, one is the Gold Sovereign, minted by the Bank of England, and the other is the South African Krugerrand. They are a bit more difficult to source since we are not able to import recently minted coins. We do have some mint condition coins from 1971. What is the total value of coins that you are considering in this purchase?"

"$45,000 dollars worth."

Mr. Hyder was very pleased to hear that number. This sale would yield him a nice commission, an unexpected commission, one that had simply walked in off the street.

"I see, well then I might suggest a mix of seventy percent newer Sovereigns, we have some uncirculated 1976 coins, and for the thirty percent of Krugerrands, I suggest the 1971 proof coins."

"Now that sounds fine, just dandy. I have my money right here. I would like to take the coins with me, today."

Mr. Hyder was not expecting this certainty. "Uh yes, Mr. Brown. Let me find out what we can come up with."

Hitting the intercom button on his phone, he ordered his secretary to bring in some cold Pepsis for his clients. He started writing down a series of numbers, while looking at the chalkboards. Paper tape spewed out of his adding machine.

They took their sodas and sipped on the bottles as the accounting maniac, Mr. Hyder, worked through the calculations. When he was finished, he pulled out a black ledger book to verify that he had the coins in stock.

At half past ten, Larry and Farmer left Raymond's Gold and Currency Exchange with one brand new brief case containing velvet separated pages laced with just shy of twenty pounds of individually-sealed Gold Sovereigns and Krugerrands; $45,000 of gold coinage.

The taxi stopped at Carol's three-bedroom rancher promptly at eleven. Carol sat waiting for them on her covered front porch. She looked worried. Her voice cracked as she spoke, "He's not doing well today. The girls will be here in a couple of hours. I hope he can last."

This news changed the flavor of the event, but Carol regained her composure to let the men inside her house.

"Carol, we have to leave and we might not get back for a while. We worry about you and want to help you through this tough time. This is for you to use in any way you need." Larry said with concern and handed her the new black briefcase.

"What have you done?" she asked as she opened the case. "What is this?"

"The case contains some gold coins, Carol. You can keep them or sell them. The name of the broker is in the bag. He will buy them whenever you want to sell some of them. The coins are a better way to keep some safety for yourself—you control it."

"But why? How did you get these?"

"Oh, don't worry Carol, all is legal. We met up with some of the old crew, and hell they think the world of Shelby. They want you to be safe. This is our way of helping you be safe. No one has done anything wrong. It is important to us for you to have it."

"But I can get by okay. I can't take your money."

"Yes you can, because we can't give it back to these people, they're all over the place now. This is what we meant to do. Please accept this as our respect for you and Shelby. You mean a lot to so many of us."

Carol reached for the rough and tough Larry and gave him a big hug. "I don't understand you men. One time you are tough as steel and the next time you are as gentle as a lamb. I know why James thinks of you as his brothers. You are closer to him than his brothers will ever be."

"Well, Carol, we asked the taxi driver to wait for us. The meter is running. We'll see Ken soon and tell him to call you. I'll even kick him out of town for a break to visit you. Please take care of yourself. I am only a phone call away at any time. Goodbye, Carol," offered Larry.

* * *

At the warehouse, Farmer set a cloth bag on the table. Today was the end of Mr. Gerald Brightman and Mr. Larry Brown. Every related document and pictures, including receipts, transfers, passports, visas and business cards went into the cloth bag.

Farmer rode by taxi, with all the camera gear, to the Greyhound bus depot. The camera gear was on its way back to the professor.

Farmer had one final stop to make. At the Hartford Insurance company, he paid his warehouse insurance for the next year and prepaid for the security monitoring of the place. In addition, he purchased insurance for two 1965 Harley Davidson Electra Glides, the last of the panhead motor series.

Larry had gone over the bikes while Farmer had been running his errands. It was just after the lunch hour when they pulled out of the warehouse on the two Harleys.

Riding down past the wharf, Farmer found what he was looking for in a trash barrel burning in an alley. He dropped the cloth bag, with their old documents, into the flames of the open barrel. Using a stick, he turned the papers repeatedly until the fire consumed them. The two Canadian reporters were officially terminated.

Back on the streets again, they took a right onto Van Ness Avenue, South onto 10th Street and onto the overpass to swing North onto Highway 80 and across to Oakland.

Just after eight, they pulled into the Medford Motel in Oregon.

It had been a long while since they had ridden the Harleys and different parts of their bodies developed new aches. It was time for a greasy beef burger, a beer, and a good night's sleep.

They were back in the US of A.

Chapter 23

Thursday, July 14, 1977

Larry finally slept soundly through the night, a first since leaving New Pontiac. Carol would be cared for when Shelby died. It still rubbed him wrong that the wife of a soldier like Shelby should have to worry about money.

Larry hadn't given much thought about the Veteran Affairs department before he saw Shelby and listened to Carol.

He had seen that the hospitals did what they could for the dying, but he wondered more about those that lived on, be it the soldier with a disabling illness, or the family of the dead soldier. What happened to them? How were they cared for? More thoughts went through his mind as the panhead motor rumbled him along Oregon's I-5.

Riding the Harley felt good. They hadn't done a road trip since they parked the bikes in 1975. Larry's body felt stiff but the ride was always the reward for new muscle pains. The aches and pains reminded him he was alive; he was free. He was going to live with more of these aches and pains in his future. He no longer carried the burden of the past. A new page had finally turned. Hell, a new chapter had begun. The key to his whole future was waiting for him in New Pontiac.

After seeing Carol go through all that she had, Farmer realized he had put May through a tough time with this trip. He couldn't tell her about why they had to leave, for her safety, but it must have been hard to understand. May accepted he was going somewhere, to do something he had to do, and she did not know when, or if, he would return. How was she supposed to deal with that? However, she had, and he knew she would be in New Pontiac when he arrived. She would not ask him about where he had been, or what he'd done.

* * *

Driving through Portland on the Harleys caused more people to look at them than they wanted. At 1:30, they met Professor at the Golden Wonder restaurant, two blocks south of the First City Bank.

Professor brought what Farmer asked of him during the telephone call last night. He handed a leather briefcase to Farmer. Farmer took the case into the washroom and locked the door.

He separated the two safety deposit box keys, and their Oregon Driver's licenses, into three pockets. Professor had been the safe keeper of their identities. All that remained in the briefcase case was the envelope containing Colonel "Harley" Henry's instructions, pictures, and the extra blank passports. Farmer knew he should destroy the information, yet he had a strange feeling that it might be needed one day. Instead, he decided he would keep all of the Quiet Thunder documentation in the deposit box here in Portland.

Into Box 175, he stuffed the envelope containing Harley's details of Operation Quiet Thunder, pictures, the three letters from President Huntington and the blank passports. He did remove the written instructions from Harley that discussed the money. Those he put back into his case. After returning the box into its storage bin, and locking it, he paid three years of advance fees for the box, in cash.

Larry and Professor walked two blocks north to enter the Bank of America to meet with the foreign account transaction manager. After two telephone conversations with the Bank of Switzerland, then a confirmation telex, $300,000 moved into a new account at the Bank of Switzerland. The remaining $290,000, plus the accumulated interest of $22,782, stayed in the original account.

For the second transaction, Larry withdrew $50,000 from the original account. The manager did not seem to be the least bit interested in why these two men were doing this; he focused on completing the tasks by quitting time. He was most efficient in his work and soon had converted the $50,000 from Mr. Larry Archer's 'inheritance account' into US bearer bonds. After placing the bonds in a brown bank envelope, he handed them to Larry and concluded their dealings.

Larry and Professor met Farmer at the coffee shop. Larry handed him the $50,000 in bonds, which Farmer put into safety deposit Box, 175, in the event they might someday need the money to deal with the paperwork that was also in the box.

* * *

The intense professor and Larry were in the middle of an animated conversation back at the coffee shop near the bank. They agreed to head back to Professor's home for dinner and a few cold ones. Professor would pick up the grub and beer in his truck. The men would head out on their Harleys.

Larry was on a high. He was on his way to building a real life. When Larry had a plan, he worked it to fruition. Professor was the key to Larry's plan and Farmer knew that in due course he would learn what they had decided. He could wait; he had no worries. Larry could run the show without his advice. After the first cold Budweiser bottles were opened, and each had taken a long guzzle, he laid out the deal.

Larry created a way to help the veterans, and the families left behind. Professor would set up a brokerage account with the initial deposit of $300,000. Annually, he would draw out the gains from investments for distribution to those in need. He would call on his old friends to bring forward names and to distribute, anonymously, the funds to the needy.

Professor and Larry ironed out details late into the night. Professor had a mission to work on and he would do so with all the liberal vengeance he possessed. He was certain he could generate $30,000-$40,000 annually from this initial deposit, but he had greater dreams. They believed that as news of this society spread, the society would receive donations and the annual payouts could increase.

This was veterans looking after veterans, anonymously, and with no interference from either Veteran Affairs or any other arm of the government. It was one way the forgotten ones would be able to live a better life in the country for which they had given so much. There were no two better, and more uniquely qualified, people to conduct such a gesture; the families would be well served by the dedication of these self-sacrificing patriots. Appropriately, they named the organization, *The Silent Veterans Society.*

Not many would have expected such an idea from Larry, but the trip had changed the man. The program suited the new Larry.

* * *

Back at the farm, the end of the day whistle blew at the mill.

May invited Starr, Leanne, Mary, George Popoff (the Mill Manager), Fred, and Ken to her house to celebrate their success at completing the week's orders a full day ahead of schedule. She served store bought beer, along with a vegetable, goat cheese, and sausage platter to her guests, while still dressed in her blue and black plaid work shirt, denim jeans and brown, steel-toed, leather boots.

May, who seldom drank alcohol, had a beer with the gang as they sat in the picnic area at the back of the house. She found it odd that this group of people had not shared a beer together before.

The team was working well together, beyond setting the record production level this week.

Working side-by-side in the office had created a friendship between Mary and Starr. Starr was a smart, dedicated worker, and she asked Mary for advice. Mary had changed too and engulfed a new view of life. She took on the new friendship, and actually enjoyed her new association.

Ken had implemented staffing changes in shipping. Susan and Brenda fit in well with Reno and his crew, so Stoner and his two friends moved to jobs inside the mill. This was a milestone in the mill's history; two women now ran forklifts full time. The department was clicking. Orders were ready for the trucks on time, they were correct, and the paperwork was complete and ready to go with the load.

Therefore, the beer flowed in recognition of many accomplishments. The new group worked well as a team. May's approach to operations worked for them.

Chapter 24

Friday, July 15, 1977

The aroma of frying bacon, eggs from free-range chickens, and hash browns from yellow potatoes, mixed with green onions, woke Farmer.

When he stepped into the kitchen, it appeared to him that the pair had not taken a break from their work on 'The Silent Veterans Society'.

Professor was now laying out the first year's investment funds of stocks, including General Electric, 3M, and Johnson and Johnson. These dividend-paying stocks would give them a safe and reasonable annual return, with a healthy growth potential. To jack up the future earnings of the fund, IBM, the Nightrider Fund, and Brickmaster Investments were added to the portfolio. The professor knew the winners from the losers. Larry had absolute confidence in his skills.

Professor was excited about this new project. It gave him reason to contact his friends from the past. It would keep him on his toes, since he didn't want to piss off Larry. His guiding management law would be, 'do what is right for the veterans, and that will keep Larry happy'. The two objectives were the same.

After one final cup of coffee, and strong handshakes with the professor, the riders hit the road again, heading north on Highway 84.

It was a great day to be on the road. The temperature sat comfortably in the mid-eighties with just a slight overcast sky. They were warm, but not baking in the sweltering heat, which often hit in mid-July. It was too far to push for home today. Instead, their older bodies would take the easy eight-hour ride and stop for the night in Spokane.

Larry always stayed at the Ponderosa Motel, beside the Exxon truck stop, just north of Spokane, Washington. The parking lot at the motel was almost full when they arrived. Larry knew Mabel and Fred, the owners of the place, so they paid the preferred member rate for the last two rooms in the motel.

The Ponderosa didn't have a restaurant. Across the road, the truck stop food was decent. However, one block away was the Steakhouse Buffet. Larry insisted on walking the block down to the meatery. The Steakhouse had an all-you-can-eat buffet that let you add a second, third, or even a fourth T-bone for an extra buck apiece. It was a hungry man's kind of place.

Larry took the second T-bone, Farmer stayed with a single well-done piece of beef. The salad bar extended down the center of the restaurant and in the line-up, the vegetables were set in the center island and then the potatoes, buns, cabbage rolls, sliced ham, fried chicken and all the other attractions continued on. The line ended at the cooked T-bone treasures.

Their corner table looked back at the motel and the truck stop. Larry had just sliced off his second bite, of his first T-bone, when a rap on the window made him jump up out of his chair. The noise had come from Jimmy's knuckles. Outside Jimmy and Gord laughed after witnessing the reaction of Larry to the surprise.

They grabbed their plates of food and sat at the table next to Farmer and Larry. The last two weeks had been good for the new driving team. They had made two more trips to Eureka. Tomorrow they were continuing south to Eureka with loads of fir beams.

The truckers enjoyed gossip. Jimmy couldn't wait to tell them about recent events back in New Pontiac.

"May took over your office, Farmer. She's at the mill at 6:30, every morning, and she doesn't leave until after 5:30. Fred's given up on trying to beat her to work or stay later than her." Jimmy took a big bite of his steak and continued, "George Popoff meets with her twice a day. I think he's taken a liking to telling her about how the mill is running."

"Tell Larry about Starr," Gord said to Jimmy to have him continue in his update.

"Oh yeah, well now Starr is keeping track of Slick and his order system. I hear Slick's first meeting with her was a bit rough. I guess no one had ever asked him to lay out what he did this week, where he was, and why he could not phone in daily reports.

"Rumor has it that he's on the wagon. They say he phones in every day, he jokes around with the women, and he makes sure Starr knows of any changes in the orders.

"Hey Larry, you had better watch that Slick, last week he bought flowers for the women in the office. He's a changed man.

"Hell, even Mary brought him in a Huckleberry pie for him to take home to the wife and kids. A month ago, Mary wouldn't talk to him. Now she is baking him pies. I think Mary found a heart while you were away. Or at least having Reverend Bob move in with her has made her more compassionate."

Larry looked at Farmer and said, "Hey man, it looks like we are out of jobs. They don't need us anymore."

"No, they did what we should have done a long time ago. We are lucky to have such strong women. It sounds okay with me. I was thinking of learning how to fish anyway," returned Farmer.

"What are you two driving?" Jimmy asked.

"The Harleys. Thought I'd bring them home for the winter," Farmer said.

"Cool hogs, man. Hey man, we're going to the Indian Lakes Casino. Guess we'll grab a taxi. You guys are in for it, right," Jimmy asked.

"Sure man, why not? You got some money you want me to lose for you," replied Larry.

"Hell no, man, you get to squeeze open that locked wallet of yours and put out your own stake."

* * *

The taxi ride was short. Inside the brightly lit casino, the neon lights and graphic signs made for an all-night party. The casino was only a couple of years old, so its polish and shine had lost very little of its dazzling luster. The slot room was filled with the clinking of handles being pulled and coins dropping down into clanging bins. The casino was its own world.

Drinks were free, as long as you played, so Jimmy and Farmer sat down at a blackjack table and ordered whiskeys to get them going. Larry's game was poker, but neither Farmer nor Jimmy would play at his table. Larry had the strongest poker face around. They never won any money when they played at his table.

Gord found a cute young woman in a middle bank of slot machines. Since there was an open machine beside her, he decided to play that machine tonight.

As midnight neared, they had consumed all the free booze they needed for the night. Farmer hailed a cab at the front door. Larry came out almost a grand ahead; the rest broke even. Gord struck out with the woman when her huge sober husband arrived and whisked his wife away.

The four of them took a vote during the taxi ride. Larry paid the cab fare back to the Ponderosa.

Chapter 25

Saturday, July 16, 1977

Breakfast at the Exxon was rushed. Each had the special, consisting of two eggs, hash browns, toast, and orange juice. They all had places to go.

Jimmy and Gord had another load waiting for them back at the mill, so this was a drop and return run for both of them—the life of a trucker—make money when the loads are available to make up for the slow times.

The bikers headed north on Highway 325 and then onto 25 to reach the Canadian border at Paterson, British Columbia.

At the inspection booth, Farmer shut off his bike, and removed his helmet, before handing the Canadian Customs agent his United States of America passport with his Canadian Landed Immigrant card inside.

The young agent sized him up, focusing on the bike and then the bags on the back of the bike. He was standing in the open, receiving direct sunlight, and sweating from the heat already.

"Have you been away from Canada for more than six months?" he asked.

"No, I came down for the 4th of July."

"Do you have a job to return to in the United States?"

"I have some businesses, but my active ones are in Canada. I own the Blue River Lumber Company."

"Oh, the company Jimmie drives for. He comes through a few times a week."

"Yes," Farmer replied to the agent who was sourcing more information than he should be, but it was harmless.

"Do you have any alcohol or tobacco in your possession today?"

"A couple of packs of smokes, no booze."

"Is this fellow behind you travelling with you, too?"

"Yes he is. He is my partner in the businesses."

Handing him his passport and card, the agent offered, "Okay, Mr. Field, enjoy the rest of this hot summer back in New Pontiac, eh."

Farmer pulled ahead as the agent asked the same questions of Larry. They were on their way home within five minutes.

It was a cool ride through the shady mountain roads. By early afternoon, they turned off the highway and onto the road into the mill site and New Pontiac. The gate was locked, but Charlie, the watchman/musician, was sitting under the tree beside the security guard's hut. He always wore denim overalls over his massive frame. Because of his size, Charlie presented a real impediment to most visitors. His image fit the role of this security position.

Farmer got off his bike and took off his black skullcap helmet.

"How's music these days, Charlie?"

"Hey Farmer! I heard you went on a trip. How was it? Cool bikes, man."

"Are you going to let us in, Charlie?"

"Oh yeah," he said as he pulled out his key and unlocked the chain around the gate.

May and Starr were in the back yard picking cabbages as they heard the two motorcycles pull into the driveway. Both looked at each other, confused, surprised, and in wonderment. Was it them?

When they walked around the side of the house, they saw their men climb off the bikes. Each ran into the open arms of their biker. May did not usually show such affection in public, neither did Farmer for that matter, but today was a joyous celebration—a reunion. They held each other close. They were together again.

Something was off with Larry as he held beautiful Starr's hands and looked at her. He looked into her sparkling blue eyes; set in her bright face, surrounded by her long blonde hair. Unexpectedly, he broke their gaze and started rummaging around in his saddlebag.

Out of his saddlebag, he pulled out a package he had obtained from Professor. With the black velvet box in his hand, he kneeled down on his left knee. He presented the gold ring, with the sparkling white diamond mounted in place between 18-karat gold claws, to his Starr.

"Starr, will you marry me?" Larry said to her as tears formed in the corner of her eyes.

"Yes, my Larry, of course I will marry you. I missed you so much. We were meant for each other," Starr replied as she wiped the tears.

Getting up from his kneeling position, Larry took his wife to be in his arms for a close hug. A kiss sealed the deal—the overdue deal for a lifetime together.

Farmer and May witnessed the proposal sequence. Although surprised, they were not disappointed. They both congratulated their friends.

"Dear, do you have any plans on when, and where, we will get married?"

"Well, I am not much for the crowds so a small wedding would do me fine. The church scene is too stuffy," replied Larry in the most cautious way he could, without derailing the sincerity of the moment.

Starr looked again at the hardened man she so loved and announced, "Well then we should get married today." Turning away from her man, she asked May, "Will you and Farmer stand up for us?"

May replied for both of them, "We'd be honored to stand up for you at your wedding. Now Starr, you run home, clean up, and come back here. I will help you get ready for this special event."

They hugged one more time and Larry got on the Harley, still loaded with his gear from the trip, and drove off to find Reverend Bob.

Starr playfully skipped her way to their house. She was a teenager in love, at the age of thirty-three. She was going to be a wife to the greatest man in the world.

* * *

After a rushed bath, Farmer held May in his arms while they lay naked on their bed. The silk sheets pressed cool against their bodies.

Even though Starr would be returning to get ready, they could not resist the time to enjoy each other. Farmer ran his rough hands along May's lithe, frame. Beads of sweat dripped from her spine after their passionate reunion. She was radiating, more than usual. Touching her now reminded him of how fortunate he was to be with her highness.

"Honey, what do you think about having children?" quizzed Farmer as he lay beside his naked wife.

May's face erupted into a big smile. "Yes, Gerry, I would like children. We will be good parents."

"Well then I guess we had better keep on working on that," he said as he kissed her smooth, narrow lips.

* * *

Starr was still bubbling in her happiness when she knocked on the door to May and Farmer's house. She carried a long, white, cotton dress; something she picked up a few years ago.

"You and Larry were made for each other," Farmer said to her as he gave her a good hug. He was dressed in the blue sports coat that May told him he had to wear, overtop his green shirt buttoned all the way up, except for the last one at the neck, and a red paisley tie, loosely tied. To finish off his ensemble, he wore new brown corduroy pants, with his polished silver Harley Davidson belt buckle on a black belt and soft brown leather shoes. He'd been allowed to tone down from May's original demands regarding his attire, but this was what she would let him get away with.

* * *

Sitting on the front porch, Larry wore a light blue suit. Starr had dressed him. He also had to wear a tie, a red one, which hung loosely at the neck. His hair had been combed and he had shaved.

"Got another of those," Farmer asked as he pointed to the beer in Larry's hand.

Larry handed him a cold one from the cooler beside him.

"Nervous?" Farmer kidded to him as he used a screwdriver to pop the cap off the bottle.

"No, not at all, should have done this last year. Now I can't figure out why I didn't. Man, Starr means everything to me. The trip made me realize how important she is to me. This is the best thing I have done in my life."

"To my best friend and his happiness," Farmer said as he clanked his bottle against Larry's in a cheer.

"Yeah, man, back at you on that! You are my best friend. We have been to hell and back a few too many times. God knows why we did it, and how we got here, but we did. I think I will like the next chapter in life just fine.

During this past week, Farmer had witnessed Larry put out more emotion than he had shown in all their years together. He was a changed man, he was in love, and now he was going to marry his soul's desire.

* * *

Reverend Bob stood before his small group of witnesses, and the bride and groom, as they congregated in front of the Bell 206 Long Ranger in Larry's helicopter hangar.

The irony of contrasts made the event as it could only be.

Starr looked like a fragile white rose in her white cotton dress. Her blonde hair was accented by silver sparkles. She wore a light blue silk scarf around her waist and shiny silver arm bracelets on both arms. May provided the sets of bracelets and the silver necklace with the pennant made from diamonds surrounding the magnificent green opal stone. The necklace had been in May's family for generations, but it became the perfect wedding gift for Starr.

The bride also wore a silver tiara, with pink and yellow roses adorning the silver banding, and daisies strewn throughout. May had given the tiara to Starr as well.

May wore a royal blue silk dress, accented by the pure silver bracelets on her arms. Her necklace hung delicately and rested above the cleavage cut of her dress. The Vietnamese traditional accessories created a warm aura around the natural beauty of the bride and her bridesmaid.

On the opposite side, in front of the Bell 206 helicopter, standing tall and straight in his powder blue suit, Larry proudly admired his radiant wife to be.

Farmer's polished silver Harley Davidson belt buckle gave their side a small amount of glitter, nowhere matching the jewelry and shine of the bride's party. Mary helped adjust the fashion imbalance by pinning a white rose on the lapel of the groom and his best man.

The large overhead shops fans circulated the air around the group as Reverend Bob performed an abbreviated service. As the ceremony progressed, the couple moved further ahead of their friends who remained in front of the helicopter. When they exchanged the rings, they were ahead of the rest of the party by ten feet. At the conclusion of the ceremony, Larry held his wife's face as he kissed her, and then hugged her as tight as he could, without harming her, to affirm his job to make sure she would be safe under his watch.

Fred flipped the passenger seat back to give access to the bride and groom to enter the backseat of his Cadillac convertible. May and Farmer joined him in the front seat. The purring 429 Cadillac engine pulled the big car away from the helicopter hangar. Some helper had tied a string of tin cans to the bumper, which rattled and smashed against the gravel roadway as they drove away. Fred accented the rumbling tin can noises with the two horns of the Cadillac as they proceeded through town, stopping at the edge of the field beside the far entrance to the farm.

Parked in the shade of the large cedar trees alongside the road, four of them lit up cigarettes, May didn't smoke. After two glasses of champagne and a fluid conversation, Fred determined he had better get them back to the hall, since Mary had set out to prepare a dinner for them and he didn't want to catch it from her if he was late with the guests of honor.

They drove to the Pontiac Hall in traditional style, again with the tin cans dragging and banging behind them.

Somehow, during this afternoon, Mary had organized an army of cooks to assemble the feast for tonight's celebration. She had men, women, and children preparing the tables, the food, and the flower placements. In this short time, they had prepared and presented a complete lasagna meal, with garden salad, corn on the cob, garlic bread, and strawberries for desert.

While they were eating dinner, Farmer opened his toast by informing the attendees that Larry must have been born with a horseshoe to find such a beautiful person as Starr, and then to get her to marry him. The men in the audience echoed Farmer's comments and toasted Larry and Starr.

Farmer then told a story about Larry. "Years ago we made a trip together to deliver a load to a base in Thailand. The old truck assigned to us by the sergeant in the Motor Pool was about the roughest truck you have ever seen. Nothing electrical worked. To start it you had to hammer on the starter switch with a screwdriver about five times.

"Larry was pissed. I just figured we would do this one run and then the truck would be the sergeant's problem again. When I met Larry at the truck in the morning, he had that big grin on his face. Those that have seen that twisted lip grin of his, you know what I mean."

A few people who had witnessed the grin clapped.

"Yes, so you know what I mean. Inside the truck, I saw new wires coming out from under the dash and going into a big coil of wires, neatly wrapped in duct tape. Larry pushed a new switch on the dash and the truck fired up. He flicked on the new set of switches, one by one to prove that the lights, wipers, horn, cargo lights, and fan, all worked from this row of switches. During the night, Larry rewired the whole truck with his own wiring plan. He did it well, since everything worked on the trip."

Farmer shook his head as he remembered the trip.

"When we returned the truck, the Motor Pool sergeant looked at the truck, and the wiring harness Larry had made himself, and he started muttering about what Larry had done. Larry stared him down and said something like, 'Why don't you just do your job, so we don't have to drive junk like this to do our job?' The sergeant's face turned beet red."

Some of the guests clapped as this was definitely a Larry event.

"But the story doesn't end there. On our way back to the mess hall, I asked Larry where he found the wire to do the job. In his best poker face, he replied, 'There was a jeep parked inside the shop that had all the wire he needed.'

"You know Larry never tells you too much, so I had to ask him, 'was there was anything special about the jeep?'

"Larry replied to me, 'Nope, it was green and it even had a nice flag with two white stars on it.'"

Most of the attendees got the significance of the stars and clapped loudly.

"Yes, there were many different days that I shared with Larry, over all these years. Larry has been a good friend. I know he and Starr will be happy together. We all wish them the best in their life together."

The audience got up to toast the new couple again.

After the dinner dishes were cleared away, and the tables moved to the side, the band started playing.

The newlyweds danced their first dance to Joe Cocker's *You Are So Beautiful*. The gate watchman, Big Charlie, belted out the tune. His voice proved to be a dead reckoning of Joe Cocker's grizzled voice.

At the commencement of the second verse, Farmer and May joined them on the dance floor, followed by Mary and Reverend Bob. By the start of the third verse, the dance floor was full.

The evening continued with children dancing and playing throughout the hall. Between the garden and the hall, the booze flowed, along with some good drugs.

* * *

Before midnight, the bride and groom were driven to their home. It had been another successful event for the Cadillac and Fred the chauffeur.

Larry carried Starr over the threshold, turning their house into their home. He carried her up the stairs to their bedroom.

Somehow, one of Mary's helpers had gotten in, decorated the room in fresh flowers, and put out candles. Larry set Starr onto their bed and lay beside her. Holding her tight he said, "My beautiful Starr, I thank you for being here with me. I will watch over you for the rest of our lives."

Starr held Larry's big hands in her tiny palms against her heart.

"This is good, and we will be good together."

She released his hands and took off her tiara. She reached down and unbuckled Larry's pants. They were soon naked, with Starr on top of Larry. Tonight felt very different for both of them. They were married now. Through the course of this night's session of love and passion, they consummated their marriage and truly, they were one.

Starr lifted herself and fell onto Larry. She ran her fingers over his face. "Honey, I don't know when is the right time to say this, but I have never been closer to you than I am right now, so here goes. Larry, my husband, we are pregnant. We are going to have a baby!"

The shock hit Larry and ran through his body. There was no hesitation as he took her mouth to his. When he released her lips and looked deeply into her eyes, a tear ran down her left cheek. "Starr this is the best day in my life. I am very happy, my shining Starr."

They entwined with arms and legs and lay together as one during their first night as husband and wife.

Chapter 26

Sunday, July 17, 1977

Sunday was a hangover day, not necessarily from drugs or alcohol, but from life itself. Starr had married one of the men best known by reputation, but the least known personally.

The greatest shock was felt by those people who thought they knew Larry Johnson. Seeing that he was actually excited, placated, and had truly found peace in his fresh bride, Starr, came as an odd surprise to all of them. The solitary man had allowed Starr to become one with him; the pairing would shine.

Larry and Starr drove away in his rare '69 Super Bee with the 426 Hemi pumping out 425 hp—one of 166 manufactured. For Larry, Las Vegas was the only place to go for a honeymoon—Las Vegas the land of bright lights, the place for stars. Where else in the world could a millionaire get a T-bone steak for $1.99 and drown it in free champagne?

* * *

May and Farmer had the day to themselves. They chose to take an afternoon walk up road alongside the river. Holding hands as they walked and talked, they reacquainted themselves with each other and confirmed the strong bond they shared with one another.

They soon arrived at a natural hot springs in the forest, off the main gravel logging road. The other residents seldom visited these waters, perhaps in respect of Farmer. He did consider this place as his personal retreat.

The rough pool consisted of a pile of rocks, which dammed the water flow back into smooth rock faces. It was a natural pool, four feet deep, with granite seats, placed by nature, on the edge.

Farmer took hold of his beautiful, and naked, princess by the waist and escorted her into the water. Outside of closed door of their bedroom, this was the only place May would appear naked. In spite of her rare beauty, she was naturally shy.

He held his princess tight in his arms in the warm hot springs water as his mind cemented the firm commitment he would not leave her again. It was time for him to close the last chapter in his past and start a new book of life.

Chapter 27

One year later

Friday, July 28, 1978

The Eagles, Hotel California played in the cassette deck, but Farmer's attempt at changing the somber mood in the truck, as they drove to Riverbend, had no effect on Larry or on Doctor Ray Miller. His passengers likely didn't even hear the tune playing as they remained slumped low into their seats and stared out their side window, their minds pre-occupied with the task ahead.

The last year had been a time of change for the farm in New Pontiac.

Sawmill orders were down. Some residents had moved away to work in the oil fields of Alberta. Others went back to the States, now that the border guards begrudgingly accepted the recent amnesty legislation.

Ken and Leanne moved to California where Ken took a job teaching at the University of San Francisco. Their child was born in May. Their life together had gone a full circle to emerge as a united and legal family living in a bungalow in San Francisco.

A most devastating incident in the spring shocked all the remaining residents of the farm. On March 28, 1978, Starr's water broke. She was in her home, in her bed, fighting the contractions, when Doctor Miller and his nurse, arrived. It looked like a quick delivery, since she was fully dilated.

Despite the regular contractions, the baby would not emerge.

Doc unwrapped his sterilized forceps, a tool he did not like to use, and used them to help the baby emerge. The baby's head finally emerged revealing that the umbilical cord was wrapped around the baby's neck. The baby was being strangled by the cord, which was also preventing his delivery.

When Doc tried to rotate the baby, Starr went into convulsions. Her heart stopped. Doc worked to resuscitate Starr, finally resorting to an adrenaline shot directly into her heart. However, her heart did not react even to that shot.

The baby died while he was working on reviving Starr. As guilty as Doc felt about the catastrophe, the autopsy revealed that the baby would not have survived the day, due to a malformed chest, which crushed upon the baby's heart and lungs.

Larry had been delivering wire spools for the power company with his helicopter when he got the message of Starr's labor. He arrived at their house an hour after Starr and their baby had died. In Larry's own way of handling situations, he kissed Starr on the forehead, walked out to his garage, and drove away in his Super Bee. When he hit the pavement, those that were listening could hear him burn rubber in all four gears. He did not return to New Pontiac until the following afternoon.

If it was possible, during the past four months, Larry had become more introverted than ever before. The 'New Larry' was gone. The Veteran Society was no longer on his radar. Starr was gone and so was Larry.

He had set his own daily regime. Early in the morning, he flew away in his small Bell 47G helicopter. Farmer figured he flew up to Starr Lake, but Larry wasn't ready to have someone pry into what he was doing, so Farmer let it go. At one o'clock, he went out to his rifle range, in an old gravel pit, and shot off a box or two of ammo using one of his rifles from his personal armory. Everyone stayed away from the rifle range in the afternoon to give him his space.

At six o'clock each day, Farmer took him a plate of dinner and a half sack of beer. Larry was always waiting on the porch. He didn't say anything while he ate his dinner and drank the beer with Farmer.

Farmer recounted the operations of the day while Larry ate and drank without entering the one-sided conversation.

The process was repeated day after day, with Larry expressing so few words during these evening sittings. He had become a torn man; a man who had his very reason for existence taken from him.

This field trip to Riverbend was an unwanted break in Larry's routine. Doc had discovered significant pain in Larry's stomach when he performed his pilot's medical examination last month. He forced Larry to get an x-ray at the Riverbend hospital. They were on their way to the follow-up appointment with the radiologist.

While Larry and Farmer thought there might be something to it, Doc Miller had a more sobering assessment. The last appointment on Friday afternoon was always reserved for bad news–the waiting room would be empty so the patient would not have to endure the walk of rage past other patients.

Doc Miller and Larry met with the radiologist at 4:40 that Friday afternoon. The technician had the x-rays of Larry's stomach clipped on the light panel. The three silver dollar-sized black circles around his liver and his left kidney were cancerous tumors. Doc Miller knew the diagnosis before the radiologist explained it to Larry. They were inoperable tumors.

This was a death sentence to be served over an unknown number of years. Tumors intertwined with organs were inoperable. When the pain got too bad, Doc would give him the morphine to get through it. In just ten minutes, Larry had been transformed from a living, though mourning, man, to a prisoner with a death sentence.

Farmer was reading the Reader's Digest in the waiting room. He recognized the long faces of both Doc and Larry as they emerged from the office. He did not need to be told the results.

Farmer was quite aware of the recent news about the carcinogens in Agent Orange killing off those that thought they had survived the war. However, the focal point of his thoughts went back to the Candle and Operation Quiet Thunder. He was now convinced of the reason no records were ever kept of that mission. They knew the team would all die from cancer from the radiation leaking from the bomb. The history of the operation would be buried in five coffins.

Farmer could not help but selfishly wonder if he was the reason that May had miscarried their baby before Christmas, and she had not been able to conceive this year.

As they left the hospital parking lot, Larry announced more words than he had spoken in a sentence since Starr's death.

"Take me to the bank and then to the liquor store."

Doc Miller bit his lip. He was a realist. Larry could not change his fate. There was no sense in pushing the guidance of eating and living healthily, and promoting false hopes of recuperation. Instead, just today, Doc decided that preaching was bullshit. Let a dying man eat, drink, and smoke whatever he wants. Pain and life will end regardless. The wisdom he had advised in the past was in question in his own mind as he witnessed Larry's fate.

Living an extra day in significant pain, because you drank vegetable juice instead of tasting fine bourbon and Cuban cigars, no longer justified the prescription. Doc would offer better advice to his patients from now on.

By the time Farmer drove his Blazer truck down Main Street, in New Pontiac, each of them had finished their two-dollar Cuban cigars and were well on their way into their second forty pounder of Crown Royal. Fortunately, Larry had planned ahead and picked up a few extras at the liquor store.

The truck stalled short of Larry's driveway, in the middle of the road. They stumbled to the front porch while Doc's fine-tuned hands carried the remaining bottle and half of whiskey.

Inside the house, the breeze through the open windows cooled the front room from the day's blazing heat. Each of them took a recliner. With greatly handicapped coordination, they managed to extend the leg rests to accommodate their exhausted souls and bodies.

Larry broke the silence.

"Farmer, I ain't going to go the way Shelby did. I ain't going to go as a shell of a man."

"What the hell are you saying, man? You don't know that, you could have years."

"Farmer, I ain't going to go the way Shelby did. I ain't going to check out that way."

* * *

At 5:45 the next morning, just as the sun cast its light on the farm, Farmer's throbbing head woke to the sound of Larry's Bell 206 helicopter circling the town. Out the bedroom window, he watched the helicopter circle a second time and then climb in elevation, away from the farm, heading north.

The place will never be the same, Farmer thought to himself as Larry and his helicopter disappeared behind the mountains.

The End

About Doug Hedman

Doug Hedman started working with machinery at a young age and at heart remains a gearhead, interested in everything with an engine that moves. In his journey of working in the oil, trucking, and construction industries, he was offered the chance to meet people with tremendous history under their boots and learned from the wisdom these people offered to him.

Moving through a colorful career, Hedman retired from the corporate offices of a large international manufacturing company.

His travels, and the diverse collection of friends he met along the way, afford him the raw resources. Incredible world events yield the relevance. Melding the two provides the basis for his writing.

* * *

The real and lasting victories are those of peace, and not of war.
Ralph Waldo Emerson

www.ingramcontent.com/pod-product-compliance
Lightning Source LLC
Chambersburg PA
CBHW070807180626
46818CB00001B/146